The Red Wheelbarrow

"Richly engaging, original, and full of heart, *The Red Wheelbarrow* is a book that sneaks up on you, sketching the characters' lives in scenes and fragments that gradually build in interest and mystery. Amy and Paul, two separate, seemingly unremarkable people, marry, work, and raise families over decades. Unaware of one another, each of them nurses a quiet, almost secret, hope of another dimension to their lives, in which their own creative gifts might flourish. Matthews masterfully weaves Paul's and Amy's stories through a series of nonsequential scenes that build a world large enough to contain both their hopes and their disappointments, guiding us to a surprising and gratifying conclusion. This book moved me in unexpected ways. The sheer decency of Matthews's characters and their hard won willingness to claim happiness for themselves as well as those they love make this novel a triumph of the spirit as well as the heart."

—Cynthia Huntington, 2012 National Book Awards Poetry Finalist and author of *Heavenly Bodies*

"Matthews' novel has me looking at the world differently. The story's two protagonists, Amy and Paul, each have their own compelling trajectories, guided by their conscious choices, moral compasses, and shifting circumstances. But in Matthews' artfully crafted story, the daily drama and decisions that make up these characters' lives are also guided by another force—call it destiny for lack of a more nuanced word. How masterful, to achieve a novel that opens the reader's eyes to the significance of our everyday actions...but also the mysteries of the universe. One of the most thought-provoking and affirming novels I've read in a long time."

—Joni B. Cole, author of *Party Like It's 2044*

"*The Red Wheelbarrow* is a book you will want to give someone who needs to be reminded of hope. It is an affirmation that, though we may not understand it, there is a force for order and meaning at work in the world. In this novel, Matthews reveals a force moving through the story that keeps us riveted for what is around the next corner of a person's life.

This novel is a joy to read and a reason to celebrate…the story calls us forward into possibilities. You'll be fortunate to settle in with the characters and ride along without any naivete or forcing a theme.

It is, without sentimentality, a story of serendipity and mystery. Matthews' characters are ones we identify with and come to cheer for, bringing comfort and realization of our own hope for a life of meaning and a place in the world. The book and its characters capture the long, circuitous path toward what is most meaningful and lasting: connection with another. The characters take an ordinary journey toward the extraordinary ending of possibilities we all long for."

—Lani Leary, PhD, author of
No One Has to Die Alone: Preparing for a Meaningful Death

"Matthews, a master of description, places her novel *The Red Wheelbarrow* beautifully, in alternate locations, set between Hawai'i and New England, and achieves an elegant balance as the two main characters subtly come together and move apart over their lifetimes, their dance resting offstage like an unfinished promise, tantalizing. Matthews knows how to keep the tension in a skillful, deft way, as these characters interweave, make mistakes, mature, grow, evolve through life's challenges, in a story told always in prose lit with poetic images, like a red wheelbarrow, its paint chipping, or a cloud of butterflies, lifting above a field."

—Laura Foley, poet and author of *It's This*

"Matthews guides us from Hawai'i to New England where one woman's stories of honest domestic rage and defiance emerge amongst a teasing historical scrapbook of what love can wage. Here is a novel about families living with the fallout between coming-of-age and the written page years later; a lifelong birth of personal liberation, fraught. To the protagonist, a teacher, there is travel and glamour after she has ruled out expectation and the social cues of her mother's generation. Secret thoughts, rumors, and private ambitions remind us that we're each buying time to finish the giant canvas of our lives. Take *The Red Wheelbarrow* with you to the edge of the sand, to the road and field and pond, and into night."

—Peter Money, author of *Oh When the Saints*

The Red Wheelbarrow

A Novel

Marjorie Nelson Matthews

Rootstock Publishing

Montpelier, VT

Release Date: March 26, 2024

Printed in the USA.

Published by Rootstock Publishing,
an imprint of Ziggy Media LLC
Montpelier, Vermont
info@rootstockpublishing.com
www.rootstockpublishing.com

Paperback ISBN: 978-1-57869-162-3
Hardcover ISBN: 978-1-57869-163-0
eBook ISBN: 978-1-57869-164-7
Library of Congress Control Number: 2023921053

Author photo by Geoff Hansen.
Cover and book design by Eddie Vincent, ENC Graphics Services.

Cover Art: "Sun Setting over a Lake" 1840, Joseph Mallord William Turner. Oil paint on canvas, 911 x 1226 mm. Accepted by the nation as part of the Turner Bequest 1856. Rights and Reproduction: © 2016 Tate, London. Photo: Tate.

For permissions, or to schedule a reading, contact the author at marjoriematthews@me.com.

For Jim

Prologue

October 1960, Lisbon, Vermont

"Bet you never had a wheelbarrow ride before." Paul jumped up from where he sat cross-legged on the grass beside Amy Barnes. His family's corn, hay, and pumpkin fields lay spread out before them, and across the Connecticut River the green hills of New Hampshire were softening into the blush of fall. He headed for the barn before Amy could answer.

The Barneses, visiting from Hawai'i, were staying with friends nearby. Paul's parents had offered them a glimpse of Vermont farm life and, because he and Amy were somewhat close in age, he nine and she seven, Paul had been saddled with showing her around.

He sensed Amy's hesitation but kept going, half hoping she wouldn't follow. He grabbed the wheelbarrow's handles and rested the braces on the ground.

"Go ahead. Climb in. I'll hold it steady."

"It's dirty and the paint's chipping off."

Paul brushed out the debris. "There."

Amy still seemed unsure.

"You scared or something?"

"No!"

"Then get in."

Red paint chips flaked off in her hands as she grabbed the sides.

"Not too fast, Paul Rideau," his mother called from out front of the house where the others had gathered.

Paul started out slowly. Once they rounded the far end of the barn and were beyond the adults' view, he began to trot, rocking the barrow gently, so that Amy yelped and leaned back for better balance. Turning the cart onto a cornfield stripped of its crop, he headed down a soft dirt furrow, the dry cornstalks flashing past.

"Put out your arms and fly," he told her, increasing his speed, his legs churning, kicking up dirt.

Amy hesitated, then lifted her arms into wings. She laughed and leaned her head back, sunlight warm on her face.

"It does feel like flying."

He rounded the row's end and pushed the wheelbarrow down the field toward the pond. From the marsh reeds curved around the water's edge rose a massive cloud of butterflies, gilded by the late afternoon light. Paul slowed and stopped, still grasping the handles, as the mass hovered over the reeds. He wanted to reach out his hands, feel the flicker of those tissue-thin wings.

Amy looked back at him, her cheeks bright red. "I think that's the best thing I ever saw."

When the butterflies settled again, Paul helped Amy climb out and they walked back side by side, Paul pushing the wheelbarrow. Something had shifted. He felt comfortable with her now, almost sorry he wouldn't see her again.

He propped the wheelbarrow against the barn. Amy reached into her jacket pocket and pulled out a broken seashell.

"I found this on the beach where we're staying in East Haven. My mom says it's the heart of a shell."

"I once saw the ocean from a pier in Boston, but I've never walked on a beach."

"Just like I'd never been in a wheelbarrow or seen a million butterflies all at once." She spoke so softly he had to lean close. "A shell's not as good as being at the beach, but you can keep it as the next best thing." Amy set the shell in his hand. "Maybe someday you'll come to Hawai'i and I can show you how to ride a wave."

Paul nodded, though he couldn't imagine ever going to a place so far away. He slipped the shell in his pocket.

As they rounded the barn's corner, the western sky opened before them. Huge cloud tendrils streaked neon pink across the sky. Amy stopped, head back, her eyes raised. Paul was surprised. He thought he was the only one who noticed when colors lit up the sky.

Chapter One

March 2001, Clifton, New Hampshire

Amy picked bits of tissue off the clean laundry. "Can't be bothered to empty his damn pockets." She shook out a blouse. "Mind's too full of deep thoughts." At least it wasn't a felt-tip pen this time. She'd lost her favorite pair of slacks when Martin left a red one in his jeans.

She hung the shirts and pants for ironing, folded the tees and jeans. When she slid open a dresser drawer to stow her underwear, she found a pink paper heart nestled among her panties. Martin's handwriting. "Wish I were here." She smiled. She was forty-eight, married sixteen years, and her impossible husband could still charm her.

Twenty minutes later the phone rang.

"Mrs. Whaley?" a young female voice asked.

"Yes, this is she."

"You don't know me, but I'm one of your husband's students. Jennifer McDaniel."

Amy's internal alarm kicked in.

"I'm afraid Martin's away at a conference this week."

"Yes, I know. I was calling to speak with you."

Amy sensed no nervousness beneath the girl's assertive tone. Perhaps she merely wanted to convey a message to Martin about an assignment.

"If this is an academic matter, it's probably best you speak with the department secretary or another professor."

"Actually, it's personal. You're the one I need to talk to. I was hoping we could meet."

Amy sat down on her bed. *Damn him.*

"Why don't you come by the house." Amy didn't want to risk a public scene in their small New England town. "We're easy walking distance from campus."

Even as she said it, Amy realized the girl probably knew exactly where they lived. She ripped up Martin's note and tossed it in the toilet.

Jennifer circled the kitchen as Amy prepared their tea. She studied the family photo gallery that covered one wall and asked Amy to identify everyone.

"That's Will and his friend Sam dressed up as Power Rangers for Halloween. They must have been about four or five then. And Kara's two in this one. The requisite pumpkin farm shot."

Amy hoped she sounded calm, as if she had no expectations for this conversation. No harm in reminding this girl that Martin had a family, an entire life in which she played no part. Amy wondered if Jennifer was imagining the space as her own, picturing the wall of history she wanted to create with Martin.

Amy could have picked Jennifer out of any group as the woman Martin would approach. She was attractive in an understated, bookish way. No makeup, a mass of messy curls, black-rimmed spectacles telegraphing her serious attitude. She was the kind of visibly intelligent, striking woman Martin preferred. A younger, prettier version of herself.

"So what year are you?"

"Senior. English major. That's why I know Martin so well. He's been advising me."

Amy gestured for her to take a seat at the kitchen table and placed a cup of tea in front of her.

"So what is it you need to discuss with me?"

Staring at the girl across from her, Amy marveled, as always, that a man Martin's age could still attract a woman nearly forty years younger than he.

"I don't know any good way to say this, so I'll just put it out there. Martin and I are in a passionate relationship. We're deeply in love."

They were always so sure it was mutual. Even these pseudo-sophisticated, sexually experienced young women needed to believe this was about love and soulmates. But then, of course, so did Martin, at least for the moments he was with them.

"I see." Amy tried to smile as she spoke. "And all that's keeping Martin from being with you is his fear of hurting me and our children? You see him as a good man trapped in a bad relationship he's too honorable to leave?"

"No, not at all." This was unexpected. "I'm here because I think it's wrong for us to be sneaking around. I have no desire to break up his marriage and family."

Amy could feel a tremor starting in her leg. This girl wasn't like the others.

"I don't understand."

"I'm not looking for a long-term or exclusive relationship with Martin. Far from it. What I'm hoping I can do is spark his writing. This connection he and I share has had a powerful effect on his work. Have you been reading his poetry this past year?"

Martin had long ago stopped sharing his early drafts with Amy, but she had no intention of revealing that to this girl.

Jennifer continued, seemingly unfazed by Amy's silence. "Since being with me, he's begun delving into parts of himself he's run from all his life. He's never written more honestly. He knows I'm good for him, but he's afraid at the same time. It's scary stuff he's unleashing. And he doesn't want to hurt you and your kids. I came here hoping you would agree his poetry matters above everything else."

What makes you presume you know anything about what I might think or feel, Amy wanted to snap, but she said instead, "And you think you alone can inspire him."

"No. I'm just the one who inspires him now. Clearly, you did for a while. His work the first five years you were together is some of his best. I only know his writing became vigorous again once we connected. Most of the time he's with me, he's writing. It's like he's drugged."

Amy pictured Martin seated at her tiny dining table in Honolulu seventeen years earlier, his pen flying across a legal pad. She knew what Jennifer was experiencing—the intoxication of lighting a spark in this respected poet, of being the trigger for a creative breakthrough. The difference was that Amy had always valued most what that said about her. Jennifer seemed genuinely focused on what it meant for Martin's work.

"And you aren't concerned about the harm your relationship might cause others?" Amy wished her voice sounded as cool as Jennifer's.

"It doesn't have to hurt anyone."

Amy was unaccustomed to such dispassion.

"As I said, I have no interest in taking Martin away from you or your children. I know he needs and values all of this." She gestured around the kitchen. "I'm not naïve. I may ignite his passion now, but it won't last. We could have kept this hidden, but I am an honest person. I have to be true to myself."

The girl's audacity stunned Amy.

"Bottom line—Martin's a great poet and if I can help him produce more great work, then I can live with any fallout."

Easy for you to say, when it isn't you or your children who are the fallout.

"I'm sure you want the same for Martin, Amy. We should be able to work out some kind of arrangement."

Amy considered mentioning that Martin might not find Jennifer quite so exhilarating absent the forbidden aspect of the liaison, but she doubted this was so. She knew Martin would find such an arrangement rather perfect. *I just have to be open-minded and sophisticated enough.*

"Mrs. Whaley," Jennifer said, her voice for the first time showing some strain, "I am no threat to you. I only want to be a small part of Martin's life for as long as I am helpful to him."

How does any twenty-year-old woman come to be so self-assured and fearless, so certain of her right to step into our lives with a plan? Amy had been more nervous on job interviews than this woman was as she proposed sharing Amy's husband.

Tiny balls of hail pinged the windowpanes.

"I will need to speak with Martin," was all she could manage. She reminded herself that she owed this girl nothing, not even a fight.

"I'm not sure Martin will choose to put his work first."

Jennifer said this as an accusation, as if Amy would forever carry the guilt of failing to love enough for art to flourish.

"I won't pretend to know," Amy answered. She had lived far too long to think she knew anything with such certainty.

"It's too cold to think." Martin put down his book.

Amy could feel his eyes on her, but kept her focus on the paper before her, the last essay in the pile she had to grade. The floor's old wood planks groaned as he plodded to the kitchen. She listened for the sound of the kettle being filled, but it was the glass cupboard he opened and then the freezer.

"For you."

He stood before her, arm extended, offering a tumbler of scotch and ice.

"Thanks."

Not like him to fix her a drink but also not like him to be home at five. He'd even emptied the dishwasher that morning. *How many gestures will it take to release us both from this claustrophobic dance?*

"You're not having one?"

He began piling kindling and logs in the fireplace.

"Once I get this started."

Outside the sky was spitting ice and rain, the kind of ugly March mix that made for treacherous driving.

I should close the shades. The thought floated by, but she stayed in her seat. Let the neighbors and passing cars catch a glimpse of their interior. *Nothing to see, folks. Just a middle-aged couple going through the motions.*

When he settled back in the leather chair that his father and grandfather had worn into softness, a scotch in hand, Amy briefly felt an urge to wrap her arms around him, comfort him.

How does he do that? She studied his profile, the drooping eyes and sloping shoulders that suggested he carried a heavy load. *Behaves outrageously and still manages to leave me aching for him.*

She hadn't asked that he end things with Jennifer. They hadn't even discussed Jennifer when he returned. She had only mentioned that Jennifer had come by for tea while he was away, had added, "I understand your writing is particularly powerful these days."

They had been standing side by side at the airport carousel, waiting for his bag to drop onto the belt. At the mention of Jennifer, he'd taken off his glasses, rubbed a handkerchief over them, buying time, rocking back on his heels as he polished the lenses. She could see his struggle for composure; the blinking, the inability to meet her gaze. The suitcase, as black and anonymous as every other one circling before them, slipped quietly down the chute. Martin let it do a full circle before retrieving it. And then they were on their way, out through the sliding doors and into the brisk March wind and a long, silent drive north.

He's frozen. She sipped her scotch, trying to regain her focus on the essay in front of her. She knew he hadn't written a word since his return.

"Amy," he said, still in his chair, but turned toward her now, the fire blazing in front of him. She couldn't stand the pain that underlay his every word.

Don't ask it. She braced for the request or the offhand statement. Would it be "I need to stretch my legs," or "I noticed we're low on tonic?" Which excuse would he offer as the key to free him from her and this house on a grim spring night?

"Hmm?" She gave him a quick smile, then studied again the paper before her. *Don't ask it.*

"Come sit." He opened his arms, inviting her onto his lap, a place she hadn't been since the children were young enough for early bedtimes.

She hesitated. *No. Can't you see I'm in the middle of something? Can't you feel I want to pummel you, that the last place I want to be is pressed against you?*

She set down her pen, took up her scotch, and walked into the awkward embrace neither of them knew quite how to arrange now that their bodies were no longer slender or supple. She finally settled, tense and uncomfortable, on his lap, her legs looped over the chair's arm, her head tucked beneath his chin, his heart thudding in her ear. He wrapped an arm around her, his drink in his other hand. They stared into the fire.

"I do love you, you know," he finally said. "I don't mean to hurt you."

Amy knew she was supposed to say she loved him as well and forgave him, but she couldn't. It was difficult enough to quiet her hip joint complaining about holding the position and her neck already protesting the bend required to keep her head against Martin's chest. *One step at a time,* she reminded herself, and awkwardly sipped from her glass.

April 2001, Clifton, New Hampshire

Amy spotted Kara beyond the cluster of seniors gathered around her desk.

"Give me a sec, guys," Amy said to her students and led Kara to the back of the classroom. "What's up, hon?"

"I saw Dad walk out of the building last period. Is everything okay?"

"Everything's fine. Actually, better than fine. He has some fantastic news. He's been appointed the Rothwell Poet-in-Residence for Summer 2001. He's over-the-moon happy."

"Seriously? He came by just to tell you that? Was that like the first time he ever stepped foot in this place?"

She had a point. Martin never visited the high school. He refused to suffer through open houses, student performances, and holiday concerts. He bowed out of teacher conferences once the kids finished elementary school. He considered public high schools toxic places, designed to limit rather than advance learning. And yet somehow he managed not to mind his own children attending them or Amy teaching at one.

"This is big news for him," Amy said.

"Why? He's a resident poet somewhere every summer."

"The Rothwell is different. On a practical level, it comes with a lot of money, but it's also very prestigious and no one at Stafford has ever been chosen before."

Kara rolled her eyes. "He must love that. He's going to be insufferable."

"Kara, please."

"What? I'm just telling the truth. You know I'm right. This is all he'll talk about now. Of course it would be even worse if he hadn't gotten it."

Amy wrapped an arm around her. "How about this for a strategy. We'll make a huge deal of it tonight. Take him to the inn for dinner. Give him a massive balloon bouquet. The place will be packed with people wanting to know what we're celebrating and he'll get to tell people over and over. He'll feel like the center of attention for everyone in Clifton. Maybe he'll feel so recognized he won't have to dwell on it."

"Yeah, right. We'll just be feeding the monster. He's insatiable."

"Indulge me. I'll keep this meeting brief and be home soon. All you have to do tonight is smile and gush."

Kara groaned.

"Hey, come on. Enough. Be happy for your dad. And proud. This is a big deal. Your dad's an important poet. That kind of makes all of us important, too."

Kara stared at her as if she'd lost her mind.

"Shoot me if I end up being a weak woman like you, living off some man's glory. I'm so out of here." She made a show of stomping out the door.

"You'll never make any man happy" had been Amy's mother's curse when at sixteen Amy exploded at having to stay home to help clean the house while her dad and brother went sailing. "You can do whatever you want once you're an adult," her mother added, practically spitting the words at her, "but you'll end up alone and miserable if you don't put your husband first."

Amy exhaled.

"It gets better," Regina, editor of the school's literary journal, said. The journal staff had turned their attention to Amy.

"I know, I know. I remember when all of you were impossible ninth-graders." Except none of them had been as adept at twisting the knife of truth.

"So bring me up to speed on distribution. I need to head out soon."

Amy tried to pay attention as Madeleine reviewed plans for getting journal copies to all the students, but Kara's snarky comment had hit its mark. Amy nodded and tuned them out.

Sarah Rideau leaned against her husband Paul. "Just like being in Boston, right?"

Paul shrugged. "It's not like I've ever dined in a fancy Boston place, but definitely looks different from anything around here."

Recent renovations had transformed the Clifton Inn's dining room from

New England cozy to big-city chic. Paul couldn't have said what exactly conveyed that sense—perhaps the slick marble floors instead of deep pile carpets or the textured gray wallpaper where there'd been floral patterns. Maybe it was the waitstaff dressed in black. Paul didn't see the point of affecting an urban sophistication. People came to Clifton for charm, not a cool vibe.

"Any seating preferences?" The host plucked two menus from her stand.

"Window if you've got one," Sarah said. "Then we can people watch." Unlike most small towns, Clifton boasted pedestrians on its sidewalks, at least for a few busy times of the day and year. "When I grab drinks here with the girls," she told Paul, "we sit in the bar area. I've always wanted a seat by the window to check out the sidewalk action."

Paul loved seeing her so animated. They rarely ate out. Full-time jobs and managing a farm left them little free time, and money was always tight. Usually they celebrated their anniversary at home. Paul grilled steaks, Sarah baked his favorite cherry pie, and they splurged on Sam Adams instead of Millers. This year their kids had presented them with a gift certificate for dinner at the inn. "So you can celebrate in style," was how their daughter Maddie put it.

"I don't suppose it'll stay this quiet," Sarah said as the host handed her a menu.

"No, it's a bit early for us. It'll pick up, but Tuesdays are usually on the slow side."

Sarah was still scrutinizing the special drink menu when a waiter appeared beside her. "May I interest you in cocktails before dinner?"

"Yes, absolutely. This menu makes me feel like a kid in a candy store. What would you recommend?"

It's going to be an expensive night, Paul realized as Sarah ordered cocktails for herself and him along with appetizers. The tab was already over fifty dollars. Yet, when Sarah declared her Old Fashioned the best ever, he shut off the frugal side of his brain. Whatever the tab, it would be worth it simply to see her so happy and at ease. They didn't talk about it, but they both knew they were celebrating more than their twenty-seventh wedding anniversary. Sarah had also reached her fifteen-year mark of being cancer-free.

"Here's to us." She clicked her glass against Paul's. "You're still the only one for me, Paul Rideau."

Paul grinned and sipped from his Stafford Full Moon, a bourbon-based concoction Sarah talked him into trying. He knew he should make some kind of declaration himself, but the words never came easily for him, especially in public settings. "Not half bad. I see why people pay the big bucks to drink here."

"Right?" Sarah gleamed. "I know it's extravagant. I usually get a beer if I come with the gang after work, but tonight is special. This evening couldn't be any better. We practically have the place to ourselves, we're sipping fabulous cocktails, and I bet these sliders are to die for." She bit into one of the mini burgers the waiter had placed between them. "Now that is divine."

Paul had to concede the bite of beef went down easy, but what he loved most was her unfiltered pleasure. He'd been missing that. Though her exuberance and delight in being the center of attention had often left him uncomfortable in their younger years—she was always the first to sing at the karaoke bar or to step out onto the empty dance floor—he now missed that flamboyance. *A casualty of the cancer,* he supposed. But maybe not just the cancer. Decades of life's challenges had quieted her spirit as well as his own.

A family of four—mom, dad, and a couple older kids, a boy and a girl—settled at a nearby table. The mom carried a single Mylar rainbow balloon with the message "Congratulations!" She tied it to her seat back.

"Pretty expensive place to bring kids," Paul said.

"Must be something special. At least they aren't noisy toddlers like that time in Quebec City." Sarah reached out a hand for his. "They can't spoil our evening."

The world outside their window had darkened, the streetlights came on, and the line of cars eased, but the foot traffic stayed busy. Paul wondered what brought out all these people, most of them students. Where were they headed on a weeknight? To the many restaurants, he guessed, or the bookstore. He'd heard good things of *Crouching Tiger, Hidden Dragon,* currently playing at the local theater. They lived less than five miles away, but Clifton felt like a different world from theirs.

Though they hadn't yet finished their drinks, a waiter arrived with a second round. "Courtesy of some folks at the bar." He nodded toward a group of young men and women who waved. Sarah waved back.

"So much for having a night to ourselves," Paul said. "Will they want to join us?"

"No, they wouldn't dare. But I should go and thank them."

"Interns or med students?" Paul asked.

"I'm not sure from this distance. I promise I'll only be a sec."

As a senior nurse in the emergency department, Sarah informally shepherded med students and interns through their ED rotations, mostly making sure they didn't kill anyone. Paul had never observed Sarah on the job, but he guessed she ran her section the way she managed their home, family, and farm business—with a firm hand, high standards, and zero tolerance for arrogance or laziness.

Paul watched as Sarah chatted up the group, standing close enough to engage but keeping enough distance to underscore the roles that separated them. Her quiet authority and ease with the young doctors moved him. One thing to witness her daily grace as a partner in parenting and working a farm, another to witness it with these gifted strangers.

Their waiter arrived with a plate of fried calamari as Sarah returned to their table.

"Perfect timing. Miss me?" Sarah scooped up a helping of squid.

"Desperately, but I'm resigned to sharing you with your public. The price of marrying a star."

She grinned. "It's true. Celebrity can be a burden."

"All joking aside, I like getting a glimpse of your life away from us." He raised his glass. "To the incredible Nurse Sarah."

A pear-arugula salad followed the calamari, complemented by a bottle of chardonnay.

"We should try making this at home." Paul speared a bit of blue cheese and arugula.

"And by 'we' you mean me?"

"I'm thinking maybe even I could pull it off, provided the walnuts come already candied."

"Right. I want to be there when you poach a pear in wine."

The waiter replenished their wineglasses and cleared their plates. "Your risotto will be right up."

Amy fished an envelope from her purse and handed it across the table.

"You already gave me a card this morning."

"I'm being extravagant. This year you get two."

Before their first anniversary, Sarah had proposed they buy a vacuum cleaner as a mutual gift. "I don't need flowers or jewelry," she'd said. "I'd much rather pick something together that will improve our home." Plants and small appliances dominated the early years, with big splurges on the key anniversaries—a refrigerator with ice maker for their fifth, a king-size bed for their tenth, a bathroom renovation for their twentieth.

He slid a card from the envelope. Tucked within it were two tickets to the American Folk Exhibit at Boston's Museum of Fine Arts.

"Seriously?"

Sarah beamed. "You like?"

"I love it." He kissed the palm of her hand. "I thought we'd decided on a porch swing for this year."

"We'll still get that. This is a little extra something. And don't panic. I'm doing a Sunday evening shift to cover the cost. We can even splurge on lunch in the North End. Dr. Gallo gave me the name of his favorite place."

"But you hate art museums and the MFA is huge."

"I know, but you hate rom-coms, yet you still take me to them. I thought maybe if you explained why you consider the folk art pieces to be so special, I might appreciate them more. And if I'm dying of boredom, I'll go sip coffee in the cafeteria."

The waiter arrived with their risotto.

"That smells so good." Sarah spooned a serving onto the extra plate the waiter provided, placed the rest in front of Paul, and dipped a fork in hers. "Bon appétit." Her smile dissolved. "What is it, hon?" She leaned forward, placed a hand on his arm.

He knew he would lose it if he looked her in the eye, and he sure as hell wasn't going to be the guy bawling his eyes out in this fancy place. He held tight to her hand and after a few moments calmed himself enough to say, "Love you."

"Love you, too. To the moon and back. Now eat your risotto."

He was happily numb to the figure on the check when it arrived, and, softened by Sarah's generosity, he tipped well. *Worth every dime.*

On their way out, they passed the family with the balloon. "You won't believe the cottage I'll have all to myself," the father said to a man who'd stopped to talk with them. "Right on the water, meals delivered. It's going to be three months of heaven."

"Please note," the teenage daughter interjected, "that my father's idea of heaven is no family."

"As you can see, Kara's become quite the wit," the father said, and continued with his description.

Paul did not miss those stormy years when his kids were prickly teens.

The large dining room was nearly full now, buzzing with animated conversations. *What a gathering of drama is contained in this one space.* Paul imagined the swirl of emotions, the exchange of words and actions at these tables, some of it tender, some vicious, and no doubt some sad enough to tear lives apart.

"Thank you for our life," he said, as they stepped out into the brisk April night. He pulled Sarah tight beside him. He knew he was a lucky man.

"You're home early," Amy said with a glance at her watch. "Not even eight." She was curled up on the living room couch, a book in hand. Martin's colleagues had gathered for Friday drinks to continue the celebration of his Rothwell award.

"Turns out we can't celebrate as long or as hard as we once did." Martin tossed his briefcase onto a side chair and eased out of his shoes.

"Big turnout?"

"Decent. Of course, Jocelyn and Herman were there. Parker even showed. I wasn't expecting that." Parker was the college's president, new to the job and an outsider.

"That's nice of him. Shows he's trying to fit in."

Martin grunted. "I expect he's like all the rest. Can't be bothered unless you do something that reflects well on the college and thus him."

"Anyone else important show up?"

Martin plopped down on the couch beside her and laid her feet across his lap. "Mostly just the department. No big surprises." He pulled off one of her socks and began rubbing her foot. "Or were you asking about Jennifer?" He dug his thumb along her arch.

"I was wondering more generally, but sure, I'd like to know if Jennifer was there."

"Are you also wondering if she'll be in Maine with me?"

"It didn't occur to me that you would have her or anyone with you in Maine. I think I have a right to know if that's your plan."

"You can relax. In the past month, Jennifer apparently found her soulmate, or so she claims. A wealthy Italian in the MBA program. She'll be summering with him at his family's villa near Sorrento. She did stop by, though, to raise a glass, with her Romeo by her side."

Amy nearly said she was sorry, as if Martin deserved sympathy.

"And to save you asking," Martin continued, "I will be going to Maine alone unless you want to join me. You could find something for the kids to do, somewhere for them to be for three months and we could spend a glorious summer together. Leisurely days and nights of doing whatever we want, whenever we want."

A classic Martin strategy. Make a grand romantic gesture, but be sure it's a gesture that required something she couldn't or wouldn't choose to do, thus making it her fault he was lonely and tempted by other women.

"You know the kids already have somewhere they are going to be." Kara and Will were going to Hawai'i with her as they did every year, and they were both signed up for classes at Amy's alma mater, McNeil Academy. Kara would take an all-day U.S. history course, eliminating a major course requirement for the school year. Will was signed up for typing, a drawing class, and an afternoon soccer training program. During the week they'd stay in the cottage she'd called home as a child and young adult. It was part of her maternal family's Nu'uanu compound. On weekends, they would head to the family's Kailua beach house. The plan had been in place since January.

"Let your aunt and mom take care of them," Martin said. "Why do you need to be there?"

Amy's mother suffered from dementia and lived in a memory care facility. Amy's Aunt Gretchen was already generously providing space for Amy and the kids. Amy wasn't about to dump more on the poor woman who managed all the family's properties and visited Amy's mother multiple times a week. Part of the point of Amy being in Hawai'i was to give her aunt a break. Besides, Will and Kara were only thirteen and fifteen. But Martin knew all this, just as he knew Amy would never agree to being away from the kids for an entire summer.

She wanted, though, to call his bluff, say yes, of course, she'd spend the summer with him. See the panic in his face. Instead, she offered a compromise.

"How about, if Gretchen's willing, the kids could fly out on their own and I can be with you in Maine for the first two or three weeks. Then I'll join them in Honolulu for the rest of the time."

She didn't usually risk testing him. It was too exhausting and humiliating to play games with their lives. But she was also exhausted and humiliated by the cycle of betrayal. If he really wanted her there, this was a chance for him to prove it.

It didn't surprise her that he hesitated, but it stung. She could have narrated his thought process. Three weeks of a wife hanging around at the start of the residency might spook interesting romantic prospects. Never mind that he would hate sharing his living space with Amy when he was trying to write. She wondered if it came as an actual surprise to him that when given the serious option of having her with him, he realized he didn't want that at all.

She put him out of his misery as his silence dragged on. "Relax. I'll go to Hawai'i with the kids. You can have Maine to yourself." She swung her feet to the floor. "I'm going to take a shower."

"Thanks for understanding, love. I'd be grateful for any day I could get with you, but having you there only part of the time really might muck up the dynamics. Such a delicate dance of bonding has to happen at these things and your departure could disrupt it. I'm afraid it's either you there the whole time or not at all."

"Maybe it will be good for us both to have some time to ourselves," Amy said, hoping he heard the whiff of a threat.

"You're the best." He blew her a kiss. He then aped at clutching his heart. "You know you are my eternal love." Amy smiled at his effort. The only thing she knew to be true was that he wanted to believe he loved her and always would.

May 2001, Lisbon, Vermont

Weedwacker in hand, Paul moved slowly along the side of the big red barn across the drive from the house. Cutting back weeds was part of the cleanup he hadn't gotten to in the fall. He carted the stalks to the debris pile, then assessed the state of the barn's siding. It was going on ten years since its last paint job, and he figured it was good for at least another year without risking deterioration of the wood or the neighbors' disapproval. The color had faded some, but nothing was flaking or peeling.

It could be a giant canvas, he thought, studying it. With the help of ladders and a bucket loader, he could create a work of art on it, a huge mural, something on the scale of Rivera's and Orozco's work. And it wouldn't have to be political in purpose or even representational. He could create a work of pop art or geometric abstraction. He imagined such a piece of art surrounded by green fields.

He walked back a dozen feet to get a wider perspective. *Not a traditional mural,* he decided. *Something unexpected, whimsical, maybe even funny. That would be better.* He could design it first on canvas, map it out, then recreate it on the barn itself. He wondered what kind of paint would be best. But then, that would depend on the design itself, whether it called for something glossy or flat. *Would take a lot of paint. Wouldn't be cheap.*

"What are we studying? You thinking it's time to bite the bullet and paint it?" Sarah had come up beside him without his noticing. She'd been cleaning up her vegetable beds and was, like him, drenched in sweat and spattered with mud. She moved closer to the wall, squatted, and felt the lower section for moisture. "I'd say we could get by another year, maybe even two?" She looked up at him expectantly, so unsuspecting, so grounded in the reality of their lives that she could never conceive of doing something as absurd as painting a giant mural on a barn's broadside. In their world, barns weren't canvases.

"That's my thought, too," he said. "No need to paint it. We'll be fine for at least another year."

"Have to say, it's a relief to take that off this year's list, what with all the work we should do on Chris's place. That roof really needs replacing." She peeled off her work gloves. "I'm going to take a break and grab some lunch. You hungry yet?"

"I could eat." Paul followed her to the house. Nothing said he couldn't play with ideas about what he might design if he were painting a huge mural. *Could be a kick just sketching out an image. Wouldn't have to actually do it.*

He left his boots on the little porch outside the kitchen door, then headed for the big utility sink in the mudroom. *Nothing hokey,* he told himself as he scrubbed his hands, arms, and face. *Nothing that screams Vermont.* This would have to be something completely unexpected. Even if he never painted it on the barn, he wanted to be sure he got it right.

May 2001, Clifton, New Hampshire

"We're waiting on Ryan and one more teacher," Jess Wong told Karen Pitchford as she joined them in the library conference room.

The "team"—Ryan Pitchford's teachers, special ed case manager, guidance counselor, and mother—were meeting with Ryan to discuss the prospects of his graduating in a month. Amy hated these meetings. No one, least of all the faculty, wanted to see a kid fail to graduate.

"Ryan's not here yet?" Karen Pitchford placed her purse and folder on the table, but did not take her seat. "Should I go look for him?"

Watching Karen, Amy marveled again at the seeming effortlessness of her appearance and manner. They'd served together years before on the PTO's board, back when Kara was a mere first grader and Ryan already in fourth. Though Ryan was a handful even then, Karen was always a study in serene elegance. Today she wore a navy striped skirt that fell just below the knees, a crisp white shirt, and a navy cardigan. Her blond hair was cut in a no-fuss chin-length bob, and if she wore any makeup, it didn't call attention to itself. The only wrinkle in her demeanor was her attention to the library's front door. Normally, her manner suggested there was nowhere she'd rather be, nothing on her mind other than the people before her.

"His last class was with John Bello," Jess said, reading the schedule before her, "so they're probably headed over together."

Karen tucked a loose strand of hair behind her ear, then as fluidly as a dancer might rise on pointe, she pulled back the chair and slid onto it. She opened the leather folder before her and Amy could see the neat stack of memos, a blank sheet of paper ready for note-taking, a pen tucked into its holder at the seam. Karen beamed across the table at Amy.

"How've you been?" Amy said.

"Hanging in there, thanks."

Despite her polish, Karen's manner never seemed false or forced. She cupped a hand against her cheek, a huge grin on her face. "To think we may be just weeks away from his making it through!" She spoke as if she and Amy were intimate conspirators in this effort to see Ryan graduate. And in a sense, they were, having survived together Ryan's first year of English as well as this last semester of creative writing. Everyone had agreed Amy was Ryan's best hope for meeting his final English requirement.

Amy didn't know how Karen kept it together. In the past year her husband, provost of Stafford College, had dumped her for the young rising star of the government studies department. Martin claimed the faculty was laying bets as to which of them, Michael Pitchford or his new love, would land a college presidency first. Karen was banished to Divorce Hill, a cluster of grim condos on the town's edge, a kind of way station for the newly abandoned or newly arrived. Such was the price of being the spouse of a college employee whose home was college provided. If she decided to leave Martin, she would be the one displaced to shabby quarters, and she sure as hell couldn't pull off showing up at school conferences dressed for success. Karen tapped a perfectly manicured nail, tastefully short and buffed, on the conference table, her smile less steady.

"Sometimes appearances matter more than reality," Amy's mother had once advised her in a well-intentioned effort to persuade Amy to care more about her image. Amy had never been convinced her mom had that right.

As predicted, Ryan arrived alongside John Bello, the popular printmaking teacher. Ryan was the dark to his mother's light. Today as every day, he had achieved the appearance of a neglected, desolate young man perched on the margins. His hair hung greasy and long against his sparsely bearded cheeks, his stretched and ripped T-shirt fell practically to his knees, and he refused to look any of the adults in the eye. He pulled a chair from the table, making sure to drag it over the linoleum so it screeched, and then he fell onto it, his back slouched and arms crossed. The way he sat every day in Amy's class.

"Hey, buddy," Karen said and touched his arm. He jerked it away.

Karen pulled her hands back to her lap and sat up straighter in her chair, her smile gone. Amy studied the agenda before her. She hated these intrusions into a family's intimate misery.

After the meeting, as Amy crossed the school's long entrance hall, bound for the front door, her arm aching with the weight of her African tote bag stuffed with papers and books, she spotted Karen exiting the girls' bathroom. Though the hallway was dimly lit, Karen slid on a pair of sunglasses. Her smile was as large and warm as ever despite the grim prospects outlined in the meeting and Ryan's apparent desire to keep them all guessing right to the end.

"Thank you as always for your patience with Ryan. I know you've tried to engage him and been incredibly generous with your time."

Amy wanted to offer her assurances that Ryan would outgrow this, that something would click into place and he would again thrive, but she couldn't pretend she knew what lay ahead.

"I so admire and envy you," Karen continued.

"Me?" Amy knew better than to envy Karen her life, but she admired the grace with which she lived it. She couldn't imagine what Karen might find to admire in her.

"Of course I do. You don't give up, even with kids like Ryan. You just keep plugging away, trying to reach them. What you do makes a huge difference in people's lives. So many teachers don't care what happens to them."

"Thanks. I hope something gets through, but nothing matters more than parents who love their kid. Ryan's lucky he has you as an advocate."

Karen shone her beam on Amy again, as if her delight in life had not faltered for a moment. "I hope so. Sometimes it feels I only make it worse for him, no matter what I do." She laughed and waved a dismissive hand. "Ignore me. Pity party. So tiresome." She pushed open one of the school's giant glass doors and held it for Amy. "And look at me not even offering to lend you a hand. Can I carry something?"

Amy shook her head. "I've achieved a delicate balance. One change and it will all fall to ground."

Amy headed for her Subaru and Karen for a two-door Civic against which Ryan leaned, glowering. Amy appreciated Karen's words, but thought they said more about what Karen wished were true than Amy's dedication as a teacher. Was a time she aspired to more, a time when she strove to make a meaningful difference in every kid's life, but she was a long time off that trajectory. After enough defeats, even the most passionate teacher loses her edge. She'd settle for keeping the balance sheet positive with her own kids. She dug for the grocery list in her bag and climbed into the driver's seat.

Chapter Two

June 1960, Oakland, California

Amy brought the pencil to her lips and exhaled a white plume in the chilled air. She had never seen her breath before. With hot chocolate in a coffee cup, she was pretending to be a secretary, sipping her coffee as she smoked a cigarette.

"Time to start class, everyone," her cousin Erica called from the terrace. Pads of paper, pencils, and crayons were laid out before her on a wrought iron table. When the moms had ordered them all outside for fresh air, Erica had decided they would play school and she would be the teacher. Only Amy didn't want to play student to Erica's teacher. All Erica cared about was being the boss, the one telling them all what to do. Amy was the one who imagined stories and poems and, with her mother's help, captured them on paper. She didn't need pretend school.

Amy balanced on the edge of a garden bench, her legs crossed as if she wore a tight pencil skirt, her toes pointed to suggest they were stuffed into heels. Her brother Kimo abandoned the stick he was using to probe an ant hole and climbed up to kneel as directed on a chair. Erica's younger sister Beverly took the chair beside him.

Amy ignored them all. She stayed in her pretend world where she was a secretary in a big New York office, and maybe after that she'd play at being a poor orphan girl, sent off to live with rich relations on an English estate. The French doors and terrace rimmed with rosebushes had immediately reminded her of *The Secret Garden*, the book her mom was reading to her every night before bed. In the morning mist, she could imagine expansive lawns beyond her aunt and uncle's home, tall hedges and locked gates, and that she wore a long full skirt that swished as she moved in her laced boots.

But first, she would play secretary and pretend her fingers were flying across a typewriter. She would be the kind of secretary who, after work, donned a black cocktail dress and sipped martinis beside elegant men in softly lit bars with high stools.

Erica rapped a ruler against the terrace table. "Today I am going to teach you about poetry."

Crayon in hand, Kimo drew on the pad of paper before him. Beverly sucked her thumb. Amy could see her mother's face at the kitchen window behind Erica, checking on them. They were guests this week, visiting her mother's sister Gretchen and family in Oakland before they began their journey east to Connecticut, where her father would do a sabbatical year of study at Yale. Amy was to do her best to get along with her cousins and brother—"so I can have some uninterrupted time with my sister," was how her mother had put it. Erica squinted at Amy, but Amy turned away and stared at the grass. After all, she wasn't interrupting or stopping Erica. She couldn't see any harm in staying where she was.

Erica held up one of the volumes she'd brought out with her. "*Now We Are Six*, by A. A. Milne."

"Amy's got that book, too," Kimo said.

"Of course she does. Grannie gives each of us a copy when we turn six." Amy wondered how Erica knew this. Erica was only two years older, but she talked as if she knew everything about everything.

Many of the pages in Amy's copy back home were ripped or had Kimo's scribblings all over them. He'd even drawn on Amy's favorite poem, "Wind on the Hill." Erica's copy appeared to be unscarred. Something else that made her better than Amy.

Erica picked up the other volume, *When We Were Very Young*.

"I think I will read you a poem from this book, called 'Disobedience.'" Squinting, Erica stared hard at Amy, then began reading the poem in a voice that sounded as if she had a clothespin squeezing her nose. "James James, Morrison Morrison, Weatherby George Dupree."

Amy set down her mug and pencil and stepped onto the damp grass. Her Keds wicked up the moisture. She tried to shut out the sound of Erica's voice as she circled the yard. Over the previous days, she had become familiar with the garden that was so different from Hawai'i's gardens, had been drawn to the snapdragons and petunias, the walnut tree. The colors muted by morning fog, the scent of rose mingled with eucalyptus, and the two-story house itself all spoke to her of mystery and adventure.

She wandered up the stone walkway to the honeysuckle hedge dividing the front from the back. A white gate bridged the space between hedge and house. She imagined the gate as locked and the hedge too tall to see over. There might be a garden hidden on the other side, just like in *The Secret Garden*.

"Auntie Clare," Erica yelled. "Amy's not cooperating."

Amy, her hand on the gate, hesitated. She didn't want to start the day being in trouble. She heard the door to the terrace open, looked behind her to find her mom, arms crossed, with the look that said, "I don't want to come out here again."

As she turned back, Amy caught a glimpse of something red fluttering, a bit of fabric stuck to the house's rough wall. The sandpapery surface scraped her fingers as she tried to remove the scrap. It looked to be a bit of tulle, like the material in her crinolines. She wondered if, as happened to her, Erica's petticoats had slipped below her hem and caught on the wall, or perhaps it was a bit of her Aunt Gretchen's crinoline. She touched the wall again, feeling the prickly points beneath her palm. She had never seen walls like these. Houses in Hawai'i were made of wood or cement block. A few like her own had rusty corrugated tin roofs.

Rubbing the fabric between her fingers, she took her place at the table, settling onto a cold, hard iron chair. Erica had begun another poem, "Come Out with Me," which Amy liked well enough. She leaned her head back, face to the sky, and closed her eyes. Only one more day of Erica. Tomorrow they would pack up the car and begin the drive to New Haven and a year living in a place where it snowed in winter and she would have to wear shoes.

As Erica droned on, Amy imagined herself in a blue satin dress, a trace of red crinoline visible at the hem. And how would she come to brush too close to the hungry wall ready to capture a careless little girl? Dancing, she decided. She would be much older, maybe twelve or thirteen, and waltzing on the terrace with a handsome boy who lived next door. As they whirled across the stones, she would sweep past the wall and feel the tug, the petticoat caught. Her prince would have to wrest her away, rescue her from the stucco, tear the fabric.

"Sit up and pay attention!" Erica snapped. Amy opened her eyes.

September 1960, Lisbon, Vermont

Paul held his breath and counted *twelve, thirteen, fourteen.* At sixteen, he broke through the water's surface, gasping for air.

"Hey!" his grandfather yelled from the riverbank. "Cut it out. You're scaring away the fish."

Paul dove under again and swam upstream, pushing hard against the cold current.

The cold couldn't stop a navy frogman. Just like his uncle, he was trained to endure every extreme, to hold his breath longer than any average Joe, to sneak up on an enemy target unseen and unheard. His mission now was to blow up the massive ship ahead. He would plant explosives on its hull and be gone without detection. When he reached the boulder, posing as an enemy destroyer, he planted an imaginary device on its underside, then pushed off with his feet, bound for the fishing craft waiting to whisk him to safety. He glided underwater as long as his breath lasted, then surfaced near shore. Ready to warm up, he climbed onto a rock and spread out beneath an unusually warm September sun.

He was far enough upriver that his grandfather couldn't see him. He'd stowed his gear and clothes just up the bank. Once dry he planned to spend the rest of the afternoon looking at the book he'd stashed in his knapsack. The day before, the school librarian, Mrs. Wetzel, had handed it to him as he was checking out his reading book for the week.

"Thought you might enjoy the paintings in this one," she'd said.

Paul had stood, perplexed, the book open on the counter before him. He wasn't a good enough reader yet for a book like this.

"I noticed you spend a lot of time studying the prints in the hallway," Mrs. Wetzel had explained. "Those prints are from paintings by an artist named William Turner. He's one of my favorites."

One of the book's images of a ship in port at sunset caught his attention. He liked the way the colors swirled around the boat, filling the canvas. He could see they were meant to suggest sky and water, and yet there was more, an energy in the movement and color that he liked.

Paul hadn't shown the book to his parents. He didn't think his dad would approve. Not because these were bad pictures, but because there was always too much work to do on the farm. His father Cam didn't tolerate any activity, including reading, that took Paul away from his chores.

Dried off and dressed, he collected the book, found a tree to lean against, and propped the book open on his thighs. He handled it carefully, the way Mrs. Wetzel had shown him, mindful not to leave fingerprints, and studied the artwork. Turner's early paintings were more like the landscapes Paul had seen before, but it was his later work Paul liked best. Turner used so few details and yet his skies and seas felt alive.

Paul did not look up again until he heard his grandfather calling from downriver. He jumped to his feet and returned the book to the knapsack. As he trotted along the riverbank, bag and fishing rod in hand, he wondered what it would be like to imagine such scenes and have hands able to bring them to life. Would Mrs. Wetzel know how he could learn to move a paintbrush the way Turner did?

"Thought you'd gone and drowned on me," his grandfather said as he kicked dirt on the fire they'd made earlier. "You seem in a mighty good mood. Got some fish stowed in that bag of yours?"

"Nah. They weren't biting for me."

While his grandfather packed up his gear, Paul walked out to the river's edge and crouched down to study the colors in the water. He felt Gramps's eyes on him. How had Turner made it look as if the water reflected the sky, he wondered, as he trailed after his grandfather. If they got back to the farm before sunset, he planned to climb the hill behind the farm and catch a look at the sun as it dipped below the horizon. He wanted to see if Vermont's sunsets were like the Venetian ones Turner painted.

September 1960, East Haven, Connecticut

"Dear Lord," Mrs. McCutheon muttered as she passed between Amy's and Jeb Spoone's desks.

She stopped beside Jeb. "You reek, child. Does your mother ever bathe you?"

Jeb shoved his hands under his legs.

Amy had complained to her mother about Jeb after the first day of school. "There's a boy in the class who smells bad and wears dirty clothes."

"It's not his fault," her mother said, looking up from the sandwich she was making. "Please be kind and say nothing about the smell."

"But it's so bad it burns my nose."

"Then breathe out of your mouth. That boy does not need you making his life harder than it already is." Amy hadn't mentioned him again.

"Look at me when I speak to you, Jeb Spoone," Mrs. McCutheon continued. "That's what decent people do. They have the courtesy to look a person in the eye."

Keeping her head down, Amy glanced over at Jeb, who did as the teacher told him. He looked up at her, his face blank, his eyes far away.

Mrs. McCutheon frightened Amy. A steely spear of a woman, she didn't hesitate to wash a mouth out with soap or paddle a bottom.

Amy burst out crying her first morning of second grade when she couldn't fill out an information card Mrs. McCutheon placed in front of her. Her handwriting was too large for the tiny blank spaces.

Mrs. McCutheon had said, "Well, I guess this is what happens to little girls when their mothers don't follow the rules. If your mother had registered you properly before school began, you wouldn't have to be doing this."

She had snatched the card from Amy's hands.

"Spell me your name, child."

She went through the entire card, snapping questions at Amy as the whole class watched.

"Tell your mother to be more conscientious in the future. Do you know what that word means? Conscientious?"

Amy shook her head.

"It means she should meet her responsibilities. If she's going to have babies, she'd best be ready to be a proper mother to them."

Amy had shared none of that with her mother.

Mrs. McCutheon chewed her lip, as if weighing her options. Amy lowered her gaze to the floor, studying the teacher's black lace-up shoes and thick ankles squeezed into an orangey pair of stockings.

"The other children can't possibly concentrate with such a stench in the room. Amy!"

Amy sat up straight, terrified that attention had turned to her.

"Take Jeb to the principal's office. Tell Mrs. Rinaldi that this is what I've been talking about. No child should be allowed in the school if they smell this bad."

When Amy hesitated, the teacher added, "Now!"

Amy and Jeb rose from their seats. Amy felt the eyes of the other students follow them as they crossed the room. She knew she was as much an outsider as Jeb. She was the new girl from Hawai'i whose clothes were too thin and who, as Mrs. McCutheon regularly reminded them, was a show-off when it came to schoolwork. Amy learned not to raise her hand if she knew the answer to a question. All the same, Mrs. McCutheon called her "little miss smarty-pants." That morning, when Amy got a hundred on her spelling test, Mrs. McCutheon had sniffed. "Smart enough to spell right, but not smart enough to wear wool in the winter."

Jeb hung back as they walked down the long corridor of the old building. The school was not large. In fact, its small size meant the district had to run two sessions of classes a day. They were part of the morning group that met from 7:30 to 11:30. At noon, the next session began and another class of second graders occupied the room until four.

"Come on," Amy whispered to Jeb, who lagged behind and wouldn't look at her. He walked with his hands in his pockets and his eyes on the gray linoleum floor.

Amy paused outside the door. "Principal's Office" was painted in black across the frosted glass. She didn't know if she should simply enter or knock first. This school, the way it looked and its rules, was nothing like her school in Hawai'i. At McNeil Academy, classrooms were large and each had its own covered patio and yard. She didn't even know where the McNeil lower-school principal's office was—no one was ever sent there. She decided she should knock. Nothing. She knocked again, a bit louder and longer.

"What?" a voice within barked. "Turn the knob."

Amy opened the door and held it for Jeb.

"Oh, it's you," the secretary behind the counter said when Jeb entered. "And who are you?"

"Amy Barnes. Mrs. McCutheon told me to bring Jeb here."

"What's the problem this time?" The woman peered down at Amy over her glasses.

Amy didn't want to say. She looked at Jeb, who was staring out the window.

"Mrs. McCutheon wants Jeb to see the principal. She says he needs help getting cleaned up."

"He's rather ripe, isn't he?"

She turned to Amy. "Okay, you did your job. Trot along back to your room and no dawdling. You go straight to the classroom."

Amy couldn't imagine what else the woman thought she might do.

Jeb hadn't moved. He still stared out the window at the cement playground ringed with skeletal trees.

Amy put a hand on his shoulder. He jumped, startled.

"It'll be okay, Jeb."

He looked at her for a moment then dropped his gaze to the floor. She followed his eyes, saw that his sneakers were separating. His big toe stuck out of the right shoe. He wore no socks.

"Go on now, get back to class." The woman motioned Amy out the door. "Come on, Jeb. You know what to do."

She held a small wooden gate open for him and he followed her to the principal's private office.

Amy headed back down the empty hallway, the murmur of voices drifting through the doors and walls of classrooms she passed. She looked down at her shiny new saddle shoes and the lace-trimmed socks carefully folded at her ankles. She pushed her fingers into the corners of her eyes. She didn't want Mrs. McCutheon calling her a crybaby again.

December 1960, New Haven, Connecticut

Amy waddled more than walked, the elastic waistband of her tights down at her hips, the crotch at her knees. She barely noticed. Her head was filled with images of tiger pits and racing with ostriches.

"Why's she walking so funny?" her Aunt Sally asked. Sally and Amy's mom Clare were walking a few paces back with Kimo.

"You okay, pumpkin?" her dad asked, his hand in hers.

Amy nodded. She didn't want her mom trying to pull her tights up right there in the middle of downtown New Haven. She could make it to the car. She didn't want anything to slow down their return home, not when it was already dark on Christmas Eve.

She had not been hopeful about this Christmas ever since her aunt's arrival from New York City the day before. She wanted to like Aunt Sally, had waited eagerly with her mom at the train station, hoping this time her aunt would be friendlier than during past Christmases in Hawai'i or when they had visited her on a recent day trip to the city. But so far Sally was acting just as strangely as she did in Honolulu and New York.

"She looks mean," Amy had told her mom the night before as Clare tucked her in bed. Amy wasn't sure if it was Sally's black clothes, her tiny fringe of angry bangs, or the giant gold hoops hanging from her pierced ears that scared her most.

"She's not so tough as she looks," her mom promised.

Amy didn't quite believe her. Her mom and dad were quiet around Sally, and when Sally poured herself another glass of wine after dinner, finishing the bottle, her mom had looked ready to say something, then rubbed a hand over her forehead.

"It'll be a good thing," her mom had said when she told Amy's dad that Sally was coming to Connecticut rather than Hawai'i for Christmas. "I'll make sure she behaves."

"Good luck with that," her dad had said.

None of that mattered now. Her fear that this odd aunt would ruin Christmas had been erased when she saw *Swiss Family Robinson* on the Palace Theater's marquee. Everyone at school had been talking about the movie, and though Amy had asked Santa for a white muff she'd seen at Macy's, what she really wanted most of all was to see this movie. She hadn't dared ask her parents. They'd been clear from the moment they left Hawai'i—no extras like movies this year, no presents that weren't essential, no treats. But the miracle had happened. Her deepest wish came true.

"Thanks, Daddy," she said, planting a kiss on his cheek as he helped her into the back seat. "That was the best Christmas present ever."

She caught her aunt rolling her eyes as she slid across the passenger seat up front.

"I feel a diabetic coma coming on," Sally muttered.

Amy's mom, squeezed into the back seat between Amy and Kimo, reached a hand over the seat back and laid it on Sally's shoulder for a moment.

As they drove home, Amy chattered to Kimo about what they would do once there.

"First we'll put out a bunch of carrots for Rudolph and the other reindeer. Then cookies and milk for Santa."

"I'm guessing Santa might prefer scotch," Sally said, staring up at the car's ceiling, her head resting on the seat back.

"What's scotch?" Kimo asked, leaning over the seat back so his head was beside his aunt's. He kept his feet perched on the back seat cushion.

"Sit down, mister," his mom said, grabbing him by the waist and wrestling him back onto the seat beside her.

"And we have to write a note," Amy said, "reminding Santa what we want so he leaves the right stuff." She remembered she'd just gotten her secret Christmas wish. "Except I guess we already had our Christmas, didn't we?"

She felt the giddiness in her fade. She shouldn't want more stuff, but it wouldn't be Christmas if there were no presents under the tree in the morning.

"The movie was a gift from Mommy and me," her father said. "I imagine Santa may still have something in his bag for you two."

Sally sighed loudly.

"Something you want to share?" Amy's dad asked.

"I'm thinking they must have added 'mother's little helper' to the water supply here. Forget Disneyland. This is the happiest damn place on Earth."

Amy was uncomfortable in the silence that followed.

"Cut it out, Kimo," she said when her brother stretched out across their mother's lap and pressed his feet against Amy's leg. "Can't we go faster, Daddy? It's getting pretty late." Even Amy could hear the whine in her voice.

"On our way, sweetheart." He fiddled with the radio station until he found one playing Christmas carols.

"I don't suppose anyone wants to go to the late service tonight?" her mother asked. She kept one hand on Kimo's head, stroking his hair. Amy could see he was nearly asleep. No one answered.

"Don't fall asleep yet, Kimo, or you won't be able to sleep later, and if you're awake, Santa won't come," Amy finally said, moving her leg so it pushed against her brother's feet.

"Bossy little thing," Sally said from the front seat. Amy's mom pressed her free hand on Sally's shoulder again.

Bossy little thing. She was a bossy little thing and that was not a good thing to be. Only the week before, her mom had told her to stop telling Kimo what to do. "No one likes a bossy girl," she'd said. It hadn't hurt so much the way her mom said it.

She wondered now if Santa thought she was bossy, too. Maybe he didn't bring presents to bossy little girls. She would have to be very careful for the rest of the night and say nothing mean to Kimo. She looked up at the sky, half hoping, half fearing she'd see Santa's sleigh racing by.

December 1960, Lisbon, Vermont

Paul used his thumb to spread the pink icing over the bell-shaped cookie's surface. With a toothpick, he experimented with drawing delicate lines in the frosting, decided he didn't like the effect, and smoothed it out again with a knife. He squeezed some orange food coloring onto his thumb and stamped the cookie's center with a thumbprint. He liked the effect.

His sister Peg, across the kitchen table from him, was icing a Christmas tree cookie. She'd smoothed green frosting over its surface and then piped the edges in white. Paul knew she would next pick up silver candy balls with her tweezers and place them in an orderly pattern over the green surface, just as she'd done with every other tree cookie that afternoon. She looked at his bell and sighed deeply.

"Christmas trees are not blue," she'd declared earlier when she saw a tree he'd decorated. His was highly textured with deep-blue splotches and flecks of white to suggest snow.

"They're blue at dusk," Paul said, wishing she'd be quiet and leave him alone.

Their mother Adele sighed as she washed the bowls and cookie sheets she'd used for baking. Dozens of cookies cooled on racks. Dozens more were piled before Peg and Paul. They couldn't possibly decorate them all that day. Most would be sprinkled with colored sugar, a few set aside for the cousins to ice later after sledding.

Adele leaned over the table to gauge their progress, drying her hands on the Santa Claus apron she always wore on Christmas Eve. "Lucky people getting these for Christmas."

Peg scoffed. "Check out his pink snowman." She nodded to a snowman cookie frosted in swirls of pink and orange with blue eyes.

"It's a snowman at sunrise," Paul said.

"Of course it is," Adele agreed, smiling. She held up one of Peg's snowflakes. "The piped icing makes this look just like lace."

Paul could see his sister's hand was steadier than his, her lines smooth where his were uneven and broken, but she had no imagination. It didn't seem fair that she was the one with good hands. He set aside his bell and picked up a snowflake. He hadn't done one yet. He reached for the bowl of purple frosting and swirled the purple thickly over the cookie. He then took a small spoonful of yellow icing and with a toothpick, mingled it in with the purple.

"That's just ugly," Peg said, leaning over the table to look. Paul wanted to yank her braids.

"You're just ugly."

Adele struck her knuckle against the kitchen counter. A warning. Peg dropped another silver ball on her tree and Paul sprinkled gold sugar over his snowflake.

The storm door slapped against the frame. Cam Rideau leaned into the kitchen, keeping his boots planted in the mudroom.

"Folks are here."

Peg jumped out of her chair and, tree in hand, ran over to show her father.

"Real pretty."

Paul continued working on his snowflake, adding a coating of pink sugar.

"You coming?" his dad asked.

"I want to do a couple more."

Paul picked up a cookie to show his dad. "How do you like this?"

"Looks like it fell in five cans of paint. Come on. Get suited up."

"He'll be out in a bit. Let him finish," Adele said.

Paul watched his parents exchange looks.

"I'll be out soon, Dad. I promise."

Cam studied his son's hands. "Pretty manly look you got going on there. Don't let the cousins catch you with that pink goop hanging from your fingertips."

"Cam," Adele cautioned.

"Just saying. Coloring cookies when he could be out sledding? Seems pretty girly to me."

Paul walked to the sink, not looking at his father as he washed the frosting from his fingers.

"What?" Cam said to his wife. "A boy should be outside, not in the kitchen making cookies."

Paul hauled on his snow pants, jacket, and boots. As he slipped his hands into mittens, his mother came to the doorway between the kitchen and mudroom.

"Want me to set some aside for you to do later?"

"Nah. They're just stupid cookies."

Paul could hear Peg and their cousin Diane squealing outside. He hoped Peg flew off her sled and into a snowbank. "I like the cookies you made today, Paul. They're real pretty."

Paul felt his mom watching him as he finished lacing his boots. Pretty was about the last thing he wanted his cookies to be.

May 1963, Honolulu, Hawai'i

The little kids bunched up close to Amy at the crosswalk, the boys in aloha shirts, the girls in bright mu'umu'us, all of them with leis draped around their necks. Their excitement level was high, and Amy had to warn them to cut out the pushing and crowding. Once she had a sizable group beside her, she signaled to her partner, blew her whistle, and lowered her stop sign. She held it in front of her as the kids passed from the playground to the classrooms housing grades one through four. When her partner, Herbert Pang, nodded, she blew her whistle again, having to first separate it from the plumeria lei she wore. The cars moved on.

It was May Day. There would be a lower-school pageant complete with a Hawaiian royal court and a series of hula performances. The cafeteria would serve laulaus and poi. Amy's mom had sewn her a new mu'umu'u and she'd strung the lei herself the night before.

No clouds hung over the Ko'olaus thanks to the stiff trade winds that snapped the flag to attention overhead. The shower trees were flaming yellow canopies.

Amy heard the first bell ringing over at Storrs Hall. The fifth and sixth graders could now enter the building. As always when she had junior police officer duty, she'd be the last one into the classroom.

Across the road from her, Janice Shimabukuro resisted the tide of kids headed to Storrs and bounced on her toes next to Herbert. Once he and Amy had lowered their stop signs, she raced across to Amy.

"Guess what, guess what?" She hung on to Amy's arm as she jiggled beside her.

Amy blew her whistle and raised her stop sign.

"What?"

"Jay's got a carnation lei for you! The thick kind."

Amy frowned. "Why would he do that?"

"Duh, cause it's May Day! It means he likes you."

Amy rolled her eyes. “I doubt it.”

She was secretly pleased. She liked Jay, too. It helped that he was the tallest boy in the class and the only one taller than she. She also thought he looked exactly like James Shigeta.

“He’s waiting outside Storrs for you. He got a pink one cause he knows it’s your favorite color. His mom had to go all the way to Maunakea Street to find a pink one. They were all out at the Mōʻiliʻili shops.”

Amy was impressed. Her parents never went to the trouble of shopping at Chinatown’s lei stands.

“I can’t leave yet. I have to stay till the five-of bell.”

“That’s okay. I told him you had JPO and he said he’d wait. Even if it means being late.” Her eyes widened as she said this. “He must really like you.”

A swarm of elementary school kids had formed around Amy, and Herbert was trying to get her attention. She nodded and they both blew their whistles.

“Okay, I’ve got to go.” Janice dashed back across the street ahead of the little kids.

“No running allowed,” Herbert snapped at her.

As Amy raised her sign, Craig Rodriguez yelled out to her, a football tucked under his arm. “Hey, Amy.” He and some of the other fifth-grade boys were heading to Storrs from the playground. He smacked his lips together. “You going to let Jay kiss you?”

“Very mature.” She turned back to watch the road. She’d despised Craig ever since the day she’d first worn a bra to school. Not knowing any better, she’d put on a white blouse thin enough to reveal the bra’s outline, and Craig made sure to point it out to everyone. She’d been snickered at all day, not understanding why until Kelly Peterson clued her in.

“Your lover boy’s waiting for you,” Craig crowed before he and the other boys brazenly crossed the road several yards down from the crosswalk.

Amy didn’t want that stupid lei now. It meant she’d be teased again.

When she’d put away her gear and headed over to Storrs, Jay was still waiting at the side stairs. She considered going around to the front, but he’d already seen her and waved. She had to go through with it. At least no one else was around.

“Hey,” he said, his binders in his left hand and a plastic bag with the lei in his right.

She could see he had a new aloha shirt. Amy knew Janice would make some comment on how well their fabrics went together—hers blue with yellow and white blossoms, his blue with white tiki blocks.

"Without being too matchy-matchy touristy, you know?" she could hear Janice squeaking.

As always, Jay's dark hair was neatly combed to the side and his cheek twitched even as he tried to act cool.

"Hi." Amy clutched her books to her chest, crushing her plumeria lei, and was grateful the bodice of her new mu'umu'u went up to her neck.

Jay held the bag out to her. "Here. Happy May Day."

"Thanks." She held the bag, unsure what to do with it. "Should I put it on?"

He shrugged. "I guess."

He held her books as she pulled the lei from the bag. Before placing it over her head, she took off her plumeria lei and held it out to Jay. "Want this?"

He shrugged again. "Sure." The yellow plumeria looked good against the blue shirt.

"Some reason you kids aren't inside?" Mr. Johnson, the middle school supervisor, had come up behind them. "Get going. It's after eight."

Craig started making smacking noises as soon as Jay and Amy entered the classroom. Mrs. Parsons turned from the board where she was writing out the day's assignments.

She looked over her glasses at them. "I know you had JPO duty, Amy, but what's your excuse, Mr. Tanaka?"

"Sorry, Mrs. Parsons. I lost track of the time."

There were a few snickers.

"We'll discuss it later. Take your seat."

Amy could feel the other kids' stares as she walked to her desk. She expected to see sneers when she looked up, and mouths screwed up to make kissing noises, but the reactions surprised her. Girls who usually ignored her smiled. Except for Craig, the boys' faces suggested respect. No one snickered. Something about the lei made her different, and while the attention made her squirm, it also pleased her. For the rest of the day, the other girls were a bit shy around her. Sometimes when she looked up, she would find one of them staring at her, as if she had captured the gold.

At the end of the day, as she gathered up her books, Mrs. Parsons asked her to stay behind. She waited until the other kids had gone before she spoke.

"I've already talked with Jay about this, and Mr. Johnson will be calling Jay's parents."

Amy was confused. "Because he was late? He was just talking to me, Mrs. Parsons. He wasn't doing anything bad."

"No. I spoke to Jay and to Mr. Johnson because I'm concerned about what happened today."

Amy stared at her, not understanding what this was about.

"You're maturing early, Amy, and that's causing the boys to notice you. But not in a good way. It's not the kind of attention you want to encourage."

"You mean the way they teased me about wearing a bra?"

"Exactly."

"But Jay didn't tease me." Amy felt even more confused. *How was it that Jay was in trouble and not Craig?*

"I heard during class that Jay gave you the carnation lei you're wearing."

Amy nodded.

"You two are very young to be exchanging gifts of that nature. Do you understand what I mean?"

Amy shook her head. She didn't understand any of this. On the verge of tears, all she wanted was to get out of that room.

"I think Jay gave you that lei to show that he likes you. The way an adult man might bring flowers to a woman he is dating. Only you and Jay are still children. It's not appropriate for him to be giving you that sort of gift."

"I don't think he meant to do something wrong. He never says bad things like the other boys do."

"That's good to hear. Maybe Jay simply needs some guidance on these matters. You don't have to worry. He's not in trouble. I only want to be sure you both understand the difference between what is and isn't okay at your age. It's not merely something Jay needs to learn. There's a lot you could do to keep the boys from talking and behaving inappropriately around you."

Amy, who'd been studying the floor tiles, looked up at this. She wanted to know how to silence boys like Craig Rodriguez.

"You must make sure you never wear dresses or blouses that are too sheer. You know. The kind of clothes you can see through. And sometimes, your necklines are lower than they should be. You need to keep your chest covered."

Amy blushed. She hated it when any part of her breasts showed, but she couldn't help it with some of her scoop-neck dresses. Her bra straps and the tops of her breasts were forever inching up and spilling out.

"It's fine," her mother always said if Amy complained about her cleavage. "You're one of the lucky ones." Only Amy didn't feel lucky.

"If you are careful to stay well covered up and keep your skirts down to your knees," Mrs. Parsons continued, "you'll be telling the boys you're not the kind of girl who welcomes crude remarks and inappropriate attention."

Amy felt queasy. All the snickers and whispers had been her fault.

"The next time a boy offers you a gift as an expression of his affection, you should decline it. There'll be plenty of time for that when you're in high school and college."

Amy wanted to leave. She could feel the tears welling up again in her eyes and didn't want Mrs. Parsons to see her cry. She nodded, keeping her eyes on the floor.

"Okay, you can go now." Mrs. Parsons turned back to her desk and Amy scurried out the door. She feared Janice might have stuck around to find out why she'd gotten in trouble, but the hall was empty.

As she headed down the corridor, she jerked the lei off her head and threw it in the large trash can at the hall's end.

"Stupid lei," she muttered, heading down the staircase, the lei's scent lingering on her mu'umu'u and hair.

June 1965, Lisbon, Vermont

Paul set the large paper bag down on the kitchen table. He'd already stuffed in his pajamas and a change of clothes. His birthday gift for Adam, a Matchbox truck wrapped in red store-bought paper left over from Christmas, sat beside it. Too busy with relations and friends crammed into the house, Paul's mom had given him a dollar and sent him off to Woolworth's with his dad to pick out something for Adam.

"I'm adding your toothbrush," his mom said as she wound a tissue around the brush and set it at the bottom. "Be sure you brush. Before bed and after breakfast."

Paul's dad leaned back against the kitchen counter.

"The boy will be fine, Adele."

"I know." His mom looked wound up tight as the tissue on the brush. The way she'd looked ever since the phone had rung at dinnertime two days earlier. "I want to be sure he has all he needs. Oh, I almost forgot."

She reached into her pocket and pulled out a quarter.

"I expect the Tremonts will pay for your movie ticket since they invited you, but you should have your own money just in case. If you don't have to pay to get in, you and Adam can go buy yourselves a treat."

"Thanks, Mom."

The coin felt heavy in his pocket. His mom never let him buy candy when he went to the Saturday matinee westerns. He wondered if the concession stand at a drive-in was like the one at the theater in town.

At the sound of tires on gravel, Paul gathered up his pillow and sleeping bag. He let his mom carry the paper bag and gift. He was surprised to see Mr., not Mrs. Tremont at the wheel. His own dad never went to the movies. They tossed everything but the present into the Tremonts' truck bed and Paul climbed into the cab. He handed Adam the package.

"Thanks." Adam held the gift unopened in his lap. Paul wanted him to rip off the wrapping, but he kept quiet.

After she'd visited a moment with Mr. Tremont, Paul's mom came around to the window and leaned in.

"You be good and do as Mr. Tremont says," she said, her head cocked to the side for emphasis.

Paul nodded, hoping she wasn't going to lean in and kiss him.

"Thanks again for having him, Ralph." She stepped back from the cab, pulling her ponytail tight.

Adam's dad lifted a hand as the truck headed down the drive. Paul was glad the cousins and aunties had stayed inside.

Paul looked over at Adam and Mr. Tremont. Both sat stone-faced, eyes on the road, so he kept quiet.

Ralph Tremont had a small sack wedged beside his seat and the gearshift. He raised it in Paul's direction.

"Little secret between you boys and me. Mrs. Tremont's not a fan of the spirits, so I take my pleasures away from the house."

He took a swig.

Paul nodded. "I won't tell anyone."

As they headed up Route 5, the sky darkened to a deeper blue behind the hills. Once they were on an open stretch of road, Mr. Tremont picked up the bag again. With his left hand on the wheel, he lifted the bag to his mouth and took another nip. Paul could tell from the smell it was something stronger than beer.

Paul knew his mom wouldn't approve of Mr. Tremont drinking while he was driving. He wondered what she was doing now. Probably making coffee or listening to people tell stories about Kurt. Paul was sick of stories about Kurt. Kurt was all anyone talked about now. One minute the world had been normal—he and Peg setting the table, pouring milk into glasses, their mom carrying potatoes from the stove to the colander in the sink—and then the phone rang and everything changed. "How" was all his mom had said into the phone. She'd listened and then told Paul to fetch his dad.

Their cousin Kurt, only nine, had been seized by an asthma attack and died before his parents could even decide about taking him to the emergency room.

People had begun arriving nearly as soon as his dad sat down at the table.

"Eat up now," he'd told Peg and Paul. "There won't be time for it later."

Their parlor immediately became the gathering place where his grandparents and uncle met with relations and friends who dropped by. His aunt and uncle's trailer couldn't hold everyone, and without anyone saying anything, people knew to come to the family farmhouse. Aunt Jill, Kurt's mom, didn't want to see anyone. She sat alone in the kitchen, a cup of cold tea on the little table beside her.

The next morning the food began arriving. Some people simply dropped off dishes, the braver ones entered the house. Paul had run away from it all to the grass slope near the pond, keeping his head turned away from the drive so he wouldn't see the cars coming and going.

As he lay there, a gust of wind swept down from the west. Paul watched as the trees swayed, the pines shaking off clouds of yellow pollen, the kind of pollen that had killed Kurt. Paul couldn't understand how the day could be so sunny and the clouds so white. Shouldn't storm clouds creep over the mountains and the wind howl when someone dies?

When they pulled up to the ticket booth, Paul read the sign: KIDS

UNDER 12 FREE. All the same, he offered Mr. Tremont his quarter and Mr. Tremont took it.

They drove onto a grassy field dotted with short metal poles. A giant screen towered over the field's far end. Mr. Tremont pulled up alongside one of the poles and parked. He rolled his window halfway up, then lifted a box from the pole and hooked it to the window so it faced out.

"The speaker," Adam explained to Paul. "The sound will come out of this thing. We can grab the folding chairs from the back and set them out on the grass."

It looked to Paul as though other people were staying in their cars with the speakers facing in. Once they'd set the chairs beside the truck, Adam grabbed a basket and small cooler.

"Mom made us some popcorn and lemonade," he said, passing Paul a sack.

When the sky reached its deepest blue, the screen lit up with a commercial for the snack bar. Paul was disappointed he wouldn't get to buy any candy.

"You kids able to hear okay?" Mr. Tremont asked, leaning out of the cab.

"Yup," Adam said. Paul thought the man's words were getting a little fuzzy, the way Uncle Murray's did when he stopped by to visit with Paul's dad.

The movie started up and the words *Old Yeller* filled the screen. A dog appeared on a ledge. Adam nudged Paul.

"Looks just like your dog."

Paul nodded. His dog, Lightning, wasn't quite so big as that, but he was just as light in color. Paul leaned forward, elbows on his knees. He didn't move much again for the length of the movie except to refill his sack with popcorn and help himself to lemonade.

Twenty minutes into the movie, Mr. Tremont began snoring loud enough for the boys to hear him. Paul figured that was a good thing. Better sleeping than finishing off that bottle.

An hour and a half later, as the boy Travis walked away from the camera into the blue smoke, his dog Yeller dead, Paul wrapped his arms around himself and dug his thumbs into his armpits. No way he wanted Adam or Mr. Tremont to catch him crying. He didn't understand why he felt so bad about some dog's pretend death in a movie when he couldn't even cry for his own cousin.

The day before Kurt's death, Paul and Kurt had sat together on the bus so Kurt could show Paul one of the fishing flies he'd made the weekend before. *How was it,* Paul thought, staring up as the movie's credits scrolled by, *that one moment a person could be talking to you, everything normal and regular, and then almost as quick as a snap of the fingers, he was dead?* Paul could come home from school one day and find both of his parents dead from a fire or a bum furnace or a collapsed roof.

He felt as if he was going to be sick. He put his head between his knees and took deep breaths, willing the nausea away.

"You okay?" Adam asked quietly.

Paul shook his head.

"Want to go home?"

Paul didn't want Adam thinking he was some kind of baby who couldn't sleep over at another kid's house, but all he wanted was to be home in his own bed, Lightning asleep on the rug beside him, his parents in the room next to his, and Kurt still alive in the trailer up the road, wrapping thread around a hook, lashing feathers in place.

Spring 1966, Lisbon, Vermont

Paul tossed a baseball back and forth with Adam as they waited for the coach and other players. A hawk circled overhead, dove into the tall grass beyond the field, and rose, a mouse in its beak. Paul missed the days when he could lie out in a field with nothing to do after school but study the passing clouds and the way they changed with the light.

Cars began to arrive. Coach Harrison pulled up in his sleek '59 El Camino. "Most ridiculous thing I ever saw," Paul's dad had said of it. "Couldn't haul a load of groceries."

Paul understood what Harrison's choice of truck said to men like his father. This was a truck that would never carry hay, grain, or deer. It didn't help that Harrison was the kind of guy who'd never owned a pair of Carhartt's and was always late paying his bills.

But unlike his dad, Paul understood why the truck appealed to Harrison.

He'd run a hand over its sharp silver fins the first time he saw it. Harrison might be a clueless, fancy-talking flatlander, but Paul knew he had an eye. Harrison and his wife had bought the old Peterson spread a few years before and poured a ton of money into it, employing every quality craftsman in the area. Some said it was a fool's errand, restoring an old place like that. Paul disagreed. He thought they'd turned a run-down farm into something like he'd only seen in picture books.

"Trust fund babies," Paul's dad had declared them, but Paul listened to his mom who said, "Don't be so quick to judge. Just cause they do things different from us doesn't mean they've got it wrong." All the same, his mom never did more than nod at Mrs. Harrison.

Harrison's son Matt was a good guy so far as Paul could tell. When he'd started school, Matt had dressed like a city kid. Someone had set him straight pretty quick or he'd figured it out for himself. He blended in fine now.

He could even throw a ball. Everyone figured the coach would make him pitcher, even if Dave Jensen's arm was better.

"Rideau, Tremont," the coach called. "Come grab a couple of these bags."

Paul hauled a sack of bats over to home plate.

"Anything else, Coach?"

Harrison ignored him.

Paul wanted to like this guy. He tried to do as his mom said, find something to like in everyone, but much as he admired Harrison's style, he could be tough to take. He wouldn't look a kid in the eye and would interrupt a kid when he was talking, as if what a kid said didn't matter.

A long line of cars filled the drive now.

"Let's pick up the pace, guys," Harrison shouted, clapping his hands together though the boys were already jogging to where he stood.

"Practice starts at four on the dot," he had told them all at the first practice. "No excuses, no exceptions."

When Jack Taylor arrived ten minutes late, Coach Harrison ordered him to run two laps around the outer field.

"But it was my mom's fault," Jack protested.

"Make that three laps for questioning me," the coach said. "It's your job to make sure your mom gets you here on time."

Paul hadn't understood how any adult could think a kid could tell his mom what to do. He had his doubts about this team from the beginning. Before this the kids had played for fun. Now that they were all in seventh grade, the town was running the show and Harrison was coaching like this was high school or college-level sports. They'd even made the kids try out so they could create an elite team.

"We play to win," Harrison told his select group. "We're going to be up against towns like Patchway and Clifton. I don't want people thinking we don't know the meaning of hard work here in Lisbon. We'll show them we're as tough as any of those teams."

Some of the boys had cheered this pep talk, but Paul couldn't figure out what Harrison was talking about. Most of the kids had been working hard since they could walk. They could toss bales of hay, chase cows, haul feed, and clean out barns. Nobody would call these guys soft. Paul figured the coach and his son Matt were the only ones there who might never have put in a long day of hard physical work.

"Jumping jacks, gentlemen. Give me a hundred."

As Paul jumped in place, he watched the coach stroll in front of them, his hands in his pockets, his shirt collar turned up, a sweater tied around his neck. Looking as if he'd never done a jumping jack in his life. *Can't judge a book by its cover,* he could hear his mom saying.

"Okay, twenty sit-ups. On your butts."

Before Paul dropped to the grass, he saw a bike approaching on the dirt drive between the highway and field. A small cloud of dust trailed behind. Dave Jensen tossed down his bike and ran onto the grass as Paul came up for his tenth sit-up.

"You're late, Jensen," the coach yelled. "Give me four laps now. You'll stay late to do the rest of your workout."

Dave didn't move. The other boys stopped doing their sit-ups.

"I said I want four laps, Jensen. You looking to make it five?"

"No, sir. I'm sorry I'm late, but I got here fast as I could."

Dave was breathing hard, his face red with exertion. Paul knew he'd had to pedal hard to cover the four miles from home.

"I can't stay after practice, sir. I have to leave by six to help my dad finish up the chores."

Dave's mom had passed away the year before and he had no older brothers to help. It was just him and his dad handling the farm.

"Sounds to me like you're saying you either don't care about this team or you think you deserve some kind of special treatment."

"No, sir. I just have other things I have to do. I need to get home to help my dad."

Everyone knew the coach needed Dave if they were to win any games. Dave was their best pitcher and hitter. Even if the coach put his son in to pitch, they'd need Dave to give them runs.

"I told you to give me four laps."

Before Dave could move, Paul stood and walked to stand beside him.

"What the hell you think you're doing, Rideau?" Harrison's jaw was tightening.

"What Dave said is true, sir. He has to help with the chores. He's the only help his dad's got. You shouldn't punish him for doing what he's gotta do."

Adam Tremont and Peter Washburn came up to stand with Paul and Dave.

"Okay. Four laps, all of you."

The boys took off, following the field's perimeter. Paul didn't look back. He kept his pace even with Dave's and his eyes on the line between mown and tall grass. None of the four boys said a word. When they had completed four circles, they rejoined the team where the coach was hitting balls for the players to catch. He continued as if nothing had happened.

When Harrison called the team together to give them Saturday's lineup, Dave approached him.

"I have to go, Coach."

Paul wondered if Harrison could feel the team watching, if he realized how much hung on what he said now.

"Be here Saturday at eight," Harrison said without looking up.

"Yes, sir. What position will I play, Coach?"

"You'll start as pitcher."

Dave nodded, picked his bike up off the grass, and rode off. Paul looked over to Matt, the coach's son, who was grinning with relief.

Harrison began reading from his roster as the drive again filled with cars, their engines rumbling.

"Tremont, catcher. Rideau at first. Parsons at second."

The boys neither cheered nor moaned as the coach read off the assignments. The roster was fair and they accepted it.

Paul carried the bats to Harrison's truck, tossed them into the back, and then crossed to where his mom waited in their wingless old Ford. Nothing but rust to rub on its sides, but it looked right to him. Like the soft mitt in his hand, it fit.

Summer 1966, Anaheim, California

Amy leaned against the toilet stall door. She had tried to dab the blood from her panties and shorts, but it hadn't helped. They still had brilliant red oval stains. She had no money with her to buy a sanitary napkin. All she could think to do was stuff a wad of toilet paper between her legs and hope her mom came looking for her. It was that or let everyone at Disneyland see her stained white shorts. She'd rather die than do that.

People came and went from the stalls on either side. The place was busy. She would never be able to sneak out unseen.

"Someone's been in there forever," a woman outside the stall said.

Someone tapped on her stall door. "You okay in there?"

Amy unlatched the door and with eyes on the ground, as if that might make her invisible, walked over to a sink and washed her hands. She didn't dare turn to see in the mirror how her shorts looked from behind.

She slipped out the door and stood with her back against the patio wall of Aunt Jemima's Kitchen.

Look up, Mom, she said silently, willing her mother to glance her way. Of course it was her brother Kimo who spotted her. He made a big commotion with his waving, causing people to look her way. *Typical.* When her mom turned, Amy motioned for her to come.

"I got my period," she whispered once her mom was beside her. "And my pants are stained."

"Oh, hon." Her mom's eyes seemed almost amused. She led her back into the restroom. "You wait here and I promise I'll be back fast as I can."

Amy stood for what seemed an eternity, her back against the bathroom's far wall, until her mom returned with a parcel. She pulled out a pair of panties and shorts. "The salesperson already cut the tags off." She also pulled out a sanitary napkin and safety pins. "You go in the stall and I'll stand guard."

Amy still felt self-conscious when she returned to the table. Kimo was bound to ask questions.

"What took you so long?" Kimo asked.

"None of your beeswax." Amy's mom placed a hand on Amy's arm, her signal that Amy needed to bring it down a notch.

"Amy and I are going to head back to the motel for a bit and have a rest," she said.

"I don't want to go yet." Kimo kicked the table leg.

"Nobody's saying you have to, dimwit."

"Enough. Both of you." Her mother glared at Amy as if she were the one causing trouble.

Amy's dad pulled out the ticket books. "We've got four E tickets and four D tickets left besides all the As. Are you going to want to come back and go on any more rides?" he asked Amy.

She shook her head.

"I want her tickets then," Kimo said.

"Not unless I say you can have them," Amy snapped back.

Her dad put up his hand. "We can all go back to the motel and give these tickets to some better-behaved child."

"How about you and Kimo go ahead and use the tickets," Amy's mom said. "Amy and I will go have a swim."

"Mom!" Amy stared hard at her. How did she expect her to swim if she had her period?

Her mother exhaled loudly. "Right, no swimming. We'll find something else to do."

"Let's go on the Matterhorn," Kimo said. "Okay, Dad?"

"No fair, I wanted to go on the Matterhorn." Amy slumped down in her seat, arms crossed, tears welling in her eyes.

Her dad studied the ticket books in his hand. Amy was afraid he'd tear them up to teach her and Kimo a lesson.

The paper from a drinking straw sailed over their table and tapped her dad's cheek. His head jerked up. A chorus of muffled laughter erupted from the table next to theirs. The boy who'd blown the paper off the straw, called out, "Sorry." He was obviously part of some group. He and all the boys at three nearby tables wore matching tees that said LISBON HORNETS. They looked to be a bit older than Amy. One of the adults with the boys yelled out, "Rideau!" and pointed at Amy's dad. The boy who'd shot the paper stood and walked over to Amy's father. He extended his hand.

"Sorry, sir. I was aiming for my friend."

"No harm done."

Amy kept her head down, certain the boy and all his friends and everybody at Disneyland could tell what had happened to her. It was all so unfair. Boys never had to worry about embarrassing things happening to them, things they had no control over. Being a girl was the worst.

"Can't we go?" she whispered to her mom.

Her mom wiped her napkin across her mouth and laid it beside her plate.

"I gather you guys are some kind of team," Amy's dad said.

Amy didn't understand why her dad had to keep talking to this kid.

"Yup. Baseball. We came out here to play a couple LA teams."

"You win?"

"Nah. But we get to see Disneyland, so we aren't complaining."

When the boy finally moved on, her dad said, "Okay. This is what we're going to do. Right now it's too hot for this to be fun for anyone. We're all going back to the motel. People can swim, take a nap, or go shopping. We'll come back later in the afternoon or early evening and use up the tickets then. Okay?"

Knowing better than to challenge his plan, Kimo and Amy silently followed him out of the restaurant in the direction of the park's entrance. Amy held the shopping bag with her soiled clothes, waiting for Kimo to ask what was in the bag and how come she got a souvenir and he didn't. Life was so unfair. Nothing bad ever happened to Kimo.

"What's your problem, pickle face?" Kimo said when she bumped against a lamppost.

She wanted to pound him. She looked to her parents to say something, but they only exchanged glances as if they were the ones suffering. She hated being a girl.

July 1966, Nuʻuanu, Hawaiʻi

When the phone rang, Amy's mom yelled, "Can you get that, Amy?" She was out front, clearing a section of bamboo crowding the dirt driveway.

Amy set her book down on the coffee table.

"Hey, princess. How's my best girl?" It was her dad.

Though he didn't teach in the summer, Brent Barnes still spent most of each day painting in his university studio. A call from him at three meant he might be ready for a break, might even take her and Kimo swimming.

"Are we going to the beach, Dad?"

"Not today, sweets. Some former students stopped by. Could you tell Mom they'll be coming home with me for dinner?"

Amy looked out the window at her mother's backside and twisted the phone cord. Why did she have to be the one to tell her? Her mom was not going to be happy.

"Was that your dad?" her mom called over her shoulder when Amy stepped out onto the front porch.

"He says some old students came by. They're coming for dinner."

Her mom sat back on her heels and inhaled deeply.

"Did he say how many?"

Amy sighed. She should have thought to ask. "No."

Her mother rose and jerked the gloves from her hands. She threw them, and the hand weeder, into her small cart then wheeled it into the backyard. Amy followed.

Without speaking, they unclipped the sheets drying on the clothesline, working opposite one another just as they had earlier when they pinned them to the line. The fabric was still damp where it had folded over the rope. It didn't matter. With company coming, it all had to come down. Clare Barnes wasn't going to have guests catch her with laundry hanging on the line.

Amy followed her mom's lead and instead of folding the items, simply dumped them in the wicker baskets. She knew from the set of her mother's face that this was not a time for talk.

"We'll have to stow these in your room," her mom said as they carried the two baskets into the house. "I'll deal with them later."

Her mother patted a hand over her scalp, feeling beneath her curlers. "Still damp. Damn. And I've got to get to the store."

She grabbed a chiffon scarf from a dresser drawer and tied it under her chin. Amy knew how much her mother disapproved of women who went out with their hair in rollers.

Her mother's hair was still damp when they returned an hour later with the fixings for dinner—round steak, cream of mushroom soup, and frozen turnovers to bake for dessert. Kimo disappeared to play in the back as their mother headed to the bathroom for a shower. Amy washed her hands and began slicing the steak. Next she would set the table and stack Louis Armstrong and Charlie Parker albums ready to play on the stereo. She knew the drill. Her mom must look stunning, dinner must be ready, and the house neat and tidy when her father came through the door.

By the time he arrived home, a gaggle of aspiring artists in tow, Amy's mom was a woman transformed. She greeted the guests with an enthusiasm that suggested she'd been waiting weeks for the pleasure of their company. *She's just like Laura Petrie,* Amy thought, not for the first time as she watched her mother usher them in, her black shantung silk pedal pushers hugging her hips, the air thick with Chanel No. 5. If her damp curls drooped, Amy didn't think anyone would notice.

Amy retreated to the kitchen to stir the stroganoff, pull the turnovers from the oven, and collect the potato chips and onion dip to pass as her father made his signature martinis, perfect pearl onions tucked into each glass.

September 1966, Lisbon, Vermont

"Wait'll you see what me and Adam found at the truck stop," Gordon told them during lunch. "Couple copies of *Caper* and three *Playboys*."

The boys were grouped around the flagpole in front of the school. Adam glowered when a fifth grader came too close.

"Did you bring 'em with you?" Peter asked.

"Don't be a moron. Course not. No way I'm gonna risk getting them taken away. I got them in a safe place."

"How come you got to keep all five? Why didn't you divide them up?" Paul asked, not quite believing Adam and Gordon had gotten that lucky. He checked the truck stop nearly every day and never found anything that good.

"I let Gordon take them because my mom's always cleaning up my room. I can't hide anything. Gord's mom doesn't care what he's got stashed under his mattress."

Adam meant this as a good thing about Gordon's mom, but Paul knew it bugged Gordon when they talked about her. Fran Dowsett didn't do most of the things the other moms did, things like keeping a vegetable patch or sewing scraps into quilts. Stop by the Dowsetts' place and she'd be watching TV or reading a book, not at all embarrassed to have people see her messy house.

The guys sure didn't care if the place was a mess. Besides providing them with the occasional bag of chips or candy, Mrs. Dowsett never kept tabs on them. Best of all, Gordon's dad Gil had built a small cabin deep in the woods of their property. His hunting camp, he called it, but it was mostly a place where he could go drink without a wife hollering at him or kids being underfoot. The boys could slip back there while Dowsett was at work and no one would come snooping to see what they were up to.

"Come on over after school and I'll let you take a look," Gordon said. "Got anything good to bring yourself?" he added to Paul.

Paul shook his head.

"I bet me and Paul can swipe a couple beers from the grocer on the way over," Adam offered. "And if my dad's got any cigarettes in the barn, I'll grab a few."

Paul didn't want to be stealing anything, let alone beers, but he kept quiet. Better to let them think he was willing to add something to the pot.

When Adam swung by the farm on his bike later that afternoon and hollered to Paul in the milking barn, Paul told him he'd catch up with him later.

"I have to finish washing down the barn before I can take off." Paul deliberately hadn't asked his dad if he could skip out on the work.

Paul could tell Adam was pissed Paul wasn't going to help him snatch beers, but Adam just gave him a look and headed on toward Gordon's.

"You going someplace?" Paul's dad asked.

"Just over to Gordon's," Paul said, hoping he sounded nonchalant. "After I finish up my work."

He could feel his dad studying him. He'd be able to tell something was up.

"You're being mighty responsible today. You could have gone off with Adam, if you wanted."

"That's okay, dad."

"Not saying it's so, but if those boys are up to something you want no part of, you can say I made you stay and do more work."

Paul didn't answer.

By the time he got to the Dowsetts' and quietly ran down the trail to the cabin, it was nearly time to turn around and head home for supper. He could smell the fire the other boys had lit even before he saw its smoke drifting above the tiny building that was barely more than a shed. He wondered at first why they'd bothered. It was nearly summer, but he figured they probably needed it for the light. Paul found them seated in a semicircle before the sad little woodstove Gordon's dad had installed. Each had a magazine in hand and they were passing a cigarette around. They made room for Paul. The cabin was hot and stuffy. The chimney pipe didn't vent well. A veil of smoke hung in the air.

"Want some whiskey?" Adam asked as Paul sat cross-legged beside him on the unfinished wood floor. Adam held out a nearly empty bottle of Jack Daniels.

"How'd you get that?" Paul asked. "They don't sell hard stuff at the grocer."

"I didn't." Adam nodded his head at Peter. "Peter grabbed it out of his uncle's truck."

Paul had tried beer a couple times, but he'd never taken a swig of hard liquor before. He feared he'd choke on it the way wimps did in the westerns. He raised the bottle to his lips and let a small amount trickle into his mouth. Managing to swallow it without gagging, he nodded his head and said, "Good stuff." Pushing his luck, he took another swallow.

"So when do I get to look at one of those," Paul said, nodding at the *Playboy* in Adam's hands.

"Here." Adam handed it to him. "Check out page 137. Looks just like Sarah Tanner."

The cover had a blonde holding up her hair to make it look like she had bunny ears. The blonde Adam was talking about did look like a grown-up, filled-out version of Sarah, he guessed. At least her smile did. It was tough to imagine Sarah would ever have boobs like that, though she'd started wearing a bra that year. As he flipped through the pages and opened up the centerfold,

Paul hoped his face wasn't flushing red.

"I'm hungry. You guys want to see if my mom's got food enough for all of us?" Gordon asked.

"Your mom cooks?" Adam said aloud what Paul was thinking.

"Course she cooks, asshole."

Paul checked his watch. "Thanks, Gord, but I've got to get back. We're eating at six. And my dad knows where to find me if I don't show up on time."

"You can't head out yet. You haven't even looked at the other magazines! Don't think I'm letting you take any with you."

"Nah, I know. Besides my mom would probably sniff them out if I tried bringing any into the house. I'll check them out another time."

Paul was dying to look through the rest of the magazine lying open before him as well as the others laid out on the floor. But he didn't really want to be looking at them with the other guys around. Maybe Gordon would sell him one once he'd finished with them and Paul could stash it in the barn.

Before Paul had even stood up, there was a knock on the cabin door.

"Hey, Gordon? You guys in there?" It was Gordon's dad Gil. "Cam's here looking for Paul."

Gordon scrambled to hide the whiskey bottle and magazines. Adam flicked the cigarette into the fire. Paul went over to the door and opened it.

"Hey, Mr. Dowsett. Dad." He stepped aside so the men could enter.

Gil and Cam looked around the cabin. Gordon had managed to pile the magazines in a way that left one of the centerfolds sticking out from the pile. It seemed to Paul as if both men were trying not to laugh.

"I needed to drop off some bales for Gil and thought maybe you could use a ride home," Paul's dad said. "I already put your bike in the back of the truck."

"Okay. Thanks." Paul turned to his friends. "So, guess I'll see you guys at school tomorrow. Thanks for inviting me over, Gord."

Cam didn't say anything more. The two of them hiked the path back to the truck and drove the three miles home.

As Paul opened the cab door, his dad said, "You'll find some mouthwash in the cupboard under the barn sink. You might want to use some before you head into the house. Your mom's got a good nose on her."

"Right."

"And Paul?"

"Yeah?"

"You'll find some other stuff in the right-hand drawer of my desk. If you promise not to share them with the other boys or bring them in the house, you can take a look. I'm glad to see you taking a normal interest in the female body. Just be respectful of your mom, okay?"

"Sure."

Paul figured his dad had some kind of girlie pictures stashed in his office. Probably like the ones he hung in the barn. Lots of girls in two-piece bathing suits. He wasn't prepared for the stack of *Playboy*s he found later when he slid open the drawer.

Chapter Three

June 2001, Lisbon, Vermont

"You're not cutting down my tree, Paul Rideau."

Judith Clement sat in a lawn chair beneath the maple tree that shaded her front lawn. The maple tree in question was in fact not Judith Clement's property. It belonged to the town and Paul, as groundskeeping supervisor of Lisbon's properties, was responsible for it. His crew checked on the town trees regularly, trimmed their branches when they threatened to damage people or property, cut them down when they died, and planted new saplings in their place.

"Good morning, Mrs. Clement," Paul said. "I'm sorry we've upset your day." He held out his hand. She kept her hands folded in her lap. Though her hair was now white and her face more lined, she looked much the same as Paul remembered from high school. She still wore her hair pulled back in a neat bun and a well-pressed oxford shirt tucked into her chinos.

"Last summer your people chopped off half its branches. Why can't you leave it be?"

"I love this old tree, too, Mrs. Clement. No tree in town could match its fall show of flaming red leaves. But last summer, a lot of those leaves were turning in July. Some just went straight to brown. I hoped cutting away the dead branches would help it recover, but look up there."

He peered at the canopy of bare branches above them, where there should have been a sky of green.

"Those bare branches are going to start falling on passing cars and pedestrians. They'll make a mess of your yard. It's my job to prevent those problems."

He gave her a frank, direct look, hoping to reassure her he meant no harm.

He dropped to the grass near her so he could look up, not down at her. Plenty of townspeople considered Judith a nuisance because of her passion for political causes, but he knew sincere convictions drove her actions. As his ninth-grade social studies teacher, she'd taught him what it meant to be a responsible citizen, and that included listening to opposing views. If she was set on saving this tree, Paul owed her the courtesy of hearing her out.

"Help me understand why you want to keep a dead tree instead of letting us plant you a new one."

She rested a hand against the trunk. "Because it's a thing of beauty and it has served us well. It may be past its prime, but it still stirs the soul. I turn the question back to you. How can you so callously destroy a part of creation?"

"I don't think I am callous, Mrs. Clement. It pains me to lose a tree, especially a town landmark. I promise I wouldn't do this unless it was necessary. A long time ago you taught me we all have an obligation to contribute to the well-being of our communities. And that can mean setting aside our own feelings for the greater good. My contribution includes keeping our town safe and sometimes I have to do things I don't like doing." He studied the tree. "I don't want to say goodbye to this tree either. It's given shelter and shade, maybe even sap. Did you ever tap it?"

"A few times, back in the early days when I taught second grade. We would do a class unit on sugaring."

Paul smiled and turned to his crew, who were restless to get to work.

"You fellows are too young to remember, but Mrs. Clement taught in our school system for what, forty years?"

"Closer to fifty. Ten in the elementary school, thirty-six at the high school."

He turned back to the crew. "She taught me and generations of Lisbon folks the responsibilities that come with the privilege of citizenship."

She smiled. "You're trying to flatter and distract me out of my protest, Paul Rideau."

"I promise I'm sincere. Back in 1965, you had us create a memorial garden and hold an event to honor Jonathon Daniels and the other civil rights activists who'd died fighting racism."

Daniels, from across the river in New Hampshire, had been shot and killed in Alabama only weeks before the start of Paul's first year of high school. Mrs. Clement had used the incident as the centerpiece of her civics unit.

"You showed me we all have an obligation to make a positive difference," Paul continued. "I'm no Jonathon Daniels. I'm sure not going to change the world, but I can at least help care for my town."

Judith allowed him a faint smile. She was no longer the formidable woman of his youth. She was steely enough to have cowed three men into setting down their saws, yet Paul read anxiety in the twisting of her hands and fear in the rigidity of her posture. She was ninety and alone. For decades, the massive tree had buffered her from prying eyes, shaded her home during hot summers, given her children branches to swing from. Everything of value in her life was being chipped away and now she was going to lose even this, her beloved tree.

"Would it help, Mrs. Clement, if you chose the tree we use to replace this one? I've got a few well-established ones set aside."

"How many decades before any of them will approach the splendor of this one?" she asked, but he heard in her voice the understanding that this was not a battle she could win.

A car pulled into the driveway of the house opposite. The driver, Kathy Jefferson, got out and waved to Paul, then crossed. Another woman got out and stayed beside the car.

"Hey there," Kathy called as she approached. "Are you guys having a get-together and no one thought to invite me?"

Paul had in fact called Kathy as soon as he heard Judith was blocking the crew from their work. He'd tracked her down at Clifton High School where she was cleaning out her room for the summer. She was not only Judith's neighbor, she was one of the few people Judith trusted. "I may need your help with Judith," Paul had told her, and she promised to head over.

"What's going on?" She directed her question to Judith.

"You're just in time to watch them destroy my glorious maple."

"Oh, love." Kathy sank down and pulled Judith into a hug. Only Kathy Jefferson would brave such a bold move with Judith. "I'm so sorry. How can I help?"

Judith pushed herself out of her chair. "Give me your arm so I can walk to my kitchen door with a stitch of dignity."

"I can do better than that." Kathy grasped Judith's elbow. "You remember my teaching buddy Amy? She and I are heading out for a celebratory lunch. School's officially done for the year. Come join us. It'll be a fun distraction."

"You don't want a tired old lady tagging along. You have stories to swap. Gossip to share."

"My dear, no one tells a better story or knows more gossip than you. Let's go inside and you can freshen up. Then we'll grab your purse, and go pig out on onion rings and clam strips."

Judith turned back to Paul. "I have your word I can pick the tree I want?"

"Yup. And we'll wait till you guys leave before we begin."

"No. I've no patience for fragile people who can't face hard realities straight on. Do what you have to do. Take it down. And just so you both know"—she looked sternly at Paul and Kathy—"I'm on to you. I know when I'm being handled. But seeing as how you're bribing me with fried food, I'll trust you. Don't make me regret that decision."

"No, ma'am," Paul said.

The door closed and Paul signaled to the crew they could begin.

A huge branch crashed to the ground before Paul had even started his truck.

June 2001, Nu'uanu, Hawai'i

"This place should be condemned." Kara slammed her computer shut. "The internet's out again. Even if it comes back up, there's no place I can put my computer. Everything's soaking wet."

Pots and mixing bowls were scattered throughout the dilapidated cottage in a vain attempt to catch the drips from the rusted roof as rain pounded the island for the fourth day.

"Think optimistically. Maybe the mice will leave to avoid drowning." Will batted a volleyball over his head.

"I'm sorry, guys. I know this sucks big time." Amy didn't want to give up on the tiny Nu'uanu cottage she'd called home for the first three decades of her life, but she had to admit, whatever charm remained was overwhelmed by its miserable state. Faucets offered trickles of water that were, at best, lukewarm, requiring that they heat pots of water to wash dishes. Lights flickered in what seemed more a throbbing fire alert than a reliable source of light and the counters, kitchen and bathroom, were a thick carpet of tiny roaches as soon as they turned off the lights for the night. The structure, originally constructed to house the property's caretaker, was at least seventy years old and it showed.

"It's not livable," Kara said, as if anyone needed persuading.

Gretchen's familiar firm knock sounded at the front door, and she entered, a huge bouquet of torch ginger and bird-of-paradise stalks in hand.

"I come bearing flowers and to see how you're holding up. This rain is something else. Feels more like March than June." She paused in the kitchen's center where they had gathered and surveyed the pots and pans, the dripping ceiling. "Oh my." She did a quick check of the other rooms. "So basically, you're about to float away. I feared this place was past salvaging, but I was hoping we could manage one more summer. Nothing for it but to pack up your things. You're moving in with me."

"Aunt Gretchen, no. We can't do that to you. We'll stay at the Kailua beach house and commute to McNeil. I can park myself at the library while the kids are in class." Amy's work for the summer was revamping the curriculum for her tenth-grade English class. She could do that anywhere that provided an electrical outlet, table, and chair.

"Don't be silly. The Kailua place is barely habitable even on weekends. There's no way the kids can get their work done there and trust me, you do not want to be doing that daily commute. You'll stay here at the main house with me. I've three empty bedrooms on the side opposite mine. We won't even see each other. It's settled." She headed for the front door. "I'll open the garage door so it's easy to ferry stuff in."

"Are you sure? The last thing I want is to impose on you." Amy followed her aunt to the door.

"You're never an imposition. Now pack up before you drown."

She hustled out the front door, the long-stemmed flowers still tucked under her arm, and headed up the drive.

"You guys okay with this?" Amy asked as she stuffed course materials and textbooks into a tote.

"Hell, yes," Kara said as Will sang the theme song to *The Jeffersons*.

As she packed a small case with toiletries, Amy resisted the sadness that enveloped her and tried to tap into the kids' delight. Of course they would be more comfortable at Gretchen's, and Amy loved that house. It was a work of art—had been featured in *Architectural Digest.* No traditional New England colonials for her grandfather—"What use is a house designed for Boston to someone living in the tropics," he would sputter. Gretchen's recent upgrade had elevated it to a home of supreme comfort as well as aesthetic grace, but it had never been and never would be Amy's home. For her, it would always be her grandparents' house, the setting for family Christmas and Thanksgiving dinners, the stunning location of her high school graduation party and her cousin's wedding. Its purpose, grander than their everyday life, seemed always to require a bit more of its occupants.

She packed up the kids' bathroom supplies, their toothpaste and brushes, the shampoos and conditioners, the blow-dryer, combs, and brushes. The mildew in the tiny bathroom was thick in the tile grout, and flushing the toilet required the precision of a safecracker, but memories saturated the space. This was where she splashed as a baby and where she prepared for her senior prom. She and Martin first bathed together in this tub, the same tub over which her mother had held her brother Kimo's hand after he sliced a finger open trying to peel an apple.

The floors sagged and the rotted window frames were disintegrating. The building was done, well past the point of patching and repainting. There was nothing for it but to take it down, and she didn't think she could bear to see it go.

July 2001, Hale'iwa, Hawai'i

"Please tell me you plan to hang on to this one."

Amy handed her brother a dripping bottle of Heineken.

"Good to see you, too, sis."

He flipped a line of thin teriyaki beef strips, then stepped back as smoke enveloped him.

"Sorry, let me rephrase that. She seems a keeper."

"Trust me, I'm a fan. The question is whether she'll put up with me. Portia's got these odd ideas about relationships, and I don't always get it right."

Amy chuckled. "Don't tell me she has grown-up expectations, little brother. I've heard that can happen if you date someone who's not a teenager."

Kimo slid the cooked pieces of beef to the grill's edges and added fresh ones, triggering a fresh cloud of smoke.

"Laugh all you want at me, Ames, but we both know which of us is happier."

The barb stung, but Amy waved a dismissive hand. She'd heard it all before. He was the passionate one who embraced life in all its messy glory. She was the one born a mini adult, ever sensible and dull. She conceded Kimo knew plenty about life's pleasures, but he had a lot to learn about meaningful happiness.

"So, Zorba, how'd you meet the lovely Portia?"

The wind shifted and the two of them moved to avoid the smoke. The trades could be a nuisance, but it would have been intolerable standing beneath a scorching midday July sun if not for the cooling breezes off the water.

"In the ER, of course. I managed to slice my foot on some coral. She was part of the team that sewed me up. Never thought she'd give me her phone number, but it turns out, Hale'iwa isn't the hottest dating scene for a professional woman. Especially one over forty."

Portia was delivering glasses of lemonade to Gretchen and Kara, who lounged on the covered lanai nearby. She'd already set out bowls of shrimp chips, wun tun strips, and wasabi peas.

Amy could see she'd instantly charmed Kara, who turned awkward and quiet around the tall, slender woman, a sure sign Kara liked her. She wondered if Kara was charmed by Portia's look—the wild mass of dark curly hair caught up in a red silk scarf, her impossibly long arms and legs, her startlingly green eyes—or was it the focused attention Portia had given Kara when they arrived? As if she'd waited a lifetime for the chance to meet this young woman from New Hampshire. She greeted Amy with the same intense welcome. Amy sensed no artifice in her voice or expression. She was exactly as Aunt Gretchen had said, "the fantasy of what a truly authentic, centered person would be like if you were ever to meet one." Gretchen had added, "I wish I could trust that she's for real." Amy hoped so, too.

"Whatever magic brought her into your life, little brother, I'm happy for you. Really. I swear you even look like a grown-up. Not a single hole in that

T-shirt."

"Right? Add an aloha shirt and I'll be doing lunch meetings at the Honolulu Business Club."

The two of them burst out laughing. Amy wrapped him in a tight hug.

"Dream on, little brother. Dream on."

Every summer on the fourth of July, Amy and the kids, along with Gretchen and any other family members who happened to be in town, made the trek out to the family's North Shore cottage where Kimo lived. After a short stint at college, he'd announced he was done with classrooms, was born to surf, and was going to stay true to that calling. In exchange for his sweat equity to maintain the house, the family agreed to let him move in as caretaker at age nineteen. The temporary arrangement became permanent and twenty-five years later, he was a fixture in Hale'iwa, and his surf shop a thriving enterprise. He was by no means well-off, but he could handle the cost of his modest lifestyle. To everyone's amused surprise, he was living his boyhood dream, complete with stunning bikini-clad women young enough to find his surfer persona irresistible.

Amy had to hand it to Kimo. He was aging well. He didn't carry a pound more than he had at eighteen, nor were his shoulders any less broad or his muscles less toned. She understood why women, young women, turned stupid around him. She also understood why they didn't stick around. Even the young ones eventually wanted assurance of a future.

Portia snagged a beer from the tub of iced drinks and joined them, hooking an arm around Kimo's waist. "Smells scrumptious."

"Let's hope it tastes the same. The beauty of having a sister here is I can blame her for distracting me if they turn to charcoal."

"Right," Portia said. "A man is always more attractive when he regresses and blames his sibling rather than accept personal responsibility."

"I like this woman," Amy said, and she meant it, even if it stung to see how tenderly Kimo looked at Portia even as she heckled him. Tender was not a part of the vocabulary she and Martin shared.

Portia hooked her arm in Amy's. "You and I need to get acquainted. Let's spare Kimo any dangerous distractions." She led Amy to chairs clustered in the shade of a lauhala tree. "Has Kimo told you I spent my childhood summers in Vermont?"

"Kimo tells me nothing. What part of Vermont?"

"Southwestern. We lived in New York City, but my grandparents had a summer place, so we kids got shipped there every June once we were semi-civilized. It was nothing fancy. And, of course, it's not the same as year-round Vermont living, but it had a big impact on me. All that Yankee decency and directness. My grandparents were big on the health benefits of nature, so we got an early dose of outdoor living."

"Kimo thinks I'm nuts to live in New England, so maybe you can help convince him of its good points."

Portia waved a dismissive hand. "I adore your brother, but he's cursed and blessed with a single passion. He can't see why anyone would choose to live anywhere but on the North Shore or do anything but surf." She shone her penetrating eyes on Amy again and asked, "What binds you to New Hampshire?"

There was no underlying tone of irony, no subtext of judgment, only what seemed sincere curiosity.

"The directness. People don't play games. They tell you straight-out what they think. The old-timers anyway. It kind of intimidated me at first. And, as you said, there's that sense of decency. They tolerate one another and lend a hand when it's needed without making a big deal about it. Everything is so town based that the individual can have a meaningful say in how things are done. Just a few weeks ago, I saw a classic example. An elderly woman, a retired teacher, stood up to town workers who were going to cut down a tree on her property. She physically blocked them from doing their work. No one called the police. No one got hot under the collar. The guy in charge just talked to her. Showed her some respect and compassion. I've gotten used to people acting that way. Of course, the real reason I stay is we have no big malls. My kids have been spared mall culture as a lifestyle. I'd endure winter just to keep them from thinking of shopping as what Saturdays are for."

"Amen to that. But couldn't you find at least some of those benefits on one of the outer islands?"

"Maybe, and I admit there's tons I miss about life here. Still, I admire the grit and resourcefulness of New Englanders. Like the Brits, they stay calm and carry on."

"I expect that stoicism comes at a cost."

Amy nodded. "Doesn't everything? And what about you, mystery woman? How did you acquire this special gift for getting people to share their deep thoughts?"

Portia waved a dismissive hand.

"Trust me, I'm just another person treading water, trying to get to some shore. The sheer number of possibilities paralyzes me. I keep hoping someone else's story will help me find my path. I'm jealous of Kimo. It was all so easy for him. He knew his bliss and he followed it. That has to be a kind of genius." *Or was it merely a failure of imagination*, Amy wondered.

Portia pushed herself out of her chair. "Enough with being so serious. Time to refill glasses. What are your thoughts on when we should eat? Should I be setting food out yet?"

Kara and Gretchen had begun a game of checkers. Will was on the lawn practicing soccer moves.

"As long as it doesn't ruin the food on the grill, I'd say let's give it an hour or two. We usually eat midafternoon."

Kimo was already covering trays of grilled meat with foil and setting them to the side of the fire to stay warm. Salads and deviled eggs were chilling in the fridge, pies resting on the kitchen counters. All the pieces for dinner were in place. They could do as they wished for a while.

"Hey, Will," Kimo called to his nephew as he kicked off his flip-flops. "Is it time?" Will was in motion before Kimo spoke the magic words. He reached the path to the beach seconds ahead of his uncle.

"Eat my sand dust, old man," Will yelled as he headed for the packed sand at the water's edge.

"In your dreams, boy."

"A family tradition?" Portia asked.

Amy nodded. "The annual testing of the generations. While they do their testosterone thing, the rest of us amuse ourselves as we please. I usually climb in a hammock and read or nap."

"Perfect. If you're okay amusing yourself, I'll squeeze in some yoga time."

She grabbed a mat from the lanai and spread it on the lawn where she could look out at the ocean.

Amy climbed into a hammock hung in the shade of the side yard. She tried not to stare as Portia glided between challenging yoga poses. An infuriating despair enveloped her as she watched. This was not how the script was supposed to go. She was the responsible one, the one who always played by the rules. She'd earned two college degrees, married a tenured college professor, juggled a career and motherhood. Kimo, by contrast, was the college dropout, an aging bachelor stuck in permanent play mode. How was it possible that he should be rewarded with the love of a kind, insightful goddess? Amy hated feeling such petty jealousy. Only pathetic losers resented other people's good fortune. She counted herself better than that, except, obviously, she wasn't.

Her eyes stung as her tears mixed with sunscreen. This misery was all Martin's fault. He'd turned her into a bitter, resentful woman. For the previous eight days, he'd ignored her calls, texts, and emails. Didn't even answer the messages she left with the workshop's administrator. Of course, it was typical Martin behavior. He would have solid reasons to explain away his silence—his phone broke, the schedule was so packed he hadn't a moment to himself, there was poor cell coverage on the island. The essential message never changed. She was not his priority. Never had been. Never would be.

She made herself breathe slowly and deeply. She was being ridiculous. She knew better than to fall into the trap of comparing her long-term marriage to her brother's fresh relationship. Kimo and Portia were in the dreamy days of early love. Of course they beamed with happiness. But Amy's efforts to explain away her feelings did not quiet the annoying truth. Had Martin ever looked at her with the kind of joy she saw pass between Portia and Kimo?

Stay in the moment. She breathed deeply and slowly, shutting out everything but the sensation of the breath itself, the canvas supporting her, the breeze on her skin, the scraping of the ropes against screws as the hammock swung back and forth, back and forth. *Deep breath in. Deep breath out.*

July 2001, Lisbon, Vermont

"What next, sweetheart? Lettuce? Spinach?"

"Basil, please."

Paul tugged a seedling from its plastic cell, loosened the roots, and handed it off to his granddaughter, Samantha. She set it in the loose, rich soil she'd softened with a cultivator and carefully tucked the dirt around its slender stalk.

She threw her arms in the air. "Ta-da."

"I keep saying it. You're a natural farmer, just like your mom. Another basil?"

She nodded.

Paul held up one of the tiny pots. "Want to try pulling it out yourself? I think you're ready."

She shifted her weight, moving from crouching on her haunches to resting on her knees for better balance.

"Help me," she said as she took the basil.

"Tip it a little bit. Now squeeze the pot and give it a little shake."

The basil slid into her palm. "I did it, Gramps. It came out perfect."

She turned her dimpled, mud-streaked face to him. For Paul, this four-year-old charmer was joy incarnate. Since the first moment when, at six weeks, she smiled up at him, she could wheedle anything out of him she wanted.

"You sure did, angel. What comes next?"

"The roots?"

Paul nodded.

As if she were performing microscopic surgery, she delicately separated the tangle of roots, loosening the bundle. Without so much as a glance his way, she set the plant in place and patted soil around it.

"Easy peasy," she said, sitting back on her haunches. "Lettuce next."

The summer before, Paul had set Sam up with her own space within Sarah's large, fenced vegetable patch. This year Sam vetoed the space-consuming pumpkins and sunflowers of the previous summer.

"I want salad stuff I like to eat," she'd declared, so they began in June with carrots and gradually added peas, cucumbers, green beans, and now salad greens.

Summer evenings they weeded, checked for pests, and gently watered the tender plants. On Saturdays they rested, but on Sundays they squeezed in garden tending before family dinner.

On this particular Wednesday, they were working in the garden at noon because it was a special day—the Fourth of July. Sarah and their daughter Maddie and son Chris were staffing the family's roadside farm stand and store with help from Maddie's husband Ray. The Fourth was always a busy day as locals swooped in to pick up strawberries on their way to barbecues, and tourists stopped in for Vermont cheeses, baked goods, and creemees. Care of the four grandkids fell to Chris's wife Emily with help from Paul.

"We're done," Sam announced once the flat was empty and she'd set the last of the spinach in place. She raised her arm to Paul for a high five. "The crops are in."

Paul nodded, as serious as he would have been if surveying a farmer friend's field. "Well done. May your yield be good."

"Time to water." Sam bounced up and headed for the faucet, setting her watering can beneath it.

Paul knew better than to offer his help. Sam insisted on fetching the water herself, even if it meant creating a muddy path as she skidded the full can along the ground.

"Get back here, you little worm," Emily screeched from inside the house. Cooper squealed with laughter.

Sam exchanged grimaces with Paul. "Oh, no," she said. "He's at it again."

"I better see if your aunt Emily needs some help. You okay out here on your own for a sec?"

"Of course." Sam shut off the faucet and started dragging the can. "After all, I've done this a million times, Gramps. I'm very good at this."

A buck-naked eighteen-month-old Cooper screamed by Paul as he entered the house, but Paul managed to scoop him up. Cooper squealed and squirmed, trying to escape.

"Looks to me like you could use a diaper, mister wiggles."

Emily, her infant daughter Elsbeth strapped to her chest, emerged from the kitchen.

"I made the mistake of trying to change him on the floor instead of in the nursery. Little monkey got away from me. Hanging on to him's like trying to catch a greased pig." As Elsbeth began fussing, Emily began swaying. Just looking at Emily wore Paul out. She was still a young woman, barely twenty-two, but her eyes were vacant and her bottom lip chapped and red from her constant biting and picking.

"I'll get a diaper on this guy and put him down for a nap," Paul said. "I shouldn't have left you with all three kids. It's too much."

"That's just a normal day for me." And, of course, it was, until midafternoon, when Sam finished preschool and Emily had all four kids to watch. Maddie and Ray paid her, of course, for childcare, but that didn't make it any less exhausting.

"Morgan asleep?"

"Yeah, she's the easy one. Out like a light soon as her head hit the pillow." She stroked the baby's head. "I need to feed this one, then she should sleep for a good stretch."

Cooper jerked his head back, one of his escape tricks, but Paul held tight. "Nice try, buddy, but this ain't my first rodeo. Like it or not, a diaper's headed your way. Go put your feet up, Em, and nurse Elsbeth. You should squeeze in a nap, too, once they're all down."

"Nice thought, but those strawberries aren't going to slice themselves. It's okay, Dad. I'll grab a nap after we eat."

This time the scream came from outside. "Oh no, Holy Mary, Mother of God. Gramps, Gramps, come quick. I need you."

"Geez Louise." Paul could tell by the colorful phrasing that this was more a theatrical emergency than a dire one. "How does she come up with this stuff?"

Emily shrugged and reached out her arms for Cooper. "The 'God' stuff's probably from Ray's side. His folks go to church, but who knows? Could be from preschool or something she just made up to get your attention. She knows exactly how to manipulate you and the rest of the family."

Paul didn't have time to respond to what seemed to him a rather unfair characterization of his amazing granddaughter. Cries of "Gramps, Gramps" began again.

He managed a "Back in a flash" to Emily, then a louder "I'm coming" for Sam, whom he found sobbing beside her garden patch, the empty watering can dangling in her hand.

"I drowned them, Gramps, I drowned them." The flattened seedlings were immersed in muddy pools. "I couldn't hold it steady and it all came out in one big swoosh."

"It's okay, pumpkin. No biggie. They'll all be fine." He folded her in his arms. "The sun will dry them out and they'll pop up again. I promise."

She dug her wet, snotty face into his chest and wrapped her arms around his neck. "How can you ever love me, Gramps. I'm such a stupid-head."

Her crying swelled to loud wailing. Paul was glad she couldn't see his smile. So like her grandmother. A first-rate drama queen.

"I will always love you, my darling girl," he said. "Nothing you do can change that, but you must promise me one thing."

Her chest still heaving, she sputtered, "What?"

"You must never call yourself stupid again. Okay?"

She nodded, her head still pressed against him.

"Let's get you cleaned up, then you can help me get Cooper down for a nap. I might even let you help me prepare the barbecue fire for later."

She perked up and put a hand on both sides of his face so he couldn't look away. "Really? You promise? Can I roll the newspaper and light it with a match?"

"No lighting paper on fire, but you can definitely roll the paper. First things first though. Let's wash off the mud and get you in some clean clothes. They've got Aunt Emily outnumbered in there."They always had Aunt Emily outnumbered. He wouldn't dare try watching all these kids alone.

Sarah had always made it look so easy. Paul realized, as he rinsed the mud off Sam's legs, arms, and face, how much he took for granted her ability to juggle the impossible demands of cleaning, caring for kids, cooking, doing laundry, tending vegetable gardens, and helping with the farm. Once their kids were in school, Sarah had added a full-time nursing job to her mix. Emily was not the first to have too much asked of her, but it was visibly depleting her in a way he didn't remember seeing in Sarah.

He grabbed a towel from the pile Sarah kept in the mudroom and tossed it to Sam.

"Dry off and pick out something to wear, okay, kiddo?" He nodded at the dresser Sarah kept in the mudroom. Each grandkid had a drawer filled with "just in case" clothes. "I'll get Cooper."

He found Emily in the rocking chair of the guest room Sarah had converted into a nursery. Morgan was still asleep in the toddler bed, and Cooper was working half-heartedly on a bottle as he fought to stay awake. Baby Elsbeth was still nursing. Emily gave him a thumbs-up.

When Sam emerged from the bathroom, dirty clothes dutifully in hand to dump in the laundry pile, Paul put a finger to his lips and led her to the kitchen. "How's about, while the little kids nap, we grab some of Grandma's molasses cookies and read on the back porch."

Supplies in hand, they settled side by side on the cushioned porch swing. Sam handed him *The Secret Garden* by Frances Hodgson Burnett. "It's one of Mom's big-kid books, so I need help reading it."

"I remember it well," he said. "Your mom loved it." He opened the book to chapter four and the spot Sam pointed to.

"We stopped right here, when she's walking through the gardens."

Paul swayed the swing gently with his feet. Sam leaned against his side, her legs curled up beside her.

"'How could a garden be shut up? You could always walk into a garden,'" Paul read:

> She was just thinking this when she saw that, at the end of the path she was following, there seemed to be a long wall, with ivy growing over it. She was not familiar enough with England to know that she was coming upon the kitchen-gardens where the vegetables and fruit were growing. She went toward the wall and found that there was a green door in the ivy, and that it stood open. This was not the closed garden, evidently, and she could go into it.

"A vegetable garden just like mine, Gramps." Samantha grinned up at him.

A breeze cut through the day's hazy warmth as Sam's breathing slowed. Her cookie lay forgotten on her lap. Paul read on.

> Presently an old man with a spade over his shoulder walked through the door leading from the second garden. He looked startled when he saw Mary, and then touched his cap. He had a surly old face, and did not seem at all pleased to see her—but then she was displeased with his garden and wore her "quite contrary" expression, and certainly did not seem at all pleased to see him.

When Sam's eyes closed and he was sure she was sleeping, Paul closed the book and set it beside him.

Emily's words nagged at him. Did he spoil Sam by indulging her whims? He squeezed one of her tiny bare feet, recalling her ferocious objection earlier that day when Emily insisted she wear boots to work in the garden. Paul had stayed out of it, but if it weren't for Emily, he'd have happily let Sam run around barefoot. He wondered if Emily's snippiness was simple jealousy. Did she think he favored Sam over the other grandkids? His own grandfather had been like that, shown him, as the youngest of the grandkids and the one born during his retirement, the most attention. He'd taught Paul to fish and keep a vegetable garden, let him keep watch beside him in his deer stand, even taken him to Boston's Museum of Fine Arts so he could see a Turner painting in person. *Dover Castle from the Sea* wasn't so brilliantly colored as Paul's favorites he'd seen in books, but it didn't matter. To stand so close to it, to see the artist's strokes had mesmerized him. He'd never been to a major art museum, hadn't known what it was to move through rooms filled with art, more art than his mind could process. His grandfather had opened the door to what became Paul's quiet passion. The family had made a joke of Paul getting so much attention, dubbing him "Golden Boy," but maybe it hadn't been funny to his sister Peg and their cousins.

He must make a point, he decided, to spend some time alone with each of the grandkids. Cooper would make sure they all noticed him, but Morgan and Elsbeth might slip through the cracks. Though tempted to stay there rocking beside Sam, he scooped her up, cookie and all. She could nap on a bed—she did not need him beside her. While she slept, he would see to Morgan, who was due to wake and would need some cuddle time to ease back into the day. He would read her the books she loved best, maybe even fill the baby pool out back so she and Cooper could splash about.

He laid Sam on Maddie's old bed upstairs, opened the windows, and set a fan to whirring. For the moment, the house was quiet. He was tempted to stretch out on his own bed, but headed for the kitchen and the bucket of ripe strawberries waiting to be washed, sliced, and sugared.

August 2001, Honolulu, Hawai'i

"Gretchen," Clare Barnes said when she saw Amy coming toward her.

As Amy leaned over to kiss her mother's cheek, she recoiled from the overwhelming metallic scent. The smell of depression, the doctor had called it. Her mother was losing more than her memory.

"It's Amy, Mom."

"Don't be silly. Amy's dead."

Her mother's childhood friend, for whom Amy was named, had died twelve years before.

"I'm the other Amy. Your daughter." Amy tried to say it gently, but all the same her mother teared up.

"I don't even know my own daughter."

"It's okay. You knew I was someone you love. That's what matters."

Amy could see the tears retreat as the moment evaporated for her mother. The mercy of having no short-term memory was that emotional wounds didn't linger.

"And what shall we do today, Amy?" She linked her arm with her daughter's. "Maybe you could read to me from Sara's poems. I do love her poems."

"An excellent idea." Amy settled her mother in a comfortable chair tucked in a corner of the common space. She pulled from her bag the small, worn binder of poems Amy carried with her for this purpose. "What is your preference for today? Will 'The Crystal Gazer' do?"

"Yes, yes, that one," her mother said.

Amy opened the notebook to Sara Teasdale's poem and began reading.

"'I shall gather myself into myself again, / I shall take my scattered selves and make them one.'"

As she neared the poem's end, at the line "And the little shifting pictures of people rushing," her mother joined in just as she always joined in at this point and recited with Amy to the very end: "'In restless self-importance to and fro.'"

How was it that her mother could flawlessly recite this and other beloved poems, yet somedays not remember she'd birthed two babies?

"Would you like to take a walk now?" Amy asked. "No rain today. We're in luck."

"A walk would be lovely! It's been so long since I've visited your Oakland gardens." Her mother beamed. "You've always had such a green thumb, Gretchen. I bet your roses are spectacular."

Amy smiled. "I hope you like them." There was no point in reminding her mother that Gretchen hadn't lived in California for years.

As they strolled down the paths lined with hibiscus bushes and plumeria trees, she wondered when or even if her mother would register them as cues she was not at Gretchen's Oakland home. Her mother stopped before a flowering bush of double yellow hibiscus.

"I do so love the frilly ones," she said, leaning close to a blossom, her fingers fluttering. "But mustn't pick them. They don't like being picked, you know. They wilt right up."

Amy was reminded of a poem she'd written about her mother years before, during her novice teaching days at Pumehana. She'd compared Clare's fingers to butterfly wings, delicate and fluttering, one of her tools for communicating with the world. Amy's father had hated that poem, said the woman she described was nothing like the woman he knew. Amy had never understood the source of his anger.

Clare stopped again, this time beside a giant Singapore plumeria tree. She stretched to reach a branch and plucked a crisp white blossom.

"Remember making leis with the ones from our backyard?"

Amy nodded. Seeing the white sap ooze from the stem in her mother's hand reminded her of the sticky, bloody fingers she associated with lei making. She was forever pricking herself with the needle, and nothing but time could completely clean the sap from her fingers.

"Remember how we'd float leis in the tub to keep them fresh?" she reminded her mother. "The bathroom would be so fragrant."

"Hmm," her mom said, smiling. "And your dad would get grumpy if he had to take a shower and there were leis in his way."

"Do you suppose anyone strings their own anymore?" Amy wondered.

Despite the mess, making leis had never seemed a chore to her. She loved climbing the trees, snapping the blossoms from fat clumps, and then dropping them into the large paper grocery bag her brother Kimo held open below. They would spread the flowers on newspaper so the best blossoms could be selected and strung together. She couldn't remember the last time anyone had greeted her at the airport with a lei. Not like the days when friends and family came to the airport or the ship terminal and piled them so high her face nearly disappeared.

She turned to her mother. "How about we make a lei, Mom? Assuming they let us pick the blossoms."

"But who would it be for?"

"For you, of course! And if there were enough flowers, one for me as well. What do you think?"

"That would be lovely. Absolutely lovely." Her mother beamed.

"Then let's go see about getting permission and a bag for the flowers."

They turned and headed back to the building. This visit was turning out so much better than Amy had anticipated. Most visits dragged on interminably and Amy left feeling wretched.

"Gretchen!" Her mother had stopped beside a croton bush. "What has happened to your rosebushes? These leaves are so odd and there are no blossoms."

Amy placed an arm around her mother's shoulders, forcing herself to stay close despite the repugnant odor. "It hasn't been a good year for the roses."

"Such a shame. Yours were always so fragrant."

They continued on, the terrace just ahead of them.

"Perhaps we could make some banana bread today, Amy. You always liked my banana bread." Her mother patted the hand Amy still had cupped over her shoulder.

"That would be lovely. Absolutely lovely," Amy said, her mother's shoulder so small and fragile beneath her grip.

August 2001, Kailua, Hawai'i

Amy woke with an oppressive sense of dread. The night before, the Clifton High School principal had emailed the faculty news of Ryan Pitchford's death by suicide. Amy's first thought was of his mother Karen and the hell she would be going through. Her second was of her own inadequate support of Ryan. His failure to graduate had saddened her, but not enough for her to consider what more she could do to help. She hadn't checked in with Karen or bothered to raise with the principal, counselors, and fellow teachers the question of how they could respond more effectively to kids with serious behavioral health issues.

"We can't save them all," her friend Kathy had said back in June. Amy knew she was right, but all the same, she felt a bitter guilt and sense of inadequacy.

She forced herself to get out of bed. It was her and the kids' last morning at the Kailua beach house. One more week of summer school before they'd be heading home.

"You're up early." Amy was filling her travel mug with coffee when Kara appeared in the kitchen doorway.

"I wanted to hunt at least once during this visit," Kara said.

Amy held up the coffee pot. "Want a mug to bring along?"

"No thanks. I'm going back to bed after this."

Combing the beach for glass balls was part of their summer ritual at the Kailua house, but Amy was usually the only one who set out regularly before sunrise. The kids always intended to join her, but rising from a warm bed on a dark, windy morning was challenging, especially that summer when they were staying at the Nuʻuanu house during the week and only stayed at the beach on the weekends. Despite a lifetime of effort, Amy had yet to find a glass ball, but she rarely missed a morning hunt.

They zipped up their sweatshirts and Amy flicked on her flashlight. She handed Kara the larger flashlight that cast a wide swath of light across the beach. A mean wind pushed straight at them as they headed across the lawn and down to the shoreline. Kara drew the drawstrings of her hood so only her eyes and nose showed, though her long legs were bare but for a pair of short shorts. Amy stopped herself from suggesting sweatpants.

Amy rarely had the beach to herself. Since fishermen stopped using the balls as floats, finds were rare, but devotees scoured the sand all the same. At least that morning there were no signs of others out ahead of them.

"This summer went by way too fast," Amy said.

"You say that every year, Mom."

"True." A melancholy always settled on her during the last days of summer, but this year was especially rough. She dreaded the tension ahead with Martin, didn't know what to make of his radio silence all summer, and now Ryan's death would hang over them all.

"I've got so much reading to do before my final exam," Kara groaned. "I don't see how I'm going to get to it all."

"For what it's worth, I'm impressed you've stuck with the class. Seven hours a day is brutal."

"At least it means I won't have to take it from Mr. Jarvis."

"Oh, come on. He's got some good points."

"But does he, Mom? Does he really?"

Amy tried to defend her colleagues as best she could when her kids complained, but Jarvis was a tough sell. She had to laugh. "Let's just be glad you've had a good experience at McNeil."

They walked slowly. Kara swept the flashlight back and forth over the sand, and they both looked for a glint of light, something reflective.

"Did you hear about that creepy kid Ryan?" Kara said. "The one who always looked like he'd strangle you if you tried to talk to him?"

Amy had hoped the news wouldn't reach the kids until they got home.

"Yeah. They sent the faculty a notice. I had Ryan in class and I didn't find him creepy, just awkward socially. And very alone. I don't think he had any friends."

"Big surprise. Who wants to be friends with someone who glares at you. I heard he didn't even graduate."

"You know I can't talk about that, but I don't think we did well by him. No kid should suffer the way he did." Amy broke down. "Damn. I'm sorry, hon." She hated crying in front of the kids. She breathed deeply, trying to calm herself.

Kara, a good three inches taller than Amy, enveloped her in a bear hug. "It's not your fault, Mom. Some kids are just messed up. You can't save them all."

"I know, love, but it still sucks. Too many kids slip away from us, even the ones whose parents love and care for them, and I feel impotent. Promise me you'll talk to me if school and life ever get overwhelming. Let me know if you are hurting."

Kara looped her arm around Amy's waist. "Of course. I'll make sure you suffer right along with me."

Amy chuckled. "I vote we dodge those problems altogether if we can." Their progress slowed in the soft sand.

"Killer workout for the thighs," Kara said. "Can we walk closer to the water?"

"But then we'll miss the debris left by the tide. That's where the balls hide. Trust me. This pain and suffering will only make our eventual victory all the sweeter."

When they reached the beach's end at the cliffside, the sky was lightening on the horizon line. Amy climbed onto a boulder. "Let's sit a sec. This is my favorite part, catching the day at its first moment. Right now the slate is still clean. Not a blemish."

Kara pressed up against her for warmth. "Do you ever think maybe you won't find a glass ball? Maybe there aren't any left out there."

Amy shrugged. "Maybe. But I like looking. Maybe it's more about the search than the finding."

Kara groaned. "Is that your deep thought for the day?"

Amy kissed the top of Kara's head and breathed in a fragrant mix of Herbal Essence and Coppertone sunscreen. "Okay, the less pretentious answer is that no, I do not give up hope. But it's also true that hunting doesn't cost me anything. It would be different if I didn't enjoy the search."

A spot of light bounced in the distance. "Another hunter," Kara said. "Time to give up for today?"

Amy hopped off the boulder. "Sure. Let's get you back to bed."

They half-heartedly checked piles of debris for buried glass as they retraced their steps. By the time they reached the path to their cottage, they didn't need the flashlight. The morning had fully arrived.

"Love you, puddin'," Amy said as Kara headed for her room, her sweatshirt still zipped tight against the cold.

Kara mumbled a reply.

A fresh cup of coffee in hand, Amy headed back to the beach. The day would grab hold of her soon enough. She wasn't going to waste a single one of her remaining sunrises.

Chapter Four

June 1966, Clifton, New Hampshire

Revenge drove Paul to slip out of the house at one in the morning and bike the four miles to Clifton High School. This was payback for those snotty jerks, those Clifton baseball players and fans who'd mocked him at the last Lisbon-Clifton game.

"That's all right, that's okay, you're going to pump our gas someday," they'd chanted when Paul hit a home run his second time at bat.

Paul's plan was simple. Clifton had a banner hanging over the back door to its gym that read CLIFTON HIGH CHAMPS. He would use white and black paint to change the *a* in "Champs" to a *u*.

He'd deliberately chosen a clear night with a nearly full moon. No one but the deer and raccoons would be able to see him on the school's backside and he might not even need a flashlight. He'd strapped a milk carton to the front of his bike to give him the bit of height he'd need to reach the banner.

Paul opened the small can of white paint and stepped onto the carton. His anger still felt fresh and raw. His homer had brought two runners in and secured Lisbon the win, making him the game's hero, but the boos and taunts drowned out the applause. "Ignore them. Rise above," his coach had said, but Paul didn't know how to do that.

It took only a minute to white out the unneeded parts of the letter *a*, and seconds to add a black stroke for the *u*. He stepped back from the building to see how it looked, to make sure the letter mimicked the style of the others. The *u* fit perfectly. He wondered if anyone would even notice the subtle change, and if they didn't, would it still count as revenge? *Yes,* he decided, *because I will know it's there.*

"What's that you got all over your hand?" his dad asked the next morning as he passed Paul a box of shredded wheat.

Paul looked down at the black splotches on his right hand. He'd need turpentine to get it off.

"School project," he muttered. He figured his dad would buy it. He never asked about Paul's schoolwork. But he had to get the paint off before his mom saw it. She'd know there was no project.

Paul waited all day for something to happen. The Clifton school janitor or one of the coaches might easily spot the edit, tell the principal and the word would be out, but nothing happened. No announcements were made. No one called him out of class. He rode the bus home, listening to Gordon talk about how Chas Heyer got to third base with Pamela Sturgiss. The girls behind him chattered about decoration themes for the ninth-grade dance. He didn't know whether to be relieved or sorry the prank didn't cause a stir.

His dad was waiting by the barn when the bus dropped him off. "See you for a minute?"

Paul followed him into the barn. Cam motioned for Paul to take a seat beside his desk. "I'm thinking you might have something you want to tell me. Before you say anything, you should know that I heard you come home in the middle of the night. You really need to oil that bike."

Paul sometimes wondered if his dad had extrasensory perception for mischief.

"I painted something on a banner at Clifton High School. Changed a letter so it says 'Chumps' instead of 'Champs.' Probably no one will even notice it."

"Why do it then?"

"Because I had to do something after all the crap they were yelling at the last game."

"Do you feel vindicated now?"

Paul shrugged. "I don't know. I couldn't figure out what else to do. We're not supposed to fight them, but it feels weak to let their insults slide."

"I get that, but it doesn't excuse defacing someone's property. It'll probably be the janitor, not those fans, who'll have to fix it. What do you plan to do to make it right?"

Paul shrugged. He knew he was supposed to say he'd take responsibility for his actions.

"I'm not sorry I did it."

Cam nodded. "You don't have to be sorry, but you made your point by damaging someone's property and creating work for someone else. The responsible action now is to acknowledge you did it and accept the consequences."

"Which are?" Paul feared his father might make him quit the baseball team.

Cam placed the phone beside Paul and handed him the phone book. "Step one, you choose who you want to inform—the Clifton police or the Clifton principal. I expect, at the least, they will want the banner repaired or replaced."

Paul flipped open the directory and found the school's number. Maybe he'd get lucky and the principal wouldn't report this to the police.

"I can take you over there now to clean it up, if that's what they want," Cam said. "I'll round up the turpentine, rags, and paint."

Paul glanced at the clock. It was nearly four o'clock. The Clifton baseball team might be holding practice. The team would see him repainting the banner and have more cause to mock him. He dialed the school's number.

"May I speak with the principal, please," he said. "My name is Paul Rideau.

July 1966, Kailua, Hawaiʻi

When Amy woke, she thought she was alone on the beach fronting her family's Kailua house, and was a bit surprised that even Kimo had disappeared. She could feel her back burning and her face damp against her forearm. She rose, intending to run down to the water, then saw her aunt Sally sitting cross-legged a few yards away. Sally held a giant glass ball in her lap and was scouring barnacles off it with a paint scraper. Amy wondered how she had the energy. Nearly skeletal, her head shaved and wrapped in gauze, her aunt seemed frail enough for the trade winds to knock over.

"You're awake. Good. I was afraid you'd turn into a broiled lobster and your mom would kill me for letting you burn."

This was the first Sally had spoken to her in the two days since Amy had arrived. The family had gathered because of Sally's brain surgery a month earlier. Aunt Gretchen, Erica, and Beverly had flown in from Oakland, and Clare, Kimo, and Amy were spending the week at the beach house with them. Sally had kept to herself, staying alone in the small cottage that visiting artists sometimes occupied. If she came outside, she lay on one of the lounge chairs set apart from everyone else.

Amy shouted so Sally could hear her over the wind and surf. "Did you find that glass ball?"

She couldn't believe Sally had managed the walk along the beach, let alone hauled the glass float, the size of a basketball, back with her.

"Yup. I snuck out this morning before Gretchen and Clare could tell me not to overdo it. I had to hide it in the naupaka. They still haven't seen it."

"It's huge."

"No kidding. Big as I've ever seen. Wait'll your mom sees it. Little Miss Do Right is going to be jealous her lazy, no-good sister scored the big one."

Amy didn't know what to say. Her aunt had always made her uncomfortable. She talked and acted so tough. Now that her skull was bald and bandaged and her ribs showed, Sally was especially frightening. Amy decided she couldn't keep talking from so far away. She moved her mat across the hot sand and sat down beside Sally.

Without looking up, Sally asked, "They tell you I'm dying?"

Amy shook her head. "Only that you had an operation."

"Of course. Mustn't frighten the kiddos. But that's why we're all congregated here. It's the big goodbye, the last supper, the grand send-off."

"What's wrong with you?"

Sally laughed. "You mean besides being the crazy one? Brain tumor. Cancer. Figures, right? I've always been the one who's messed up in the head. They can't make it go away. They've tried to cut it out a couple times, but it keeps growing. Just a matter of time."

Amy considered this for a few minutes. She felt like she should cry or something.

"Are you scared?"

"Yeah. But I'm always scared, so that's not a big change."

Amy nodded. Though it was unsettling the way her aunt talked to her as if she were just another person and not a kid, she kind of liked it, too. She wanted to act as if she understood the things Sally said.

"You want to try your hand at this?" Sally offered her the scraper. "I'm losing steam."

"Sure." With the ball cradled between her knees, Amy slowly and gently pressed the scraper against the glass.

"Press down harder. Short scratching strokes. It's a tough old bird. You won't hurt it."

Sally lifted her face to the sun, then sighed and put on her wide-brimmed hat. Amy preferred her that way. She didn't like to look at Sally's head for fear the gauze might slip or a line of blood seep through.

"You don't like me much, do you?"

Sally didn't seem angry or upset as she said this.

"It's okay not to like me. Consider that my gift to you. Permission to have your own feelings and opinions. They'll try plenty hard to take them away from you, you know. Keep you from trusting your own sense of things and tell you there's only one way to live your life. I'm not going to be around in six years to be a bad influence and tell you it's okay not to follow their scripts. So I'll say it now even if you are just a kid."

Amy kept digging the scraper into the grit.

"God, what I wouldn't give for a cigarette. Mustn't smoke, you know. Not good for you, especially right after surgery." Sally laughed. "I wouldn't want to risk dying of lung cancer. Even a condemned man gets a last smoke, but not in Pollyanna land."

Amy heard the sneer in Sally's voice as she said "Pollyanna."

"You didn't like *Pollyanna*?" Amy stopped scraping. "It's one of my favorite movies."

Sally snorted.

"I love every Hayley Mills movie," Amy said. "Have you seen *Summer Magic*? I liked it even better than *Parent Trap*." Amy wondered if her aunt had noticed that Amy's hair was styled exactly the way Hayley Mills wore hers.

"*That* good, eh? I'll have to make sure I see it before I kick the bucket." She rested her chin on her knees, as if she couldn't hold her head up any longer.

"So tell me what's so great about Hayley Mills?"

Amy shrugged. She feared her aunt was making fun of her now.

"I'm serious. Why is she such a big deal to you?"

"I guess because she always plays the one who's a little bit different. Not so girly-girly. She gets into trouble and is smarter than the other girls who only care about boys and how they look."

"Fair enough. Not just another Goody Two-Shoes princess, eh?"

"It's not like she's bad or anything. She's just not fake good. You know how some people can be like Eddie Haskell and talk nice but be really bad when no one's looking? Hayley Mills is never like that. And she's the one who knows the truth about really bad people. Like in *Parent Trap* when the icky woman wanted to marry their dad for his money and was only pretending to love him." Amy could hear herself talking faster and faster as she got more worked up.

"Okay." Sally raised her hands in surrender. "You've persuaded me. Hayley Mills isn't a phony. Or at least she doesn't play phonies. She's a regular female Holden Caulfield."

"Who?"

"A guy you'll read about in English class someday. I'm guessing in a couple years Hayley may be a bit less interesting to you than Holden. Or at least I hope you'll think so."

Amy chipped away and for a while they both were silent. It was the first time she'd ever been with Sally and not wanted to run away.

Sally groaned softly and lay back on the sand. She curled up, her knees nearly touching her chin.

"You okay?" Amy could see something had shifted in her aunt's face. Sally had closed her eyes and her body trembled.

"Get your mom for me, kiddo?"

Amy ran up the path to the house, calling for her mother, and didn't realize till she reached the cottage porch that her arms were still wrapped around the glass ball.

"You found one!" Her mom swung open the screen door, her face glowing.

"No. It's Sally's. She's on the beach. She needs you. Something's wrong."

Clare called into the house, "Mom! Gretchen! It's Sally. There's some kind of problem." She let the screen door slam, ran down the steps, and took off for the beach.

Amy settled on the grass, sheltering the ball in her lap, and resumed its cleaning. She liked the sound of the metal scratching the glass and the satisfaction of digging through to a glint of green. She didn't want to hear or see what was happening on the beach.

"I'm hungry," Kimo said without looking up from the jigsaw puzzle spread across a card table.

Amy glanced at the clock on the wall, the one her aunt Gretchen had decorated with small seashells back when she and Amy's mom were kids. It was already six o'clock. No one had called from the hospital to tell them how Sally was doing or when they might be home. Through the huge plate glass window that faced onto the ocean, she could see her cousin Erica in one of the lawn chairs, bent at the waist, brushing her hair over her head. She was doing her one hundred strokes, the same as she did every day. And every day she wrote her boyfriend Steve back in Oakland, touched up her nails, and flipped through the *Tiger Beat* magazine she'd brought with her from California. If this was what it meant to be a teenager, Amy wasn't interested.

"I'll get dinner started," Amy said. "I bet the moms will be home soon."

She'd much rather stay with Jane Eyre, but she put down her book and climbed out of the big armchair she'd occupied since her mom, Aunt Gretchen, and grandmother had taken Aunt Sally to the hospital. Not for the first time that week, she wished her dad wasn't spending the summer studying in California.

"Keep an eye on the young ones," her Aunt Gretchen had told Erica. "No one swims while we're gone." Amy's mom, already in the car with Sally, issued no directives.

Amy's younger cousin Beverly sat curled up on the couch, buried in a Nancy Drew mystery. Amy was grateful Beverly was nothing like her sister.

Cans of food and a big bag of corn chips sat on the kitchen counter. Tonight was her mom's night to fix dinner. Judging from the cans of spaghetti, chili, corn, and olives, Amy figured it was Mexican casserole night. She dug around the utensil drawer for a can opener, rinsed the tops of the cans, and began removing the lids.

"What stinks?" Erica leaned against the doorframe, her hands in the pockets of her tight short shorts, her long blond hair swept over one shoulder. "Smells like dog food."

Amy pulled out a large bowl into which she dumped the cans' contents.

"I'm making my mom's casserole."

"Gross. I'm not eating that."

"Fine with me."

Amy added the entire bag of corn chips and stirred the concoction with a giant serving spoon, then squatted before the large cupboard that housed the cottage's pan supply, a collection of garage sale cast-offs accumulated over the many decades the family had owned the beach house. She hauled out a large baking pan, dumped the mix into it, and evened out the surface before setting it in the preheated oven.

"You can set the table," Amy said, nodding toward the utensil drawer.

"I told you, I'm not eating that. I'll have an orange."

As far as Amy could tell, Erica rarely ate anything at all. In the morning she might have a slice of dry toast, at lunch she ate carrot sticks and undressed salads.

"You could have a stomach like mine," she'd told Amy the day before as they lay on the beach. She ran her hands over her concave belly, lingering on her protruding hip bones. "You just have to stop eating chips and ice cream. They make you fat and give you pimples."

Though she envied Erica her skinny body, Amy had made a point of taking a large pile of potato chips when they ate lunch a short while later.

Amy dug out forks for herself and the two younger kids. She set the utensils and napkins on the table, then pulled out plates and glasses.

"Supper should be ready in twenty minutes," she told Kimo and Bev. They both grunted.

Erica had disappeared into the room she, Bev, and Amy shared. Not that Amy was ever there except to sleep.

The cottage felt stuffy and claustrophobic. Amy didn't blame Aunt Sally for choosing to stay in the tiny, airy cottage beside the work shed. She wondered who would get to be there now if Sally didn't come back from the hospital. She felt guilty immediately for such a bad thought.

"I'm going to go down to the beach for a few minutes," Amy said aloud. Neither of the younger kids looked up. "I'll be back before the casserole's ready."

She plopped down in the sand in the same spot where she and Sally had talked earlier that day. The glass ball Sally had found was safely nestled by the back porch until it could be cleaned up enough to bring indoors. Amy wondered how close Sally was to dying. Was she dying right that minute? The thought scared her.

Don't be afraid to write your own scripts, Sally had told her. Amy wasn't sure what that meant. Life was something that happened to her. She didn't control it. As for Sally's advice to be herself, Amy had no idea who that was. She could look at other people, people like Erica or Sally, and see them as fully-formed, separate people. But she couldn't see the same in herself. Was there someone buried inside her that she had to dig out and set free? It was all so confusing.

Amy was drying the last of the dishes when the car pulled up.

"Mommy, Mommy," Beverly cried, running in from the living room.

She wrapped her arms around her mother's legs. Aunt Gretchen and Amy's mom both looked as if they'd been crying.

"Look at you, all ready for bed! Good girl." Aunt Gretchen hugged Beverly tightly.

"Amy made me and Kimo take showers and put on our pj's. And she wouldn't let me have any ice cream."

Gretchen beamed at Amy. "Then good for Amy."

Amy's mom squeezed Amy's shoulders. "Thanks, sweetie, for keeping an eye on things. You guys eat?"

"Yup. I made your casserole. The leftovers are in the fridge if you're hungry."

Clare shook her head. "We grabbed something at the hospital." She kicked off her slippers and sat down at the kitchen table. Gretchen took two beers from the fridge, passed one to Clare, and sat opposite her. Amy settled between them at the table's end and Beverly leaned against her mom.

"Kimo in bed already?" Clare asked.

"I'm in here," he yelled from the living room. "Amy's been a bossy pants all night."

Clare gave Amy a questioning look.

"I just made sure they had dinner and got ready for bed."

"Where's Aunt Sally and Gram?" Beverly asked, climbing onto her mother's lap.

"The doctors want Aunt Sally to spend the night at the hospital, so Gram's staying with her." Gretchen buried her face in her daughter's curls as she spoke. "Where's your sister, pumpkin?"

"In her room reading Stevie-poo's letters for the millionth time. She said dinner smelled like dog food."

Amy caught her aunt's grimace. "I bet it tasted great."

Beverly nodded. "Yup. Amy even put Fritos in it."

"Fritos, eh? Sounds like you lucked out big time. Good thing Amy was here to take care of you all." Gretchen swung Beverly off her lap and stood. "Let's get you and Kimo into bed, missy. It's nearly ten."

Amy stayed at the table while her mom and aunt saw the younger kids off to bed. She didn't feel good. The day had been confusing.

"Is Aunt Sally going to die tonight?" she asked when her mom returned. She wished she were little like Beverly and could sit on her mom's lap.

"I don't know. She might. If not tonight, then soon." Clare reached across the table to cup a hand on Amy's face. "But Gram's with her. Lying right on the bed beside her to keep her warm. She's not alone."

They stayed there at the table, Gretchen joining them. The sisters sipped beers and Amy copied by slowly drinking her root beer. The fridge murmured, gusts of wind slapped the venetian blinds against the window frames, and the harsh fluorescent light hummed overhead. Only when she could no longer keep her eyes open did Amy kiss her mother good night. She wanted to fall asleep quickly. She didn't want to picture Auntie Sally lying in the hospital bed.

September 1968, Honolulu, Hawai'i

"Be the wind," Mr. Curtiss said. "What would you see? Think about the sounds, the sensations."

He paused, all twenty pairs of tenth-grader eyes glued to him. Amy would gladly have stared at him all day.

"Looks just like Mr. Novak," her friend Malia declared the first day of school. He was only one year out of college, which they figured made him something like twenty-two or twenty-three. Old but not too old.

"Now let those images flow onto the paper," Mr. Curtiss continued.

Amy wanted to impress Ben Curtiss. He might never notice her looks, not with Ginger Mendes in the class, but she fantasized about the day when he'd read one of her essays and declare her brilliant. So far his B-pluses suggested he was as underwhelmed by her mind as by her beauty.

Amy tried to imagine herself as wind sweeping down Manoa Valley, headed for the ocean. She'd see green, lots and lots of green. There would be the smell of ginger, the cool Manoa stream, then hot asphalt and concrete as she, the wind, emerged from the valley and spread over the baking city. She pictured herself twisting around the tall hotels, skipping trash along the sidewalks, sending a tourist's hat sailing. She wrote it all down in the stream of consciousness style Mr. Curtiss favored. In the final five minutes, she reviewed her writing, tweaked a few lines, and added a last dramatic flourish of settling the hat on the crest of a wave.

"Pencils down."

Mr. Curtiss rose from his seat and, hands in pockets, strolled behind the circle of their desks.

"Anyone want to share what you wrote?" He looked around the room. Amy resisted the impulse to raise her arm and shout, "Me, pick me!"

When no one offered to go first, he turned to Ginger. "How about you, Miss Mendes?"

Of course he'd ask her. He had gotten Ginger's name down pat the first day. If Ginger so much as shifted in her chair, every guy in the room turned to look.

"Mine's terrible," Ginger said, blushing, covering the paper with her hands.

Natch. Amy chewed on her pencil.

"You know the rules, no putting down anyone's work, your own included." Mr. Curtiss picked up Ginger's paper. "Let's see what you've got here."

"I am the wind, the breath that stirs the spirits. I glide through tangled kiawe, dissolve in morning Koʻolau mist." He continued on, the words sounding even more poetic for being spoken by his lips. Amy doodled in the margins of her paper.

No way, she thought, *absolutely no way Ginger wrote something like that.* She glanced over at Ginger. For once she wasn't leaning back in her seat, her long legs extended in front of her for the guys to admire.

Mr. Curtiss handed back her paper.

"Beautiful, Ginger. Another fine piece. Thanks for sharing it." He looked around. "Who's next?"

Amy stared at the floor. No way was she following that.

"How about you Mr. Chun?" Mr. Curtiss asked Marcus. "Want to read yours?"

Terrific. Nothing Marcus liked more than to be called on to read one of his ridiculous rants.

As she expected, Marcus stood and trumpeted in a dramatic voice, "I am the wind god, hear me roar, beware the power of my lungs, you mere mortals."

Amy looked at her own piece of writing. She wanted to toss it in the trash. What was she thinking? Nothing she wrote would ever impress a grown man. As Marcus droned on, she began a new line on a fresh sheet, her pen flying over the page. Lost in her writing she didn't even notice when Marcus finished. Mr. Curtiss stood behind her now.

"Looks like you're on fire. Your turn."

All eyes were on Amy.

"Sorry. I couldn't make it work."

"Come on. No excuses. The whole point of these exercises is to write without judgment."

He picked up the sheet she'd scribbled on.

"No, not that one," she protested.

It was Amy's turn to blush and stare down at her desk.

"Would you like me to read it for you?" Of course he would rescue her. He was that kind of man. She nodded.

"I am not the wind. I am the grass it flattens, the leaves it tears from the limb. I have no power. The wind snaps me, drowns my voice, somersaults me over buildings. I am the dandelion puff carried from my home. I disappear above oceans and fields."

Amy cringed as he read. She hadn't even done what they were supposed to do. Be the wind, he'd told them. She hated the melodramatic, self-pitying tone.

"I like that you went in a whole other direction. This is a good example, everyone, of stretching the assignment, letting go of obvious expectations. Excellent work."

He moved along, picked up someone else's paper. Amy felt a rush of pride. He'd noticed her, recognized her as a maverick, a creative spirit.

At the end of class, Amy took her time gathering up her books. People filed out. Mr. Curtiss packed up his briefcase. As Rachel Schmidt passed, he glanced up and said, "Good work today. I liked the way you went to that 'I'm not the wind' idea."

"That was Amy Barnes, not me," Rachel said, making it clear she didn't appreciate being mistaken for Amy.

"One of these days I'll get you all sorted out," he said with a laugh, following Rachel out the door.

Amy stood by her chair, books pressed to her chest, feeling utterly invisible.

May 1969, Lisbon, Vermont

Paul pressed lightly on the gas pedal. The back right wheel spun again. Nothing.

"Shit." He got out of the car, careful to step over the mud, and crouched beside the tire.

Sarah leaned out the passenger window. "How's it look?"

"Not good. It's in deep."

He had pulled off to the side to let a large truck pass on the narrow dirt road, forgetting that even in May the ground on these back roads was still spring soft.

Before he could ask, Sarah hitched up her prom gown and climbed over the gear shaft and into the driver's seat. Paul opened the trunk, hoping his uncle might be carrying some kind of board he could prop under the tire. Nothing. "Couldn't just drive to the prom in the truck," he muttered to himself. *Had to impress Sarah with my uncle's Mustang. Be the big shot going to the prom in the cool car.*

He took off his tuxedo jacket, tossed it into the back seat, and rolled up the sleeves of his shirt.

"Count of three," he called to Sarah. He planted his feet, his hands braced against the back right fender, as she turned the key.

"One, two, three." At three, he pushed hard against the fender, rocking the car loose, as Sarah gave it some gas. The spinning tire sprayed him with mud and gravel.

The car lurched forward. Sarah steered it onto the dry roadbed and stopped.

"Looking pretty slick, Rideau," she said, smirking.

"Good thing your mom took pictures before we left your house. How bad is it?"

Paul could see the splatter on his shirt, but the jacket would hide that. What he couldn't tell was just how much he'd gotten on his face and hair.

"I've seen you worse."

Sarah handed him a pack of tissues. She leaned her elbow against the windowsill, her hand cupping her chin, and watched as he crouched in front of the side mirror, dabbing at the mud. *Cool as a cucumber,* Paul thought. Nothing fazed Sarah.

"You're missing spots. Step away."

She opened the car door, took the tissues from Paul, and finished wiping his face.

"There. All better." She headed around the front of the car, her skirt hitched up with both hands, and Paul climbed back into the driver's seat.

"Ah, geez," she said softly, her hand on the passenger door, her teeth clenched.

"Step in it?" Paul pictured her high heels, the ones she had the store dye pink to match her dress, buried in mud.

She pulled open the door, sat down, careful to keep her feet out of the car, and slipped off the shoes. She picked them up off the ground by slipping a hand in each.

"Thoughts?" she said, holding the shoes in front of her, the heels and soles packed with mud.

"Can you hold 'em like that till we get to the gas station? I can try rinsing them off in the john."

"Sure thing."

Paul reached across to close the door for her, then pulling her face to his, kissed her.

"Strawberry?" he asked.

She shook her head.

"Watermelon. Trying to keep things interesting."

How did I ever get this lucky, Paul thought as he started up the engine and headed down the road. Most girls would be flipping out if their prom date was mud splattered and their high heels ruined.

He drove slowly, sticking to the center of the dirt road. The Archies' "Sugar, Sugar" blasted from the radio. Sarah sang along, making the shoes in her hands dance in time with the music. She elbowed Paul.

"Sing!" she ordered.

"I don't sing."

She waved the shoes at him.

"Sing or I'm wiping these shoes off on your shirt."

Paul grinned. "Okay then. You asked for it." He turned the volume even higher and joined in as they swung out onto the main road, headed for town.

June 1969, Haleʻiwa, Hawaiʻi

Tiny as a chickadee, Paul thought, as Amiko Akutagawa handed him a paper plate piled with thin slices of grilled teriyaki beef, two mounds of sticky white rice, a scoop of macaroni salad, and two generously buttered slices of white bread. Amiko wouldn't look him in the eye, but before she darted away, she smiled and seemed almost ready to say something. He'd never seen a girl so delicate. He liked the way she ducked her head, letting her long hair fall like a veil of black silk over her face. *Give it a rest,* he told himself. No sense messing with a local girl when he'd only be there for the summer.

The work his first morning at Akutagawa's General Store had been easy but monotonous. All the same, it was a welcome relief from playing endless rounds of Go Fish and Chutes and Ladders with his nephews. Hawai'i had sounded pretty fine on the muddy, cold March day when his sister called and asked him to come for the summer. Her husband was shipping out to Vietnam and was worried about leaving his wife and young sons alone. Paul hadn't been prepared for the claustrophobia of a tiny military base house or the tediousness of childcare. He was grateful his sister had agreed to his finding a part-time job.

After the lunch rush, Amiko appeared again, this time carrying a cone of yellow shave ice. Her primary job at her father's store was operating the ornate shave ice machine. She turned a giant wheel that rotated a blade beneath a huge block of ice. Thin, fine shavings fell in a pile below. These she scooped up and packed tight as a snowball in paper cones, then finished with a generous topping of syrup. Paul figured it would take him the entire summer to try all the flavors and combinations. Some were familiar—root beer, strawberry, and vanilla—many were exotic—coconut, lilikoi, and guava. The glass bottles of syrup, each a different, brilliant color, lined two shelves beside the machine.

Looking at Amiko now in the white afternoon light, her hand outstretched with the yellow ice, Paul wondered how she could be so beautiful without any makeup. Her thick, arched brows and dark lashes made her eyes startling against her porcelain complexion. His girlfriend Sarah wouldn't leave the house without layers of eye shadow, mascara, and blush.

"Pineapple," she said, her eyes averted so that her lashes brushed her cheeks.

Paul bit into the top. "Pineapple snow."

He was glad when she didn't rush back into the store.

"I've never seen snow."

She slid a small silver cross she wore around her neck back and forth on its chain. It was a simpler crucifix than the type girls wore back home.

"Well, this is what snow's like. Only in Vermont, we put maple syrup on it."

The bell on the front screen jingled, calling Amiko back to her spot behind the counter.

At six Mr. Akutagawa called out "Pau hana" and turned the sign in the window to CLOSED. Paul had emptied all the boxes and flattened the cardboard into a tall stack. He gathered up his things and headed to the front. He wanted to speak to Amiko before leaving, but she was busy wiping down the shave ice machine and he couldn't catch her eye.

"I'll be heading out now," he told Mr. Akutagawa, who nodded without smiling.

"You did good work today."

Paul slapped the doorjamb, called out, "See you all Friday," and looked back at Amiko and her aunt Miyoko. Both smiled and dropped their gazes.

He felt good as he headed to the bus stop. He had done more than was asked of him, had been careful and neat with his work, would have more spending money at week's end, and best of all, would see Amiko again soon.

June 1969, Honolulu, Hawaiʻi

"What're you up to in class, Barnes?"

Though he sat next to her, Brad Wilcox never spoke to Amy. She pretended she didn't know what he was talking about.

"You know," he said. "That sheet of paper you keep pulling out of the desk."

She considered her options. Explain her game for surviving this summer chemistry class and risk Brad telling others what a nerd she was or stop the game. It would be a deadly four more weeks if she had nothing to ease the boredom.

"Idioms," she said. "I keep track of the idioms. You know, the clichés Mrs. Donahue uses." She could have added, "As in, Brad is not the brightest bulb in the room."

"Huh?"

Amy wondered if it was the word "idioms" that baffled him or if he had really not picked up on their teacher's penchant for trite, overused expressions.

"Ever notice how many clichés Mrs. Donahue uses? Like when she excused us for break, she said 'I want you all back by ten on the dot'?"

Brad looked at her blankly.

"Or how every morning she says, 'Okay, people, let's get this show on the road'?"

"Yeah, I guess." Brad still looked confused.

"Well, I keep track of them. You know, write them down as she says them. And I keep score of the ones she repeats. There are ones like 'in a nutshell' that she uses about a dozen times a day."

"Why?"

Amy figured she must sound like the biggest weirdo ever.

"To stay awake. To keep from screaming out of boredom."

"Bitchin'," he said, bobbling his head at her. This surprised her. She wondered what about this seemed "bitchin'" to him—that a nerd like her was doing something mildly subversive or that he saw a way to kill some of his own boredom?

"Yeah. Real bitchin'."

"Can I have a look?"

She slid the list out of her desk.

"How long you been keeping track?"

It was only the third week of summer school.

"Since the second day."

Mrs. Donahue arrived, carrying a stack of papers fragrant with mimeograph ink.

"As luck would have it, people," she said, "the mimeo machine messed up these quizzes." Amy took back her list and made a mark next to "as luck would have it." This was Donahue's twelfth usage. "There's a fold midway that makes question four tough to read. I'll write it out on the board."

Brad smirked at Amy. Coconspirators with Brad Wilcox! A dimwit, but a cool one. A bona fide member of the "in crowd." *Means nothing,* she reminded herself. Donahue passed out the quizzes.

"I don't mean to sound like a broken record, but books closed, papers away. There should be nothing on your desks but a pencil."

Brad elbowed Amy and she nodded. Once Donahue had passed, she dutifully marked her sheet. Brad gave her a goofy grin. She looked away quickly and studied the quiz before her. *Don't be stupid,* she told herself when Brad's arm brushed hers, setting her pulse racing. *He's an idiot.* She stared at the equation Mrs. Donahue was writing on the board, forcing herself to concentrate. *Next thing I'll be blubbering about how he makes me go weak in the knees and takes my breath away.*

As the mingled scents of Brut and Lifebuoy washed over her, she shifted her body away from Brad and worked her way through the quiz. *Nose to the grindstone, Barnes. Nose to the grindstone.*

July 1969, Hale'iwa, Hawai'i

"So what's that you're reading when you sit up front at the register? That book you keep tucked under the counter?" Paul asked Amiko as they ate lunch, he with his chicken katsu plate, she with a small bowl of rice and vegetables.

Amiko was perched a couple steps above him on the staircase leading to the store's back door. The trades blew hard next to the beach, bending the palm trees and spritzing them with ocean spray. Amiko kept her skirt gathered between her legs so it wouldn't billow, her tiny feet in their dainty white sandals and her knees set tightly together.

As she talked, she let her hair fall forward over her face, used it as a shield when she smiled. If Paul said something that amused her, she would, with a flick of her head, send her hair sailing back over her shoulders, her dark eyes looking straight into his for a brief second.

She shrugged. "Just a book."

"Oh, one of those books."

She blushed and let her hair fall forward.

"Relax, I'm just kidding. I'm curious, that's all."

"It's called *A Selection of Poems.* They're poems by E. E. Cummings."

Now it was Paul's turn to be uncomfortable. He knew a little Robert Frost, but poetry had not been his thing in English classes.

"You know, the poet who wrote 'somewhere i have never travelled, gladly beyond'?"

He shook his head. "Sorry. Don't know it."

"Then you're missing out," she said with a flash of conviction, her face emerging from its curtain of hair. Her intensity was so out of character, he had to smile.

"Okay then. How about you read it to me while I eat?"

It was her turn to laugh. "No way am I reading poetry to you. Especially not that poem."

"Oh, I get it. It's one of those poems."

With a deep sigh he felt sure was exaggerated for his benefit, she rose and said, "Okay, but it might just sprain your brain."

"Yeah, yeah, yeah. Quit stalling and get the book." Paul liked that she was teasing him.

Amiko returned, book in hand, and held it open to the poem. "Here."

He shrugged and lifted his plate. "Sorry, hands full."

She perched herself back on her step, book propped on her knees, and began reading. She began with a silly poem, one with words like "mud-lucious" and then another about a Molly and a Milly and some other girls with M names.

"And," he said when she'd finished those, "the one about traveling?"

She opened the book to "somewhere i have never travelled, gladly beyond" and, without looking up, began reading it, her initial discomfort fading as she read. When she had finished, she sat silent for a moment. Finally, she closed the book and took the empty plate from his hand. Her fingers brushed his. "What flavor today?"

"Lime," was all he said.

For the rest of the afternoon, Paul worked at a keen pace. He not only finished stocking shelves, he collapsed all the boxes and swept out the storeroom. He needed to keep moving. Listening to the poem had flooded him with an unsettling energy. He moved out into the main store area and swept the aisles, careful not to watch Amiko too closely. He carried a letter from his girlfriend Sarah in the back pocket of his jeans. Promises had been made. Promises that meant he needed to be careful his flirting didn't cross lines. He just wasn't sure where those lines were exactly or if he still wanted to stay on the right side of them.

Midafternoon the front door's bell rang and a group of teens entered. The pack's leader, a kid with streaked hair that drooped over one eye, sunglasses perched on top of his head, his shirt unbuttoned and hanging over baggy surfer trunks, swaggered up to Amiko at the shave ice counter, hands in his pockets. Paul wanted to smack him just for the way he walked.

"So, guys, what's it going to be? Amy, a vanilla, right?" He looked back at a girl near the front door and winked at her. "And Mandy's gotta be cherry."

Mandy, an Ann-Margaret look-alike, wore a T-shirt tied at her waist over her bikini. She smirked and draped an arm over his shoulders. "Ha ha. Very funny. Make mine root beer."

The other girl, the one named Amy, hung back and answered, "I'm good, Brad. I'm going to get myself a Coke."

Unlike Mandy, this girl wore modest shorts and a tee. She radiated none of the affected coolness of the other teens.

"Tell us, Brad," Mandy said. "How good *is* Amy? I'm guessing not very if she's hanging out with you."

Brad snickered. The girl named Amy had pulled a Coke from the cooler and gone to pay at the cash register. She stared out to the street as she drank from the bottle, pointedly ignoring the others.

Amiko made three shave ice cones for Brad, Mandy, and the other kid. If she had an opinion about this group, she didn't let it show.

Cone in hand, Brad called ahead to his friend, "Hey, Carl, can you pay the papasan? I'm a little low."

Paul looked up, first at Mr. Akutagawa and then Amiko. Their faces were blank. Paul wanted to say something to the kid, but he figured it wasn't his place. He waited for Mr. Akutagawa to say or do something, ready to back him up.

"I'm busted, man. I got nothing," Carl answered as the three headed to where Amy stood near the front door.

"Don't look at me," Mandy said before Brad could ask.

The girl named Amy pulled out her wallet.

"Thanks, Barnes. I owe ya." Brad blew her a kiss as he and the others headed out the door.

"I'm sorry," the girl said to Mr. Akutagawa.

No one spoke after she left. Mr. Akutagawa resumed his work, Amiko wiped the counter, and Auntie Miyoko continued to chop vegetables in the kitchen. Paul wondered if there was something here he was missing. Was the papasan reference not an insult? If not, then why had the Amy girl apologized? The more he thought about it, the angrier he was. He wasn't even sure why he was so angry. Was it Mr. Akutagawa's passive response that offended him or his own sense of impotence?

Amiko didn't bring him a shave ice that afternoon. By four, he'd finished all the work there was for him. He hesitated before leaving to catch the bus, thinking he should say something to Amiko or her father. When he couldn't find the words, he said a simple "See ya tomorrow," waved a hand at Amiko, and let the screen door slam behind him.

A few minutes later Amiko came out the back door and crossed the lawn to the bus stop.

He dug his hands into his pockets.

"You seem angry. I don't understand."

"This afternoon that kid referred to your father as papasan. That's an insult, right?"

Amiko shrugged. "Could be."

"And yet your father didn't say or do anything."

"What do you think he should have done?"

"The kid was a jerk. He insulted a grown man in his own store. How is that okay?"

"I'm not saying it's okay, but what do you think my father should have done?"

Paul didn't speak. He wanted to say *Be a man.* But he would never say that to Amiko and he wasn't even sure what exactly he meant by it. It wasn't that he thought Mr. Akutagawa should have pounded the kid, but he could have said something, stood up for himself.

"My dad has learned to ignore people like that guy. Either they want to get a rise out of him or they're so clueless, they don't even know how insulting they're being."

"Where's his dignity?" Paul finally asked. "Letting some punk get away with that—it's wrong."

Amiko stood before him, her hands clasped tightly.

"He was trying not to be a part of it, to rise above. He can't control what other people do or say. He can only control himself."

Paul considered this.

"Look, I'm sorry, okay? I was being dumb. I've no right to judge your dad. I just wanted to clobber that kid."

She softened. "I know the feeling."

"I didn't mean to show any disrespect to your dad."

He held out a hand to her. "Friends?"

She shook his hand.

"You need to grow a thicker skin, you know, if you're going to hang out with us Japs."

"You've got a sick sense of humor, Akutagawa."

"Better than no sense of humor, Rideau."

The last line of the Cummings poem repeated in his head as he watched her go: "nobody, not even the rain, has such small hands."

July 1969, Honolulu, Hawai'i

"How do you celebrate a moon landing?" Paul's sister Peg asked over dinner. "Champagne?"

Something crashed against the wall separating them from the apartment on the duplex's other side. His three-year-old nephew Craig covered his ears.

"Kaboom," Paul said, smiling and splaying his fingers to suggest an explosion. "They're already celebrating the man on the moon next door." He didn't know if trying to make light of the neighbors' fights was good or bad for the kids.

"Can we set off firecrackers?" Kevin, the six-year-old, was suddenly interested.

Peg began clearing away dishes. "I've got a better idea. You boys eat all your dinner and I'll take you over to Liliha Bakery. You can pick out some special desserts. What do you say? Cream puffs? Cake?"

Peg kept smiling as the yelling escalated. She winced at the "you sorry-ass motherfucking cheater." Paul tipped his chair back to reach the television set and turned up the volume. When he first arrived in Hawai'i, he'd wondered why Peg never turned off the set. Lazy, he'd thought at first, using the TV to babysit her kids. He'd learned soon enough how paper-thin the walls were in the military base housing.

"You go ahead and take them to the bakery," he told Peg. "I'll clean up."

When he'd finished with the dishes, Paul headed out to the swing set in the backyard as he often did in the evenings. The tiny duplex could become impossibly small even when the neighbors weren't going at it. He could still hear the screaming along with the other neighbors' televisions and stereos, but at least he didn't feel trapped when outside. Swinging gently with his face to the sky, he tried to imagine what the Apollo crew was feeling as they prepared for the next day's landing. Were they afraid? Or did the wonder of what they were about to do trump every other emotion? He had no desire to trade places.

A month earlier, he might have envied them. For as long as he could remember, he'd wanted to see the world, escape the suffocation of the Vermont hills that blocked horizon lines. He'd been sure a more enticing world lay beyond the stone walls of his family's farm.

"Put that down or I swear to God, I'm calling the cops."

Every fight it was the same. The woman next door grabbed a kitchen knife. The husband threatened to call the cops. Fifteen more minutes and he'd slug her or push her out the front door and Paul or some other neighbor would call the MPs.

This summer in Hawai'i was meant to be an escape from what he saw as the drudgery of his Lisbon life. He planned on joining the navy as soon as he turned eighteen, but until then, he had to put up with farm chores, boring high school classes, and a social life that consisted of drinking beer with his buddies and making out with Sarah at the drive-in or down by the river. Home wasn't looking so bad now. He was even reconsidering his idea about joining the navy. If Honolulu felt foreign and unsettling, how would he ever survive Vietnam? But it wasn't as if he had much control over where he'd end up in a year. Unless he lucked out in the lottery, he would be in some branch of the military.

He wondered if the moon was still visible over his family's farm thousands of miles away. For the astronauts looking down at Earth, Hawai'i and Vermont mustn't seem all that far apart. Did the entire planet become home when seen from space?

A door slammed. They were taking the fight to the front yard. *Good,* Paul thought. Let some other neighbor deal with it. Maybe the MPs would lock up the pair for the night and give everyone some peace.

He didn't understand how military families survived living in these close quarters. Even with good neighbors, there was too much intimate knowledge of one another's private lives. His sister didn't complain, but he knew it ate at her. She'd grown up on the farm, too. He thought of those men in space squeezed into that tiny craft.

The squeal of tires from the street told him the fighting couple had taken their quarrel on the road. However their evening ended, he hoped they'd finish it, not bring it home for them all to suffer through. Maybe the astronauts did have the right idea. Get away from it all.

It cheered him to think something extraordinary was about to happen. Tomorrow the *Eagle* would land and a man would be on the moon. No matter how broken the world might seem, there were still people striving for something better, even at great risk to themselves. He wanted to fall on that side of the line, be a person capable of hope and wonder.

He heard Peg's car in the drive, took a last swing, and headed in. At least he would be back on farm fields in a month, not like these servicemen, wives, and kids enduring a sardine life. And Monday he would see Amiko again.

"So what did you get me?" he called as he pulled open the screen door.

Not much of a moon, Amy thought, looking up at the crescent revealed by parting clouds. The beam of Kainalu's flashlight illuminated the wet ledge ahead, but Amy would have welcomed the light of a full moon. She wouldn't voice her fear aloud, but it terrified her to walk along the slippery stone shelf on such a dark night. She could hear waves crashing below, feel their spray in the wind.

"Torch fishing," Kainalu had suggested as an alternative to catching a movie. "We can go out on the ledge by Portlock when the tide goes out."

Amy was dressed for seeing *True Grit*, not for torch fishing. The hem of her long dress was drenched, a dragging weight, and her thin zoris caught on the jutting rock. She wanted to walk barefoot so she'd have a grip, but she knew the rock would shred her feet.

Kainalu and Janine moved confidently along the ledge, as if it were no more challenging than sprinting across a sunlit lawn.

"Something over there," Kainalu yelled, moving toward a small pool. He shone his flashlight into the water and raised his spear. With a whoosh, he plunged it into a squid.

Amy had to look away from the gelatinous mass hanging on the spear's tip, its tentacles squirming. She lifted her skirt and moved closer to the wall of ledge farthest from the ocean. Maybe the squid would be trophy enough and they could head back to Janine's house. Janine's parents, out for the evening, didn't even know they were out on a cliff instead of inside a theater. A wave could sweep them off and no one would know.

Kainalu swung the flashlight's beam over the surrounding ledge, shone it directly into the few other pools of water, and found nothing.

"Got one at least," he said, shrugging. A wave, hitting with a boom like thunder, showered them in salt water, the spray reaching as far as Amy. *Enough already,* she decided.

"I'm getting cold," Janine said, her teeth chattering. "I need to get into dry clothes."

Grateful she wasn't the first to suggest leaving, Amy echoed her. "Yeah, I'm soaked and freezing in this wind."

Kainalu left the squid dangling on his spear. Amy could tell he was pleased, showing off for Janine's benefit. She figured it would work. He looked sexy enough in his surfer trunks, his bleached hair long and wild around his face. Unlike Brad, he was the real deal, an actual surfer. Amy wished some cute guy wanted to impress her as much as Kainalu wanted to impress Janine.

As they headed back, she walked as fast as she could, trying to stay far ahead of the couple. Not because she was such a generous friend, giving them their privacy, but because she couldn't stand the false squeal in Janine's voice.

"Stop it," Janine giggled, clearly not wanting Kainalu to stop whatever he was doing.

Amy kept her eyes on the sidewalk ahead. Living rooms glowed blue as she passed. She expected everyone was watching news coverage of the Apollo mission. Right now three Americans circled the moon, preparing to be the first humans to step onto its surface. What made a person brave enough to do that, she wondered. To do what had never been done before, risk burning up in a rocket or springing a leak in a space suit or floating off untethered. She felt small and inconsequential by comparison and wondered if maybe, someday, she would have the kind of courage that helps change the world.

She checked her watch. Already 10:35. She needed to be home before eleven. Usually she resented her curfew, but tonight she was grateful she had to leave. All she wanted now was a hot shower and dry clothes.

She slipped in the side door they'd left unlocked, collected her purse and keys, and was back outside before Kainalu and Janine had made it up the driveway.

"You're going?" Janine seemed genuinely surprised, even annoyed.

"I have a curfew."

"You can't go. My mom'll have a conniption fit if she finds me here alone with Kainalu." Her whining irritated Amy.

"And my mom will have a fit if I'm late. Sorry. I can't stay."

"Some friend you are." Janine all but stomped her feet.

Amy headed down the driveway, everything a blur through her tears. *Are you kidding me?* She wanted to say. *You use me as a way to spend an evening with your boyfriend, you ignore me completely, and you expect me to get in trouble so you won't?*

She held her tongue and climbed into her car.

"Don't blow the clutch, don't blow the clutch," she muttered as she turned the key. She eased the Corolla forward from the curb, shifted smoothly into second, and drove off.

Am I a bad friend? she wondered. Did a good friend do whatever she could to help out, even if it meant getting in trouble? In chapel the week before, the school chaplain had stressed the importance of being true to oneself and not being swayed by others to violate one's own code. But she wasn't always sure what her code was exactly. It felt like there were different codes, a code for what her parents wanted her to do, a code for her friends, even a code for how to treat strangers. How was she supposed to stay true to herself, when she was only sixteen and had no idea what her true self was.

At the intersection of Portlock and Kalaniana'ole Highway, she turned left toward the glow of Honolulu's city lights and scanned the sky for signs of the elusive moon. At times like this, when she felt keenly how little she knew of herself and the world, she could not imagine ever being an adult capable of managing everyday life, let alone performing great deeds like riding a rocket to the moon or writing a great novel or saving a human life. How would there ever be time enough to know all she needed to know to live her life well?

Chapter Five

September 2001, Clifton, New Hampshire

Amy's computer beeped. A new message. She continued her slow stroll between the rows of desks, watching her students' hands fly across their papers. Pop quiz on the summer reading. As she passed her own desk, she paused to read the message. It was from her friend Kathy.

"You guys free for dinner Saturday? I thought I'd grill—" Kathy had left the sentence unfinished then added, "Just started hearing some horrible news. They say two planes crashed into the World Trade Center and the pentagon is on fire. This is so scary."

Amy typed, "Is this for real?"

The computer beeped a few seconds later. This email was addressed to Amy as well as Kathy's brother Steve. "Now they're evacuating the Capitol and Treasury. VP and admin may be in situation room and not known if they're still in WH. Air Force 1 is in the air."

Amy struggled to process what Kathy was writing. Was this more hysterical cable news coverage, or was something serious happening? She glanced up. Ivan Markowski, one of the guidance counselors, paused in the doorway to her room and nodded for her to step out into the hall.

"Have you heard?"

"I got an email from Kathy about some kind of attack. Is it for real?"

"As best we can tell. We're asking teachers to keep their students in the classrooms. We don't want anyone leaving until we know what we're going to do. We're not in lockdown mode, but we want everyone to stay put. There'll be an announcement on the PA system."

Amy nodded.

"Do the best you can to stay calm and keep the kids calm."

Ivan headed down the hall to the next room.

Heads popped up as Amy entered the room. It wasn't like her to leave the class in the middle of a quiz. She was known for being a hard-ass about such things. She glanced at her watch. A bit before ten.

"Okay, guys. You've got another ten minutes." Several people groaned. "Come on. If you did the reading, this is easy stuff. If you didn't read, extra time isn't going to help you figure out the answer."

Several students had finished and turned over their papers. She collected those and let the kids read as the others finished. She walked back to her desk as calmly as she could and checked her email again.

"They have tape of the second jet crashing. No word if passengers were on board. They're evacuating the state department now. Another tower exploded. Just happened. Lower Manhattan is enveloped in smoke. They think the tower collapsed."

Her computer beeped.

"DC now in attack mode. They evacuated the Sears Tower in Chicago." Amy straightened up and looked out at the students. Carrie Kim smiled at her and Amy made herself smile back. What was happening with her own kids? She tried to recall what class Kara would be in.

At ten after ten, she clapped her hands and said, "Okay, people. Make this your last sentence. Check that your names are on your papers and pass them up."

As the students moved their quizzes forward, Amy paced at the front, impatient. *Come on, come on,* she said silently to the principal. *Make the announcement. Tell us what we're supposed to be doing here.*

"I have everyone's quiz?" She held the stack up in her right hand. "Yes? They're all here? Okay, then let's see how you did." She proceeded to go through the quiz question by question, soliciting answers from the class. She was interrupted at question four.

"Good morning, everyone." Finally, it was the principal, Helen Swenson, speaking over the PA. "Some of you may have already heard that terrible events have occurred in New York City and Washington, DC."

The students quieted.

She proceeded to summarize the news, much of it exactly as Amy had read in Kathy's emails.

"Until we know what is happening, we are asking that you stay in your classrooms. We don't want you leaving campus or making phone calls. Mr. Holden is setting up televisions in the library and auditorium. Once those are in place, we will let you watch the news coverage if you would like. Teachers, we leave it to your discretion as to whether you proceed with what you had planned or do something else. If any students are anxious and would like to talk to a counselor, the guidance staff will be available in the cafeteria to meet with students."

They can go watch TV, Amy thought, *they can go talk to a counselor, but I'm supposed to keep them in my room? Kind of confusing, Helen.*

For the rest of the day, Amy sat in the library with Kara, students, faculty, and staff, watching the news or checking her classroom computer for news from other family members. She'd emailed Martin immediately but gotten no reply.

At precisely 3:02, the students streamed out of the building and her cell phone rang. It was Hayden Brookstone, the priest at their church.

"I'm in Barre, getting on the interstate. I want to get the church open for people to gather. Are you free to do that?"

"Yup. I have to collect my kids and then I'll head over."

"Good. Open up the doors. Make it obvious people are gathering. I'll call Deb and get a phone tree going to the congregation. Could you also light the altar candles?"

"Will do." Amy was grateful for the assignment. It would help to stay busy and be useful. "See you in an hour."

The phone rang again. This time it was Martin.

"You getting the kids?"

"On my way now. Hayden just called. He's asked me to open up the church, so we'll head over there."

Martin sighed.

"You don't have to join us," she said, irritated that even at a moment like this all Martin could think of was his own comfort level. "We'll be home for supper."

"I may need to stick around here. In case students come looking for someone to talk with."

Don't do this. The world's blowing up, and I know this is how you handle your fears, but please, not this time.

"I understand," she said, knowing he would hear the warning. She snapped shut her phone and immediately it rang again.

"Mom!"

"Hey, Will. I'm on my way. Everything's going to be okay."

Paul didn't see Sarah pull the arterial line from her arm though he was sitting beside the bed. He must have nodded off. By the time the machines began wailing and nurses filled the room, Sarah and the right side of the bed were drenched with blood.

"Step outside, please," a nurse, the kind one, said, leading him gently to the door. "We'll let you know when you can come back in."

He wandered down the hall, through the ICU's giant automatic doors, and from a picture window looked out on a perfect September day. A cast encased his own left arm, the arm he'd fallen on. His entire left side, face to foot, had been scraped raw on the gravel. The swelling had nearly closed his eye. He'd spent most of the previous day in the ER being patched up. When they finally released him in the evening, it was to go with his daughter Maddie into the ICU, where they'd brought Sarah after her surgery.

He had walked away from the wreckage, but not Sarah. She had taken the full brunt of the vehicle as it sideswiped her bicycle. He'd only suffered the collision between his bike and hers.

The night before, the doctors didn't think she would make it to morning. When the sky lightened and she was still with them at five, Paul sent his kids home. Maddie had protested, but he'd insisted. "I need you rested. And the farm looked after. I'm counting on you and Chris to fill in."

No sense in having an army of people hovering around when no more than one or two of them could go into the ICU room at a time. Though now, with the full weight of being alone, he wished that someone had stuck around. His legs were shaky, and he could use an arm to help him down the hall.

"Mr. Rideau." It was the kind nurse again. The one with the gentle eyes. "We've got her cleaned up. You can come back in."

He nodded and followed her back to the unit with its beeping machines and weeping visitors.

"Go ahead." She nodded toward Sarah's room. "You can go on in."

Only he didn't want to go in. He didn't want to look at her colorless face or the tube taped to her cheek extending to a pouch. For the fluid draining from her brain, the doctor had said. The woman on that bed wasn't recognizable as his wife of twenty-seven years. All Paul wanted was to run away. Drink a beer. Eat a sandwich. Climb into his own bed.

"Dad." Maddie had come up behind him. She gave him a hug. "You look awful." Her husband Ray was with her. "How about you let Ray take you home? I'll stay with Mom."

Paul shook his head. "No. I shouldn't leave. Got to keep an eye on her."

This time it was Ray who put an arm around him. "Seriously, man. You need to get some food and sleep. Nobody's going to leave Sarah alone. We'll call you if you need to come back."

Running a hand down his face, Paul finally nodded. He didn't have it in him to pretend he could keep doing this.

"Okay, but you stay here with Maddie. I've got the truck. Chris left it last night." He watched Maddie and Ray exchange looks. "Seriously. I'll feel better if Mom has both of you here. I'm okay to drive."

"Before you go, Dad," Maddie said, putting an arm around him. "There's something you should know. Nothing for you to worry about now, but there's been some kind of attack in New York and DC. No need to concern yourself with all of that now. Just go home and rest."

As he passed the visitor's lounge, Paul glanced up at the TV screen. Buildings were crumbling. He stopped and stared. People were running.

An orderly had stopped as well. "They flew planes into the World Trade Center and Pentagon this morning."

"Who did?"

The man shrugged. "Arabs, I guess."

Paul couldn't make sense of this. He was too tired to grasp that this misery was unconnected to his own. Something was making the whole world collapse.

But nothing he saw in the streets outside the hospital suggested a world turned upside down. Traffic moved as it usually did. Drivers did not appear panicked or distraught. Paul made his way through Clifton, across the bridge, and meant to get on to Route 5, but missed it. He pulled into St. Stephen's parking lot to turn around and saw that its giant red doors were pulled wide open. Cars were entering the lot, adults and children headed up the church steps.

Paul shut off his truck engine and sat for a moment. He wanted to be home, fed and in bed, but he needed another kind of comfort as well. He climbed out of the cab and followed the others into the sanctuary, taking a seat in the last pew. People knelt or sat hunched over, hands clasped or holding open prayer books and Bibles. Candles flickered on the altar and in votives placed along the windows. A woman moved slowly up the center aisle, greeting people, hugging some, grasping others by the hand. Paul lowered himself onto the kneeler and stared straight ahead. The woman greeting people crouched beside him. He turned to look at her. *More kind eyes,* he thought. *Frightened eyes.*

"Are you okay? May I get you something?"

He wanted to tell her no. He was nothing close to okay. Instead, he shook his head and managed to say, "No thanks. I've been treated. Just came from the hospital." She patted his arm gently and then slid into the pew beside him.

"If it's okay, I'd like to sit here with you."

It was fine with him, but he had to resist the desire to rest his head on her shoulder.

He could hear the shuffle of footsteps around him as the church filled. The shadows lengthened until the church was nearly dark but for the flickering candles.

"Mom," a young voice said. A girl stood beside the pew, a younger boy behind her. "Can we go home soon?"

"Sure, Kara," the woman said. "You and Will wait out front for me and I'll let Hayden know we're going."

The woman turned to Paul. "You sure you're doing all right? Would you like someone to give you a lift home?"

He shook his head. "Thanks. I'll be fine."

He wanted to move on, follow the woman and kids out the church to his truck and drive home, but he couldn't find it in himself to move. He slumped back onto the hard wood pew and closed his eyes.

He would later describe it as coming like a gust of wind, as if someone had lifted wide a window or swung open the door. He felt it with his entire body, an enveloping rush and then a profound absence. He knew Sarah had passed. It was not an inkling, not a fear, simply cold, hard knowledge.

"On behalf of Emma and Josh, I welcome all of you, their family and friends, as we gather to celebrate the happiest of occasions in a most beautiful location," Kathy Jefferson, the officiant, said.

The wedding guests were seated on white folding chairs fanned out on a well-mown field overlooking the Connecticut River.

"As beautiful as this fall day is, as joyous as we feel for this couple ready to pledge themselves to one another, it may feel odd, even wrong perhaps, to celebrate so soon after the attack on our nation."

Martin pinched the bridge of his nose. He looked ready to cry, which puzzled Amy. He was usually able to mask his romanticism with well-honed disdain. All around them, handkerchiefs and tissues were being pulled from pockets and purses. Amy relaxed. Kathy Jefferson had the wedding well in hand.

Kathy continued. "Josh and Emma could have deferred their wedding plans as some suggested. They could have waited for a time when our shared trauma was not so acute. Instead, they chose to trust that love triumphs over hate and hope defeats despair. They said no to fear. So on this spectacular fall afternoon, nestled in the hills of Vermont and surrounded by their loved ones, they are promising to love one another for the remainder of their days. They invite us to share their faith in the future and witness their commitment, but we are not here merely as audience members. As witnesses, we are also called upon to support them in their commitment and do all we can to nurture their love in the days ahead."

Amy had had a pit in her stomach all day worrying about the event. She loved and admired Kathy, but feared the day's task might overwhelm her. Setting a joyous tone amid collective grief seemed more than even a seasoned minister could be expected to manage—and Kathy was a new justice of the peace. Not that Kathy had confided any fear to Amy. She was, as she always was, calm and quietly self-assured.

Amy also feared Martin would find Kathy easy to mock. Yet here he was, seemingly overwhelmed by emotion. He was clearly blinking back tears, his eyes glued to the distant horizon. Kara and Will were more difficult to read. They were paying close attention, but then, they both knew and loved Kathy. They were also close to Josh and Emma, whom they knew as their former (and favorite) teachers, Emma for second grade and Josh for eighth-grade algebra. This circle of Clifton teacher friends was the closest thing to family they had in New Hampshire. It was that sense of family that made it matter so much to Amy that Martin not ruin the day for her or anyone else there.

As Kathy led the couple through their vows, a doe and her fawns, in the glow of late-afternoon sun, galloped across a field close by. The crickets chirped away, but otherwise the world kept silent and still as promises were made. The couple chose the familiar, traditional vows from the Episcopal church's Book of Common Prayer. They promised to have and hold, to love and cherish, but it was the promises said with the giving of the rings that seemed to Amy the most eloquent. *I give you this ring as a symbol of my vow, and with all that I am, and all that I have, I honor you.* This was when Amy welled up, but not with tears of joy. It stung to be reminded of how far she and Martin had drifted from honoring one another, how little they gave of themselves to one another.

Kathy finished with Boris Pasternak's poem "The Wedding," from *Doctor Zhivago*, and let a moment of silence linger before signaling the band. As the wedding party danced down the aisle to "Walking on Sunshine," the guests clapped and followed, many of them dancing as well, including Kara and Will. Amy wrapped her shawl around her shoulders. The day's warmth was fading with the sun and the sheltering shadows of the ash and maple trees were now more nippy than pleasant. She and Martin strolled to the open lawn still awash in gold light where waiters circulated with champagne and appetizers. For all the glories that Hawai'i's natural world offered and which she missed, Amy could still be struck by the quiet eloquence of the New England countryside on an afternoon in fall.

"Well done, well done," Amy cried, as she gathered Kathy in a bear hug. "Best wedding ceremony ever."

Martin offered Kathy a peck on the cheek. "I can't imagine a more onerous task than to render a convincing affirmation of eternal love. Hats off to you,

Kath. You could make a person believe such a thing exists."

And there it was, Amy thought. He couldn't help himself. He was incapable of delivering a straightforward compliment. There must always be the thrust of the blade. This time he managed to wound her as well. Collateral damage.

Amy was past feigning surprise or objecting. This was the Martin she had married, the man she'd called husband for sixteen years. Martin had seduced her with this very behavior—affecting arrogance to hide his vulnerabilities, then revealing his tender sensitivities in the most intimate of moments. So enticing to imagine she alone could penetrate his well-protected heart.

"You don't fool me, Martin, dear," Kathy said. "We all know you are the supreme romantic. Now be a love and fetch us some champagne."

Martin took a moment. He was deciding, Amy knew, whether to push back or yield.

"Your every wish," he finally said with a slight bow to Kathy.

"You know that's precisely the sort of exchange he considers foreplay," Amy said.

"Hah!" Kathy shook her head. "He would be such a love if he weren't such an ass. Offer still stands, you know. There's always room enough for you and the kids. Anytime."

"Can you at least pretend you hope my marriage can be salvaged?"

Kathy made no secret of her opinion that Amy should end it with Martin.

"I appreciate your generosity," Amy added. "Really. You are the truest friend in all the world, but I haven't given up completely yet. Besides, it seems in bad taste to discuss divorce at someone else's wedding."

"Good point."

A passing waiter paused. "Champagne?"

"Thanks, no, we have some on its way. Or at least I think we do."

Amy scanned the crowd. Martin had drifted off to the far end of the lawn, cell phone to his ear. The call was brief and he soon returned in good spirits, two flutes of champagne in hand. "For you, lovely ladies. Enjoy." He was pleased with himself. Couldn't stop grinning. He loved playing the gallant gentleman. "I checked out the buffet while I was in there. You are in for a feast. Makes me sorry I can't stay and indulge."

"What are you talking about?" Kathy said. "You can't possibly be leaving so early."

"Afraid so. Classes start Wednesday and I'm buried in work. Amy and I've already discussed it. We even brought separate cars so she and the kids can stay and enjoy themselves." He pecked Amy's cheek. "I may be late, Ames, so don't wait up."

Amy waved him off, then downed her champagne in one gulp. "Well, that was mortifying."

"Had he really told you he was leaving after the ceremony?"

Amy shrugged. "Sort of, only it was more like a 'let's take two cars just in case' scenario, not a plan."

Kathy reached out an arm, but Amy stepped away. "Please, no. I'll totally lose it if you hug me or say something kind. I need distraction."

"You got it. Let's get some food and see what the kiddos are up to."

From the buffet line, Amy watched Kara and Will taking and posing for pictures with a small circle of teens. The bride had provided each table with a disposable camera, and guests were directed to capture the wedding's candid moments. Clearly, the camera was a hit with the younger set.

As Amy piled food on her plate, she imagined taking Kathy up on her offer. What if she told the kids she was leaving their dad that very night and the three of them would be staying at Kathy's? She rather liked the idea of Martin coming home to an empty house and feeling the sting of abandonment, but she couldn't put her kids through something so painful and melodramatic. Besides, she wasn't ready to take that step. Maybe he did have to catch up on work. If and when she decided to leave him, she would go with civility and dignity.

She sat down beside Kathy at a table of their work colleagues. Conversation had already drifted away from the wedding, and they were sharing stories of friends and family who'd witnessed the falling towers. There were happy accounts of good deeds being done—Vermonters heading to New York to evacuate loved ones or deliver supplies for the rescue efforts. Health professionals volunteering their medical services at ground zero. Mostly though, the stories were grim—a friend who disappeared when the towers collapsed, an NYU student traumatized as she watched a plane fly into a tower, someone's teenage son trapped in the city for days with no way back to Vermont. They hadn't meant to wander from the spirit of the celebration, but the wounds were fresh and there was so much yet to process.

Amy turned her attention to Kara, who was now on the dance floor with the bride, rocking out to "Girls Just Want to Have Fun." Tough to believe, watching that exuberant young woman, that she was the same person who so casually and frequently speared Amy with her barbs. When she let her veneer of adolescent cool slip away and forgot to worry what others were thinking, she could be a delight.

"Hey, Mom." Will grabbed both of Amy's hands. "You have to dance with me." He hauled her out of her chair.

"You want to be seen on the dance floor with your mother?"

Amy feared this was a pity move on his part, that he felt obliged to make up for his dad's desertion. Either that or someone had put him up to it. She decided his motivation didn't matter. She kicked off her shoes and let him lead her to the center of the dance floor.

The DJ switched to "Honky Tonk Woman" and people abandoned their dinners for the dance floor. Amy couldn't remember when she'd last danced packed tight in a crowd, the collective energy obliterating worry and pain. This was how it felt to have fun, a sensation that had gone missing with Martin. Smiles, everywhere smiles and movement as together they escaped, if only for a few moments, the days of suffering and embraced joy.

October 2001, Lisbon, Vermont

I live in a domestic graveyard. Paul surveyed the kitchen, coffee mug in hand. Sarah's sweater still hung over a chairback. The book she had been reading, Mary Higgins Clark's *Before I Say Goodbye,* lay on the counter. Except for the dirty dishes, it was exactly as it had been the morning they'd gone for a bike ride.

Maddie kept badgering him to let her come in and clean up.

"You tell me what you want left as is, Dad, and I swear I won't move a thing. But you've got to let me at least do the basic cleaning. It's been weeks."

She had said this as if his health might be in jeopardy if his toilet bowl didn't get scrubbed. As if there were something worse that could happen in his life, something a good cleaning might prevent.

He had to admit Sarah would be appalled to see her kitchen in such a state—dishes piled in the sink, dirty pans on the stove, a muddy path from the kitchen door across the white linoleum. He hadn't the energy to wash up the few dishes he used, let alone run a sponge over a counter or a mop over the floor. What was the point now? Hank was the only person who ever came in, and Hank sure didn't give a goddamn if newspapers were left stacked on the kitchen table.

He peered out the kitchen window. A thick fog still enveloped the farm.

His day had begun in early darkness as he helped his son Chris haul pumpkins and corn to the road stand. As well as he knew every inch of the farm, he'd still struggled to keep track of where the field ended and the road began. Paul knew he should now see to some of the bills piling up on his office desk in the barn. Once they finished haying the lower field, his day would be gone and he'd have no interest in desk work. As he crossed the dirt drive between house and barn, he heard a whoosh overhead and looked up, startled. He could see nothing.

The voices came next. Paul paused again. The whooshing sound and then, clearly, a man's voice said, "Head for the light, the patch of green."

For an instant, Paul imagined it was a heavenly voice speaking to him. He even looked around for a shaft of light. Later he would make a joke of it to Hank, but at that moment, he wanted to believe an angel hovered above him. Maybe Sarah had found a way through the divide.

He studied the dense grayness above, aware of how ridiculous he was being and yet wanting all the same to believe. He swiveled to look around the yard, the coffee sloshing in his mug. No one spoke, nothing moved. The whooshing sound continued. He followed it, moving down the hillside.

As he descended into the field, a hot-air balloon, its basket suspended below, appeared through the thinning fog, skimming a few feet above the ground. *Of course.* He should have known. Balloons had landed on their fields before, but this was the first time he'd heard one before seeing it.

From the hill behind him, a man cried out, "There! You can just make it out," and then two men, strangers, ran past him, headed for the balloon. Paul didn't run with them. He had seen his share of balloon landings, had done his part to help crews secure them. This one was a rainbow spiral, brilliant in the sun's spotlight. The men on the ground wrestled with the ropes. A passenger jumped out to help.

Paul turned and headed back up the hill. They would offer him champagne in appreciation for the use of his field, the passengers would gush about the patchwork of fiery leaves seen from aloft, and he would have to pretend he shared their joy. Better to hide in the barn. He'd send Hank out to lend a hand and drink the reward.

November 2001, Lisbon, Vermont

Amy smoothed the fair linen across the altar. *Concentrate,* she told herself. This was sacred work, not a time to get lost in her own emotions.

She returned the candlesticks to the table's ends and set the prayer book back on its stand, open to Eucharistic Prayer A. She laid the corporal on the fair linen, centered the chalice, then draped the purificator over the chalice and set the paten on top. Hayden would raise first the paten and then the chalice. She pictured his hands. The strength of them.

Enough, she told herself. *Be done.*

She moved to the sacristy. From a large wooden box, she extracted cardboard numbers for the psalms and hymns, using a service program on the counter as a guide. "Lord of All Hopefulness." "God of Grace and God of Glory." Two of her favorites.

Footsteps in the hall. Hayden opened the sacristy door, the late afternoon sun sliding in through amber glass. No eyes kinder than those. He wore his usual Saturday jeans and faded flannel shirt.

"Hey," he said.

"Hi."

"You working solo today?"

"Yup. I figured my last time on duty I should spare someone else having to come in." The job didn't really require two people, but custom dictated the guild work in pairs. The shared work fostered fellowship.

She busied herself finding the last of the numbers she needed, hoping to hit the right tone of nonchalance.

"Can I put those up for you?"

She handed him the cards and a program.

"It must feel odd to be doing this for the last time," he said as she followed him into the nave.

Lost was the word she would have used. She felt lost, but she couldn't tell him that, any more than she could explain why, after a decade of active service to the church, she was stepping away, abandoning him and the small congregation that so desperately needed members to keep the church running. "To devote more time to my family" was the reason she'd given, but it rang false every time she said it.

While he slid the numbers into place, she set out the collection plates, stacked programs at both entrances to the sanctuary, and made sure there were prayer books, hymnals, and programs in place for Hayden and the service attendants.

"How do they look?" Hayden slid in the last of the numbers.

She stood in the center aisle, a few feet back, and assessed the symmetry.

"Fine." She gave him a thumbs-up, then checked the numbers against the program in her hand. "Bingo. You got them all right."

Side by side, they stared at the altar as if making further evaluations. Amy tried to focus on whether the lectern dressings were evenly spaced, if the candles were straight, but it was a blur. "Kindred souls" he had once said of their friendship. She liked to imagine he meant more, but she knew she was being absurd. Hers was a silly, one-sided schoolgirl crush, triggered no doubt by her struggles with Martin. She was wounded and desperate to feel loved, even more so as Martin drifted further away. It was easy to mistake Hayden's kindness for something more, but it was nonsense to entertain such thoughts and deeply unfair to Hayden, who was never anything but appropriate with his friendship. She couldn't stay on at the church, not while wrestling with such feelings.

"I have something for you." Hayden slid a small package out from under his arm. From a paper sack she pulled a slim volume of poems. *Like the Dew* by Hayden Brookstone.

She raised her eyebrows in question.

"Long time ago. While I was in seminary. I doubt they sold a hundred copies."

She flipped through it, unable to focus her eyes enough to read any of the print. She saw he'd written something on the title page. "You've an actual book of your poems. How did I not know this?"

"Embarrassing stuff now, of course, but I thought you might like a copy."

"Of course. I'm honored. What a triumph to create something like this. I fear I haven't anything to offer in kind." All those years of aspiration and she hadn't so much as a single poem to give him.

"You've given me and the church so much. Those poems are just a feeble attempt to say thanks." He paused as if considering whether to continue, then added, "Whatever is weighing on you, if I can be of help, please reach out. The church is here for you."

She couldn't help but smile. He was indeed a good Episcopalian, too well-mannered to press her on her reasons for leaving. He felt larger to her, standing there so close beside her in the aisle, like a sheltering tree, his concern stitched across his face.

"I promise I'm not dropping off the face of the Earth. You'll see me at services from time to time." She didn't want him to worry about her.

"Hayden! There you are. I could use a hand with the tables." John Cowan stood in the doorway to the parish hall. "Hey, Amy." John coordinated the men's group that met once a month for a Saturday potluck supper.

"Hi, John. We've just finished up. He's all yours." She placed her hand on Hayden's arm for just a moment. "I'll finish and lock up. Have fun tonight, you guys."

"How many tables do you suppose we'll need?" Hayden asked, his voice fading as the two men moved away, and she headed for the sacristy.

"Shall we give thanks, folks?" was all John needed to say for conversation to stop and the other men to gather in a circle, link hands, and bow their heads.

Paul had never held another man's hand, but he did as the others did, even bowed his head. John hadn't mentioned this was part of the deal.

"For what we are about to receive, may the Lord make us truly thankful and keep us always mindful of the needs of others," the group said together, and then with John as the lead, they followed by singing something called the doxology.

Paul hoped his face wasn't as red as it felt. He was reminded of football games as a kid where he mumbled his way through the national anthem. He should never have let John talk him into coming to this thing. "It'll do you good," John had said. And when Paul protested he wasn't a churchgoer except for Christmas, John insisted this wouldn't be church. "Just happens to be at church. It's a bunch of men talking with other men about the challenges in their lives and how to manage their burdens." Even then Paul had resisted. He didn't want to be part of any support group with everyone feeling sorry for him. "Not a support group," John said. "Just regular guys talking about their lives. No one gives out advice. No one feels sorry for you."

Paul relaxed a bit once they finally started making themselves plates of food. He'd done as John suggested, picked up a cherry pie at the general store. It looked pretty sad with its plastic top next to the platters of cookies and brownies and even a massive apple pie still warm from the oven. For the main course, there was a lasagna big enough for twenty and a pot of chicken and dumplings, as well as a plate of ham slices beside a basket of warm biscuits. Paul reminded himself these guys had wives who did the cooking for them. No one would expect him to produce anything like this himself.

"Did I hear right that you got that big remodel job in Clifton?" the minister Hayden asked one of the younger men.

"Yup. Our biggest job yet. And they want it done before Christmas. I think we'll be doing a lot of six-day weeks."

Over dinner the talk continued to be mostly about work and sports and other personal interests, but finally, when they'd cleared away the dinner plates and settled down with their desserts, talk shifted to a book they had all read called *The Tipping Point*. The idea wasn't to discuss the book so much as to use it as a way to think about their own lives.

"I've been thinking about times in my life when something shifted in a consequential way. I've had plenty of small moments, like switching to a new beer or deciding it's time to update my jeans, but there have been some really big points of change, like when I left a perfectly good job and started over in another part of the country or when I switched my college major or even when I married Joyce. I'd sworn marriage wasn't for me," a guy named Jeremy said. He apparently was the group leader for the night.

Others shared their own moments, some so mundane Paul couldn't imagine sharing them, others were so huge—opting to leave a marriage, adopting three kids, enlisting in the military, that Paul felt his own life choices were boring by comparison.

"Something I realized," Hayden said, "is how much I've changed in what I let affect me. And it keeps changing. In some ways I'd be more willing to make a bold change now than when I was younger and had less sense of what mattered most to me. It seems counterintuitive, but I've become more uncertain and open to change as I age."

Paul didn't know what to make of the group. He couldn't remember ever talking with other men this way. Sure, he'd done his share of what-ifs in jest with the guys. A few beers and he'd play along with "What if you had a free pass for one night, what woman in this bar would you pick?" or "If you could relive one moment from the past, what would it be?" but he'd never spoken seriously about possibilities and choices with other men. He was surprised by their candor and willingness to admit their mistakes.

He stayed on after to help with the cleanup and even lingered a bit with John and Hayden when the others had left.

"I'm no churchgoer," he said to them as they switched off the hall lights and headed to their cars, "but I enjoyed the discussion tonight. Might even manage to read a book before the next one if it's okay for me to come back."

"You're always welcome," Hayden said. "I promise no one's going to try to convert you."

"Well," John said slowly, "we do have one guy. He wasn't here tonight. He can lay it on a bit thick, but he's basically harmless and means well."

Hayden nodded, clearly knowing who John meant. "The point of this group isn't to preach or talk scripture, it's to learn through reflection and discussion. About ourselves. About our aspirations. You don't have to belong to the church or go to services or even believe in God. You're still welcome."

Driving home, Paul realized that for the first time since Sarah died, he'd felt no physical pain for almost two hours. For the first time in weeks, he could imagine relief from suffering, if only for brief stretches, was a possibility.

Paul couldn't help himself. He dipped the brush in the can of paint, then swept it across the blank wall before him. The surface demanded definition.

This was, after all, what he had wanted—a giant blank surface equal to his vision. He began with strong, bold strokes of red then turned to the black. He let the paint run where it wanted. He could not switch the brushes or move the color fast enough.

At four, he heard the kitchen door open downstairs, remembered the kids were coming for supper.

"Upstairs," he yelled without interrupting his stroke of cobalt blue.

He heard someone climb the stairs and cross the few feet to his bedroom door. His son Chris stood in the doorway. Paul turned to him, the giant brush dripping onto the canvas mat.

"What are you doing?"

"I had to paint it."

"But Maddie's ordered wallpaper. Two days." Chris raised his voice and said again, "Two days it took us to prep these walls. We lost a day of mowing because you couldn't bear to sleep in this room if it looked the way it did when Mom was here."

Paul wilted before him, turned, and saw the wall through Chris's eyes. An act of madness. It challenged everything his family knew of him. Yet for him it was also a thing of beauty. The upper right corner with its splash of yellow breaking through the blue, the contrasting brush sizes, the broad reds and the thinner blacks, it was all as his interior eye said it should be.

Stepping away from it, he felt more than saw the work. It might as well have been his soul stretched and pinned to the wall. He had taken something from within and made it visible. And yet Chris was right. In the world they shared, this was foolish, a waste of precious resources. Who they were as a family did not include pouring oneself onto a bedroom wall.

"Maddie will be here in an hour," was all Chris said by way of direction. Paul knew to clean up the room and himself, climb back into his jeans and T-shirt, and be ready to help at the grill when the rest of the family arrived. Paul would close the bedroom door, sparing them.

He dropped the brushes into a pail and gathered up the cans.

Chapter Six

October 1974, Honolulu, Hawai'i

"Just call me Cricket," Sarah Rideau said, leaning against the doorjamb in the strapless dress—turquoise patterned with giant black hibiscus—she'd bought that afternoon.

"Works for me." Paul grinned at his wife.

With her nearly platinum blonde hair and deepening tan, Sarah was a ringer for Connie Stevens, star of the old TV show *Hawaiian Eye*. Ever since middle school, when someone first told her she was a Connie Stevens look-alike, Sarah had deliberately tried to emphasize the resemblance.

"You need one of those old cameras with the big flash to complete the look."

"What I need is some kind of big flower to put behind my ear and you in that shirt I bought you." She glanced back at the clock beside their bed. "The luau starts in ten minutes, bud."

Sarah had planned every detail of this delayed honeymoon, insisting they stay at Hilton's Hawaiian Village, even asking for a room in one of the original towers used in the television series. Her long list of things to do in Honolulu included attending a luau, getting drinks at the Polynesian Lanai, and learning how to do the hula. That evening they planned to check out the Polynesian Lanai after the luau, and she had signed up for a hula class the next day.

For his part, Paul didn't begrudge Sarah any of it. When she chose an April wedding day for the fresh hope of spring promises, Paul didn't have to remind her an April honeymoon was impossible. Already attuned to farm life, she understood they would have to wait for fall.

"Which ear says I'm taken?" She grabbed one of the purple orchids that had decorated their room service breakfast plates and stuck it behind first her left and then her right ear.

"No idea." Paul picked up the aloha shirt she'd laid out on the bed. "Seriously? You want me to wear this? Not only the gaudiest color and pattern I've ever seen, but you're turning us into the Bobbsey Twins?"

Sarah didn't even bother trying not to laugh as he buttoned it up.

"I wish I had that camera. We look ridiculous."

Sarah dabbed her eyes with a tissue and checked her makeup in the mirror.

"We are quite the pair tonight, Rideau."

Drawing attention to himself was not Paul's idea of a good time, but Sarah's good spirits were infectious. *This is my wife,* he thought. *Mother of my children-to-be.* Life was not going to be dull.

"That may be the ugliest piece of fabric on the face of the Earth, but it looks plenty good on you," he said, bending over to kiss her.

"Play your cards right, mister, and you just might get lucky tonight."

She wrapped an arm around Paul's waist as they headed out the door. A conch shell called from the lawn where the luau would be served and tiki torches flickered. Paul reminded himself that no one at this dinner would know him. At least he wasn't wearing shoes and socks with his shorts or a camera hanging from his neck. Besides, with Sarah beside him, he could face anything.

October 1974, Honolulu, Hawai'i

Congressman Conrad Suemori read aloud the numbers on each mailbox as Peyton drove the Lincoln Mark IV at a snail's pace up and down Ala Ilima. No number 1257. Amy knew blame would fall on her. A predictable end for a day that began bad and never got better.

"Did you know the first house tonight is out of district?" Peyton had asked her at seven that morning.

"What are you talking about?" Amy was typing Conrad's cheat sheets for the day, the little index cards she prepared so he knew whom he was meeting at each event.

"Look." Peyton showed her the street map of Oahu. Sure enough. The first hosts for that night lived in the second district. It was too late to change the event.

"Who invites a candidate to their home when he isn't even their congressman!" She punched her typewriter. "I suppose I have to call Rosie and let her know." Rosie was the senator's administrative aide in Washington who called all the shots.

"I shouldn't have said anything," Peyton said, folding up the map. "Then you could have claimed ignorance. If I were you, I'd keep quiet. Chances are no one will figure it out. Besides, he's going to run for the Senate in two years. You can always claim you were thinking ahead."

Peyton had been right. If Conrad realized they were out of district, he hadn't said anything and no one at the event seemed aware he wasn't their congressman. *What he is,* Amy thought, *is a colossal bore in love with his own voice.* As always, they were running nearly an hour behind schedule because Conrad couldn't stop talking. Rosie demanded two events a night, which meant asking the second crowd to turn out at 9 p.m. on a weeknight. What they never warned them of in advance was that the guest of honor wasn't apt to show before ten. And now they were lost and would be even later. Lost looking for Conrad's sister's home. *Who doesn't know where his own sister lives,* she wanted to scream. *And why should it fall to me, a college kid, to sort out the mess?* She would at least get course credit for the campaign work. She'd taken off the fall term of her senior year and needed the six credit hours her advisor had promised her in exchange for a written analysis of her experience.

Two days left in the campaign and she was exhausted. It didn't help that the island was socked in with Kona weather—hot humid air with no trade winds for relief. Amy craved a cold shower and sleep.

"What now?" Peyton asked, looking at her through the rearview mirror.

"Pull over," she said. "I'm going to borrow a phone."

Not allowing herself time to think about what she was doing, she strode to the nearest house with its lights still on and rang the bell. When a middle-aged couple, already in their nightclothes, appeared, Amy extended a hand.

"Good evening. Sorry to disturb you so late. I'm Amy Barnes, a member of Congressman Suemori's staff, and we seem to be lost. I was hoping I might use your phone?"

The stunned couple stepped aside and pointed to the kitchen. As she flipped through the phone book, Amy wondered how much trouble she would be in for doing this. Taking independent action was well above her pay grade.

As she dialed, she heard Conrad at the front door. "Aloha, I'm Conrad Suemori. How are the two of you this evening?"

She felt a rush of appreciation. Good old Conrad. Sometimes he surprised her. He might be furious as hell, but he would do his part to salvage the situation. She listened for any current of anger in his voice, but he soldiered on, as comfortable as if it were a Saturday morning canvassing call. The couple bobbed their heads, all smiles, clearly honored to have their congressman paying them a visit.

"So sorry, so sorry," Conrad's sister June gushed on the phone to Amy. She'd forgotten to mention the house sat on a cul-de-sac off of Ala Ilima. *Not as sorry as those thirty waiting people are.* Most of them probably had to be up at five the next morning. She glanced over at Suemori. His hand was now on the man's shoulder, his demeanor relaxed. She could see he was confident he'd saved the day.

"This young lady's quite the whippersnapper," Conrad said as she joined them at the door. "Only a senior at the university and yet she bosses me around. Anyone would think she's the one who's in Congress. Something tells me she will be someday."

Everyone laughed, because nothing could be more absurd than the idea of a young woman telling this seasoned pro what to do.

"All set?" Suemori asked.

"Yes, sir. It's just a few houses up the road. We're very close." She glanced at her watch. It was now past ten. "And we have a houseful of people waiting for us." She dared to place a hand on his arm to signal they must not linger.

After handshakes and bowing all around, they headed down the walk to where Peyton had kept the car idling. He smirked as she climbed in. The ribbing the next day would be relentless. She only hoped the newspapers wouldn't get wind of it. She could imagine the headline. "Suemori Team Tries New Campaign Strategy: Late-Night Canvassing." Probably better than the other possibility: "Suemori Campaigns in Wrong District." *Deep breaths,* she told herself, *deep breaths.*

The hosts had set out a special armchair for Conrad, so he resembled a king on his throne, some of his subjects cross-legged at his feet on the lauhala floor mat, the others standing at the room's edges, his sister June a flurry of useless energy. Amy had tried to suggest Conrad simply circle the room, do handshakes and hellos, and then let the people go. It was too late for a Q&A let alone a policy lecture. Despite the glazed eyes staring back at him, Conrad droned on. *Nobody here gives a rat's ass about tax law,* she wanted to yell. Watching him at these small gatherings always made her squirm. She tried not to listen and fanned herself with a campaign brochure. Why did the Washington staff think these coffee hours were a help? She was pretty sure they lost votes every time she brought him to one.

The tiny house was cramped and stuffy with no breeze for relief. Peyton, his back to the congressman, began making faces at her, mimicking Conrad's pretentious speaking style in an effort to make her lose it. She narrowed her eyes at him and looked away.

At least Peyton was on her side, not like most of the drivers who resented her as too young and too haole. Though he was wrapping up his final term at UH and also volunteering for the other district's congressional race, Peyton still was her number one volunteer, always willing to pitch in if she needed a driver or an envelope stuffer. That he also saw the humor and absurdity in the whole enterprise didn't hurt.

She felt the rain before she heard it. The trades suddenly kicked up and blew moisture through the screen door beside her. As it increased, the drumming began on the house's metal roof.

Conrad paused in his oration.

"Are the shoes okay?" he asked, looking over at Amy. All eyes were on her.

Everyone had, of course, taken off their shoes and left them either just outside the door or in piles beside where she sat. She smiled and signaled she had it under control.

Peyton leaned over and whispered, "Move the shoes, flunky. Chop-chop." Amy bit her lip and pulled the shoes in from the porch, not all that sorry to be out in the rain.

Why had she ever thought political work would be exciting? She spent long hours being a glorified gofer and babysitter to a man old enough to be her grandfather. For this she had given up everything she enjoyed? She hadn't read a book, seen a movie, or had dinner with a friend in five months.

"Where to now, general?" Conrad asked once they were back in the car.

"I'm done giving orders for the night, sir. Your choice."

He turned to Peyton. "What do you say? Shall we go ring some more doorbells or grab us some food and a drink?"

"I'm ready to eat," Peyton said. Amy realized she hadn't eaten anything since her morning doughnut.

"How about the Polynesian Lanai," Conrad suggested, loosening his tie, and glancing back at Amy. He knew how much she disliked the tacky tourist dive with its black velvet paintings and garish tropical cocktails served in plastic coconuts. If this was his revenge, at least it was good-natured.

Drunk tourists packed the Waikiki bar. Conrad loved late-night restaurant drop-bys. Most nights they ended up at some diner where locals showered him with attention. It could be a real spirit booster after an evening spent putting audiences to sleep. However, locals only went to the Polynesian Lanai after work. By ten, the bar was mostly tourists and servicemen.

Oblivious, Conrad moved down the line of mainland haoles at the bar, shaking hands and acting as if they must all be thrilled to see a congressman in person. Peyton and Amy stood against a wall watching the confused tourists shake the hand of this friendly, well-dressed Japanese gentleman. Finally, the manager, who did recognize Conrad, found them a corner table and directed a waitress to take good care of them.

Amy ordered a burger and began going over the next day's events. A walk-through of the Kaimuki storefronts in the afternoon—she gave him his index cards—and then a couple evening coffee hours like tonight's. Though Conrad put his head close to hers, Amy could see he was too tired to absorb the information. He finally shrugged and Amy knew they were done with business for the night.

"So, Peyton," Conrad asked, "you finish up this term or next?"

Peyton explained, not for the first time, that he'd graduate from the University of Hawai'i in December and then head off for San Diego, where he'd begin graduate work in political science.

"So you've got two months to convince Amy to marry you before you go?"

Amy kept her eyes on her food. *Not good form to glare at a congressman.* She could feel her cheeks flaming.

"Well, sir, Amy and I kind of have an understanding. You see, she'll never say yes, and I'll never ask."

What the hell was that supposed to mean? Amy assumed this was Peyton's way of telling her he had no interest in her. She was sure he had a thing for a woman named Lena who worked on the other congressional campaign. A strident feminist, Lena wore no bra or makeup, had an intimidating depth of knowledge on every issue, and could hold her own doing tequila shots. Amy's preference for wine coolers and carefully ironed dresses made her feel the queen of dull by comparison.

"Well, you're a fool, if you let her get away. Trust me, you won't find a better woman." This was a surprise to Amy. Maybe Conrad didn't consider her an idiot. "I'd marry her off to my kid if he was worthy of her."

"If you two are done planning my romantic life, we should eat and get back to the office. You still have letters to sign." Even as she said it, Amy knew she hadn't a prayer of getting Conrad to do more work that night.

As they ate, a trio of Hawaiian musicians started up, joined by two dancers in bikini tops and tea leaf skirts. They began with a spirited version of the "Hawaiian War Chant," complete with 'uli'uli, the red and yellow feathers swirling in the dancers' hands. A well-endowed young blonde in a too-tight, garish turquoise dress faced the dancers and tried to mimic their movements, spilling much of the drink in her hand as she flung her hips around. Amy had to turn away. Conrad and Peyton were transfixed.

Excusing herself to visit the ladies' room, Amy made her way along the edges of the room.

Having identified the star in the crowd, the trio's lead singer handed a microphone to the blonde, who began a painful rendition of Don Ho's "Pearly Shells." A young man sporting an aloha shirt in the same awful turquoise print leaned against the wall between Amy and the restroom. Clearly partnered to and amused by the blonde, but also intent on staying out of the spotlight, he was oblivious to Amy standing beside him. Before she could lean over and ask him to move, the crooning blonde came their way, the spotlight following her. She pressed up against the young man, microphone in one hand, the other pulling him to her as she sang.

Now it was Amy's turn to try and blend into the background as all eyes focused on the couple. *Honeymooners,* Amy figured. *Why did mainlanders act like such fools when in Hawai'i?* Once the blonde had pulled her husband away, Amy ducked into the restroom.

She stared at herself in the mirror as she washed her hands.

"Not at your best," she said to her reflection.

Sweat and humidity had curled her hair into a frizzy mass and smudged her makeup. Everything about her felt and looked wilted. No one would ever stare at her in a crowd, not with her granny glasses and high-necked peasant dress.

What the hell had Peyton meant when he'd said she'd never say yes?

"Would definitely say yes," she told her reflection, but knew as she ran a brush through her hair that she lacked the courage to ever say it to him. Besides, he'd said he would never ask.

Paul paused for a moment before the stone lions and the wrought iron fence they guarded, even though Sarah had walked ahead and up the staircase. This building was nothing like the museums he'd visited in Boston. He had seen enough pictures to know that except for the Guggenheim, curved like a seashell, most museums were the same—big and boxy. More than anything else, the Honolulu Art Academy resembled a sprawling villa, its architectural style the same as so many buildings in Honolulu, blending with and opening up to its natural surroundings.

He joined Sarah in the open courtyard at the top of the stairs. A towering stone sculpture of an immense woman stood before them. He would gladly have sat for a while to contemplate its elegant curves, its simplicity, the way the sculptor's choices communicated something essential about a woman's grace.

"I don't get it," Sarah whispered. "What's so great about a massive woman?"

Paul wondered if he'd made a mistake asking to stop here. Art wasn't exactly Sarah's thing. Though she knew he'd taken art classes in high school, she'd never expressed much interest in what he produced. He told himself they didn't have to share everything in common. After all, he had no interest at all in her favorite topic—Jacqueline Kennedy Onassis.

Despite their differences, Paul had plenty of reason to count himself lucky to be married to Sarah. His mom called her vivacious, and he knew she meant that in a good way. He considered her complete lack of fear to be Sarah's most striking quality. It knocked him out the way she'd sung the night before in front of all those people in a Waikiki bar, as if she performed in public all the time. He'd never be as gutsy as she was. That courage carried over to her ER work. She thrived on the adrenaline rush that came with serious cases.

He liked to think that someday, after this honeymoon, when they'd settled into their life together and grown more comfortable as husband and wife, she might let him sketch her. He imagined winter Sundays with her stretched across a bed or a sofa, a fire burning, and him capturing on paper the curve of her hip or the elegance of her hands, hands he knew would, soon enough, grow rough from farmwork.

He decided he'd best keep this visit brief. No sense making her miserable. He opened the brochure and showed her the building's map.

"Asian and Hawaiian art to the left, American and European to the right."

Sarah turned right and Paul followed.

They stepped into the first gallery, an intimate space with works by Monet, Degas, van Gogh, and other impressionists, many of whose names Paul didn't recognize. Sarah seemed to like these well enough, but she moved along quickly. When they reached the more modern artists, she wrinkled up her nose at a Picasso and a Modigliani.

"Why do artists make women look so weird and ugly?"

She cupped a hand over her mouth as she spoke, as if a guard might read her lips and bounce her for not liking the art.

When they reached the gallery exhibiting the modern American artists, Sarah ran her eyes quickly around the room, said, "Yeah, right," and moved on to the next gallery.

Paul stood frozen before a painting by Hans Hofmann. Instead of following Sarah, he perched on a bench before the painting *Fragrance*, overwhelmed by its intense effect. This beauty was an original creation in itself, drawn solely from the artist's imagination. Paul wanted to understand how this explosion of colors became something that could stir him. He moved up close to the painting, examining the brushstrokes until a guard asked him to step away. Someday he would create a work that would speak this powerfully.

Sarah appeared at the gallery door, calling him with her eyes to follow, and he did.

February 1975, Honolulu, Hawai'i

Peyton twirled the lazy Susan again and the eight nearly empty dishes of food went spinning past Amy. Her parents sat to her right, Peyton's parents to her left, and Peyton across the table between two donors none of them knew. Obviously, they weren't big donors if they were stuck in Siberia with Peyton and Amy. "The less-than-VIP Table," Peyton had whispered to Amy as they all found their seats. The gigantic hotel conference room was filled with fifty other tables just like theirs—white tablecloth, a lazy Susan at the center, each boasting a bottle of Jack Daniels and space enough for an eight-course family-style Chinese dinner.

For once neither Amy nor Peyton had to work. This was the big thank-you banquet, ostensibly meant to shower appreciation upon the volunteers and donors who'd helped get the congressman reelected. If some, or rather most, of those attending had chosen to donate big sums to defray costs, that was simply a nice bonus but officially not the objective. No longer on staff, Amy was counted among those deserving of thanks, so she got to sit and enjoy herself without worrying about the logistics.

After its second rotation, the lazy Susan began to slow and Amy noted Peyton hadn't taken any of the dishes. She looked across at him and he signaled for her to look at the turntable. A note. He'd written her a note. Everyone else at the table was engrossed in conversation. She stuck a hand between the sweet-and-sour pork and lo mein and fished out the folded cocktail napkin.

"I heard Conrad singing 'Let's Get It On' to the new blond receptionist."

She smiled across at him, shook her head, and wrote, "How dare you blaspheme our congressman! Shame on you!" and returned it to the lazy

Susan. She was definitely going to miss Peyton. She already did. It had been two months since the election and they'd only gotten together once for a beer along with a horde of other campaign people. She'd barely managed to share two words with him that night. She was hoping there'd be dancing after dinner, providing the opportunity she'd been waiting for, the moment when, thanks to music and lighting, he might finally see her as something other than a pal.

He read the napkin and mouthed to her, *I did. Really.*

She gave him a skeptical glare and tried to implant telepathically the idea of his standing up, walking to her seat, and taking her by the hand. She felt a tap on her shoulder. It was Rosie Kagawa, the congressman's administrative aide, the woman in charge of everything, including Conrad.

Rosie said nothing, merely wiggled her finger for Amy to follow. As she rose, Amy shot a look at Peyton that was meant to say, "Oh my God, what does she want of me now?" She could see from the smirk on his face that he knew exactly what she was thinking. Why couldn't he have read her thoughts a minute earlier?

Rosie was the terror of the DC office and the campaign. To hear the words "Rosie on line four for you" was akin to "Principal's office, now." Amy followed obediently to a table so close to the dais that Amy knew these were the really big donors, the guys who could call the office and get an appointment with Suemori any time they wanted. She recognized several of the key players. One of the men at the table stood and joined her and Rosie.

"Amy," Rosie said in the singsong voice she used around powerful men, "this is Jake Remillard, a close friend of the congressman's. Mr. Remillard has taken note of your hard work throughout the campaign and wanted to meet you."

Amy smiled and extended a hand. He was not the typical donor. Those men wore suits, worked downtown, and lunched at the Oahu Country Club. She'd taken minutes at all the campaign meetings those men attended and had never seen Remillard at one of them. He was certainly as old as the others, much older than her own father, Amy guessed, but his presentation was completely different. Where their idea of casual was a Reyn's aloha shirt paired with gray flannel pants, Remillard wore baggy linen trousers and a retro silk aloha shirt unbuttoned far enough to show off the gold chain nestled on his hairy chest. He leaned in too close when he shook Amy's hand and ran his left hand from her shoulder down her spine, nearly letting his hand brush her derrière before resting it at the small of her back.

Hands to self, she wanted to say. She shifted away from him.

Rosie drifted off, leaving her alone with the guy, who proceeded to carry on about how successful Amy had been at staging Conrad's appearances.

She interrupted him to ask, "How do you know so much about my work on the campaign?" It wasn't as if she was a high-profile player within the organization, let alone beyond its borders.

"Why from Conrad, of course! He pointed you out to me at an event a couple months ago. Told me what an asset you'd been to the campaign and what a fine young woman you are. I've been wanting to meet you ever since."

Flattered but wary, Amy nodded as Remillard told her more than she wanted to know about a campaign he was helping with in California. She would do her job, play nice for Conrad's benefit.

With a hand now on her elbow, Remillard leaned in. "So we're going to be moving this party back to my place when we wrap up here. I hope you'll join us."

Amy smiled and shifted away from him. "It's kind of you to include me." She couldn't say an outright no and risk offending a big donor. "I'm here with others though, and we have plans for the rest of the evening." She waited for him to assure her she could bring friends, but instead he told her to come later, no matter what the hour, and handed her a card with his address. "It's right on the beach beside Diamond Head," he added. "Mine's the one on the top floor." *Wouldn't mind checking out that view,* she thought. She had never been in an apartment that took up an entire floor.

"I'll see how my evening goes and will pop by if I can." With nods all around to the other donors, she slipped away.

"What happened to everyone?" she asked her parents, now alone at their table. What she really wanted to know was where the hell Peyton was.

"They needed to get going, hon, and we weren't sure how long you'd be tied up. Peyton said to tell you he'd send a postcard."

Amy couldn't believe Peyton had left. He was flying to California the next day. This had been her last chance, the one hope for getting him to see her as more than his campaign buddy, and he hadn't even been enough of a friend to say goodbye in person.

"I think we'll be heading out, too, princess." Her dad leaned over to kiss her on the cheek. They'd come in separate cars. "You stay and have a good time."

The conference hall was emptying. No signs of a band. No dimming of lights. This party was definitely wrapping up. So much for her fantasies. She headed for the parking garage.

Jake Remillard caught her arm as she passed. "Tell me you'll be stopping by my place. I'm counting on it." He looked at his watch. "I should be there in fifteen. I'm thinking we could have some real fun." He leaned in so close she could feel his breath warm on her ear. "I promise I'll make sure you have a very good time."

Amy forced herself to smile. "I don't think we have the same idea about what constitutes fun, Mr. Remillard." She fished her car keys out of her bag. "Good luck with the campaign ahead."

As she rode the garage elevator, Amy considered what she'd done. Probably angered a big donor who would complain to Rosie. Maybe blown any chance of a recommendation or a job on the Hill when she graduated. Worst of all, she'd lost any chance of being with Peyton. She wasn't crushed exactly. It wasn't as if there'd been anything but friendship between them. But he'd seemed a real possibility. Possibly even a perfect match, if there were such a thing. "Have to hope there's more than one," she said as she started up the car.

Olivia Newton-John was singing "I Honestly Love You."

"Ick, barf." She turned the dial and got The Three Degrees asking, "When will I see you again?"

"Are you kidding me?" she yelled at the radio, but she didn't bother searching for another song. Might as well wallow in the whole miserable mess that was that evening. She eased the car out of its space and headed for the Kalakaua exit.

September 1976, Honolulu, Hawai'i

Mind pressed in darkness

waits deep in shadow
while life softly whispers,
come—
join—
it's tomorrow.

Amy stared at the words she'd scribbled on the back of an envelope. She'd woken that morning with the lines in her head. The words were meaningless to her as she committed them to paper. She couldn't fathom where they came from, couldn't tease out what event of the previous day might have prompted them. She hadn't written a word of verse since her undergraduate days. Why now and why this?

She looked over at her office mate Rachel, who, despite the piles of student papers on her desk, was staring out the window.

"Can I ask you something?"

"Hmm?" Rachel turned her way.

Amy jiggled the envelope in her hand. "Have you ever woken up with a completely formed poem in your head? With line breaks and everything?"

"I wish. Why? That happens to you?"

"Never before, but this morning—boom. I woke up with a set of lines in my head. Not necessarily good lines, but still, it was fully formed. It's the weirdest thing. I don't want to sound all Age of Aquarius, but I can't figure out if it's my brain telling me something about myself or my brain's trying to be creative when I'm not looking. It almost feels like this is something I read somewhere and it just popped up again in a dream."

"What's it say?"

Amy read her the lines. "It doesn't even sound like me. It's like a line out of an inspirational poster."

"Or maybe some part of your brain is screaming for attention. Do you write much poetry?"

Amy shook her head. "Not anymore. I had fantasies of being a writer when I was a kid and got a couple poems published in our college literary magazine, but nothing since."

"Seems to me you should get back to it. If you're interested, I've been thinking about starting a small writing group here if only to push myself back into a regular practice. I get so swamped by the endless paper grading that I neglect my own work. If I can find one or two others who want in, would you be game?"

Amy was flattered. Rachel was at least ten years her senior, had a PhD, and taught lit classes as well as a creative writing section at the local community college. As a lecturer with only a master's, Amy was limited to teaching the survey lit course and a basic writing skills class.

"You sure you want me in a group like that? I'm hardly in your league."

"Oh please. It's not like you're ever going to read a poem of mine in *The New Yorker* or in any literary journal that matters. They didn't hire me because I'm a gifted poet. I got the job because I could handle a range of twentieth-century lit courses in a tiny department top-heavy with men who haven't read anything beyond the Western canon. We both know whatever you write is going to be better than the stuff our students turn in."

"I wouldn't be so sure. I've got a woman in my Western Lit class who terrifies me. She's in the Women Starting Over program and is brilliant. She did two years at Stanford before dropping out to get married a decade ago. Her writing blows me away."

"Yeah. I've had a few of those—the hidden gems who are only here because life tripped them up. Maybe we could brave a mixed group of faculty and students? What a concept." She laughed. "I'll give it some thought and see if I can come up with candidates."

A young man rapped on the doorframe of their tiny office space. "Ms. Barnes?"

Amy recognized him from her writing skills class. "Yes. How can I help?" Amy could hear the eagerness in her voice. A student! At her office! Asking for her! Students rarely sought her out during office hours despite her repeated invitations to stop by.

"Sorry to interrupt, but I need your signature on the drop-class form." He handed her a half sheet of paper.

"Sure thing." She hoped her disappointment didn't show too much. If one more student dropped, they'd have to cancel the class, and she needed to be teaching at least five sections to cover her living expenses. Before signing, she gave it one last shot. "If you're finding the class a struggle, I can help you find ways to manage it."

"Thanks, that's not the problem. I got a job working afternoons, so I've got to transfer to the evening section. I'm bummed. Word is you're way cooler than the night dude."

Amy dutifully signed the consent form.

"Hear that?" she said to Rachel once the kid had moved on. "I'm way cooler than the night dude."

Rachel laughed. "Well, that is what it's all about. But then, you do realize that anyone is cooler than the night dude?"

"Doesn't matter. I'll take any compliment I can get. I'm a happy camper if even one student in the room looks up at me while I'm talking. Remind me again why we do this work?"

"The money. It's all about the big bucks they pay us." Rachel picked up her pen. "And the opportunity to read amazing work like this." She held up the essay she was grading. "We are blessed."

"You jest, and yet this was the only English lecturer spot open this year. In the entire UH system. It's a miracle I got the job. I just have to figure out how to live on the pennies this great honor provides me."

She pulled out the roster for her writing class. She was right. Only ten students remained. *Please, please, please, let the class fly,* she begged any angels that might be listening. She could not afford to lose a single course that term, not when her car brake pad was going straight to the floor.

"Is your nine o'clock class meeting today?" Rachel asked with a nod to the clock, which showed the time as a minute short of nine.

"Oh shoot!" Amy grabbed her bag, stuffed her class materials into it, and slung it over her shoulder. "Catch you later." So much for grabbing a cup of coffee on her way to class.

It's better than being in DC, she reminded herself, and she did believe that to be true even if she was making half what a congressional job would have paid her. She slowed as she neared her classroom, hoping to appear less rattled than she felt. There was always the job opening at Pumehana, one of Honolulu's elite prep schools. Unlike her current situation, they were offering a permanent job with benefits. The pay wasn't a lot better, but a friend who taught there had told her the school provided free coffee and orange juice, as well as bread and peanut butter, which effectively meant she could have free breakfasts and lunches. That would allow a buffer for car repairs, unexpected medical costs, and an occasional drink out with friends. She really did have to think seriously about that option, but for now she had to think seriously about *Mrs. Dalloway* and hope at least some of the class had done the reading.

October 1977, Lisbon, Vermont

"I don't think so," Sarah said, looking up from the sink where she was scrubbing carrots.

Paul grinned. "I took off my boots."

"And if you want to step into my clean house, you'll take off the rest of those filthy things."

Paul and his dad had spent the day plowing. On a day like this, when the wind blew hard and cold, every part of him was caked in grit.

"Next thing you'll be telling me I can't get a welcome-home hug either."

"Not like that you can't. Undress and get yourself into the tub. Then we'll see about your welcome home."

Paul appreciated the way Sarah had taken ownership of the household, stepped confidently into her role as homemaker. When his parents had offered to move into the smaller house across the street, Paul had thanked them but said no, that was too much. His parents persuaded him they preferred the newer, smaller house. "Much easier to maintain," his mom had insisted. "And almost new appliances. Besides," she'd added, "now you can host all the big family gatherings. My turn to rest."

Both Paul and Sarah had feared his mother would have second thoughts once she saw another woman in her kitchen, but it had proved an easy transition. Adele Rideau was quite happy to hand over the place with its temperamental furnace, uneven floors, and tired pea green walls. Though they weren't even a year married, Paul thought he and Sarah were already showing they would be mature, capable stewards of the family homestead.

"At least come help me out of this gear."

Sarah looked at him skeptically, but shut off the faucet and crossed to where he stood grinning in the mudroom entry. Paul unbuckled his jeans and pretended to pull his long T-shirt over his head, but once Sarah was close, he grabbed her and held her against him.

Rubbing his face over hers, and his arms up and down her back as she squirmed, he said, “Who’s too dirty to touch now?”

“Let me go, Paul Rideau.” She pretended to pull away.

“Take off my pants and I’ll consider it.”

She pulled down the dungarees, not even trying to escape as he stepped out of them.

“Shirt,” he directed, and she pulled it up over his head so he stood before her in his jockey shorts, his body clean and pink below his throat and above his wrists and ankles. He grabbed hold of her again as she tossed the shirt to the floor, and nibbled at the base of her throat.

“Stop,” she said laughing, but didn’t pull away. He began unbuttoning her blouse but paused when the doorbell rang.

“Sarah?” they heard his mother call from the back steps.

“Busted,” Paul whispered, and before he could haul on his pants, his mom opened the door to the mudroom.

Paul and Sarah stood in place, still locked together. Flustered, Adele stopped at the threshold and turned her head away from them.

“Oops, bad timing. Sorry.” She backed out, pulling the door shut as she went.

Paul’s first impulse was to call to her to wait, not leave, assure her it was fine for her to walk into the house that had been her home for nearly thirty years. He felt the slightest pressure of Sarah’s hand at his back. This was their home now.

“I’ll stop over a bit later, Mom, okay?” he called.

“Sounds good,” she answered. The door closed and she was gone.

“Thank you.” Sarah slipped her hand beneath the elastic of his shorts.

Paul picked her up by the waist and Sarah wrapped her legs around his waist. He carried her through the kitchen and up the staircase, taking the steps two at a time, never mind that he’d just put in a ten-hour day.

“Careful there, tiger,” she yelped halfway up. “I won’t be much use to you if you drop me down a flight of stairs.”

“No chance that’ll happen.”

When they reached the bathroom, she directed him to get in the tub.

“You’re not getting in too?”

“Hold your horses. Don’t be in such a doggone hurry.”

She ran the bathwater, slapping at his hands when he reached out to touch her. He forced himself to look and not touch, playing along with her game. She leaned over to test the water's temperature. Light from the setting sun streamed through the bathroom window, casting a pink glow over her tanned arms. He eyed the lace of her bra cup through the armhole of her cotton blouse, the curve of her hip, the lean stretch of thigh.

Paul felt sure this was how their marriage would always be. They wouldn't become one of those couples who tear one another apart in small bites or become comfortable roommates, more brother and sister than lovers. His own parents weren't exactly mean to each other, but they sure never looked like they were in love anymore. It wasn't ever going to be like that for him and Sarah.

Chapter Seven

November 2001, Lisbon, Vermont

The bike came at Paul with a whoosh, knocked him to his knees, and skidded to a stop. Paul recognized the rider, Nathan Washburn, his childhood friend Riley's son.

"What the hell are you doing?" Paul yelled as he examined the shredded knee of his dungarees. He wiped away the gravel embedded in his palms.

"Sorry, Mr. Rideau. I didn't see you."

Paul followed Nathan's eyes to the crest of the hill where three other boys on bikes stared down at them.

"Those boys chasing you?"

Nathan stood silent, his eyes glued to the boys, his entire body on alert.

"Least you can do is give me a hand getting back to the house."

"You hurt that bad?" The kid finally seemed to notice he'd injured Paul.

"No. But it wouldn't hurt to let those friends of yours think I am. Give them a reason to get out of here."

Paul pretended to lean on the boy's shoulder as they headed down the drive, Nathan pushing the bike.

After setting out milk and doughnuts for Nathan, Paul peered out the kitchen window, looking for signs of the others. He didn't see anyone.

Nathan doodled on a paper napkin as he ate.

"Some reason those guys are after you?"

Nathan stared Paul straight in the eye, as if challenging his pretense that the situation was anything other than absolutely clear. The kid was right. Paul knew exactly why boys would harass him. He invited ridicule with the long, blue-tinted bangs he wore swept over his face and his all-black getup, including black wristbands. Paul figured it was probably a good thing Riley didn't know how his kid had turned out. It didn't take much imagination to know what Riley would think of a twelve-year-old who looked like one of those emo kids Paul had read about in *Newsweek*. Maybe if Riley had stuck around instead of running out on his second wife and kid, the boy might have avoided being a target for bullies.

Paul nodded. "You don't exactly blend in."

Nathan shrugged and continued with his doodling, showing no interest in leaving. Paul finished up the breakfast dishes he'd never gotten to and tried to figure out how to get the kid moving along. Nathan set down his pencil.

"Okay if I use your bathroom before I head home?"

"Sure. It's down the hall to the left."

Paul studied the napkin drawing on the table. It was a rendering of Paul's face, achieved with an efficiency of stroke that humbled Paul. His own labored drawings were neither as accurate nor as sensitive in capturing character. This was more than a replication of Paul. Even Paul could see Nathan had captured something true about him in the tilt of the head, the piercing stare of the eyes.

When Nathan returned, drying his hands on his jeans, he was more animated. "What's that painting you got in the living room? The one with the wild colors?"

"You like it?"

Nathan nodded. "How come you got something like that here?"

Paul laughed. At least the kid was honest. Nothing about Paul or his house matched his artwork.

"Because I painted it," Paul said, enjoying the surprise in the boy's face. He wanted to add, "You're not the only one who doesn't blend in."

When Nathan headed for the kitchen door, Paul was ready to see him go, but the napkin on the table gave him pause.

"Any interest in earning some extra money?" he asked.

Nathan looked at him with suspicion. Like he was some kind of predator. *Damn,* Paul thought. *When did the world get so twisted that kids think every old guy is a pervert.*

"My uncle can always use a hand over at the milking barn," he offered as reassurance. "And I've got plenty of small projects that would go faster with someone to help."

Nathan shrugged. "I guess."

"We can start by getting the outside Christmas lights hung. Always good to do that before snow flies."

"Today? It's already dark."

"You got something better to do?" Paul asked, headed for the door. "We can at least get a string or two up around the front porch. I'll turn on the outside beams. Snow's going to show up one of these days."

When they finished outlining the porch in white lights, Paul paid Nathan and told him to put his bike in the back of his truck. He didn't want him riding home in the dark. Nathan had told him his mom usually got home from work around 5:30 or 6. The small cabin was set deep in the woods, off a long dirt drive. A thick stand of pines blocked even the midday light. *Grim enough to make me put a bullet through my skull,* Paul thought. He never understood why Riley didn't clear more of the land when he built the cabin. He figured the last place this kid needed to be alone on dark winter afternoons was in this secluded cave of a home.

"Ask your mom if it's okay for you to work afternoons, okay?" Paul said as they climbed out of the cab. The boy nodded.

"You don't have to," Paul added. The kid being here alone seemed a bad idea to him, but he wasn't going to push it. Nathan had to want the work.

"Sure. I'll talk to her about it."

Paul lifted Nathan's bike out of the truck bed.

"Getting awful dark and cold to be riding this thing. How about I swing by for you on my way home from work? I'm off by three most days."

Nathan nodded and carried the bike up the front steps, parking it in a corner of the porch.

"Thanks, Mr. Rideau," he called. Paul waved.

As he turned down his own driveway, Paul wished he'd left the lights on in the kitchen. Even with the Christmas lights, the dark interior looked empty and cold. Chris was forever lecturing him about wasting electricity, as if it hadn't been Paul who'd taught his son the value of conservation, as if Paul were merely being careless when he left the lights burning. A dark house at the end of the day was just another reminder that no one waited inside.

December 2001, Clifton, New Hampshire

"I thought we weren't doing Christmas decorations," Martin said, as Amy set the Hawaiian angel on the tree's peak.

"I know, I know. And I'll be sorry come January when I have to put it all away, but it just doesn't feel like Christmas without the tree."

For the first time in forever, they would not celebrate Christmas at home or in Hawai'i that year. Martin had decided he wanted to visit his sister and her family in London. Given how rarely they saw any of his relatives, Amy had no objections, was even looking forward to it now that his sister and her husband had a spacious flat.

"How about you and I get dinner at the inn tonight," Martin said. "I've already run it by the kids and they're fine having takeout pizza here."

"That's a lovely idea." Amy set down an ornament and hugged him. "Are we celebrating something?"

"Nothing special. It's just that we're overdue for a conversation." Amy wanted to be delighted, but something put her on alert. This was odd behavior for Martin who never suggested dinner out, just the two of them, unless it was Valentine's Day or their anniversary. Evenings away from the kids usually meant meeting up with friends. His friends.

"I made the reservation for seven and gave Kara money for the pizza."

"You thought of everything." Amy tried to look and feel happy but bells and whistles were going off in her head.

Martin lifted his glass. "Cheers." He clicked it against Amy's.

"So what exactly are we celebrating tonight? You're being very mysterious." She half hoped he'd arranged a room at the inn as he once did when the kids were little. A surprise getaway. A gesture to show he was sincere about repairing their marriage.

"Here's the thing, Ames." Martin took her hands in his, his face somber. "You will always be the great love of my life and our lives are forever linked by the kids, but we both know our marriage doesn't work anymore. It hasn't worked for a long time. You are desperately unhappy and you blame me. I want the suffering to end. For both of us."

Amy pulled back her hands. He might as well have slapped her—it felt as unexpected and searing.

"You're leaving me?"

"I'm setting you free."

Amy didn't think Martin could surprise her anymore. He always swore that, despite his infidelities, he would never give up on their marriage.

"How kind and generous of you. Always looking out for me."

"See? My point exactly." He raised his hands, as if in surrender. "You feel nothing but contempt for me."

He was right, of course. At their best, they were awkward and uncomfortable together.

"I thought the plan was to work on this. You asked me not to give up on you, to stay."

"Right, that was the deal, except you can barely tolerate my presence. I don't call that working on it."

Amy couldn't disagree, but relationships didn't heal overnight. "It takes time to rebuild trust."

"Here's the thing." His tone was different, more confident. "I don't want to wait anymore to be loved. I deserve happiness and I've found someone who loves me as I am. No conditions."

Spoken like a lovesick eighteen-year-old boy. "Of course you have," she said. "Who is she? A new one or a former?"

Martin wouldn't look at her. With a tiny straw, he dunked the ice in his scotch and glanced in the direction of the bar. Amy followed his gaze to a young woman seated alone at the end.

"Is that her? Why is she here? Were you planning on introducing us?"

"There's no reason we can't be civil about this, Amy. It's no one's fault. And yes, that's her. She knows this is agony for me and is here to provide strength and support."

Amy laughed. "And make sure you actually go through with it? You can't even end your marriage like a grown man. You sure you don't want her to come over and have this conversation for you?"

"You see, this is why I'm done. Your jealousy and insecurity have made you small and mean. Sharon has shown me what real love looks like. She knows how to give abundantly and without expectations."

Sharon. Amy recognized the name. The new hire. A poet.

"Wow. That didn't take long. She's been here all of four months."

"Actually—" Martin started, and Amy finished the sentence for him. "—She was at the residency in Maine with you." She sat back and stared at him. "You're such a lying weasel. All that guilt you piled on me for not being with you last summer."

"I was hoping to keep the drama out of this. Let's not forget that you opted not to be with me. I gave you a chance and you threw it back in my face." He finished his drink. "Look, there's no point rehashing the past. We need to focus on the future. Sharon and I want to be fair to you."

"God. You make it so easy to hate you, Martin."

"I'm not going to sink to your level, Amy, and let you draw me into a fight. I'm doing you the courtesy of being candid about my plans. Sharon and I will take the kids to London for Christmas, which gives you a couple weeks to find a place to rent, get packed up and moved out. You realize, the college won't let you stay in the house since it's linked to my employment."

Amy signaled the waiter. "I'll take another martini, and could you bring me a cheeseburger with fries? No ketchup, no salad." She turned her attention back to Martin.

"No. Here's how we're going to do this. I'm calling the shots, not you, and certainly not some woman I've never met. Go to London with Sharon. Take the kids if they want to go, but I'm going to be in Hawai'i for Christmas and the kids can come with me if they'd prefer that option. When I get back, I am going to continue living in my home until the divorce is final and I have my share of its value. Until then, you are the one who's moving out. Sharon can put you up, starting tonight. I want you to leave now. I'm going to eat my dinner alone at this table, which means you have an hour to go to the house and pack up what you need for the next few weeks. I'll find an attorney and have her be in touch. Now go. Get out of here."

"I didn't figure you for the vengeful sort, Amy. I hoped you'd see this is for the best."

She reached out and took his hands as he had earlier taken hers. "I do see that divorcing is for the best, Martin. Truly. But I'm not letting you and some child-woman decide what's fair or right for me." She let go and sat back, surprised by how clear and determined she felt despite her trembling body and voice. "Collect your girlfriend and pack up quickly. I don't want you at the house when I get back."

Picture windows opposite Amy framed a giant Christmas tree centered on the college green and haloed by moonlight cutting through a rising fog. *I should find that lovely,* she thought, but it seemed merely ominous. When her dinner arrived, she forced herself to eat slowly though she had no appetite. She picked at her fries and nibbled at the burger for a full hour before asking the waiter to pack it up, then ordered a dish of ice cream with cookies. All she wanted was to be home, soaking in her tub, but she forced herself to stay for two hours. Only then did she brave the walk home. The kids would need her.

December 2001, Lisbon, Vermont

Two birds with one stone was how Paul thought of it. The project had begun as something for himself, but had evolved into being something for the boy as well.

Over recent weeks, he'd transformed a section of the small barn. He'd hauled junk away and then with Chris's help, added insulation, set up a pellet stove, and hung large fluorescent lamps from the ceiling. He replaced the old utility sink with a large stainless steel basin and put up shelving for supplies, storage racks for canvases, and a hazardous waste locker for the more dangerous materials. A week ahead of Christmas, the space was ready and stocked with paint, brushes, and canvases.

He invited Nathan and his mom Lydia to join him and his family for an early Christmas gathering at the farm. Paul would spend the holidays with his sister and her family in Hawai'i, so Maddie insisted they celebrate before he left. He knew the rest of the family would have plenty to say about his including the "weird" kid, but Paul didn't care. He'd grown attached to Nathan. Get past the hair and clothes and there was a decent, talented kid there, eager for someone's attention. When Nathan and Lydia arrived, Paul sent Lydia inside and asked the boy to get a few logs for the fire.

"I've got some dry wood out in the small barn," he told him.

He watched as the boy slogged his way along the slushy driveway and slid open the door. The building burst into light. Paul waited for some sound or for Nathan to come running back. Nothing. He made his own trek to the barn. Nathan was circling the room, checking out the supply shelves with their paints and brushes, eyeing the different-sized canvases, the stacks of drawing paper and sketchbooks.

"You fixed this up?"

Paul nodded. "I thought we both needed a place where we could draw and paint without upsetting anyone."

"I can use it, too?" The boy had stuffed his hands in his pockets.

"Anytime you want. Except when you're supposed to be at school or doing work. I don't want your mom coming after me because you're not doing your chores or letting your homework slide."

Nathan ran the hairs of a new paintbrush over his fingers. Paul pulled a blank canvas out from the rack and put it up on one of the easels.

"Merry Christmas, Nathan. Come on back to the house when you get hungry." He gave the boy a pat on the shoulder as he passed.

"Why did you do this?" There was accusation in the boy's voice.

How many weeks had it been now that Nathan had worked almost daily alongside Paul? And yet, he still couldn't quite trust that Paul didn't have ulterior motives.

Paul shrugged. "Maybe because no one did it for me. You've got a gift. I don't think that should go to waste. Best thing you can do to show your appreciation is use this space. Help me keep it in good shape. Deal?"

Nathan had a pencil in hand and was sketching on the canvas as Paul closed the barn door. Light spilled from the worn structure so that it sat like a star amid the other outbuildings. Paul forced himself to open the kitchen door and go in, much as he wanted to be back in the barn painting beside Nathan. *Tomorrow,* he told himself. *Tomorrow you get to play for a day before flying off to Hawai'i.*

December 2001, Kailua, Hawai'i

Amy slipped out of her robe and ran straight into the surf, not pausing as the first wave crashed over her. The moon, a brilliant coin just above the horizon line, cast a gold path across the water. She turned her back to it, let the waves lift and drop her, a gentle roller coaster.

Don't think, she told herself. *Let it all go.*

It had surprised her, even hurt, that the kids didn't hesitate to choose London over Hawai'i. How could they want to spend Christmas with Martin and his girlfriend, a stranger to them? She told herself they had chosen time with their cousins in a big city. Hawai'i couldn't help but look stale by comparison.

What she hadn't anticipated was how strange and empty it would feel to be alone in Hawai'i. She'd flown in a few hours earlier and followed her usual routine: picked up a rental car, stopped at Foodland for basic groceries, unpacked her small suitcase, and donned her bathing suit. Nothing different from if the kids were with her, except it felt completely different. So much silence and empty space.

She could have stopped by the Nu'uanu house, but she wasn't ready to face Gretchen and her cousins. She would celebrate Christmas Eve with them, but she dreaded seeing them, even Kimo. She hadn't the energy to pretend to be festive or the capacity to maintain her composure. Except for regular visits to her mother's nursing home, she had no obligations and no invitations.

At least being in the water felt familiar and comforting. New Hampshire seemed far away, and her dark, low-ceilinged New England cape home claustrophobic compared to this expanse of sea and sky. *A cave,* she thought. *I live in a cave.* She slid down the slope of a muscular wave, her stomach fluttering with the motion. Her eyes closed, she willed the tension from her body. Betrayals, worries, uncertainty. She let the ocean absorb it all.

When she tired, she rode a wave to where she could stand and slowly climbed the sandy slope to her crumpled robe. She slipped it on, tied the sash around her waist, and headed back to the house. *Remember how this felt,* she told herself. *Don't forget. Write it down. Capture it.* This was exactly how she should spend this time alone—imagining, observing, recording. And maybe, with practice, she could even begin creating again.

She had only stopped to introduce herself. It felt odd to have a stranger on the property. She'd never been at the beach house when an artist was in residence. Rather than hire a groundskeeper to watch over the property when the family wasn't using it, her Aunt Gretchen regularly provided artists short-term housing and workspace.

Now Amy was sipping iced tea with the man on the porch that encircled the single-room structure. She didn't know much about him beyond that his name was Brian and that he was a sculptor.

"Does that hurt?" he asked, staring at the base of her neck.

"What?" She put a hand to her throat.

"That bump?" He reached a hand out but didn't touch her. "There, by your collarbone."

She ran a finger over the small colorless bump.

"No." If Martin had ever noticed, he hadn't said.

It was a simple question, but something shifted with its asking. This man who had been merely peripheral came into focus. She felt brought into focus herself. She wondered if seduction were really so simple, requiring only the capacity to let another person feel seen.

"You're still on East Coast time. I saw your lights on at four this morning." He stretched out his legs.

"Yeah, I've definitely not adjusted to the time yet. It's actually good though. I always say I'm going to get up early and hunt for glass balls while I'm here, but it's tough to get out of bed before six. I was on the beach well before five this morning. Not that I expect to find any. It's just part of the ritual."

"You never know. It happens. There are still some caught in the currents, circling the globe."

"You must be up pretty early yourself, if you saw my lights on."

"I work better in the mornings."

"And I'm interrupting your work. I'll get out of your hair." Amy drained her glass and rose.

Brian stayed seated. "No need to rush off. I just finished a piece, which means I'm done for the day."

"Do you let people see your work?"

"Sure."

He led the way across the lawn to the studio. He wore only a pair of swim trunks and zoris. Amy noted the hard line of his shoulders and was immediately embarrassed. When had she last noticed a man's body?

The studio space was as she'd remembered from when it was her grandfather's shop. The metal roof would have made it an oven if not for the sliding doors along the walls that pulled back to create a room without walls through which the trade winds rushed. It was a difficult space for a painter—canvases and papers had to be secured so they didn't go flying—but for a sculptor working with stone and wood, it was perfect. Materials and completed pieces could easily be moved in and out. Even doors left open in a storm did not spell disaster. Brian clearly meant for the work to be displayed outside and seasoned by the elements.

A tower of stones at least three feet tall sat on a worktable in the room's center. A thick wood dowel rose from its center to support a mobile of bobbing wood pieces sliced thin enough for light to penetrate.

"What fun!" Amy clapped her hands as a little girl might and immediately felt foolish. Perhaps he didn't mean for the piece to be seen as whimsical.

"Perfect response." Brian gave the mobile a gentle push so that it bobbed even more vigorously and, it seemed, even joyously.

He pulled out a large black portfolio from a desk at the back of the shop.

"Photos of my work," he explained. For nearly an hour, she stood at his shoulder as he showed her work that dated as far back as the seventies. Several of his larger pieces graced the entries to buildings in Honolulu and West Coast cities. More recently, his work had been on a smaller scale and captured a sense of play. She wondered if it reflected a new sensibility or the realities of a man no longer young enough to lift stone easily.

"I was thinking of heading out to Waimea and Pūpūkea this afternoon to collect driftwood. You're welcome to ride along if that's of any interest," he offered as he put away the third portfolio he'd brought out.

Amy considered the invitation, not because she had any time commitments, only because it had been so long since any man had invited her somewhere. At least Brian knew nothing of her situation. She would not have to explain herself.

"Sure. Okay. That would be fun."

She felt a bit giddy as she changed later into her swimsuit and pulled on shorts and a T-shirt. She dabbed on some lip gloss and mascara, pulled her hair up with a clip, and grabbed her sunglasses and a towel. All she needed was a six-pack of Primo, a couple joints, and KPOI blasting on the radio to feel completely back in the high school days of her peers. She wondered now at how circumspect her actual life had been as an adolescent. No smoking pot or drinking beer for her. She had always been earnest and serious. She studied her face in the mirror. Did her dullness show in the lines of her face? A jet from Kaneohe Marine Corps Air Station screamed by overhead.

Universe is cooking today. Maybe her moment to let loose had come at last. *But do I really want to grab hold of it?*

December 2001, Hale'iwa, Hawai'i

"I could get used to stringing Christmas lights in seventy-degree weather." Paul hooked the strand of lights to a nail. "This is one of my least favorite jobs at home. I lose all sensation in my fingers by the time I'm done."

From his perch on the ladder, he could see over the vegetation blocking the view of the beach and the surf beyond. His nephew Craig's kids were bodysurfing and their muddled chatter, punctuated with an occasional squeal, carried across the lawn. His sister Peg handed him another section of lights.

"Yeah. I don't miss putting up lights and wreaths in the dead of winter," she said. "Maybe you should think about moving out this way. No more ice. No more cold."

Paul grunted. "Tempting. Might even consider it if I could." He hooked another line, then climbed down and moved the ladder over a few feet. "Day comes when I think Chris is ready to manage the farm, I may just show up on your doorstep."

He finished the last of the strands. Peg hit the switch and the lanai's entire roofline gleamed. They assessed the effect from the lawn. "Have to say, even lights don't make it feel like Christmas when it's this warm," Paul said, "but it's still pretty."

"I admit I'll never get used to Christmas without snow, but I've no complaints." Peg gathered up the boxes they'd emptied. "You really don't think Chris can manage our side of the farm? He doesn't have to be helping Uncle Roy with the dairy. They can hire someone to do that."

Decades earlier, the farm had been split with Paul and Peg's dad Cam keeping the land on the river side and their Uncle Roy taking over the entire dairy operation and fields beyond the road dividing the property. Since his parents had retired to North Carolina, Maddie had been running the farm's pick-your-own apple orchard and pumpkin patch along with the seasonal farm stand. Chris did all the crop labor and management on their property with help from seasonal hires, but he also did much of the dairy's labor for his uncle.

Paul's role was reduced to taking care of the business side of things. He hired as needed, kept the books, stayed on top of federal and state regulations, and paid the bills. During the intensive planting and harvesting times, he chipped in as needed in the evenings and on weekends. This role allowed him to keep a steady job in Clifton's public works department—a job that insured a steady income and protection during years of drought or any of the many other outside forces that sabotaged a farmer's livelihood.

"I can't see Chris taking on the full business side of it all," he said. "He's smart enough, but he's young and doesn't have the education needed. So far, he's shown no interest in learning that side of it or in staying current about best farming practices." Paul had never earned a degree himself, but he'd benefitted from the University of Vermont's programs for farmers and picked up practical business classes as needed. "Now Maddie, she could handle that part, no problem." He laughed. "How is it I never figured that out before?"

"Because you weren't brought up to think a woman could run a farm," Peg said. "You think Dad ever asked if I wanted to take over?"

Paul had never heard a whiff of complaint from Peg. And like his dad, he'd always assumed he'd be the one to run the farm once his dad stepped away. Never crossed his mind that Peg might want a shot at it.

"Maddie would be a natural at managing the business side," Peg continued. "Look at all she's done to improve the farm-stand operation. Plus she's the one with a college degree and the people skills. Seems to me your kids would do just fine running the place without you."

"I bet Maddie wouldn't mind living in the farmhouse either," Paul said, pleased by the image of his daughter with a horde of kids infusing some needed life into the old house. "It's wasted space with only me living there."

He liked the idea of handing the house off to Maddie and Ray. They could make the same swap his parents had made with him and Sarah.

"Would Chris be okay with that?" Peg asked. "Not just with Maddie running the farm, but with her and Ray living in the big house?"

"Tough to say on both counts, but the farm isn't the passion for him that it is for Maddie, and I don't see him wanting to host family events. I expect he's happy to be down on the river and away from the rest of us. Besides, he's put a lot of sweat and love into his place. You wouldn't recognize it. It's no little camp anymore."

"Good for him. And let's hope he and Maddie can find a way to make this all work. I'd sure love having you out here with us."

"Something tells me there might not be much demand in Hawai'i for a guy like me. No need for snowplowing or sanding."

"You can do a hell of a lot more than that, and you're more than qualified to help with our kind of business." Peg and her husband Chuck cared for expensive properties whose owners used their second homes infrequently but wanted them kept pristine and always ready for an impromptu visit.

"You're messing with my mind, sis. I'm here for some warmth and relaxation, and you're suggesting I turn my whole life upside down."

Peg lifted the large, now nearly empty cardboard box of holiday decorations and balanced it on her hip. "I'm going to put this back in the garage, but you keep thinking about this. Seems to me your life's already been completely turned upside down. Maybe a move like this would help set it right again. You have a chance to choose how you want the future to look."

Paul collapsed the ladder and tucked it under his arm. "We done with this?" She nodded and he followed her to the garage. "It would take some getting used to, having only a garage for storing things."

"You learn you don't need half the stuff that fills your basement and attic." Peg pointed him to the ladder's hook. "This place may be a tiny box of a house, but you can't beat the location."

"No argument there." Paul had never asked, but figured their half acre had to be worth a small fortune now. When they'd bought the house in the early seventies, it was like the others along the shore—modest and meant for weekend and summer living. Huge estates worth tens of millions of dollars now surrounded them, but Peg wasn't about to give up her spot of prime oceanfront property, no matter how much people were willing to pay. "What now?" Paul asked.

"You're off duty. Go play. Take a nap. I think I'll have a quick swim. Another little benefit of island living. You get hot and need a break? No problem. Dive in the water."

"Enough, enough. You've made your case. I promise to think about it." He gave her a hug. "I do appreciate it, Peg. And who knows? Maybe I'll do it, but everyone tells me not to make any big changes for at least a year. Let's see what I want come fall."

He thought of the new studio space he'd created back home. The opportunity he had to make a difference in Nathan's life. A move to Hawai'i would mean saying goodbye to the people he loved and a way of life that defined him.

"I don't mean to pressure you, little brother. I'm just being selfish."

"Trust me. There's plenty to lure me here. You go have a swim. If it's okay, I'm going to make a grocery run. Get you anything?"

"Let me guess. You're heading to Akutagawa's. You still carrying a torch for that girl? She hasn't worked at the store for decades," Peg teased. "Teaches at the high school now."

"Good for her, but no, romance is the last thing on my mind these days." He knew Peg didn't mean to hurt him any more than all the others who'd offered to set him up with someone. As if he could just set aside his grief. "I was just thinking I'd pick up some treats for our Christmas celebration."

Peg pulled him into a hug. "I'm sorry, little brother. That was insensitive of me. Good old foot-in-mouth Peggy does it again."

"One thing I've learned is no one knows how to do this—not the people grieving and not the people trying to comfort them. I don't want you to feel like you're walking on eggshells around me. What I hate most is that people are afraid to mention Sarah's name or talk about her dying. I want to talk about her and I need to talk about how much it hurts."

"Okay. I'll try to think before I speak and you've got my ear anytime you want to talk. I miss her, too."

"So how about you write down the type of beer Chuck likes and doesn't let himself buy and any other special treats the family will enjoy. I was thinking maybe some manapua and sushi? Where's the best place to get some out here?"

Peg laughed. "Akutagawa's, of course."

January 2002, Kailua, Hawai'i

A strand of tinsel lay on the kitchen floor.

"Lovely." Amy picked up the glistening foil. *Must have stuck to my sandal.*

The night before, a drunk young woman at Jimbo's Beachside Bar had pulled tinsel off the fake Christmas tree and decorated herself and Brian with it, ignoring Amy.

Amy filled the coffee maker. There'd be no early hunt for glass balls. She'd managed to sleep till eight. She gauged the weather. A stiff breeze bent the palms, and dark, low-lying clouds promised rain. She might have the beach to herself.

From the kitchen window, she could see Brian transferring driftwood from his truck to the studio. She'd been surprised the night before at the jealousy she felt watching him with the young woman. *Jealous of what exactly?* she'd wondered, as the girl pressed herself against him on the dance floor. Was she even attracted to Brian or did she merely resent the attention he showed to a woman so much younger and more attractive than she? Studying him now, shirtless and deeply tanned, she imagined him coming in the back door, crossing the kitchen to her, pulling her into his arms as if she were all he desired.

She could picture it all up to the moment when he embraced her, but the image dissolved before his lips ever touched hers. She didn't want to be with Brian. What she wanted was the sensation of being desired as that young woman was desired, to stop feeling like faded wallpaper. She knew this was Martin's curse. His persistent need for adoration meant he would always succumb to an attractive woman who fed his ego. Was she really that pathetic herself?

Coffee mug in hand, she slipped out the front door and into the peculiar quiet of a deserted beach on a rainy morning. She walked on the firmer sand near the water, imagining all the families behind the sliding glass doors practicing their Saturday rituals. She willed away the rising sense of self-pity. As a divorced woman she would probably spend the final decades of her life alone, her children grown and managing without her. She reminded herself of how miserable she had been with Martin, how toxic he was to her self-esteem. There were worse things than being alone.

One thing she knew she didn't need was another man-child in her life, no matter how gifted and appealing he might be. Brian's interest flattered her, reminded her of how intoxicating Martin's attention had once been, but she wasn't going down that path again. She wanted more than either man could offer and was done playing cheerleader to a male ego.

January 2002, Nu'uanu, Hawai'i

"I'm guessing you don't want to talk about it, and that's fine." Gretchen settled in the chair opposite Amy's.

Gretchen was right. Amy did not want to talk about it. She had avoided this conversation for the entirety of her two-week visit.

She focused her gaze on her cup. "If I try to talk about it," she began, her voice breaking.

"You'll fall apart," Gretchen finished for her. "I hope you know that falling apart is okay. I'd say the circumstances warrant it."

Except Amy didn't want to fall apart. She was tired of feeling fragile and weak.

Gretchen handed her a box of tissues. "We've hours till your flight."

"Hah!" Amy blew her nose. "Which means I have to keep my act together enough to manage the trip home and the mess waiting for me there."

She grabbed another tissue and wiped her eyes.

"Besides, there's really not much more to tell you beyond the basics. Same old story, but this time Martin chose the other woman instead of me. Now I have to figure out where and how the kids and I will live, but I'm stuck on pause. Paralyzed."

"And scared?" Gretchen reached across the table to grasp Amy's hand in hers. "Or at least that's how I felt when it happened to me."

Amy nodded. "Absolutely."

"The good news is you're not alone and you have options." Gretchen released Amy's hand. "Let's take a walk."

As if a walk could fix anything. But as they hiked the dirt road that looped the Nuʻuanu property, Amy felt her tension ease. Did her sense of comfort flow simply from familiarity, from all her years living in this tropical forest, or did the property itself calm her? *It doesn't matter why. Be grateful you have such a sanctuary,* she reminded herself.

"The world feels right when I'm here," she told her aunt.

"So maybe here is where you belong."

Amy knew her aunt meant well, but the dilapidated cottage where she grew up was unlivable. Assuming she could even get a job, she couldn't manage Hawaiʻi's high cost of living on a teacher's salary.

She inhaled the crisp fragrance from a stand of white ginger. "The grove is flourishing."

"Yes, and the bad news is ginger's considered an invasive plant. I can't decide whether to encourage or eliminate it. The florists want it for leis, so it makes sense to grow and sell it, but a UH botanist tells me to keep the bamboo and pull out the ginger. Even with a full-time gardener, caring for all of this can overwhelm me."

Gretchen had always been so passionate about preserving the properties and so capable in her role that Amy hadn't considered the day would come when she could no longer manage it.

"Are there tasks we can take on for you?"

"Bless you for asking. My own girls don't seem to notice I can't do as much as before."

"That's because you hide it well."

They reached the bend in the road just before the cottage. Amy braced herself for a house in ruin—a caved-in roof, a collapsed porch. Instead, she faced a construction site with a nearly finished bungalow, a slightly larger version of the house it replaced.

And the tears are back.

"Oh, love." Gretchen hugged her. "Are these happy or sad tears?"

Amy shrugged. "Both?"

Gretchen held her until her crying eased.

"It's overwhelming." Amy finally said. *Overwhelming and also painful.*

She didn't want the old place back. She knew it had to go, but all the same, her past had been erased.

"I'm sorry, love. I meant it to be a happy surprise, a reassurance you have a home here."

"And it is," Amy said, "it really is. It's fabulous."

If only you'd told me. If only I'd been able to say goodbye. She understood Gretchen's desire to surprise her, knew she meant to heighten the emotional intensity. *Only I've already an abundance of emotional intensity.*

"How did you get it built so quickly?"

"I've been planning it with an architect for a couple years. I knew it was only a matter of time before the old place would have to go. Given how bad it was during last summer's rains, I accelerated the pace and had them begin after you left in August. It should be ready by June for you and the kids."

The tears returned. *Too much. All too much.*

"Come take a look inside."

Amy wandered through the interior. A second bathroom meant Amy wouldn't have to share with the kids, and a new family room provided space enough to entertain friends.

"There's going to be a dishwasher?" Amy was studying the kitchen space. "And a built-in microwave? This could be dangerous. Create something this comfortable and you'll have us expecting upgrades to the Kailua beach house."

"I'm already on it. Still deciding whether to build new or remodel. My priority is to keep these houses livable. To save money, I let them go untended for too long. I've spoken with Kimo and we'll make improvements to the North Shore house as well."

"Seems to me that you're doing more than ever."

"I want things in good shape before I step down from this role, which is why I've a proposition for you. I know you have a lot to weigh as you decide what's next for you and the kids, but I want to add one more option for you to consider. If you want to move back here, you're welcome to live here and teach or do whatever feels like the best next step. But, if you're game, I'd like to train you to replace me as trustee and steward. The work is meaningful and the salary would be at least as much as or more than what you'd make teaching."

"Whoa." Amy breathed deeply. "I did not see that coming. I swear you're going to kill me with your surprises."

"I'm sorry, love. I know I'm dumping a lot on you, but you have big decisions to make, and I want you to know you have this option as well."

"And why me? My brain freezes when it comes to finance and I'm better at killing plants than growing them. Why not Erica or Bev?"

Amy wanted to be grateful, but she could not imagine herself in such a role. This seemed yet another opportunity for failure.

"Because you are the one most qualified. You love these properties and care about preserving them. I love my girls, but given the option, they'd sell it all before my ashes were even scattered."

Amy hated the thought of the properties subdivided and developed. How many houses would they squeeze into this rainforest? How many mega mansions would fit on the Kailua beachfront lot?

"The time may come when selling is the only viable option, but we aren't there yet, and I trust you to weigh such decisions carefully. I can teach you the technical tasks of managing it all. I can't trust my girls to act as responsibly as you would."

Amy wished she was as confident as her aunt. *I can't even make a decision about my own life.*

"Back in August, when you decided to build the new house, were you already thinking I'd consider moving back here?"

"I didn't know what you would do, but it seemed possible you'd come home. I sensed a shift in you, an appropriate anger at Martin's selfish behavior. I trusted you were figuring out what you needed to do."

"Except I didn't. Martin had to do it for me."

"Then kudos to Martin. The least he could do was set you free."

Amy wanted to climb into bed and turn off her brain. As grateful as she was for her aunt's generous offer, it felt a confirmation of how pathetic she and her life had become. Except for refusing to move out of the Clifton home immediately, she had done nothing decisive. Like it or not, she had to act, choose whether to uproot her kids, change everything about their lives, or stay in Clifton, living a diminished version of her previous life. A move to Hawai'i would require a kind of energy and determination she feared she couldn't summon, but it also offered her a chance to live where she was happiest and to do something of value. There remained the question of whether Martin would even agree to it.

The oblivion of a nap wasn't possible. She needed to visit her mother before the flight to Chicago. Clare might not know her, but Amy had to go through the motions, if only for her own sake. Each goodbye had to be lived as if it might be the last, because soon enough, it would be.

"I can't say yes or no at this point," she told her aunt. "But I promise to consider it. The responsibility scares me, but I'm honored you think I'm capable."

"We all need someone to believe in us when we can't manage it on our own. This land, this work, saved me when I was in your shoes. I believe in its power to heal you as well."

January 2002, Chicago, Illinois

A woman plopped two bags on the carpet beside an unoccupied chair at the airport gate, and directed the little girl with her to the seat. Paul guessed the girl was four, maybe five years old and presumed the woman was her mother.

Flights were running late at O'Hare due to weather issues on the East Coast. This gate, like all the others, was packed with multiple flight loads of people waiting for their planes. Paul's flight to Manchester had already been rescheduled twice with a new gate assignment each time.

He was about to offer the mother his seat directly opposite the girl, when the mother said, "I want you to wait here while I check our seat assignments," and walked away. The woman seated to the girl's right looked up and took note of the mother's departure. Paul recognized the woman as one of his own, from rural or small-town New England. Nothing fussy about her Merrells, blue jeans, and white Oxford shirt.

Taking up her crossword puzzle again, the woman pretended to give it her full attention, except she wrote nothing and kept shifting her weight, as if trying to find a comfortable position. Comfort was tough to come by with the sheer number of people packed into the small space, their assorted carry-on bags stacked beneath and beside them. The woman herself had to extend her legs over a shopping bag only partially tucked under her chair. Paul smiled, recognizing that she must be flying back from Hawai'i. The word "Mahalo" was written all over the bag in brilliant colors.

Paul tried without success to concentrate on the *Time* magazine in his hand. The man beside him, reeking of a musky cologne, put down his newspaper and winked at the little girl. The man's intense focus on the girl set off Paul's internal alarms. He knew he wouldn't have wanted this character anywhere near his own daughter or granddaughters.

The man covered his eyes with his hands, then uncovered them and said "Peekaboo" to the little girl.

The lady with the Hawai'i bag kept her head down, but Paul could see that she, too, was monitoring the interaction.

"Peekaboo." He leaned forward this time, a big grin on his face, and the little girl giggled. Ducking her chin to her chest shyly, her doll against her cheek, she leaned into the woman beside her, as if instinctively substituting her for her absent mother. The woman started to raise her arm, as if about to wrap it around the girl, but stopped herself. Instead she stared hard at the man who had eyes only for the little girl. *If looks could reduce you to ash, you would be a pile of soot, mister.*

"What's your name, sweetie?" the man asked.

The woman's eyes narrowed to slits. *Watch out, buddy. You're about to get a mama bear clawing your face.* And then, the girl's mother was back.

"I'm going to get us something to eat from the kiosk," she told the girl, nodding in the direction of the nearby stand offering pastries and drinks. "I'll be right back."

The girl nodded and shifted in her seat so she could see her mother. When her doll tumbled to the floor, the woman beside her leaned down to get it, but the man was faster.

"Here ya go, precious," he said, handing it to the little girl. "Wouldn't want you losing your dolly. She's such a pretty little thing."

The woman stiffened in her seat. Paul caught her eye and gave her the slightest of nods. Let her know she was not alone in this. He got in return the briefest fluttering of recognition in her eyes.

Paul crossed his arms and sat up straighter in his seat. If this clown had half a brain, he'd see that he was surrounded by people who weren't going to let him anywhere near the kid. He checked on the girl's mom, relieved to see her glance back to check on her daughter as she waited to pay.

"Oh damn," a woman seated behind him said. Faces had turned to the monitor overhead. Their flight had been delayed again. And moved to another gate. At least this time they wouldn't have to hike to another terminal. The woman across from him sighed, pulled out her cell phone, and began typing a message. All around them, people gathered up their bags and moved on obediently, but not the guy wearing too much cologne.

Her typing done, the woman picked up her handbag and slung an arm through it as if to go, but paused. Paul could see that like him, she didn't want to leave as long as the girl was unattended. Her gaze shifted to the kiosk where the mother was now at the cash register.

When the mother returned, food and drinks in hand, the man beside Paul grabbed his bag and headed off. The woman opposite collected her Mahalo bag and offered the mother her seat. Paul followed her out to the concourse.

"You have to trust she'll be okay," he said softly.

She smiled. "I know. I wish I could switch off my mom antenna. My daughter would tell you I'm way too anxious about everything."

"People looking out for one another seems a good thing to me. That guy sure set off all my alarms."

"Right?"

"Nothing subtle about him." Paul realized they had become a barrier to the other travelers. "I suppose we should get out of everyone's way. Have a safe trip home."

With an awkward little salute by way of goodbye, he walked on ahead to the people mover, unsure why he felt as if he were abandoning her. He leaned against the rail and stared out the giant plate glass windows at the falling snow, letting the conveyer belt carry him. Resisting the urge to turn and see if the woman had followed him, he pulled out his cell phone and hit Maddie's number.

Chapter Eight

September 1980, Honolulu, Hawai'i

A Hawaiian trio sang beneath the banyan tree, one on 'ukulele, one on guitar, one on bass. People clustered on the lawn of the headmaster's home, drinks in hand. A few lingered in the living room, but Amy wanted to be outside where it was cooler. She grabbed a glass of chardonnay and piled crackers and cheese on a plate. She eyed the spread. Between the veggie platter, cold cuts, and rolls, she could build herself a meal later. Given the choice, she would have skipped Pumehana's faculty reception, but apparently it was mandatory.

"Thank God, you're here." Barbara Chan grabbed her arm. "Preston Jacobs won't leave me alone. I'm going to scream if I have to listen to one more rant about what a backwater Honolulu is compared to New York. Why did he ever take this job?"

Amy tried to mimic Preston's pinched-nose voice. "Because he's already done Turkey, darling, and Hawai'i sounded delightfully kitschy."

Barbara, Amy's office mate and mentor, took her by the elbow and led her to chairs in a shaded corner of the yard. Amy studied Preston, who was talking to one of the new female teachers. As always, a cigarette dangled from his mouth. He wore bright madras shorts with a white Ralph Lauren polo shirt, and loafers without socks.

"I swear he wrote the damn *Preppy Handbook*," Barbara whispered.

"Trust me, he's neither that funny nor that self-aware." Amy eyed her wineglass and resolved to slow her pace. Not good to get tipsy at a school event. "So what's the protocol? We eat, drink, and make small talk?"

"That's about it. And, of course, listen to the Whiffenpoofs."

They both snickered, as they did every time someone said "Whiffenpoof."

"Preston was aghast I'd never heard of them," Amy said. "Proves I am one of the great unwashed, as he suspected. Maybe when he finds out I went to a state university, I'll be spared all future contact."

Barbara leaned close. "I hear he got hauled into Carl's office yesterday. Someone bothered to check homework assignment sheets and saw that he's been simply copying Earl's verbatim. Earl wasn't amused."

Amy didn't find this as shocking as Barbara did. Preparing weekly outlines for three different courses she'd never taught before was grueling. She'd have gladly adopted a more experienced teacher's plans if someone had offered. At least she knew better than to borrow without permission.

"What happened?"

"Got his wrist slapped. Carl's never going to get tough with one of his Ivy League darlings."

A group of scrubbed young men appeared on the lanai, exuding the enthusiasm of pups. *They would look great in tuxes,* Amy thought.

"I'm going to grab more food," she whispered as the headmaster, Joe Hossfeld, stepped up to a microphone to introduce the Yale singers.

Amy slipped around the edges of the yard avoiding eye contact so she wouldn't get drawn into conversation. She made a sandwich out of a roll and cold cuts as the a cappella group began. She held her wineglass out to the bartender for a refill, then headed back, bound for the spot where she'd left Barbara. An arm shot out and grabbed her around the waist as she passed behind a circle of chairs. Stu Vargas, red-faced and sweating, pulled her to him and planted a wet kiss on her cheek.

Amy tried to pull away. Stu, a former colleague from her days at the community college, was a notorious lech. His wife Jill seemed the only person on the island unaware that he pawed any woman he got near. Jill taught at Pumehana, which meant Stu was going to be a fixture at all faculty social events. Not a good feature of the job.

"Hey, Stu. How you doing? I'm sitting over there with a friend." Amy nodded to where Barbara was and tried to pull away.

"Don't run off so quick." He leaned closer, his beer-saturated breath warm on her neck.

"Hey there, buddy, how about we let the poor girl breathe." The headmaster had appeared on Stu's other side and wrapped an arm around his shoulder, pulling him off Amy. A former college lineman, Joe managed to move Stu a good distance. "You're missing out on all this fine singing, my friend."

Amy smiled her appreciation and moved on. As the young men in a half circle sang of pitching woo, she made a beeline for Barbara and their spot of shade. Even her handkerchief of a dress was too much clothing for this hot September day.

"Too darn hot," the lost lambs sang as she dabbed her face with a napkin. *No kidding,* she thought, and pressed her wineglass to her cheek.

July 1982, Clifton, New Hampshire

The crowd roared, so Chris did another somersault.

"Damn," Paul said softly, thinking Sarah should be there to see this.

Their three-year-old son stood in the center ring of the Big Tent Circus, so at ease anyone watching would think he did this every day. During intermission, Auntie Nelly the clown had plucked him out of the audience to join her center stage. As soon as the spotlight was on Chris, he did a somersault and then another as the crowd applauded.

Paul was always surprised by his son's utter lack of self-consciousness. *Doesn't get it from me,* he thought, watching. *That's all Sarah.*

"Did you see me, Dad?" Chris asked as soon as he sat down again.

"Yeah, buddy. You were amazing."

Chris couldn't stop grinning.

"This is the best circus ever, right Dad?"

Paul smiled. He hadn't been sure Chris was ready for this. When he saw the circus was coming to Clifton for the first time, Paul suggested to Sarah that he take Chris. What he didn't add was how much he wanted to go himself. Ever since he'd seen the movie *Toby Tyler* as a kid, he'd wanted to see a real live circus. Back then, he'd also wanted to be like Toby and run away to join one.

A woman seated behind them leaned forward and spoke to Chris.

"You were terrific out there. A real natural."

Chris nodded. "I just kept rolling and rolling."

"You're a regular somersault machine."

"Yeah, maybe someday I can get lots and lots of money for doing somersaults."

"You never know," the woman said, laughing. "You keep practicing and you could be the best somersaulter in the world."

"Yeah! And I'll be famous."

Paul could see Chris was getting wound up. There was a fine line between animated Chris and overstimulated Chris, which is why Paul had said no to cotton candy earlier. Chris climbed onto his chair to turn around and talk to the woman.

"Sit down, guy," Paul said quietly.

"S'that your special friend?" Chris asked the woman, pointing to the little girl beside her as he dropped to his knees. The girl had a thumb in her mouth.

"This is my granddaughter Molly." The woman turned to Molly. "Can you say hello?"

The little girl shook her head and wouldn't look at Chris. Paul understood how she felt. He knew he should turn around and join the conversation, but all he wanted was for them to dim the lights and start the show.

"This is my dad," Chris said, placing a hand on Paul's shoulder. "He's kind of shy."

Paul shook his head, turned back to look at the woman, and shrugged. "That's my boy."

"He's a keeper," she said as the lights finally dimmed. He wasn't sure whether she meant him or Chris.

The wow factor increased steadily into the second half of the show. The high-wire act and horse riders had Chris out of his seat and on his tiptoes, straining for a better view. When the lady astride a galloping horse exited the ring, Paul sat back, wondering how they could top that. He glanced at Chris, who had climbed back into his seat, his thighs pressed close together. The thumb in his mouth was Paul's first clue that something wasn't right.

"Doing okay, squirt?" he whispered.

Chris wouldn't look at him. He also wouldn't look at the clowns or the ringmaster. Paul wondered if the sense of danger had overwhelmed him. "Everybody's going to be okay," he assured him, but Chris didn't snap out of it.

When the show ended and the lights came up, Chris stayed as he was even as Paul collected their trash and stood. People were waiting for them to move so the row could empty. Paul bent over and spoke quietly.

"We've got to go, bud."

Chris shook his head. Paul pushed his own seat back and made as much room as he could for people to pass, saying, "Sorry, sorry," over and over as people filed past.

When the row had cleared, he sat down again beside his son.

"What's up, kiddo?"

He couldn't remember when he'd ever seen Chris remain so quiet and still for such a long stretch. Chris whispered something. Paul leaned closer.

"Can't hear you, guy. Say again?"

With a hand cupping Paul's ear, Chris whispered, "I peed in my pants."

Ah damn. Sarah had told him to take along a backpack just in case. He hadn't bothered since Chris had gone months without an accident. Now he was stuck with no change of clothes.

"Happens to the best of us," Paul whispered back.

He thought for a moment, then shook the cup in his hand. There was still a little soda left.

"Trust me?" he asked Chris. "It's going to be a bit cold."

Chris didn't look sure, but he nodded.

Paul loosened the cup's plastic top.

"Remember, I'm doing this on purpose, okay?"

Chris nodded again.

As he rose from his seat, Paul hit the arm of his chair and spilled coke and ice into Chris's lap.

"Oh man," Paul said at full volume. "I'm sorry, buddy. Your mom's going to kill me." He took a wad of napkins and dabbed at Chris's wet T-shirt and shorts. "I've completely soaked you." Chris grinned up at him.

Paul signaled to an usher. "I just spilled Coke all over my kid. Got it on the seat, too. You got something I can use to clean it up?"

"Don't worry about it, man. I got it," the guy said.

Paul led Chris out of the tent, keeping the empty cup raised in his hand like a beacon.

"Don't tell Mom," Chris said as he climbed into his car seat.

"Scout's honor," Paul promised, snapping the buckle.

June 1983, New York, New York

"If I'd only kept walking," Paul would tell Sarah later. "But I stopped to get a hot dog."

After dropping his cousin Beth and her daughter Meghan at Madison Square Garden, he'd parked the truck and headed up Park Avenue on foot. His plan was to spend as much time at the Met as he could before the museum closed and then meet up with Meghan and June after the Menudo concert.

The early Saturday evening was June at its best—warmth without steam and a fresh green hue to the trees. It drew people out. They strolled rather than rushed. Paul smiled to see little kids wobbling on skates beside parents, melting down over ice cream denied, and one struggling to master a bike. As much as he'd looked forward to this time alone in the city, he wished Sarah and the kids were with him. Watching a golden retriever haul a small boy up the sidewalk, he'd have gladly traded Chris or Maddie's hand in his for the few hours he would have alone with the art.

Later, he couldn't say if he heard screams before or after what sounded like a small explosion. All he would remember was that he was squeezing mustard onto his hot dog and then the boy was splayed on the sidewalk across the street from him.

At first he didn't register what he was seeing. But for the cars still crawling forward, the world was frozen for a moment, everyone staring at the sidewalk in front of the hotel. As people registered what was before them, the cries began, all around him, and from windows above. Some ran, desperate to get away.

"Don't look, don't look," a mother beside him said to her daughter.

Paul said it to himself, his left hand still holding the hot dog. He set it down and tried to get his bearings.

Something needed to be done, but this was not like a car accident, not like hitting a deer. No point in leaning over the body, searching for a sign of life—a breath, a pulse. No CPR would keep this boy alive.

Paul crossed the road all the same, the imperative to help too rooted for him to do otherwise. Traffic slowed. Drivers gawked. A young woman stood beside the body, an umbrella open in her hand, held low, as if to shield it, protect it. Not for the sake of the onlookers but for the sake of the life that had been.

A doorman emerged on the run from the lobby, a blanket in hand, and he spread it over the body. The young woman, her face white, her whole body shaking, put down the umbrella, doubled over, and vomited into a planter beside her. Another, older woman near her kept repeating, "No," over and over.

Paul could see hotel employees blocking people from exiting through the front door. One tall Asian man was allowed to leave and he went immediately to the two women.

"Is it Keali'i?"

Neither woman spoke, but the older one nodded.

"You know who jumped?" the doorman asked.

"Didn't jump. Fell. A student with us," the man said. "The kids say he climbed out the window. Was trying to get to another room. An accident. He slipped."

The inflection in the Asian man's voice was familiar. From Hawai'i, Paul guessed, then wondered at himself. How could his mind be processing such a useless observation at that moment? Through the plate glass, he could see a group of teenagers huddled in the lobby, weeping and holding on to one another.

"Amy and I were in the lobby." The older woman struggled to speak as she wept. "We saw the sneakers and the jacket. We knew it was him."

Paul moved away from the small group, not wanting to intrude and unsure whether he should or could simply leave. When the police arrived, he told them what little he knew.

"No," he said when asked if he saw anything before the fall. "One minute I was getting a hot dog, the next thing there was some sound and he was on the sidewalk."

"You heard nothing before? No commotion?"

"Nothing. Just the impact."

Paul glanced over at the young woman who'd been sick. She leaned against the hotel wall. *Someone needs to attend to her,* he thought, and then reminded himself, *not my job.*

What had been lovely about the evening now upset Paul. As he neared Central Park, he heard more than saw the people around him. Their laughter, the ordinariness of their conversations, irritated him. Their joy felt wrong and disrespectful. He thought of the parents receiving the phone call. Of the teacher or official who would have to make it. *At any moment, the worst imaginable is happening to some individual, some family, some community, and yet life goes on as if the order of things has not shifted.*

When he reached the Met, Paul headed straight to the pay phones and made the collect call. He needed to hear their voices, have the dull routines of his life spoken aloud. Yes, the milking was done. Yes, the hay was delivered. Yes, Maddie had eaten all her carrots at lunch. Sarah had it all in hand. His world was still intact.

March 1985, Honolulu, Hawai'i

Martin Whaley followed her to her seat at the end of the back row. Amy had stood away from the crowd in the lobby during the break, sipping her lukewarm decaf as people gathered around him, copies of his book in hand. As much as she would have liked to meet him, have him sign her copy, she didn't want to be part of that pack, a mix of adoring coeds and white-haired ladies.

When she headed back into the auditorium, Martin broke away from his circle and was suddenly at her elbow.

"I see you find me resistible."

Amy smiled. Out of all the women there for his reading, he had singled her out.

"No, no. Not at all. Highly irresistible. When they do the movie, they'll definitely cast Robert Redford. Maybe Harrison Ford if they want a more academic look." She stopped beside her seat, leaned over to set her purse on the floor, and froze. A pair of pink panties lay beneath her chair. She glanced up at Martin Whaley, prize-winning poet, esteemed Stafford professor of English. He'd spotted them as well.

"I guess I really do have a Tom Jones kind of thing going on, eh? You planning on tossing those up at me?"

She could feel the heat in her ears.

She managed to say, "Of course. I just wasn't sure of the protocol. When exactly does one throw panties during a poetry reading?"

"This may be tough to believe, but I don't actually have a lot of experience with that. My guess would be during the applause at the end?"

People were hovering inches from them, waiting for their chance to grab his attention.

"Good thought. Thanks. I'll weigh my options during the rest of the reading."

"It certainly would make this one of my more memorable appearances." He eyed the stage. "You'd need a slingshot, though, if you have any hope of them reaching that far."

A woman tapped him on the shoulder and nodded toward the stage.

"I guess they want me back up there." He extended a hand. "Pleasure chatting with you."

"Static cling," Amy said as he turned to go. "They must have been stuck to the inside of my mu'umu'u."

"Right." He grinned. "You stick with that one. Makes you seem so much more normal." He leaned closer to her. "I didn't get your name."

"Amy."

"Nice. A sweet name. Not at all what I'd expect for some strumpet who tosses her drawers at poets. You free for dinner after this, Amy?"

"I suppose I could be." Amy hoped she looked cooler than she felt. "You'd have to promise to say or do something mortifying. Balance things out a bit?"

He nodded. "Fair enough. Not to worry. I will be sure to embarrass myself thoroughly before the night is over."

Amy took her seat, scooped the panties off the floor, and stuffed them in her purse as Martin returned to the podium. All she had expected of this evening was a respite from the grind of grading papers. Every week, between her teaching schedule and debate coaching, she worked five long days as well as most Saturdays and Sundays. Her social life consisted of a rare dinner or movie with a friend, her monthly poetry group with Rachel and other former colleagues, and also thanks to Rachel, the occasional poetry reading at the university. Men floated through now and then, but none held her attention.

She'd nearly opted out of going to Whaley's reading. When Rachel canceled at the last minute, Amy figured she'd use the time to catch up on some papers. At five, though, she'd glanced out the window of her classroom as two pairs of debaters once again made the arguments they'd been making for the past seven months. This late in the competitive season, there were no fresh arguments to float, little new evidence to present. Amy didn't think she could bear to listen to one more cross-ex. She had done something she never did—ended the practice early, before they reached the rebuttals.

"Looking good, guys," she told them. "Go home, get some rest. Spend tomorrow at Hamilton, and we'll do an evidence work session Monday."

She had decided she was not going to spend another dinner hour in her classroom with a bunch of teenagers. Martin Whaley, whose poetry moved her to tears, was reading at the University of Hawai'i that evening. She was determined to be there.

Now she had managed to catch his eye. She would wait at the back of the hall. He might be a bit smooth for her taste and his hair already flecked with white, but a mature man was a welcome change from the boys she usually dated. She could get used to a man who wore a jacket and button-down shirt with his jeans.

June 1986, San Francisco, California

This is the single happiest moment of my life. Amy lifted her face to the hazy sun.

Martin lay stretched on a blanket beside her with an empty bottle of chardonnay resting against his leg. A damp paper plate boasted the discarded crowns of a dozen strawberries, a few bites of brie, and a chunk of sourdough bread.

"Have another," Martin said, offering her a piece of dark chocolate dipped in caramel.

"I couldn't eat a bite more," she protested, but she let him place it on her tongue. He lifted his cup of wine to her lips. "I do believe you are trying to get me drunk, Mr. Whaley."

Wine dribbled down her chin and Martin dabbed at it with a napkin. "My only goal, Mrs. Whaley, is to make you the happiest woman alive."

"And I am. How could I not be? Today has been absolutely perfect. Thank you."

Martin had arranged everything—planned the picnic menu with the concierge at the Fairmont, identified a secluded spot in Golden Gate Park, and booked a car service to bring them there, even brought a small cassette tape player on which he played recordings of Bach, Mozart, and Debussy. He saw to every detail of this wedding celebration just as he had seen to every detail of their city hall ceremony that morning. "Trust me," Martin had told her a month earlier. "I will take care of all the details. You need only to get yourself to San Francisco." Amy had never felt so cherished and desired.

"Now I want to hear some of your poetry," Martin said, lying down again.

"You are a dear man to ask, but I'm not going to embarrass us both by reading you my poems." Martin had brought and read some of his work to her as they grazed their way through lunch.

"I'm your husband who adores everything about you. How could I not love something you've created? I want to be inside that creative mind of yours."

Her every instinct told her this was a bad idea. "And if you hate it, what then?"

"I won't hate it because the very act of sharing it with me is what matters most. Besides, you are delicious. You couldn't possibly write anything horrid."

She wanted to believe him.

"Well, all right, but be gentle with me." She pulled a folded sheet of paper from her bag. "This first one's called 'Communion.' The obligatory nature poem." She paused. Reminded herself he loved her.

> Just to love is enough, she tells herself
> in the garden at dawn as the irises spike purple
> and the grass sweeps green across the sun washed expanse,
> just to witness and to love is enough, yet
> she wants more, she wants to pull the garden to her—
> the petals and the leaves, the sun soaked stone

and the dirt warm beneath her feet. She wants
to burrow into it all, know the electric union.

Just to love is enough, she reminds herself
on the terrace at dusk, except the lily of the valley
still emerges bowed and weeping no matter
how lovely the lilacs—it wants more.

Martin grinned at her. "So you were reading Whitman for an American lit class when you wrote it?"

Amy chose to be flattered. "I have to confess I haven't read much Whitman, but I'll take that as a compliment. And I actually wrote it post college."

"Ah. What's next?"

She sensed that, just as she'd feared, he was disappointed.

"I've just this one other short piece. A love poem." She could feel herself blush.

He beamed up at her. "For me?" He took her hand and kissed the palm.

"Okay. Here goes. 'Tender.'"

I think you could hold a moth's wing
in your hand and not crush it,
squeeze my heart in your fist
and not bruise it, slide me to paradise
and bring me home again.

I think you are the most tender man
God ever kissed awake.

Martin was silent for too long, but finally sat up and kissed her gently, dispassionately. "Very sweet and very brave of you to share that with me. Thank you."

She hoped her smile looked steady on her face and her voice sounded wry, as she said, "Shall we sample another bottle of wine?"

She stuffed the poems into her bag as Martin opened the bottle.

"Did I mention," he said, as he poured her a cup, "that I've booked us a table at Alioto's for tonight?"

Amy had confided that dining at Alioto's was one of her family's rituals when visiting San Francisco. How had she possibly won the heart of this brilliant, sophisticated man so eager to please her? And how could she ever be enough for him?

"Lovely," she said, forcing herself to take only a small sip.

July 1986, Clifton, New Hampshire

Put down the knife, Amy wanted to scream as the five-year-old jabbed the paring knife into the large block of cheddar cheese. His mother Jocelyn, who'd seen him pick up the knife, didn't even glance his way.

With her hand still on Martin's arm, Jocelyn said, "So sorry, loves, to leave you stranded here. Herman can't be torn from the studio—finishing up his masterpiece, no doubt—and I'm filthy from the garden. I'm headed for a shower. I promise I won't be a sec. Pour yourselves some wine. Nibble on the cheese if Kip hasn't destroyed it all." She paused and looked at her son, who was now attempting to peel an apple. "You be careful, pet."

"I know what I'm doing." The boy didn't look up, just kept sliding the knife along the apple's surface. Amy had to look away.

Martin bussed Jocelyn's cheek. "Don't worry about us. We'll make ourselves at home. I'll introduce Amy to your wall of books. Go. Take your shower."

"All righty then." She leaned over and buried her face in her son's curls. "Be a good boy."

With her gray hair and matronly body, Jocelyn seemed more likely the boy's grandmother than mother.

"They didn't think pregnancy was a possibility," Martin had told Amy earlier. This was a second marriage for both Jocelyn and Herman and each had kids in high school and college from their previous relationships.

Amy was nervous about the evening, their first dinner invitation as a married couple. Since they had skipped having a wedding with guests, Amy hadn't met any of Martin's friends or colleagues. She'd only been in

Clifton a couple weeks and the small town felt desperately remote and unfamiliar. She found it curious that the isolation frightened her more than the streets of Honolulu. The woods and unmarked dirt roads felt menacing, never mind that she had no support network in the community should an emergency arise.

As Jocelyn headed off for her shower, Martin poured them each a glass of burgundy, then wandered off to the wall of books at the far end of the room, leaving Amy perched on the couch beside Kip, who was now chopping the apple into bits.

"Careful," she said softly to the boy. "Don't want to cut yourself." She itched to grab the knife from his hand.

Kip brought the knife down hard against the apple. Seeds scattered.

His face buried in a book, Martin didn't even look up. Amy took a big sip from her wineglass and tried to think of a way to divert the boy's attention.

"Would you like me to read you a book?" she offered.

"I can read books by myself."

Of course. Probably already up to Twain and Dickens.

"Then maybe you could read one to me."

He looked at her skeptically, his eyes barely visible beneath the wild tangle of hair falling over his forehead and nearly to his shoulders. Amy wondered if anyone had ever bothered to cut his hair or, for that matter, wash it.

"Don't you know how to read?"

"Well, yeah, sure. I can read."

She sipped more wine. *What is wrong with these people.* They let their preschooler handle a sharp knife and didn't bother being ready when guests arrived.

Kip suddenly ran from the room and within minutes was back with *Alice's Adventures in Wonderland.* He climbed onto the couch beside Amy and opened it.

"'Alice was beginning to get very tired of sitting by her sister on the bank,'" Kip read. Though Amy had assumed he was telling the truth when he'd said he could read, she was still surprised by his fluency. He was a precocious little guy.

As he read along, he inched closer to her, spreading the book open so she could see the illustrations. By the time his mother returned, running her fingers through her wet hair, he was leaning against Amy, who now had her arm wrapped around him. The book lay open in her lap, her breast a pillow for his small head.

"Thanks for your patience. I feel human again," Jocelyn said.

She had put on a sweeping gauze skirt that nearly touched the floor and an oversized linen pullover, so wide at the top that it fell off one shoulder. Her bare feet were rough and wide. *Luau feet,* Amy thought, *like my own.* Amy's were courtesy of a barefoot childhood.

"Martin, be a dear and pour me a drink," Jocelyn said, then turned her attention to Kip, still nestled at Amy's side. "Look at the two of you! Now that's a picture."

Plopping into an easy chair across from them, she opened her arms wide, said, "Come here, love," and Kip tumbled into her expansive lap. Martin handed her a large glass of wine.

"No Herman yet, eh?" she said with an exaggerated sigh. "These damn artists with their oversized egos." She glanced at her watch. "Shit! It's already seven. The roast will be a dry lump soon." She placed her mouth next to her son's ear. "Be a love and round up your pop."

Kip bounded off through the kitchen to the breezeway connecting the house to the studio. Amy felt herself softening toward the large woman opposite her. She had expected Martin's friends to be more straitlaced than people in Hawai'i, and was pleasantly surprised by Jocelyn's informality.

"Herman'll be pissed to have his work interrupted, but them's the breaks," Jocelyn said with a laugh, then picked up a chunk of browning apple and paired it with a ragged bit of cheese. "I must not forget to pull the roast from the oven," she added, but remained seated. To Martin she said, "Did I mention I promised Jule we'd all stop by after dinner? Bunch of her students are sharing their poetry and some friend from Boston is here, plays jazz guitar, I think. Which reminds me." She rose, walked over to the staircase, and hollered, "Liv! Liv, hon!"

A distant female teenage voice yelled back, "What?"

"Can you watch Kip tonight? Herman and I are going out."

Martin winked at Amy as mother and daughter continued to scream across the space between them.

"Why do I have to watch him?"

"Because he's your brother." No answer followed.

Taking another swig of wine, Jocelyn yelped, "The roast!" and disappeared into the kitchen.

Amy quietly asked Martin, "Should I offer to help?"

"It's fine. They're always like this. She'll put you to work if she needs a hand with something."

Kip ran back into the room, a giant of a man following him. In paint-speckled shorts and smeared T-shirt, Herman was the expanded version of his son. A wild mane of hair framed his bearded face and his barrel belly overwhelmed the waistband of his shorts. His voice was as oversized as his body.

"Martin, you bastard, interrupting my artistic genius!" The wide grin on his face told Amy he was joking. His intensity rattled her some, but she could see his appeal. He enveloped Martin in a huge hug, nearly lifting him off the ground. When he turned to Amy, he held her first at arm's length, openly appraising her, then lifted her off the ground in a crushing embrace. Setting her down again, he said to Martin, "Well done, you son of a bitch. She's perfection," then to Amy added, "You ever tire of this sad sack, you come see me. Unlike Martin, I know how to keep a young woman happy."

"Leave the poor girl alone," Jocelyn said from the kitchen doorway. "Go shower. And take Kip with you. Lord knows when he last bathed. Dinner will be ready in ten."

"Stop nagging at me, woman." Herman lifted Kip to his shoulders. "And save some of that wine for me!"

"As if you haven't already drunk a bottle out in the studio!" Jocelyn yelled, and headed back into the kitchen as Herman and Kip disappeared down the hall.

Amy looked over at Martin who was grinning.

"A little out of your comfort zone, Barnes?"

She could see how comfortable he was in this space, how much this was a home to him. Which meant she needed to find her way to being comfortable as well.

"Definitely not the stuffy New Englanders I feared they'd be," Amy whispered. Martin embraced her from behind, lacing his hands in front of her waist.

From the kitchen, Jocelyn called, "Come make yourselves plates. We'll start without them."

Jocelyn crossed to the staircase where she yelled, "Dinner!"

Doors opened overhead, feet thumped down the stairs, and suddenly there were young adults grunting hellos at them and grabbing plates to fill. A large stringy pile of pot roast lay sliced on a cutting board, vegetables and potatoes in a bowl beside it.

"Do we have to eat at the table?" one of the young women asked.

"I don't care where you eat, so long as the plate comes back."

Each of the teens went off with dinner and a glass of wine.

Jocelyn shoved a plate into Amy's hand. "Go, help yourself. We'll eat in the dining room."

Amy set her filled plate across the table from Martin's. He was out in the hallway, studying a painting. She joined him, linking her hand in his. It took her a moment to realize it was an enormous oil portrait of a younger nude Jocelyn, prone on a bed.

"I fear this may all be a bit shocking for you," Martin said, seeming amused and rather pleased with himself. She could see he liked playing the part of sophisticate to her rube.

"What? This?" She gestured at the portrait. "Seriously? As I recall, you've been in my parents' home, seen my dad's artwork."

"Oh, right." He released her hand. She followed him to the dining room.

"Not to worry, my love," she whispered as she slid onto her chair. "Nude paintings might fail to shock me, but my horizons are definitely being widened. You having fun watching my reactions?" She playfully punched his side.

"Oh yeah. Doesn't get much better than watching you with this group. And the night is still young."

Jocelyn joined them, the young people all returned to their rooms. "God, it's great to have you guys here." Jocelyn placed a hand on Amy's. "Welcome to the Stafford family. Now eat! God knows when Herman will make an appearance."

Amy scooped up some strands of pot roast as Martin ran his foot along her calf and said to Jocelyn, "Tell me about this guitarist friend of Jules."

December 1986, Lisbon, Vermont

Chris and Maddie tossed logs onto the pile. They'd helped Paul load and haul the sleds full of firewood out to the field closest to the house. Paul had shoveled a clear patch in the snow and built a stack of kindling and logs to fuel a giant bonfire for that night. Clear, calm skies were forecast. The moon would rise early and full, perfect conditions for a winter fire. Paul was determined to make the night celebratory.

He glanced up at his and Sarah's bedroom window, aglow in the fading light.

"I need a moment alone," was all Sarah had said.

His mom and sister were in the kitchen roasting a turkey and preparing side dishes; his dad and Sarah's brother were stringing Christmas lights on the fir trees that stood to either side of the kitchen door. Sarah's folks had been by earlier to drop off food, and Sarah's sisters were in the living room setting up a Christmas tree. Neither he nor Sarah had asked for any of this help. His mom had proposed the two families gather for an early holiday celebration and everyone had sprung into action.

Paul had hoped Sarah would join in the preparations, but she showed no interest.

"Look tall enough to you guys?" he asked his kids as he piled the last logs on top.

"How long will it burn?" Chris said.

"Longer than you'll want to be out here on a cold December night."

Paul's folks had set up folding tables so that the whole downstairs was a series of tables stretching from the kitchen through the dining room and across the living room. The regular furniture had been shoved up against walls. They'd never before tried to squeeze this many people into their home.

Sarah's sisters, done with the tree, were now setting the tables. Everyone had pooled their good flatware, glasses, dishes, and linens. Fresh pine boughs ran down the center of each table with votives and glass ornaments interspersed throughout.

"Beautiful!" Paul declared, standing in the doorway between living and dining rooms.

Sarah's sister Betsy looked up. "It is, isn't it? Beginning to feel like Christmas!"

Of course it didn't feel at all like Christmas, which was why they were all trying so hard. They'd only discovered the cancer in Sarah's breast a few weeks earlier. In two weeks, she would have a full mastectomy, just to be on the safe side. Chemo and radiation would follow. Sarah, his unshakable, steady rock, had been leveled by the news. She'd gone through the motions of daily life, but spent much of her time alone in her room or hiking nearby trails.

Paul climbed the stairs and tapped on the door to their bedroom.

"Yup," Sarah called.

He stuck his head around the door. "Okay to come in?"

"Of course."

She sat on the floor, her jewelry box open before her with little white boxes stacked nearby.

"This looks like a project. Want more light?" Not waiting for her answer, he switched on another lamp.

"I figured now was as good a time as any to sort through all this stuff. Nothing really valuable, but lots of sentimental pieces from Granny Joyce and my aunt Regina. I'm trying to find something here for everyone."

Paul could see that some of the boxes had bows and tags attached.

"It's a challenge for the guys. Granny gave me a bunch of Granddad's rings and tiepins, but I don't think the boys will find them all that exciting."

"Maybe not exciting, but I'm sure they'll like having something from their great-grandfather."

He squatted down beside her.

"You sure this is what you want to be doing?"

She settled a pair of pearl earrings onto a square of cotton in one of the boxes.

"I can't be down there watching everyone work so hard. I appreciate it"—she reached out and touched his arm—"I really do. It's just overwhelming."

He kissed the top of her head and headed to the door.

"In case you're wondering, I always kind of liked that silver tie clasp with the fish."

She smiled, her first real smile in days. "You mean you don't want to put dibs on his high school ring?" She held it up for him to see. It was humongous.

"I'll be generous and let your brother have that one."

He shut the door quietly and left her to her work.

Dinner was the boisterous, rowdy event Paul had hoped for. They made sure to mix kids and adults at each table. No exiling the young people to the kitchen. Paul wanted them in the middle of it all, wanted them loud and unruly, silly, and oblivious to the emotional weight the adults carried. They performed their duty well. A four-year-old niece made reindeer ears out of pine boughs and sang "Rudolph, the Red-Nosed Reindeer." One of the teens made a game of refilling the wineglass of Paul's dad when he wasn't looking. Each time Cam lifted his glass, the room quieted as everyone watched to see if he'd notice his glass was always full. A couple of the boys got into a shoving match, a toddler had a full-blown tantrum, and Chris tried out a new bowling ball, rolling it the length of the hall so it bumped up against the front door. Whenever Paul looked Sarah's way, she was laughing or engrossed in the kids' antics.

By the time they finished their meal, the entire downstairs was a happy explosion of torn wrapping paper, ribbons, and dirty dishes. Paul's mom began clearing the table and his sister appeared with trash bags for the debris, but Sarah's father banged a spoon against his water glass and motioned for them to wait on the cleanup. Everyone crammed as best they could into the living room.

"Before we all get busy washing dishes and roasting marshmallows over the fire, I want to make a little speech." He looked over at Sarah, who stood in the doorway to the dining room. "Don't worry. I'll keep it short."

"That'll be a first," Sarah shot back.

"Sarah, I know how much you hate people fussing about this, but you and Paul have a long haul ahead of you. We all want you to know we'll do everything we can to lend a hand. Your cousin Beth has made up a calendar"—June held up the calendar for everyone to see—"and tonight we're going to set up a schedule to make sure the farm's covered and someone's looking after the kids. I think Paul's mom's got a schedule for meals, too."

Paul's mom nodded and said, "I have copies for everyone."

Sarah's dad resumed. "Now I'm going to turn this over to your brother."

Jerry rose from his seat, an envelope in hand. "With all you've got ahead of you, we thought it might be good if you two got away for a couple nights. So this is your Christmas present from all of us."

He handed Paul an envelope. A sheet of paper inside said they had reservations at the Château Frontenac in Quebec City for the January weekend before her surgery.

Jerry said, "We'll take care of the farm and kids."

Paul stood silent for a moment, not trusting his voice. Sarah crossed the room to him, put her arm around his waist.

"Thank you for all of this," he finally said, gesturing at the large calendar and sheets of paper with assignments spelled out. "There's no way we could make it through without your help."

"That's what family's for," his father-in-law said, fake punching him in the gut. "Don't worry. You can be sure I'm going to call on your sorry ass someday to haul me out of bed when I can't walk to the john. Not a person in this room's going to let you two get by without doing for us."

Paul's dad rose and for a moment, Paul thought he might be about to make his own speech, something he'd never seen him do. "Time to get back to the partying. Who wants to light a fire?" The kids cheered.

As Cam led the kids off to the field, Paul slipped away upstairs. It was his turn to need a moment alone. He felt as if some gauge within him had flipped, his internal control button against emotional overload had sprung straight to maximum. There was simply too much of everything. Too much fear, too much love, too much sadness, too much joy.

He could hear the kids whooping and hollering, see their bodies dancing around the fire as the flames rose, their lit faces reminding him of a Caravaggio painting. He belonged there beside them, free to dance and holler as loud as he wanted. He ran back down the stairs and grabbed Sarah's hand.

"The kids have the right idea. The cleanup can wait. Everybody get your jackets and come on out."

He didn't give Sarah a chance to put on her coat before pulling her out the front door. She wrestled it on as he led her to the field. The fire was so hot they barely needed the extra layer. He started running in a clockwise direction around the fire and the kids fell in behind him. The other adults trailing out of the house joined in, even the grandparents, all of them baying and whooping as they skipped and danced around the flames. The fire illuminated Sarah as she ran beside him, laughing so hard tears ran down her face, laughing as if this were the most magical day of her life. In that moment, she was joy itself. *Please God,* he prayed, grabbing hold of her hand, *keep her well.*

January 1987, Quebec City, Quebec

"It tastes like poo," the little girl said, pushing her plate away.

Her father, or the man Amy presumed was her father, said, "Really? Can I have a bite?" He put a forkful of pasta into his mouth. "Mmm. Mighty good poo, Susie-bear."

"I wanna eat poo, too," the diapered boy cried, standing up on the velveteen bench seat he shared with his father and sister.

The waiters in their tuxedos, hands clasped behind their backs, looked the other way.

Martin was fuming across from Amy. She wasn't sure which made him angrier—that the man had ignored the jackets-required rule or that he'd brought his children into the elegant dining room. They weren't bothering her. She thought they were rather fun, except for the hissy fit they were triggering in Martin.

It wasn't as if the dining room was exactly packed with people. Besides the two of them and the family, there was only one other couple—a man and a woman who Amy thought looked rather miserable, he in an obviously borrowed jacket and chinos, she in a tight knit dress about a size too small.

Neither smiled and they said little.

She had warned Martin that six o'clock was on the early side for dinner in Quebec City, but he had insisted he was too hungry to wait for a more fashionable dining hour.

She placed a hand on his. "Relax. They'll be out of here soon."

"It's the principle," Martin persisted, draining his martini. "The sign says jackets required and the guy's in jeans and a polo shirt, never mind that he has a couple of noisy brats with him."

"There's no hurry. We can have a couple drinks and order once they leave."

If the rest of the world only knew, Amy thought, watching him tap his knife against the table surface. The gap between the public Martin and the private one was immense. Stunningly cool, Martin as poet and charmer of women was unflappable and ever the amused observer of humankind, above and beyond ordinary human concerns. His particular allure sprang from his ability to appear always detached until that moment when he turned his full attention on an individual. Then it was as if the skies had opened, the dove descended, and the person on the receiving end of his spotlight had become the chosen one, adored and blessed.

The private Martin was less appealing. He required precision in his household. Socks and shirts sorted by color, kitchen and bathroom surfaces sanitized daily, books alphabetized by author, silence when he worked, and constant mothering of his inner child. On Amy he could and did dump the full weight of his grievances, insecurities, and terrors, yet she chose to see this as proof of the unique and resonant link between them.

She knew the diners were merely the last straw. This delayed honeymoon was not unfolding as he'd planned. He had thought himself clever to piggyback a honeymoon onto a conference, so they could stay at Quebec City's Château Frontenac on the college's dime. Their room was drab and small, the amenities few. A particularly chilling January had descended over the region and the sidewalks and roads were slick with ice. Martin had slipped and fallen earlier on the winding cobblestone road to the shops below. She guessed his back was still aching.

"Order another martini," she suggested, "and how about"—she glanced at the menu—"escargots to begin? Lots of butter and garlic to distract you."

He rolled his eyes but signaled to the waiter.

A musician, violin in hand, entered the room.

"Ah, romantic music," she said. "That's sure to chase away Dad and the kiddos."

The violinist began with their table.

"May I play something for the lady?"

Amy wasn't sure if he was asking her or Martin. When Martin said nothing, she spoke up. "How about 'The Way You Look Tonight'?"

Martin sat back and watched her as she listened. She could not tell if he approved of her request.

"I hadn't figured you for a Sinatra fan," he said when the violinist moved on.

"I like the song." From the other couple's table came the strains of a tune Amy didn't recognize. "Do you know that one?"

"'Hymn to Love.' One of Piaf's." She could see Martin was pleased he knew this.

The waiter arrived with a platter of escargots. "Compliments of the manager, with his apologies if your meal has in any way been disturbed."

Martin glowed. He liked being placated. He could feel affirmed in his indignation. He raised an eyebrow at her. She smiled, grateful to see his good humor return, and picked up a shell.

As she predicted, the father and kids soon moved along.

"Finally." Martin sat back in his chair, visibly relaxing.

Amy glanced at the other couple in the room whose hands were now linked on their table. They radiated such sadness. The violinist had moved to a corner where he played a series of old love songs.

Martin, wiping the butter from his fingers, flashed her one of his spectacular smiles, the kind that made her feel she was the most desirable woman in the world. His equilibrium restored, he could be generous to her, which is why she always forgave him his childish moments. She would forgive him much for the gift of his attention.

A week after they met and a day before he returned to Clifton from Honolulu, he had read her Cummings's "i carry your heart with me." After that, every day for four months he read a poem to her either in person or by phone, some of them his, most the work of others. But as they settled into married life and things grew busy, he had begun to forget. Now he only occasionally remembered, and usually only as a prelude to lovemaking. It had been nearly a month now since he'd recited anything to her. He pulled from his pocket a slip of paper and began to read.

"This is one of Marianne Moore's, not mine. It's called "A Jelly-Fish." 'Visible, invisible, / A fluctuating charm,'" he read, "'an amber-colored amethyst / Inhabits it.'" At the last lines, "It floats away / From you," he set down the paper and took her hand. For a few minutes, they sat just so, neither speaking.

The poem was new to Amy, and she struggled to make sense of it. She wanted to believe Martin had shared it as an expression of his love for her, but it left her puzzled and uneasy. Was she the jellyfish, elusive and cloudy? Or was he explaining himself?

He leaned across the table and kissed her, his childish temper vanquished for the moment. He was again the dashing but sensitive poet, happily admitting her within his spotlight, tucking her in his pocket.

June 1988, Lisbon, Vermont

Paul hadn't factored in time enough to find parking. The small library lot was full, as were the side streets nearby. He managed to find a spot a few blocks away and jogged back. When he pulled open the large door to the library's meeting room, he wasn't prepared for the crowd of people packed into the good-sized room. He'd intentionally cut it close, not wanting to be standing around waiting any longer than necessary, but now he wasn't sure he'd even be able to see Maddie.

He looked for a spot in the back. An arm waved at him from across the room. It was Sarah, motioning to a chair beside her. Joining her would require going up the center aisle and then either squeezing past people or asking them to stand, drawing attention to himself either way. He had changed out of his work clothes and put on a button-down shirt and slacks, but he knew he wasn't fooling anyone. He might as well have been a guppy flopping around on land. He shook his head and pointed to the back wall.

He scanned the crowd for Maddie. A well-dressed group of high school kids sat in a line at the front. He spotted her at the farthest end, her blond braid hanging over her chairback. He was relieved when she turned and spotted him. He wanted her to know he was there. He gave her a subtle thumbs-up. As out of place as he felt, she fit in perfectly. She wore her cousin's hand-me-down Laura Ashley dress and soft pink gloss on her lips. As lovely as her mother had been at the same age.

He could see the manila folder in her hand, the folder that had sat on their dining table for days now, available for any free moment when she could practice her reading. She'd worked on the poem for weeks before submitting it, tweaking drafts with the help of her English teacher, who was seated behind her.

An imposing woman, her graying hair piled in a mass atop her head, spectacles dangling from her neck, walked to the front of the room. She waited for people to quiet.

"Good afternoon and welcome," she said when the crowd turned its attention to her. "I'm Victoria Smith, one of the librarians here. I thank you all for joining us and extend a special thanks and congratulations to our young writers." At this she nodded to the group in the first row. "What a talented group they are. When we conceived the idea of a literary contest for our young people, we had no idea that we would receive so many fine submissions. I am honored to present to you this afternoon the winners of what we hope will be the annual Connecticut River Valley Young Writers Contest."

Even from where he stood, Paul could see Maddie glowed. Her cheeks were flushed a soft pink. He looked over to Sarah. She beamed as well.

"Our first reader will be Madeline Rideau, an eighth grader at Lisbon Middle School, whose poem took first-place honors among the middle school submissions. Madeline will be reading her poem, 'You Roll Your Shoulders Forward.'"

Maddie rose and walked slowly to the podium. She laid her folder on the stand and opened it. Calmly, as if she did this every day, she adjusted the microphone so it was just beyond her lips. She paused for a moment and let her eyes scan the crowd. *Her teacher coached her well,* Paul thought. His anxiety lifted.

"I wrote this poem for my mother, who was diagnosed with breast cancer a couple years ago. I am happy to say she is now doing well."

She glanced over at Sarah.

"The poem is called 'You Roll Your Shoulders Forward.'"

She paused again before the first line.

"Lie still, the lady told you. Don't move."

Paul pictured the cold room with the huge machine and Sarah stretched out on its table. There had been something comforting about that slick technology and its promise of healing powers even as it destroyed cells.

"But I could not stay beside you, thick glass between us, I watched, buttons pressed, lights flashing, watched them burn the cancer away." Paul thought of the raw red patches the radiation left on Sarah's breast.

"When they dripped poison through your veins, I stroked your arm and you sank into the easy chair, your thighs sticking to its green plastic, nothing was easy there."

The chemo treatments had taken longer but been more tranquil, Sarah lying back in that big chair, the IV in her arm, the gardens jarringly lovely beyond the glass walls.

"You want now to show me where they cut you. You say it's not so very bad, but I do not want to see."

He nearly winced to think of that angry red scar he still avoided touching.

"What I see is how you roll your shoulders forward now, like a hood to mask what they took away."

Rolled her shoulders, Paul thought, *and hid in oversized sweatshirts and tees, anything to keep eyes from lingering.*

Maddie paused when she finished, placed the poem back in the folder, and took her seat as the audience applauded. As the next reader was announced, she glanced back at Paul, her smile wide, and he nodded, his jaw locked, his cheeks trembling. He knew Sarah would be crying. He did not look her way.

May 1991, Clifton, New Hampshire

That can't be good, Amy thought. The screams had grown even more shrill. She pushed herself up from her knees and gathered her weeder and paper bag full of dandelions. Before she could stow her gear on the porch, Will came crashing through the hedge that separated the front and back yards. Stripped to his training pants and covered head to toe in sand, he shrieked when he saw Amy and ran back through the hedge. Amy jogged after him.

The sprinkler was not where she'd left it in the grass. Will had picked it up and used it as a weapon on his sister Kara, the sandbox, and the house. The sandbox was now a soupy mix and the house's clapboard pockmarked with fistfuls of wet sand that drizzled down its backside. Amy groaned. Just how much water had gone through that open window? Will climbed into the sandbox and sat down, a huge grin on his face.

Standing there in her bare feet, her tired, oversized T-shirt drooping nearly to her knees, Amy wanted to be the calm mother who, in a firm and neutral voice, took her children by the hand, put them in a time-out at the picnic table, and then quietly went about the business of cleaning up. This was, after all, perfectly normal behavior for a two-year-old and four-year-old. *I'm just really lousy at being a mom.*

Staring at the mess of sand crawling down the wall, she flopped down on the grass and told herself she would not cry. Kara walked over and, squatting beside her, ran a hand up and down her arm.

"Don't worry, Mommy. It'll be okay. We'll clean it up."

Amy nodded. Will, still in the sandbox, began jumping up and down, splashing wet sand onto the spring grass. At least she hadn't crushed his spirit. Not yet, anyway.

"Count to ten," she whispered to herself.

Closing her eyes, she counted, inhaling deeply on each number and pinching her leg to stop the tears. She could feel Kara's body warm by her side. As she reached three, another hand, this one smaller and wetter, took her left hand. She could feel Will's damp, sandy body pressed against her thigh. At ten, she opened her eyes and looked down. He knelt beside her, leaning across her lap.

"It can all be fixed, Mommy," Kara said. "It's nothing a little water and elbow grease can't take care of."

Amy smiled to hear her own words played back to her. She ran a hand through Will's gritty wet curls.

"Right you are, sweetie. How about you run inside and close up those windows so Will and I can hose down the house."

Kara skipped off to the back door and Will headed for the hose.

"Faucet off first, mister, so I can unscrew the sprinkler head. And I'm in charge of the hose."

He turned and for a moment looked to be weighing whether or not he would challenge her on this. With a finger twirling a curl at the top of his head, he continued on to the faucet, where he shut off the water. Amy twisted off the sprinkler and nodded for him to turn the water back on. It gushed cold and clear from the green plastic tubing. She let it run down the front of her shirt, then leaned over and let it run over the back of her neck.

Will squealed, his small legs galloping. "Me too!"

He bent his head forward and Amy let the water fall onto his neck. Kara knocked on the window above and Amy's stomach did a small flip. *Not so close to the glass,* she wanted to yell up at her.

"Spray her, Mom, spray her."

Amy lifted the hose, positioned her thumb over the pouring water so as to form a sweeping spray, and lifted it so the water fell in a sheet. She moved the hose right and then left, annihilating the sand bombs clinging to the wood, chasing the sand to the ground. Will jumped up and motioned for the hose.

She handed him the nozzle and watched as he struggled to make the water spray as she had. When he turned to her in frustration, she guided his thumb into place until the water plumed in an arc.

Amy looked down at her now very wet self. The bleach-stained T-shirt clung to her in thick folds. Nothing wet-T-shirt sexy about this look. She added more pressure to the water with her thumb so that it fell like rain. Will let go and stationed himself under the falling water, lifting his face to it.

Amy moved closer, aiming for his hair, searching out the sand grains. He squirmed beneath the cold water, but let her finish.

"Your turn," he said, and took the nozzle from her. Amy could see he meant it as an offering. Returning the gift of water. She dipped her head. Cold water ran down her face, shoulders, and back.

"Now shake like a dog," Will directed, and she did.

She shook her head. She shook her shoulders and hips. Linking hands with Will, she jumped in the water puddling around them. Kara burst out the back door and joined them.

This was what Amy wanted her kids to carry away from the day, this memory of their mother barefoot, soaking wet, and splashing and shaking and happy as a dog. They all needed more days like this one.

July 1995, Hana, Hawai'i

Eyes crusted shut, the mewing kittens crawled out of the brush and up the backside of the low stone wall, emerging beside the children's feet. Kara and Will had jumped up on the wall for a better view of Ke'anae Peninsula and the ocean below. Kara bent down, ready to pick one up.

"No," Amy cried out sharply. "Don't touch them. They're sick." She motioned to the kids to get off the wall.

"What's wrong with them?" Kara asked, wrapping her arms around her mother's waist.

Amy figured the kittens couldn't be more than a few weeks old. Their tiny bodies were emaciated and pocked with oozing sores. They stumbled blindly along the wall's top, turning toward the human voices. Will bent forward, sitting on his haunches, and studied the kittens' eyes.

"I think they have some kind of infection, honey." Amy ran her hand over Kara's head.

"Will they be okay?"

"I don't know," she lied. "I hope so."

Martin walked over to them. "What's this?"

He had been down at the wall's other end, pen and pad in hand, scribbling. Sightseeing with Martin required patience. He never knew when the muse would strike, and he always indulged it.

"Sick kitties, Daddy," Kara said.

"We should feed them," Will suggested.

"I don't think we have anything they would want," Amy said. She tried to corral the kids toward the car. "I'm sure their mother will feed them."

"If they're sick, we should take them to the doctor." Kara planted herself on the asphalt. "We should take them in the car with us."

"Don't be ridiculous," Martin said, continuing to the car. "We're not taking a bunch of starving, sick kittens to Hana and back."

"They're starving?" Will had followed him to the car, but stopped short of climbing in.

Amy narrowed her eyes at Martin. Was it really so wrong to sugarcoat things a bit for the kids? Kara was only eight, Will barely six. Martin did not believe in lying to children.

"Their mom's still nursing them, guys. We would be hurting them if we took them from her," Amy tried to reassure them.

As she said it, she wished she believed it. She wanted to grab one of the beach bags, put the kittens in it, and tell Martin to forget about this drive to Hana. They should go back to Kahului and find a vet, if only to have them put down humanely. This long drive on winding roads had never been on her list of things to do with the kids. But she knew to challenge Martin on this would only mean injecting tension and would worsen an already challenging day. He would not be persuaded. He never was.

"Then why did she leave them?" Kara was not going to give up without a fight. Will had climbed into the car.

"She had to hunt for some food, sweetie," Amy said. "She'll come back to where she left them. That's why we mustn't move them."

"Can she fix their eyes?"

Amy could feel Martin's eyes on her. If she turned, she knew he would be standing by the car door, motioning her to get in.

She felt the impulse to say no to Kara. Be as brutally honest as Martin was. No, the mother cat can't fix their eyes or their sores. They will die here by this wall, either from starvation or thirst or from the infection spreading through their bodies. Their mother is long gone, probably dead on the road herself. And we are going to walk away, go swimming in the Seven Sacred Pools, and try to forget these gaping, mewling mouths. But it wasn't her children she wanted to wound.

She said, "Yes, of course she can. That's what mother cats do."

Kara crouched down by the kittens. "Bye, little kitties. I hope you feel better soon."

She and Amy got in the car.

"There's another great spot about three miles up ahead," Martin said as he drove back onto the narrow road. "Marcus says the way the morning light cuts through the shower trees is transcendent."

How was it possible, Amy wondered, *for Martin to be unaffected by the kittens?* But she knew her anger was not really directed at him. It was at herself, the docile swallower of feelings. There was a time when she would have gathered up those kittens and insisted they head back to town. Or at least she wanted to believe she had once been that woman.

"I can see why Merwin settled here," Martin said. Amy wasn't sure he was even talking to her. "The sensory stimulation is incredible. It's as if the very air is supercharged. I'm itching to get these sensations on paper."

"Those starving kittens felt like poetry to me. That's a poem that needs to be set in words."

Martin only smiled.

"What? You don't see poetry in a moment like that?" His silence infuriated her.

"I suppose. But there's a bit more to it than mere description of a moment."

"Doesn't the poet's gift rest in her recognition of what resonates? We stood at that wall with a litter of suffering kittens and you saw only the beauty of the backdrop. Their misery didn't even register with you. How is it you find poetry in that view but not in the kittens' plight?"

"Do you really want to be having this conversation? You're kind of out of your element."

"Right. What do I know about poetry."

"Come on, Amy. You're just picking a fight."

He was right.

"I think I'm going to be sick," Kara said quietly from the back seat.

"Oh God," Martin said, "Just what we need with a rental."

Amy unbuckled and leaned over the seat back. She pulled sandwiches from a plastic bag and handed the bag to Kara.

"My tummy really hurts."

"Okay, sweetie," Martin said. "I'll pull over at the next spot."

He found a shoulder wide enough for the car and Amy helped Kara climb out, then crouched beside her as she leaned into the tangle of plants. Martin grabbed a water bottle and towel and came around to Kara's other side. Though surprised, Amy was pleased he'd gotten out of the car to help. Together they held their daughter so she wasn't sick on herself, soothed her as best they could with words and a wet towel to her face, and when her stomach had calmed, settled her in the front seat, plastic bag in hand, just in case. Amy climbed into the back with Will.

Martin decided on his own not to continue to the sacred pools. Amy was grateful she hadn't had to press him on that and hoped concern for Kara drove his choice more than worry over the car. As they drove back past the scenic stop, only Amy turned to look. All she could see was the wall of lava rock and spears of red torch ginger. Nothing moved. She told herself that was okay, that was the way of nature, but she knew she would see the kittens' eyes and hear their cries when she lay down to sleep that night.

Chapter Nine

February 2002, Clifton, New Hampshire

Amy let the engine run as she waited at the base of the Fremonts' driveway. The car's thermometer put the outside temperature at three degrees. She had the heat cranked as high as it would go and was grateful she'd thought to grab her heavy parka and lined boots before heading out. She peered up the icy drive, looking for signs of a body moving her way. Lights blazed in the house and she could almost feel the vibration from the sound system blasting Jay-Z. Clearly, Kelly Fremont's parents were not home.

"Please come get me," Kara had whispered when she called, her voice small, nearly drowned out by the background music. Woken from a sound sleep, Amy had only managed to find out where she was. She wished now that she'd gotten more information while she had her on the line.

She and Martin had always told the kids, find yourself in a compromising situation, call and we'll get you. No questions asked. Kara had never taken them up on it and as far as Amy knew, this was her first call from a party. It didn't surprise Amy she'd chosen to call her and not Martin, even if she was staying at her dad's that weekend. Or maybe she had called Martin, and, as usual, been unable to reach him.

"Wait at the bottom of the drive," she told Amy. "I'll walk down." From the looks of the driveway, she'd have a long slide down to where Amy waited.

Amy pulled out her phone and texted Kara for the second time. "U okay? U coming?" At least she had cell coverage.

At what point would she have to get out of the car and climb the slick slope? As a teacher at Clifton High, she did not want to see what was going on inside or who was there. If she went in the house, she would have to act as both a responsible teacher and parent. She did not want to be in the role of calling the cops.

C'mon, Kara, move your butt. Don't do this to me. How much easier it would be if she were doing a scene like this in Hawai'i. At least she'd be warm.

She imagined Kara passed out in some room of the house, other kids stepping over her. She could be lying on her back, getting sick and choking on her own vomit. Amy checked her phone. Nothing.

"Damn it." She slapped a hand against the steering wheel and switched off the engine.

Arms out for balance, she searched for the few textured areas of snow along the driveway's edge and began a slow ascent. When her foot slipped on the ice, she considered dropping to her knees and crawling to the door. She wasn't that desperate. Not yet. She stepped farther into the snow pile, seeking traction, and her boots sank deep. Hauling one foot after another out of the ice-crusted snowbank, she inched up the drive.

She put a hand to the front door and could feel it vibrate from the music throbbing inside. No one was going to hear a knock or a doorbell. She pounded on the door. Nothing. She stood on her tiptoes and leaned from the front porch to reach a window, then rapped on the glass. She could see only the backs of teens sharing a couch. She pressed Kara's number on her cell, listened to it ring, and went back to pounding on the door. A face she didn't recognize finally appeared at one of the small glass panes framing the door and then disappeared.

Amy considered again the prospect of calling the police. She made a fist and struck the door as hard as she could. This time the door opened to reveal a red-eyed Dan Borges.

"Hey, Ms. Barnes." He leaned against the door, swaying and unfocused. Amy leaned forward to speak close to his ear.

"Can I come in, Dan?"

He looked behind him.

"Maybe not a great idea, Ms. Barnes. You looking for Kara?"

She nodded. "Would you let her know I'm here?"

Dan wedged himself in the door's opening, preventing her a view into the interior.

"Hey, anyone seen Whaley?" he yelled into the room behind him. Amy doubted anyone could hear him over the music.

The two of them stood there for a few minutes, Dan alternating between his barricade stance and consultations with others on the inside. *At least I've got a coat on,* Amy thought, looking at Dan in his bare feet and T-shirt.

"Letting lots of cold air in, Dan. Can't I wait in the entry?"

"No, that's okay. It'll only be a sec. They're bringing her."

Bringing, as in unable to walk by herself.

In her best teacher's voice, she said, "You either need to let me in now, Dan, or I'm going to have to call the police."

"Chill, Ms. Barnes, it's cool. She's just a little unsteady." Dan shifted away from the door and Amy could see Kara, her arms resting on the shoulders of two boys, her head drooping.

She looked up when Amy called out, "Kara!" but Amy couldn't tell if she was fully conscious.

"Where are her coat and boots?" she asked one of the boys.

"Here." A girl handed over Kara's outerwear.

As three of them worked to slide Kara's arms into her jacket and her feet into boots, Amy studied her pale face and glassy eyes. This was new territory for her. She couldn't tell if Kara was merely drunk and sleepy or dangerously intoxicated and in need of medical care. She calculated that if she did need more than a bed and sleep, it would still be faster to drive to the ER than wait for an ambulance to make it out on this slippery dirt road. It had taken her over half an hour to get there and sirens didn't make things any faster on ice.

"Okay, I need you guys to help me get her down the hill to my car," she directed as she held Kara tightly next to her and waited impatiently for the boys to don coats and boots. Someone shut off the music and a crowd of teens watched them maneuver Kara to the door.

Before she closed the door behind her, Amy stepped into the entry and faced the group.

"Anyone know how much Kara drank or if she's on anything else?" The kids stared at the floor. "Okay. I suggest you end this party, get rid of the booze and whatever else there is, and each of you either call someone sober to come get you or stay here and sleep it off." No one looked up. "If anybody wants to leave now, you're welcome to ride with me." Again, no eye contact, no answer. "I will be following up with Kelly's parents and the school. The party is over." She closed the door and followed the boys as they moved slowly down the hill and then laid Kara across the back seat.

"Want me to come with and sit back here with her?" a boy Amy didn't know offered.

"Yes. That would be a big help. What's your name?"

"Scooter," the boy said. "I live over in Lisbon."

"Thank you, Scooter of Lisbon." Amy fished around till she found an intact plastic bag in the back. She handed it to Scooter. "In case she gets sick."

Amy climbed in and backed the car to the road, the antilocks kicking in as soon as she touched the brakes. It was a white-knuckle drive back to town and she took it slow, terrified of sliding off the road or jostling Kara too much. Thinking she should try to keep Kara awake, she talked nonstop, trying to engage her and Scooter. Kara showed no indication she heard her. "Check her pulse," she told Scooter.

"I think she's just a little woozy," he said. "It's not like she's in any danger of dying."

"And what would you know about that?" Amy snapped at the boy. "How old are you? Fifteen? Sixteen? You have a vast experience with inebriated girls?" She glared at him through the rearview mirror.

"No." He sounded close to tears. "She just isn't like that. She doesn't party like the other kids. All I ever saw her drinking tonight was a Coke."

So maybe someone had slipped something in her drink. Maybe that's why Kara had been whispering for help on the phone. She knew something wasn't right.

Amy hadn't realized how tightly she was holding the steering wheel, how intensely she'd been staring ahead at the frozen dirt road, until the glow of Clifton appeared over the trees ahead and she reached asphalt. She leaned back in her seat and stretched her spine. *Could still be black ice,* she reminded herself, *keep it slow.*

Another five minutes and she'd have to decide—head for the hospital or the house? She could call Martin, see what he thought she should do. But she knew he would say take her home, she'll be fine. No way Martin would want her involving the authorities. She knew that taking Kara to the hospital would mean questions, maybe even charges against Kara if she had been drinking, charges against the other kids and even the Fremonts, certainly questions about why she, a Clifton teacher, had not called the police immediately. She felt a wave of paralyzing anxiety. This was all too much to manage solo.

Deep breaths, she told herself, and inhaled and exhaled deeply and slowly.

You can do this. You do not need Martin or anyone else to tell you what to do. All that matters right now is making sure Kara is okay.

At the intersection in the town's center, she turned left and headed to the hospital.

February 2002, Lisbon, Vermont

"Come on, it'll be fun."

Right, Paul thought. *Fun the way bad TV comedies are fun—somebody always ends up painfully embarrassed.* There was no way going out on a blind date set up by Gordon was going to be anything but messy.

"Seriously, man, you gotta loosen up. Get a life. It's not like you've got all that much time left, you know? I'm handing you the chance to get laid tonight. How long's it been since Sarah died? Six months? You gotta be horny as hell."

Paul crossed his arms and stared at him.

"Don't give me that look. I'm doing you a favor here."

Gordon hung on to the door of his Tundra and made no move to climb back in. Why the hell did he want Paul to come along anyway? There had to be a dozen other guys he worked with who'd jump at the chance. Knowing Gordon, they weren't talking about two aging church ladies. These were sure to be women who would pass for hot in a dimly lit bar. He knew Gordon meant well, but he wanted no part of this.

"I appreciate it, Gord. Really. I know you're being a friend, but that's not what I'm looking for."

"What aren't you looking for? A woman? You gone queer on me or something?"

Paul sighed. Why did Gordon always have to push him to the point where he wanted to put a fist in his face?

"Seriously? You can't imagine any other reason why I might not want to hook up with some woman I've never met?"

Gordon stared at him as if he were crazy. "No, I sure as fucking hell can't.

And there was a time, buddy, when you would have felt the same."

"That's the thing, Gordon. I was never that guy. You just assume everyone's like you."

Gordon jumped back into the cab, still nimble. All that boozing and chasing tail and he still moved and looked like a man in his thirties. The perpetual boy, Sarah had called him.

Gordon stuck his head out the truck window.

"I won't be making you an offer like this again, you know."

"Fair enough."

Gordon pulled out of the drive with a squeal of his tires.

"What did he want?" Chris asked, emerging from the barn.

"Help entertaining two ladies tonight."

"You going?"

Paul gave his son the look he'd given Gordon earlier.

"You might have a good time, you know."

"Yup. And someone might give me a million dollars today."

They headed across the main road to the dairy barn operation to help with cleanup.

"I know it's tough with Mom gone and I miss her too, but I kind of envy you your freedom, you know?" Chris stopped at the dairy barn door. Paul could see this was about more than whether he should go out on a date.

"What's up?" Paul studied his son's face. He could see the fatigue, heard enough of the yelling even from across the fields to know Chris and Emily were in a rough patch.

"Did you ever want to leave? Just get in your truck and drive until you can't go any farther? Be alone with no one to think about but yourself?"

Paul could see Chris was serious.

"Of course. I'm sure your mom had those moments, too. I expect every parent and spouse has times when they think they can't do it anymore. Hell, you don't have to be married with kids to feel that way. There are always going to be people aggravating you, causing you stress. I'm not sure that's a bad thing."

Chris stared at Paul as if he were nuts.

"It's good to spend your life angry and frustrated?"

"I didn't say that. I'm saying that hard as it is to put up with one another, we need other people in our lives. There's no going it alone. And if you've any hope of being a decent human being, you're going to have to learn to make space for what other folks need. I'd be a sorry excuse for a man if I hadn't learned all I did from living with your mom. I've probably learned something from every person who's been part of my life, even the idiots and jerks who showed me how not to be." Paul could see Chris had tuned him out. "What is it you want that you don't have the freedom to do now?"

"I'm so buried, I don't even know, Dad. I just want out. I'm suffocating."

Chris looked defeated, as if even a smile required more effort than he could ever manage. Paul wondered if too much was broken between him and Emily. At least he and Sarah had always shared a mutual respect and affection that carried them through their tough times.

"How about I watch the kids this weekend? You and Em go spend a night in Burlington, my treat. Maddie can give me a hand if Emily thinks the kids would be too much for me alone."

"Thanks, but leave the two of us alone together and you'd probably end up having to raise our orphaned kids."

Paul couldn't remember a time when he had ever felt that kind of bitterness.

"I just want to sip a beer, watch a football game, hell, take a piss, without someone yapping at me for something. It's always 'give Elsbeth a bottle, read Cooper a story, bathe the kids.' I'm sick of it."

"But those are the good parts of parenting," Paul said, genuinely confused by Chris's grievances.

He ran a hand across his face, mystified by this version of his son. What had happened to the boy who'd somersaulted with such joy at the circus and led his baseball team to a state championship? Where was the kid who'd stayed close at hand after Sarah's chemo sessions, bringing her tea and orange slices, massaging her hands and feet, so she was never alone during the worst of the discomfort?

"Tell me what you need," he said, "and you've got it. I can help with the kids, do the milking solo, make grocery runs."

"I get it, I get it," Chris yelled, focusing his anger on Paul. "You're the best. Everybody's hero. Superman Paul Rideau can change a diaper while plowing a field. Well, good for you, Dad. Unfortunately, I'm not you. I'm the jerk who says to hell with it all."

He paced in a circle around the dirt yard, like a bull working itself into a rage.

"I can't do this anymore," he finally said and jogged back across the road. He climbed into his truck and tore off in a cloud of dust.

Paul gathered himself up and headed into the barn. The barn manager would be needing a hand with the last of the day's tasks.

February 2002, Clifton, New Hampshire

"It's lovely." Amy lifted the bracelet from its box and undid the clasp. She handed it to Kara. "Mind putting it on for me?"

The silver bracelet with its tiny heart charm was better suited to a girl of fourteen than a middle-aged woman, but Amy didn't care. She was touched by the efforts the kids were making to celebrate Valentine's Day with her. She highly doubted Martin had any hand in arranging the gift or suggesting the kids propose dinner out given how angry he still was over her refusal to vacate the house before July.

"You guys were super thoughtful to think of me today," Amy said.

Will shrugged his shoulders. "Sharon said we should get you something, that you'd probably be feeling bad about being alone and all that, so she took us down to Penny's."

"Will"—Kara elbowed him—"you can be such a jerk."

"What? It's true."

Of course. Sharon. The ever-thoughtful homewrecker who possessed a remarkable skill for winning the kids over to her side. Who could speak ill of a woman who made sure the ex was remembered on Valentine's Day?

"It's fine," Amy said. "It's a thoughtful gesture, no matter its source, and I appreciate it. Most of all, I'm glad to be with both of you." She opened her menu. "So what are you thinking you'll get? I don't know whether to just get a brownie sundae and call it dinner or go all out with fish and chips, too." She was pleased by how steady her voice was, how calm her composure.

A child shrieked in the booth behind her.

"Oh my goodness, Gramps. That is the most splendid sundae I ever saw."

Kara and Amy exchanged smiles.

"Well, I would hope so," a male voice answered. "A splendid granddaughter deserves a splendid sundae on Valentine's Day. But remember, my love, use your indoor voice, please."

"Sorry, Gramps. You must be extra sad today without Gram on Valentine's. You suppose she's watching us from heaven?"

"I'm sure she is, sweetheart. Now what do you say we tie this cloth around your neck? Your mom won't want you staining that pretty pink dress."

Amy placed a hand on her heart and Kara nodded her agreement. Will rolled his eyes and shook his head.

"I'm going to have a burger and fries," he said, and tucked his menu behind the napkin dispenser.

"I'm going to be good and have the Caesar salad with chicken," Kara said. "Sharon says carbs are super bad for you and I should stick to proteins and veggies."

Don't say anything, don't say anything, don't say anything. Kara weighed all of 115 pounds and was five six. Why the hell was Sharon talking diets to her? Amy smiled as best she could.

"Any word yet on what you might do for winter break?" Since the kids were going with Amy to Hawai'i over spring vacation, the plan was for them to be with Martin during their February holiday.

"Dad said it looks like he'll be really busy that week so maybe we should just stay with you," Will said. "He said it's easier if you take us skiing since you have time off, too."

Right, and that way he won't have to pay for lift tickets. Let me be the one shelling out for the kids' fun. What if I had my own plans for the week? Had he even considered that possibility?

Amy realized both kids were looking at her. Waiting. Were they waiting for her to blow up in anger or just hoping she'd seize the chance to be the good parent and promise them a week on the slopes?

"Obviously, I'm thrilled you'll be with me that week, and we'll have fun. I promise. Maybe a trip to the Boston Museum of Science?"

"Maybe skiing?" Will countered. "We don't have to go to the big resorts. Local's fine."

"Sure. Of course, you can have some ski time. It's just that the lift costs add up no matter where you go. I can't swing being on the slopes every day."

So much for the idea of weeding through the closets and basement or finalizing the kids' application packets for McNeil.

"Maybe we can really go wild and do some movie nights—candy, popcorn, the whole works," she added.

"Uh, hello, Mom, we're not exactly eight-years-old anymore." Will gave her one of those I-can't-believe-you-are-so-stupid stares she despised.

Moving to Hawai'i with kids in tow would mean at least four more years of being an essentially single mom with Martin seeing the kids only for vacation stretches. *I'll be the one getting all the attitude.* Better that, she reminded herself, than the unpredictability of the current arrangement. Besides, she was surviving Kara's attitude years. Will would outgrow this phase soon enough.

"Gotcha," she managed to say in what she thought was a fairly neutral tone. She smiled at the approaching waitress.

"You guys ready to order?" The waitress clicked her pen.

As the kids ordered, Amy tuned in to the grandfather and little girl talking in the booth behind her.

"You done, puddin'?"

"Uh-huh."

"So shall we head on home? I expect your mom and dad will be happy to see you."

"Can't I spend the night at your house? Morgan gets to sleep at Grannie and Grandpa's."

"That's because Morgan doesn't have to go to school in the morning."

The girl sighed deeply. "Getting old isn't much fun."

"I know, love, I know."

"And what can I get for you?" the waitress asked Amy.

"Fish and chips, please."

"What about your sundae?" Kara asked.

"I'm not ruling it out. We'll see if that still sounds good after all those fries."

She resisted the impulse to turn around and watch her dining neighbors depart. She leaned forward and whispered to Kara, "So is the pink dress as perfect as I'm imagining?"

"Oh yeah," Kara said. "Party shoes to match."

February 2002, Clifton, New Hampshire

For the most part, she had stuck to her shopping list—carrots, celery, onions, and chicken breasts for a pot of soup, a loaf of multigrain bread, salad fixings, and laundry detergent—but she couldn't resist adding a giant chocolate cupcake to the cart along with a split of champagne. It wasn't every day she ended a marriage. No harm in a little celebration even if she didn't feel anything close to jubilation. The kids were with Martin for the weekend and she needed to do something to mark the moment. At least it wasn't a weeknight. She wondered if the lawyers had deliberately scheduled the signing of the divorce papers for late on a Friday. Did they know to spare the client a day of work after what she supposed was often a night of excess? Delightful celebration for some, miserable wallowing for others.

Despite her deliberate effort to see no one and avoid eye contact, her progress through the small store was slow. It was, after all, nearly six on a Friday evening. Students, past and present, called out some version of "Hey, Ms. Barnes." Acquaintances smiled with what she read as pity in their eyes. She was sure everyone knew Martin had dumped her. She did her best to nod, smile, and keep moving. She could handle the kids and people she knew superficially. She dreaded running into a sympathetic friend, certain she would dissolve into tears at the first comforting word.

She chatted up Lorraine, her favorite cashier, and packed her groceries in the totes she'd brought.

"Nasty nor'easter coming in tomorrow. Do you have to work?"

"Thank the Lord, not this time," Lorraine said, handing her the sales slip.

"That's a relief." Amy knew Lorraine's long early-morning commute could be treacherous on wintery mornings, especially if the roads weren't yet plowed and sanded when she set out. "Let's hope it's not a bad one."

The groceries stowed in the back seat, Amy headed for the gas station beside the store. The tank was still half full, but with a storm in the offing, she was taking no chances. As she waited for the pump to finish, she did a mental inventory of her weekend's to-do list. Swing by the bank ATM for some cash. Pick up the dry cleaning. Grade the essays from her AP American Lit students.

Her cell phone buzzed. It was Will.

"I thought we were supposed to stay with Dad this weekend."

"That's the plan. Your dad was going to swing by the house to pick you up after we finished with the lawyers. He should have gotten there by now."

"Well, he hasn't shown up yet."

"And you've tried his cell?"

"Yup. No answer."

Damn, damn, damn. She wanted to scream. She'd have bashed her phone on the asphalt if she had money enough to replace it.

"I'm gassing up the car and will be home in a minute. I'll try to track him down when I get there. He probably stopped by his office and got distracted."

"Typical," Will said.

The pump nozzle clicked and the pump stopped. She shoved her phone back in her bag and climbed into the driver's seat, muttering. So was this how it was going to be? Now that he had the divorce he wanted, was Martin going to start reneging on his promises to the kids and screw with her weekend plans?

She started the engine. So much for a quiet celebration alone. As she started to pull forward, she met resistance. Great. All she needed was for the car to start acting up. She gave it a bit more gas and there was a snap, then the resistance dissolved. A loud clanging followed and a whoosh like the sound of a gushing faucet. She stopped the car and looked back. The gas hose had separated from the nozzle, which, she could see through her side mirror, was still attached to her car. A fountain of gasoline showered down upon the cars and people under the gas station canopy.

The day's destruction was complete.

March 2002, Lisbon, Vermont

Paul clipped the ends of the roses and stuck the blossoms in the tall vase he'd found at the back of a cupboard. He'd already laid out Sarah's good linen cloth on his mother's mahogany dining table and set two places with the good china and silver. He even brought out the crystal wineglasses from the china buffet for the merlot Maddie had suggested he buy.

The pork loin was in the oven. He'd already roasted vegetables he would rewarm and one of Maddie's chocolate cakes sat on a fancy glass tray in the pantry. He tossed another log on the fire, loaded the CD player, and after surveying the living room one last time, headed upstairs to shower and change.

"Acting like a stupid teenager," he grumbled to himself as he stared into the oval mirror over the bathroom sink. "Sure as hell don't look like one."

He studied the weathered face before him, ran a hand over his beard stubble. He'd have to shave again after his shower. What a bother this was, getting all worked up over dinner with a woman.

"At least it proves you're still alive," he told his reflection, and headed into the shower.

"Nina Simone," Janelle said as Paul took her coat. "I like your taste in music."

She unzipped her boots and slipped her feet into the wool clogs she'd brought with her. She also pulled a six-pack of Long Trail Double Bag from her canvas tote.

"A little something for you."

Paul was pleased she'd brought beer rather than wine. He was reminded of what he'd liked about her from the very first studio session—she had no pretensions. She wasn't one of those women who'd lecture him on the merits of different wine labels or worry over whether he was eating too much beef.

"I'll stick these in the fridge. Would you like one, or would you rather have wine? I've got a bottle of merlot." Paul was pleased with how at ease he sounded, as if he entertained women for dinner all the time.

"A beer sounds great. Anything I can help with?"

Paul shook his head. "Dinner's cooking itself for now. Make yourself comfortable in the living room and I'll be right back."

"Bottle's fine," Janelle called after him. "No need for a glass."

This may work out, Paul thought, as he popped the tops off two Long Trails. He grabbed the necks with one hand, gathered up the platter of crackers and cheese he'd laid out earlier, and headed back to the living room. He paused at the entry when he saw Janelle was sitting in Sarah's chair. *Let it go,* he told himself. It was time to move on.

"Something tells me that one's your chair," Janelle said, gesturing at the worn leather chair opposite hers. "It looks well loved."

He nodded and set down the beers and platter, not trusting his voice.

She gestured at the photographs lined up along the mantle. "So fill me in. I think I have a pretty good idea who's who from what you've told me, but I want to get it right."

Introducing his past and family to Janelle proved easy. She listened without interrupting him, asked enough questions to suggest she was paying attention without being nosy, and she softened before the picture of Sarah taken a few months before her death.

"She was lovely and she looks so happy" was all Janelle said. Paul hadn't realized he was holding his breath.

"Yes. On both counts, I think." He stirred the fire, added a log. "So do you have any pictures of your clan?"

"No, unfortunately. I need to update my wallet supply."

Janelle had mentioned a former husband, but said nothing of kids. At thirty-two she was still young enough to start a family. Maybe even wanted all of that. *You're a damned old fool,* he told himself. *Lusting after a woman too young for you, as if you'd be willing to do it all over again.*

"If there's time before dinner, I'd love to see your artwork. Or would you rather save that for later?"

This was ostensibly why they were dining together, so Paul could show her his work. Besides running the studio sessions, she was the exhibition coordinator for a gallery in Clifton. At her request the week before, Paul had shown her photos of his work after the evening's studio session. Emboldened by her reaction, Paul invited her to his place, an offer she'd accepted with enough enthusiasm to make him think she, too, was interested in more than planning an exhibit.

Paul began with the living room, led Janelle through the dining room and kitchen, which also boasted his paintings and mixed-media works. She loved it all—lingered before the individual pieces, recognized the influences, and delighted in his departures from them. He hesitated when they reached the front door. Most of his work was in the barn.

"You sure you want to brave the cold before eating? It's got to be in the teens out there."

She wrapped her shawl more tightly around herself.

"I could go with eating rather than freezing this second. But I do want to see what you've got hidden away. I've seen enough just in here to warrant a show."

Paul grinned. "You making me an offer?"

"Why yes, Mr. Rideau, I think I am." She said it playfully, with just the right smile for Paul to read a subtext in her words. "I'll have to talk it over with the rest of the staff, but I expect we will be exhibiting your work. Maybe even later this spring if you think you can manage it?"

"Works for me." He took her elbow in his hand and led her to the dining table. "Now how about I serve up that tenderloin."

Janelle insisted on helping with the cleanup after dinner and tossed a dish towel on her shoulder.

"You a dryer or a washer?" she asked.

"Washer. Definitely a washer."

"Good, because I'm a dryer." She gathered up another dish towel, and Paul filled the sink with hot water. "Those are the kinds of preferences people need to figure out before committing," she continued, leaning back against the counter, waiting for Paul to drop a clean dish in the drainer.

Paul grinned. She did like him.

"My new partner and I failed to cover that terrain before she moved in last week," Janelle continued. "Turns out we're a pair of dryers. Neither of us wants dishpan hands. Fortunately, she has other qualities that compensate for that single failing."

Paul tried to sustain his smile, hold on to the lighthearted tone of the evening, but he felt as if he'd taken a body blow, all the worse for it not being intended. How had he been so obtuse? Clearly, to Janelle he was merely an artist she admired. This was a business meeting, not a date. Probably never crossed her mind that a guy so much older would mistake her kindness for romantic interest.

"If she's a good woman, you'll want to hang on to her," he managed to say, elbow deep in hot water. "Even if she's a bad match at the sink."

Janelle took the dish and ran the towel over it. "Yeah. She's definitely a good woman. And there aren't many of them around."

Tell me about it. Paul smiled and passed her another plate.

March 2002, Clifton, New Hampshire

Amy and Kathy surveyed the pub's private dining room, now arranged into something resembling a classroom. Three rows of tables and chairs faced a large whiteboard.

"We better grab our seats or we'll end up in the front row." Kathy led the way to the two second-row spots most accessible to the waitstaff.

Amy draped her jacket over her chairback, set out a notebook and pen, then looked around for a waiter. Kathy had already made eye contact with a woman in black who was weaving her way to them.

"I'll take the house merlot and an order of fries," Kathy said.

Amy added, "And a pint of Guinness for me with sweet potato fries, please."

A striking woman in knee-high boots, skin-tight jeans, and a snug turtleneck strode to the front. She tossed a messenger bag on the table then perched beside it, beaming as she pulled back her thick mass of blond curls. In one smooth, graceful motion, she twisted and secured it in place with a jaw clip.

"The things you get me to do," Amy sighed. This was not feeling like a boost to her self-esteem.

"Would you rather we come drinking here some Saturday night instead? We could sit on the sidelines and watch the young babes get hit on."

"That would be a firm no. This is definitely better than that version of hell."

"Ignore what she looks like and the fact that she's probably also a brilliant writer and teacher. We're here to drink and do something we like. Remember, we like writing poetry."

"But do we? It's been close to ten years since I've written anything."

Kathy grunted. "So don't think about the writing, think about the deeply wise and sensitive poet you might meet tonight."

Amy laughed. "Promise you'll shoot me if I so much as glance at any man in this room. No poets for me."

Their drinks and fries arrived with a generous stack of napkins.

Amy took a swig of her Guinness. "I have to say, you do keep me from dying of boredom. Of course, I may die of embarrassment instead."

The woman at the front appeared completely at ease, smiling at people entering, chatting up those closest to her. She exuded the kind of exaggerated enthusiasm that workshop leaders need if they are to win over a group of nervous strangers. Amy thought it a rather brilliant idea to add liquor to the mix.

"If everyone can find a seat, we'll get started." The room quieted. "I'm Melinda, and welcome to tonight's Poetry in a Pub event, where we will challenge the notion that writing has to be a miserable, lonely pursuit. I promise we're going to have some fun and give our creative muscles a good workout."

"Oh God, she's a cheerleader," Amy whispered.

"Be still, nobody likes a class mutterer," Kathy whispered back.

Why was it that the people who taught these one-shot workshops were so often stunning, hip, and infuriatingly charismatic. Never in her life could Amy have worn a pair of jeans as tight as Melinda's. Even the woman's jewelry hit the perfect note, minimal and yet extravagant enough in scale—*Just how heavy are hoops as big as those?* Amy wondered—to signal she knew the trends and was comfortable calling attention to herself. Amy's single goal in public settings was to go unnoticed at all times.

"First off," Melinda began, "I want to assure you that your level of participation tonight is completely up to you. Write if you want to, share if you want to, or just observe. No pressure. This is all about what serves you. And, of course, you can nibble and sip as much as you want while we play." She grinned and repeated, "Nibble," this time with a heavy dose of sultry in her delivery. "That sounds a bit naughty, doesn't it? I do love a good verb."

Shoot me now, Amy wrote on a napkin.

Behave, Kathy wrote back.

"So does everyone have a notebook? Pen? I've some paper and pencils up here if you need any. Good. Well, let's get started." She wrote MEMORIES all in caps on the board. "We're going to start off with a quick freewrite exercise. Everyone familiar with the term 'freewrite'? Anyone care to define it?"

Someone called out, "When you keep writing without rereading or judging what's on the page and you can't lift your pencil off the paper."

"Right! Thanks. For a few minutes, I want each of you to write down as many specific memories as you can. Write just enough to cue you in to what moment you mean. For example, you could write down things like 'my first kiss, the day my dog died, shoplifting gum at Woolworth's, first time skydiving.' Don't worry yet about the details, just list as many unique events as you can think of. Everyone got it? Okay, when I say begin, you start listing them and don't take your pencil off the paper. If you can't think of something just write blah-blah-blah until an idea comes. I'm going to write my own list up here on the board, and I'll set a timer for three minutes. You can BEGIN."

"Day Kara got drugged at a party, getting lost at Ala Moana, throwing up on the Ferris wheel, meeting Martin, giving birth to Kara, picnic in Golden Gate Park." Amy kept going, even as her fingers began cramping. She glanced over at Kathy whose paper had one brief phrase on it and whose pen hovered above the page. Kathy rolled her eyes and shook her head. Amy went back to her own list, started a second column.

"Time!" Melinda called. "Finish the thought you're on, then pencils and pens down."

"I'm so bad at this," Kathy groaned. "I've got like five total. And look at you." She gestured at Amy's sheet.

"Doesn't matter so long as you've got one good one on the list."

Next they selected the moment that felt most resonant, then circled or underlined it. Amy chose the memory of watching Aunt Sally put on makeup the Christmas she was with them in Connecticut.

"For this next step, I want you to record sensory details." Melinda erased her list of memories and wrote the one she chose at the top of the board, then made a list of categories: SMELLS, SOUNDS, SIGHTS, TOUCH, TASTE, FEELINGS. "You don't have to include all of these categories, but try to remember as best you can what it was you could see, what you heard—including noises in the background—what you felt on your skin, what you felt emotionally, what you smelled or tasted." She explained how the more particular the detail was, the better it was. Not just a hairbrush, but the blond strands tangled in the brush. Not just the taste of tomato in a sauce, but the flavors laced with it—the garlic and the onion, the anchovy and the basil. "Do this for as many categories as you can. I'll give you fifteen minutes for this part."

Amy could feel the movement of Kathy's pen on the page, the jiggle of her elbow on the table, hoped the ideas were coming more easily for her now. As cramped as her own hand was, it kept moving down the page, the details pouring through her so quickly, they were nearly illegible. After ten minutes, she paused and shook out the fingers of her right hand, ate a few fries and downed some beer, then got back to it, remembering the soles of Sally's feet, the dark patina of dirt on them, the way her ankles crossed beneath her chair, her heels cracked and nearly gray, the chipped red polish on her toenails, the way she stretched her eyelids as she blackened first one and then the other.

I'm having fun, she realized, recognizing that she was in that sweet space, a space she remembered from the years before she met Martin, the days when she wrote often and with joy. She'd forgotten how glorious it felt to be in a state where time and place evaporated and there was only the pen flying across the paper, only resonant images vibrating on the page. This was what she craved. This was what she needed.

Chapter Ten

March 2002, Clifton, New Hampshire

Amy woke gasping, her heart galloping. Someone was banging on the door at 3 a.m. She grabbed her robe. This had to be something horrible. The kids were spending the weekend with Martin. They or Martin would have called if it were a low-stakes emergency—kid has a fever, kid's panicked about an assignment, kid's late coming home. What would be so urgent that someone had to come to the house instead of calling? She slowed her pace on the stairs. Wouldn't do anyone any good if she fell and broke her neck.

She switched on the front entry and outside lights, then peered through the front door's side glass. She couldn't see anyone. The banging began again, but it was coming from the kitchen door. She hated being alone in the house. If Martin and the kids were there, she wouldn't have been half so panicked, wouldn't be afraid about who or what stood outside her house. But she was alone, and she wasn't about to unlock her door without knowing what was on the other side.

She lifted the shade covering the door's glass top and braced herself. There was no one. Nothing except the storm door swinging back and forth, smacking the doorframe. Hail bounced off the driveway and against the windows. Small branches cluttered the lawn. It was only a nasty night, a typical night for March, and yet here she was, her heart pounding, assuming the worst was at hand.

She caught the storm door, latched it firmly, and shut off the outside lights. Her pulse still raced. There'd be no going back to sleep anytime soon.

Three on a Saturday morning was too late for alcohol. Better to have tea or a glass of milk. She dropped two pieces of bread in the toaster and got out the butter and cinnamon sugar. She reconsidered her drink assessment and poured a small glass of sherry. Her pulse had slowed but now it was her mind that raced. The early-morning curse of midlife, when a day's stressors and dilemmas overwhelmed the mind and derailed sleep. Only one thing could calm her monkey mind state—writing it all down. Sometimes shedding the thoughts helped calm the brain.

She made her columns of pros and cons. One set for the option of staying in Clifton and carrying on with life as it was. One for the option of moving to Hawai'i and teaching at Pumehana, assuming that she was right to be encouraged by the letter she'd gotten offering her an interview during spring break. The third option was to move to Hawai'i but instead of teaching, learn how to manage the family properties—and "take some time to consider what you most truly want to do," as Aunt Gretchen had put it, with this next chapter of her life.

Option one was easy to eliminate. She couldn't afford a home in Clifton and she itched to get away and start over. And yet. She had to be sure she'd weighed carefully what was best for the kids. They had both said they welcomed a move to Hawai'i and both had been accepted by McNeil Academy, but it would mean separating them from lifetime friends, their father, and a whole way of life. Could they really grasp the decision they were making? Martin was so focused on his new love that, as Kara put it, "He can't even pretend he wants us around." All the same, was it ultimately in the kids' best interest to have some contact with him, no matter what he or they thought they wanted?

Option two was simple and the most comfortable—return to her old job at a school she loved. The option that scared her most was taking on the role of managing the family properties. Gretchen would teach her, but it would be a huge challenge. She would feel stupid and awkward and afraid at the beginning. *But I can learn and it's work that matters,* she told herself. The family needed someone to be the next steward. Pumehana had no shortage of other qualified teachers knocking at its doors. The other compelling argument for working with her aunt was that it would leave her time to write. With no papers to grade or curriculum to create, she would have time to stretch her own writing skills.

She listed every argument she could think of for and against each choice, then wrote herself a long list of all the tasks she should do the next day no matter what she decided. As she nailed her thoughts to the page, she felt her tension ease. These were doable tasks. She did not need to worry about the day or the week or even the months ahead. At the start of each day, she needed to create a list, and by the end of each day, have a checked list. And so it would go, day by day, as she did what each day required of her.

April 2002, Clifton, New Hampshire

Paul sat in the cab of his Ford, a block from the gallery, and surveyed the people streaming toward the gallery's front door. A long line of parked cars had formed behind his truck. A silver-haired woman in a flowing batik skirt paused beside the truck, waiting for a man hurrying down the sidewalk. When he reached her, she tugged playfully on his ponytail, then standing on tiptoe, pulled his face down so she could reach his lips. Paul looked away, puzzled by how much it still stung to see happy couples.

Probably going to be a whole room full of rich Clifton white hairs in there, all of them sipping chardonnay and trying to be witty. No way he wanted to be anywhere near this crowd.

"Get your sorry ass out of that truck!" Matt Harrison, Paul's baseball team buddy who'd handled with grace his role as the coach's son, knocked on Paul's window. "The party's inside."

Paul cocked his head at Matt.

"I don't know, Matt," he started to say.

Matt opened the truck's door. "Quick, while there's a break in the traffic."

Paul climbed out. He felt ridiculous trailing after Matt, who was, of course, impeccably dressed in linen slacks and some kind of silky shirt. Matt had fit in okay back in school, but now, like his father, he dressed like a guy from the city. *No one's doubting I'm right off the farm.* At least his wrinkled button-down shirt had a collar and he'd rinsed off his boots.

Matt put a hand to Paul's shoulder. "I know this isn't your kind of thing, but trust me, you'll do fine. They're crazy about your work. Just smile and nod. They love anyone who reeks of authenticity."

Paul followed him to the main entrance, where clusters of people, plastic cups in hand, chatted on the stone terrace. Paul and Matt passed through the huge glass doors propped open on the warm spring night.

The gallery itself was packed tight with people. Matt pressed forward, but Paul hung back, uncomfortable about pushing against the people in his way. He stood landlocked between a huge woman in a brilliant cobalt caftan and a young man in a thin white T-shirt and snug red jeans. Neither sensed Paul beside them. Neither moved. Matt smirked at Paul, his arms crossed in affected annoyance, silently daring Paul to push through to the other side.

"Pretend they're cows," Matt said when Paul finally joined him at a banquet table where a young woman poured warm chardonnay into cups.

"At least I know how to act around cows. I've never even been to one of these things before."

His first visit to the gallery was to discuss the exhibit, his second was to drop off his work. He hadn't even been sure he wanted to have his work in a show. When Janelle confirmed the gallery wanted to exhibit his paintings, Paul called Matt, the only friend he could think of who might know something about what an art show required and whether Paul would be risking humiliation. Matt had shown up at the farm the next day.

"I'm not ready for this," Paul had told him. "My work's too raw. I'm just setting myself up to be ridiculed. Besides, I don't paint for others. I paint for myself."

"Bullshit," was all Matt said. He then wandered slowly around the barn, studying Paul's work.

He pointed to an immense canvas of swirling colors onto which Paul had glued soda bottle caps in intricate patterns that transformed the work into something exquisite. "Include that one." Paul wasn't sure Janelle would appreciate someone else curating the submissions, but he set aside the pieces Matt singled out and, in the end, most were selected by Janelle and a committee of artists and art educators.

Paul sipped from his cup of wine as he followed Matt into the gallery's main room. Maybe a little alcohol would help steady his nerves. Thank God he hadn't told anyone about the show, let alone the opening event, not even his kids. He could only imagine the disbelief and ribbing that would have followed. He considered telling Maddie, knew she would wish him well, and half wished she was there with him now as an anchor, but he suspected she might be as terrified and overwhelmed as he felt. She might once have been able to read her own poem before a large audience in Clifton, but that confident young lady had learned she was an outsider in these circles.

He spotted Janelle across the room, but it was a whole new version of her. With makeup on and her hair tamed into a neat bun, she looked more New York runway model than Vermont artist. Her black dress was simple and very short. She balanced on heels taller and spikier than any Paul had seen before. The effect was knee buckling.

Matt grabbed Paul by the elbow and guided him to a tall, slender man with an immense mane of white hair brushed back from his forehead. "Franklin, I'd like you to meet Paul Rideau."

"The man of the hour," Franklin said, shaking Paul's hand vigorously and clamping his left hand on Paul's shoulder. "You've got everyone talking. Come—I want you to meet Sheila Meyerson who has a major gallery in New York."

Paul turned back and caught Matt's eye, hoping his face conveyed his panic and plea for rescue. Matt simply saluted. No way Matt would be helping him now. This was precisely what Matt had hoped to help orchestrate—the launching of Paul into the art world.

"Take a look," Franklin said and gestured over the heads of the crowd surrounding them to a painting prominently displayed on the gallery's main wall. A huge red circle sat on the card beside it. "Sheila has already purchased that one for her house in the Hamptons," Franklin trumpeted. People near them turned, curious. "Sheila doesn't usually buy work. She sells it. That she wanted to own one of yours is affirmation, my friend. You are on your way."

"Sheila, Sheila," Franklin roared even louder to the woman in the blue caftan. "This is the artist—Paul Rideau."

The gallery had quieted. All he could think was *What would Sarah say to all this?* and then there was no space to think of Sarah or anything of his familiar world. There was only an unending blur of extended hands, pats on the back, faces too close, breath stale and hot, name after name after name being shared. By evening's end, eight works had sold for a take hovering at ten thousand dollars and Janelle's assurance that more would follow. He was a star.

You can do it, Amy told Jacob silently. The paper in his hand shook. He didn't raise his eyes.

For three months she had sat across a table from him in the evening poetry class. He was there to escape English at his high school. She signed up to see if she could begin again in earnest. Get serious about writing.

Shut out Martin's voice, she told herself as she shifted in her seat. *Listen to the poems.* But fear distracted her.

Tonight she and her five classmates were taking the step of reading their poems aloud to an audience of friends, relations, and a few strangers who had wandered into the art gallery, probably drawn by the possibility of free wine and cheese. They sat on uncomfortable folding chairs in the room's center, artwork all around them. Distracting artwork. Amy's eyes kept wandering to the huge canvases spray-painted with neon-bright colors and spackled with something textured, the effect much like the spidery patterns on raku fired pots. Things like gum wrappers and wrapping paper, ribbons and beads had been stuck onto the canvases. They were the work of some local farmer.

She directed her attention back to Jacob, now on his third poem. For someone who didn't want to do this, he was holding his own. Extra points, their instructor had told the high school kids in the class, if you read more than one poem.

She looked down at her feet pinched into uncomfortable black heels, uncrossed her legs to keep them from going numb. Had she turned off the iron in her bedroom? She studied the acne scars running down Jacob's neck. Brushing lint off her black rayon slacks, she thought again that she should have gone with the jeans. Never mind what Kara thought. Kara liked wearing high heels and anything that sparkled, but it wasn't Amy's style.

She caught Jacob's eye and gave him a thumbs-up as he headed back to his seat.

Java, a self-named young woman with hair to her waist wearing an oversized flannel shirt and black combat boots, planted herself at the front, crumpled paper in hand, everything about her defiant. Amy wondered if

Java had any idea how striking she was, how much Amy envied the ease with which she moved and spoke, her refusal to be invisible.

Some days, Amy half believed she looked okay for a woman closing in on fifty. Men's eyes might not linger anymore, but she could squeeze into a size ten, sometimes even an eight, and kept her graying hair styled in a short, edgy cut. She slathered moisturizer on her face before bed, wore sunscreen and lip gloss during the day, and never wore sweatpants or leggings in public. All the same, she knew she was invisible to most people. No one would be admiring her short legs or sagging chin when it came time for her to read.

She thought of Martin's fiancée Sharon, who wasn't much older than Java. Sharon definitely knew her worth. She didn't even feel the need to paint her hair neon colors or punch holes in her face, daring the world to pay her some attention. She knew they were already looking.

Stop it, Amy told herself. *Let it go.* Sharon was not to blame for Amy's unhappiness. *Focus your anger where it belongs.* As her therapist had taught her, she imagined her anger at Martin as small, compact balls she hurled one by one with all her force.

She smiled up at Java who was nearly shouting her words into the small space. *I see you. I hear you,* she tried to tell her with her steady gaze.

When Amy's turn came to read, she rose slowly and carefully, anticipating the twinge of her arthritic left hip and hoping no one else would notice the way it made her leg collapse a bit when she stood. She hobbled to the front, shaky in the heels, uncomfortable in the poorly fitted blouse she'd bought for its brilliant purple color. She tried to remember to pause, smile, look out at the audience before beginning. All the tips she fed her students. She began.

"'Shades of Black and Blue'"

She had read this aloud before to the class, but when she did, she had also shown them the three photos that informed it. She had merely been describing magazine pictures she'd used as prompts. Without that context, her words acquired an edge, a personal intensity.

The wind blows right into
empty rooms seen
through tiny windows.
Grass bends, clouds fork,

shadows bump the light,
paths disappear into dunes,
and the brick red chimney bleeds
rust across a roof....

She made herself look up at the blank faces before her as she read. Her instructor nodded encouragement from the back.

On another island,
cobalt splashed the white washed plaster,
solid walls simmered beneath sun,
and everything was still possible—
lives piled one atop the other
touching, a building block
construct of connection...

Slow down, she told herself. *Let the words settle. Don't just read it, feel it.* She continued slowly, pausing, giving the audience time to hear and register her words. She straightened, looked them in the eye. They looked back.

The next beach will be faded
to teal with angry salmon sunsets
zigzagging across sky and sand...

That's it, she thought. *Angry zigzagging.* Years of it. The pictures may have triggered the words, but the words described her life.

They will draw our story
on the soft underbelly of giant clams
and in those black illustrations,
our lives will twist and twist
and twist again into confusion—
no more right angles,
no more grounded corners,
only shapes moving, unanchored,
spinning into empty gray space.

She could feel more eyes on her. At least some in the audience were with her, perhaps imagining their own empty gray spaces.

She didn't dash from the front at the last word. She let it linger. The silence that followed was better than any applause. She read affirmation in it. Her words had resonated. When she looked up, eyes were still on her. She wouldn't try another poem. This was enough.

Back in her seat, waiting for her pulse to slow, she looked up at the work on the wall beside her. It rattled her. Who would think to create such a juxtaposition and how had he known the effect would prove so intriguing?

April 2002, Lisbon, Vermont

"Thanks for stopping by, guys." Paul handed bottles of beer to Maddie and Chris and motioned to the kitchen table. "This shouldn't take long."

"Boiled peanuts, eh? You must want a big favor from us." Maddie scooped up a small bowlful for herself. "What's up?"

"Since talking to Peg at Christmas, I've been thinking more about the future. Peg suggested I move out there to help with their business, but I'm definitely not ready for that big a change. She called this past weekend with another idea. She knows a family that lets artists stay on their beach property in exchange for keeping an eye on the place. Apparently there's a big studio as well as a tiny cottage I could stay in. They've an open slot this coming winter, November to April."

"Wow. How could you say no to that?" Maddie beamed. "Could you use a studio assistant? I'm great at cleaning brushes."

"And who exactly is supposed to take care of the farm while you two are enjoying a tropical getaway?" Chris's leg was jiggling up and down as he spoke, causing the whole table to vibrate.

"I'm joking, Chris. Geez, lighten up." Maddie squeezed Paul's hand. "I think it's a perfect plan, Dad. You can see if you like it out there without making any drastic, permanent changes."

"That's how I see it. I'd still be here to help out for the busiest stretch, but I'd get a chance to see if painting engages me enough to do it full-time. Skipping out on winter doesn't sound so bad either." Chris was studying the bottle in his hand. His leg still jiggled. "I sense you're not so keen on the idea, Chris."

Chris shrugged. "If Maddie's cool with it, then fine. You go follow your dreams, but you both need to know you can't count on me being here to pick up the slack. I've got some news of my own. I've been talking with a Marine Corps recruiter. I'm thinking about enlisting. Now that we're at war, signing up seems the right thing to do."

"That's a big step." Paul knew to respond carefully. "I'm proud of you for wanting to serve."

"But? Go ahead and say it, Dad. I'd be leaving you all in the lurch, abandoning the farm and family."

"Not what I was going to say and not what I would call it. If this is what you want, then we'll hire help. Nobody's going to force you to stay on the farm."

"What about Em and the kids?" Chris asked. "Could they stay here or would they need to move out?"

"Of course they can stay. The house is yours, Chris." Paul wondered what he'd ever said or done that made Chris expect the worst from him.

Chris's leg stilled, his shoulders relaxed. "Looks like everything's getting dumped on you, Maddie."

"It's not a problem. Really. I love the farm and I love the work. Ray feels the same. It's no burden."

"That brings me to the other thing I've been wanting to talk about with you both." Paul had dreaded this part of the conversation, but was feeling hopeful given Chris's news. Maybe it was all going to work out okay. "Again, I'm not looking to make any changes right away, but we need to think about the long-term future. My folks handed the farm over to your mom and me way before they retired, but Dad worked beside me every day until they moved to North Carolina. It meant I could take on managing the business while he was still around to guide me. I'd like to do the same. Have a smooth transition. Seems pretty obvious that Maddie's the one to take on managing the place. Hell, you're already doing most of the business side of it. Also seems like it's time for me to swap houses with you, Maddie. Ridiculous for me to be rattling around alone in this place."

"I thought you weren't going to make any big changes yet." Maddie grinned at him. "Or is this your way of getting me to host family gatherings?"

"Bingo. You know me too well. Any of that going to be a problem for you, Chris? Maddie and Ray living here and running the farm?"

"You kidding? I've been dreading telling you both that I want out. If Maddie's willing to do this then I say hallelujah. I don't want to see the family lose this place, but I sure don't want to be the one having to keep it going."

Paul raised his bottle. "I think we have ourselves a plan. Here's to our next phase." They clicked bottles, and while Paul felt immense relief and could see relief in his kids' faces as well, he felt also a wave of grief. A new phase meant they were moving on and away from the life they'd known with Sarah at the family's center.

As if he'd read Paul's mind, Chris raised his bottle again. "And here's to Mom."

"To Mom," Maddie and Paul echoed.

April 2002, Boston, Massachusetts

Amy was proud of herself. Here she was on the Red Line, bound for the Harvard stop. She feared she'd lost all her city skills after decades in a small town and just as many years married to a man who took charge when they traveled. With coaching from Kathy, who as a Boston University alum was skilled in navigating the city, she'd learned to ride the subway and buses with some confidence.

Perched on a bench in the packed car, she fingered the ring in her pocket. As she had collected earrings and a chain necklace to wear that morning, she'd spotted the ring tucked in a corner and plucked it from her jewelry box. She ran her thumb over the smooth jade. It had been her Aunt Sally's. She could still picture it on her aunt's finger the Christmas she'd spent with them in East Haven. Sally had fiddled with it all weekend, as if it were a worry bead. It had been incongruously delicate on a woman whose dress was otherwise bohemian. Amy didn't know how Sally had come to have it, only that her grandmother had decided Amy should have it when Sally died.

The ring itself was a thin band of gold. Oval cut, the jade sat within a circle of diamond chips. It had always been Kara's favorite. As a little girl, she'd sit with Amy's jewelry box open before her, loading rings on her fingers and draping necklaces over her chest. She would wear the jade ring on her right thumb, counting it the best treasure of them all. Amy couldn't afford a significant birthday gift that year and hoped this would seem to Kara a worthy recognition of her turning sixteen. She could present it at the family birthday dinner Gretchen had planned at the Halekulani's La Mer. Ever inconsiderate of others, Martin had scheduled his wedding for two days before Kara's birthday and at the start of spring break, complicating Amy and the kids' travel plans. They would catch an early flight to Honolulu the next morning.

Next stop, she told herself as the train pulled away from Central station. She tried to prepare herself mentally. This late on a Saturday night she would have to push through crowds of people as the train emptied. She'd never grown accustomed to that part of urban mass transit.

She managed to disembark without event and stepped onto the long escalator that made the steep climb to the main exit, "the pit," as Kathy called it. Amy marveled at the engineering feat that was the Boston subway system. The wonders of her life in a small New Hampshire town were natural ones, the human constructions on a scale she could grasp. Living away from the city, she found elements she'd once taken for granted—towering buildings, bridges, and tunnels—now astonished her. Her town couldn't agree on the design for new playground equipment and yet in this city, people had burrowed into the ground beneath buildings and roads and built an entire transportation system. Subway stations, especially the newer ones with their vaulted ceilings, humbled her, reminded her how insular and small her world in Clifton had become.

When she emerged from the station, she paused to get her bearings. "Head east on Mass Ave along Harvard's exterior fence," Kathy had said. The hotel would be on the vee parcel formed where Harvard Street intersected Mass. She did as Kathy had directed and found herself facing a redbrick building of modest size that seemed a Disney knockoff of a quad dorm. It was nothing like the towering glass hotels of downtown Boston or Honolulu.

The street and sidewalks were still packed on the warm April night. At home, the sidewalks would be empty but for the college kids and the throng of theatergoers headed for their cars. Hard to believe she had ever been like these people, dining at nine, clubbing well into the morning, falling into bed as the sun rose.

The walk signal had cycled through twice, yet Amy still stood at the corner, staring at the hotel. Within that building were the people she loved most in the world—her daughter and son—as well as the people she wanted least in the world to see—Martin, his new wife Sharon, and Sharon's parents, in town for the small wedding and celebratory dinner.

"We're too in love to wait," Martin had told Amy a few weeks earlier when she called about arrangements for the spring break trip. She registered the insult to her personally, felt its sting, but was also relieved by the speed with which he hopped from one marriage to the next. This was never about her personally. She and all the women before her and all the women while he was with her and all the women yet to come were simply interchangeable actors playing a part in his drama, satisfying his insatiable need to feel worshipped. Martin didn't love her or any woman, she'd realized. He loved the feeling of falling in love, the rush of a passionate infatuation that comes before any real knowledge of the other. What bitterness she felt was at the humiliation of falling for it and, even worse, enduring it for as long as she did. As her aunt Gretchen had put it, she'd forgotten who she was.

She hadn't even bothered to fight Martin about the way his sudden wedding plans had scrambled her already set travel arrangements. Didn't even complain about him costing her a night at a hotel because he couldn't make the effort to get the kids to Logan to meet her early the next morning. "For God's sake, it'll be my wedding night, Amy," he'd said. "You can't expect me to rise in the dark and deliver the kids to the airport just because you scheduled a ridiculously early flight." Easier to collect the kids herself and check in to an airport hotel.

She texted Kara and Will, "I'm here. Almost to hotel," and picked up the handle of her suitcase.

The blast of cold air when she entered through the hotel's back entrance was welcome after the unseasonably warm spring day. Her sandals clapped on the gleaming floor as she crossed the lobby to the front doors. Her phone vibrated. "See you in a sec," from Kara.

Before Amy could even turn, she heard Kara's laugh and then, "Mom!"

And there they all were, coming through the front doors. Together they were a frothy mix of heightened excitement. No mistaking the nature of this group. Martin might disappoint the kids, even wound them with his lack of attention, but all the same, they were a family unit with him, a part of this smiling clan, reveling in a special celebration. They formed a circle unto themselves, a circle that would never include her. An escalator could move people hundreds of feet, but she didn't know if she could propel herself the thirty needed to reach them.

"Hey, guys," she said, managing a smile as she pressed forward on the cold marble floor, her arms extended to Will and Kara for an enveloping hug as if it had been weeks rather than a day since she'd last seen them.

April 2002, Kailua, Hawai'i

Amy dried and stowed the last of the plates.

"Are we ready?"

"Yup. Only a hundred pages to go." Kara stuffed her copy of *A Tale of Two Cities* into her tote. "I should be able to finish it on the plane and be ready for Monday's quiz."

"I'm set." Will stashed his backpack at the kitchen door beside Amy's bag.

"Great. Inspection time." Amy grabbed the laminated list hanging on a hook by the kitchen door. Her grandmother had composed it in the 1950s when Gretchen and Clare had begun using the Kailua beach house as a getaway with their own families. Her grandmother's original penciled list hung framed on the kitchen wall.

"MAHALO FOR YOUR KOKUA. Please honor the kindness of those who came before you by extending courtesy to those who follow," it began, and after a long set of specific instructions, ended with "Give thanks always for the blessings of this land and home and loved ones."

The three of them made their way around the kitchen, the living room, bedrooms and baths, checking for any personal items they missed when packing. The bedsheets were changed, the linens washed and put away. The toilet bowls were Lysol blue and fresh towels adorned the racks. Windows were latched.

"Missed one." Kara pulled a small trash bag from the container under a bathroom sink and tied it up. "I'll take it and the kitchen trash to the bin and meet you guys out front."

"Thanks, hon. Will and I will double-check the yard for anything that's been left out."

Their inspection complete, Amy led the kids down to the beach for their ritual "Aloha Kailua" moment. For all the years of her childhood, she had performed this same routine with her parents and Kimo, and then done the same with her kids and Martin (if Martin felt generous enough to participate). *No small thing,* she thought, standing at the shoreline, Kara on one side, Will on her other, the waves tickling their feet, *that we've managed to preserve this tradition.* So much of what had once been habitual had faded with time, but this routine had the weight of ceremony, a way of honoring the land and those who came before.

"I never tire of this view or these moments. Which has everything to do with why I've chosen to help Aunt Gretchen," she said. "I hope I can do right by this place."

It would be easier if I knew exactly what "doing right" meant. Was it enough to keep the property in solid shape for the future, or should they be finding ways to put the land to better use? Open the Kailua property to more artists? Use the Nu'uanu land to help perpetuate native plants? The possibilities were many.

"And what about your writing?" Kara asked.

"It'll take some effort, but I think it's doable. Easier to write when you aren't grading papers evenings and weekends. We're all taking a big leap here. You kids are being courageous about moving far from your friends and dad and starting at a new school."

"As if Dad cared." Kara dug her big toe in the wet sand. Amy didn't contradict her. She was done making excuses for Martin. His desire to be an occasional dad was way too apparent.

"I'm pumped about being at McNeil," Will said. "Being on campus this week helped a lot." He and Kara had spent two school days of their vacation attending classes and after-school activities. "I kind of wish we didn't have to go back to finish the term in Clifton."

"I know what you mean," Amy said. "But the Nu'uanu house isn't ready yet, and we've got a house full of stuff to dump and pack over the next two months."

She linked an arm around each kid's waist and pulled them close. "I won't pretend this is going to be easy, but it feels right and we'll give it our best shot. Ready to give thanks?"

Amy began, and the kids joined her in saying the simple words Amy's grandfather had composed decades earlier.

For the blessings of the land and sea, mahalo. For the blessings of time with family and friends, mahalo. Until we gather here again, aloha.

She pulled the kids in tight for a brief moment, ready to release them quickly, but Kara reached her arm out around Will's waist to create a circle. Amy breathed deeply. *How lucky am I to have a life as good as this.* She gave a final squeeze and let them go.

"You guys go on ahead. I'm going to hang here for just a bit. I'll catch up."

She closed her eyes. Something had shifted. Her fear had eased and she felt almost at peace.

As she turned from the sea, Amy spotted a piece of driftwood in a twisted pile of seaweed and debris. She lifted it from the tangle and ran a finger along its curves. *Something so satisfying about wood worn smooth by water.* She reached out to a larger mass at the heap's center and pulled it to her, felt its curve and heft. A large ball, thick with barnacles. She scraped a tiny portion of its surface with a shell and struck glass.

Well, of course. She plopped down on the sand, the glass ball in her lap. *You appear when I'm not even looking.*

She pictured her aunt cradling the glass ball she'd found on this same stretch of beach. *Trust your own sense of the world, write your own life script,* Sally had told her, but Amy hadn't understood.

Amy lingered a while longer by the water, Kailua Bay spread out before her in a welcoming embrace. Perhaps all would be well.

May 2002, Lisbon, Vermont

"They're lovely, Dad."

Paul held a bucket full of daffodils.

"Your mom always loved them best."

Maddie carried a plastic vase of lilacs she'd cut. The vase would fit neatly into the ground by Sarah's grave, and Maddie was good about replacing the flowers regularly, so there were always fresh blooms or at least evergreen boughs.

Paul knew that keeping flowers in water was the more sensible choice, but he liked the sheer extravagance of a mass of blossoms scattered over Sarah's grave. He knew she would have appreciated so lavish a gesture.

They headed down the dirt lane that linked the farm buildings to the apple orchard and the family cemetery.

"Couldn't ask for a better Mother's Day than this," Maddie said. "Mom would have loved it. Blue skies, no black flies yet, and a stiff breeze."

"Perfect day for a bike ride. Remember? That's what she wanted to do last year. A long ride first thing in the morning before any cars were on the road, then brunch at Nellie's."

"I don't remember the bike ride," Maddie said.

"Because there wasn't one. It poured all day."

"Oh, right. And she canceled on brunch, too. Didn't want to bother getting dolled up only to have the rain make her hair go limp."

"Hell of a last Mother's Day."

Maddie grabbed hold of Paul's hand. "You know she was happy as a june bug that day, Dad, especially when Chris surprised her and showed up with the kids. That's all she wanted—her kids and grandbabies together in one place." He knew Maddie was right. So far as Sarah was concerned, she'd had the perfect Mother's Day, even if they had dined on pizza and spent the afternoon watching Disney movies.

"Pretty special piece of land we have here," Paul said as they emerged from a tunnel of maples into an open space with a view of the Connecticut curving its way south.

He thought he was ready for the step he was contemplating, and most of the time he felt sure he was. But then there would be a moment like this—a moment of keen appreciation for the place he'd called home all his life—and he couldn't imagine being away for more than a week or two. It wasn't just the land itself or special moments that caused him to reconsider. It was seeing the peace in Nathan's face each time he approached a canvas or hearing Sam's exuberant rendition of "The Wheels on the Bus" or catching the aroma of Maddie's pot roast on a Sunday evening—any of the ordinary moments of his life could make it seem impossible to leave all this behind. He told himself he would make new moments in Hawai'i, delight in new foods, witness different kinds of transcendent beauty, but the tug of the familiar was strong.

"You're not saying goodbye forever, Dad," Maddie said. "Not unless you want to. Five months may feel like a long time, but all you'll be doing is escaping during the worst of seasons. You'll still be here for all the best times. Hell, after nine months of farming and having art shows in New York and Provincetown, you're going to be desperate to get on that plane to Hawai'i."

They continued the short distance to the small cemetery. The apple blossoms were at their peak, as was the norm for Mother's Day, and the lilacs at the cemetery's edges were softening into lavender. Maddie removed the vase she'd left by the grave a couple weeks before and set her lilacs in place. Paul knelt by the gravesite and scattered the daffodils across it.

"Happy mom's day, Sarah," he said softly.

"I'm going to check out the orchard trees," Maddie said. "Take as much time as you want, Dad."

"Hear that, Sarah?" Paul said as he watched his daughter feign an interest in the trees. "Typical Maddie, always the thoughtful one. Giving us a bit of privacy." He settled into a more comfortable position on the grass. "You don't have to worry about us. We're doing okay here. Maddie's stepped up and taken the lead on every front. Chris, well, he's struggling some, and I'm no good at figuring out what to say to him. You were always the one who knew what he needed to hear. He's going to enlist in the Marine Corps. I'm hoping that's a good thing for him. Maybe some time away from us all will give him space to become his own man."

He left out his fears about the war, about what combat would do to Chris physically and mentally.

"I guess the really big news is I'm turning the farm over to Maddie, like Dad did with me. I'll still be here to help with the farming from spring through fall, but this winter I'm going to try a change of scenery. I don't want to be one of those guys who's always looking back, you know, so come November, I'm heading out to Hawai'i. Peg knows some folks with a beach place. The family lets artists stay in their caretaker cottage and use their art studio in exchange for keeping an eye on things. Now that I've got an art dealer wanting to sell my stuff, I have to produce some pieces to sell. Can you believe that? Fancy folks are hanging my art in their houses. It doesn't feel real."

How to tell Sarah that his life was unfolding in unexpected, wonderful ways, ways he hadn't even known to wish for, and yet it was also moving him further and further from the life he knew here on the farm, the life he had shared with her.

He turned to see where Maddie had gotten to and spotted her on her knees, pulling a vine off the trunk of one of the apple trees. Just like her mother. Never content to sit, always busy with some task no one else noticed needed doing. The farm would be fine in her care. Better than fine. She'd probably have whole new systems in place within a few years. She was what the farm needed—a young, fresh mind with lots of energy to keep up with the changing times. "She's our best hope for keeping the farm," he said aloud to Sarah. "She sure has a better chance of pulling it off than I do." He placed a hand at the center of her burial spot. "I miss you, Sarah. Sometimes it's so bad I think my heart's going to fall to pieces. But I'm steadily doing better, so you can rest easy, wherever you are, and don't be worrying yourself about me or the kids."

He rose and brushed the grass from his jeans.

"You're going to have to pace yourself," he called to Maddie as he approached her. "This work will kill you if you go full blast all the time."

With the back of her hand, she swept a strand of hair away from her face. "Figure I might as well make a dent in the work when I can. Just like you and Mom taught me. You ready to head back?"

Paul looked back at Sarah's grave, festive with its daffodil blanket, and said a silent goodbye.

"Yup, I've got cooking duties to attend to. Your kids are real taskmasters."

"What have they got planned?"

"You'll get nothing out of me. I'm sworn to secrecy. Let's just say your kiddos know their mom real well."

As they reentered the stretch of maples shading the lane, Paul heard a familiar song. He motioned to Maddie to stop, then pointed up. He scanned the limbs, but couldn't spot the rose-breasted grosbeak calling above them. "They're back, they're back," Sarah had cried each spring when she heard the first of them in the crab apples.

Maddie and Paul grinned at one another. "You're back, you're back," Maddie called up to the bird, laughing.

Paul didn't subscribe to notions of supernatural occurrences and had always scoffed at those who claimed to communicate with the dead. But standing in that cathedral-like space and hearing the familiar birdsong that would forever remind him of Sarah's delight, he allowed himself the indulgence. Perhaps, just perhaps, Sarah was there with them, letting him and Maddie know that all was well and they could get on with their lives.

May 2002, Lisbon, Vermont

Tires on the driveway drew Paul's attention to the window. Through the wavy glass, he could see the farmhouse and yard washed in the softening light of the summer evening. He glanced at the wall clock. Nearly eight. No wonder his lower back ached. He'd been painting for five hours. A red Honda Civic sat in front of the house, a salt-and-pepper-haired woman beside it.

He sighed, set down his paintbrush, and slid open the door. It had been weeks since he'd used the woodstove, but early May evenings still ran cool. He grabbed his denim jacket from a hook.

The woman had walked away from the car and seemed to be taking stock of the hillside sloping to the pond and fields.

"Can I help you?" he called.

She turned and flashed a smile warm enough to rattle him and defuse his annoyance at the interruption. *Something familiar in that smile.*

"I'm Kathy's friend, Amy Barnes from Clifton High. Here to collect some reeds for the school play."

"Right. Sorry. I meant to have those cut and ready for you but lost track of the time."

Amy held up a kitchen knife in her right hand. "I came prepared."

"With that? Do you know anything about cutting reeds?" Paul laughed.

"Haven't a clue. Will probably lose a leg in the process, but that's a small sacrifice for the sake of theater."

Paul shook his head. "Yeah, you're definitely a friend of Kathy's. Tell you what, how about you put that thing away. I'll grab a scythe and do the cutting. Any idea how much she needs?"

Amy circled her arms the way a young child might. "She said an armful so I'm guessing about this much."

"I'll also grab a wheelbarrow and some twine."

Paul liked this Barnes woman and was sure he knew her from somewhere. He felt such a strong connection, but couldn't place her. He was surprised when she fell into step beside him and followed him into the barn to retrieve the supplies.

"At the risk of coming across as a total flake, I have to say I feel like I've been here before," she said as Paul pushed the wheelbarrow out of the barn. She gestured to the pond in the distance. "I could swear I've seen this view."

"I bet you have, seeing as how most every farm in Vermont has a similar view. Sloping hills. Cornfields. Pond."

He was glad when she laughed. He hadn't offended her.

"I'm such a flatlander, right? You'd never know I've lived here nearly twenty years. I think I'm remembering a farm I visited when I was a little kid. The image stuck, probably because it was my first time seeing pumpkins in a field, but also because there were butterflies rising out of the pond's reeds. So many butterflies. I remember thinking it was the most beautiful thing I'd ever seen."

"I'm partial to them myself." Paul felt at ease with this woman. Maybe it was her eyes. Something familiar about the way they crinkled when she smiled. A kindness in them.

"This will sound nuts, but I could swear we know one another from somewhere. And not from a long time ago either. Recently. I can't place it. I want to say in some crowded space?"

She laughed. "Isn't that the worst? When you know you know someone but because it's the wrong context, you can't figure it out? You seem familiar to me, too. We must have met at Kathy's sometime in the past. One of these days our brains will figure it out."

He led her down the grassy slope to the pond, then set the wheelbarrow down beside the marsh reeds that crowded one end. "We haven't a lot of time. The light's fading."

The sun had slipped behind the tall hills that shadowed the farm, but pink and orange cloud tendrils fanned out across the sky.

"I promise not to be greedy," Amy assured him.

He lifted the scythe from the barrow and, aiming low, neatly caught a bundle of stalks in one swoop. Without prompting, Amy leaned in and gathered them from him, resting them across the wheelbarrow. Her blouse wicked up the pond water, but she didn't seem to notice. Her simple gesture of helping pleased Paul. He slipped the blade through another bunch, and, again, she took the stalks from him. He found her presence calming.

"One more will do," she said as the scythe sliced through one last time and the feathered stalks fell in a rustle as soft as a petticoat's.

Paul tied the bundle, then turned the wheelbarrow back toward the house. They slowly climbed the grass slope. A flock of swallows rose from the barn's roof and circled. Paul didn't have to point and call them to her attention. Amy's head was already back and her eyes scanning the sky.

"Poetry," she whispered.

"O'Hare," he blurted, thrilled he'd figured it out. "The little girl and the creepy guy."

"Yes!" she clapped her hands. "That's it! You were the guy who helped keep an eye on her."

He loved the way she smiled with her entire body. Such exuberance. Such joy at the puzzle solved.

"Wow. What a small world it is." She placed a hand on Paul's arm. "Thank you for your solidarity that day. Truly."

Paul could feel his face flush. The way she looked up at him. The conviction and sincerity in her gaze. He didn't trust himself to speak.

They lingered a moment, shifting their attention to the birds dipping and soaring until some signal cued them to line up again along the roof seam.

Paul put his weight to the barrow and continued on, feeling no rush and sensing none from her. It was as if they had a shared understanding that the tasks ahead could wait. For the first time in a long time, he knew there was time and space enough for it all.

Acknowledgments

I thank the many fellow writers, friends, and family members who read scenes and entire drafts of this work over the past fifteen years. These include fellow workshop participants at Joni B. Cole's Writer's Center in White River Junction, Vermont, most especially Jessica Eakin and Colleen Marshall.

I owe special gratitude to the many poets, most of them based in Vermont, who've inspired and guided me through the years. These include poets and teachers Peter Money and Verandah Porche, fellow poets Ina Anderson, Doreen Ballard, Beverly Breen Barton, Laura Foley, Deb Franzoni, Phyllis Katz, Hatsy McGraw, Giavanna Munafo, and participants of the Green Mountain Writers Conference.

I am particularly indebted to Cynthia Huntington, former New Hampshire poet laureate and Dartmouth College professor of English and Creative Writing, who encouraged me in my efforts to write poetry and provided tools and guidance to help me. Her faith and friendship have lifted and sustained me through the roughest of times.

Special thanks to Linda Doss, Kathy Hastings, Jim Matthews, and Norma Smith who graciously read the final pre-submission draft, and to Lani Leary Houck who helped me discern emerging themes in the work and whose passion to see this published helped sustain me through times of self-doubt.

Joni B. Cole remains my valued writing partner and dear friend. She tolerates my doubts and complaints, presses me to keep writing, and keeps me laughing through the good and bad of it all. She didn't let me drop this project and for that, I am most grateful.

Most recently, the book has benefited tremendously from development editor Marisa Keller's insights and suggestions, and I thank Sheryl Rapée-Adams, whose excellent copyediting elevated the novel and whose encouraging comments lifted my spirits. I am especially grateful to Rootstock publisher

Samantha Kolber for this opportunity to share *The Red Wheelbarrow* with an audience. Her professional guidance has been essential, and the scope of her talents amazes me.

Finally, I thank my husband Jim for his support, patience, and wisdom. The integrity with which he lives each day inspires me to do and be better.

About the Author

Born and raised in Honolulu, Marjorie Nelson Matthews resides in Hanover, New Hampshire. Her poetry has been published in *Rainbird, Across Borders*, *Bloodroot Literary Magazine*, and the 2012 New Hampshire Writers' Project's Poetry in the Windows event. *Hawai'i Calls* (Rootstock Publishing, 2022) was her first novel.

More Fiction from Rootstock Publishing:

A Reason to Run: A Novel by Mike Magluilo

All Men Glad and Wise: A Mystery by Laura C. Stevenson

An Intent to Commit: A Novel by Bernie Lambek

Augusta: A Novel by Celia Ryker

Blue Desert: A Novel by Celia Jeffries

Granite Kingdom: A Novel by Eric Pope

Hawai'i Calls: A Novel by Marjorie Nelson Matthews

Horodno Burning: A Novel by Michael Freed-Thall

Junkyard at No Town: A Novel by J.C. Myers

The Funny Moon: A Novel by Chris Lincoln

The Hospice Singer: A Novel by Larry Duberstein

The Inland Sea: A Mystery by Sam Clark

Uncivil Liberties: A Novel by Bernie Lambek

Venice Beach: A Novel by William Mark Habeeb

To learn about our titles in nonfiction, poetry, and children's literature, visit our website www.rootstockpublishing.com.

www.ingramcontent.com/pod-product-compliance
Lightning Source LLC
Chambersburg PA
CBHW020131120726
47903CB00007B/2211
9781578691623